THE RANGER'S LAMENT

The King's Ranger Book 6

AC COBBLE

Cobble Publishing LLC

Keep in Touch and Extra Content

You can find larger versions of the maps, series artwork, my newsletter, free short stories, and other goodies at accobble.com. It's the best place to stay updated on when the next book is coming!

Happy reading!
AC

Chapter One

Turgid air, thick with the smell of rot, excrement, and the copper tang of blood, hung like a cowl over the squat, stone fortress and the trampled and torn field in front of it. Each breath brought that stomach-curdling stench into one's nostrils, but breathing through the mouth was no better. Then, you could taste it.

It was enough to make you sick, to spew bile over the side of the wall, splashing down on the heaving pile of refuse and slime below, but Rew had been there for a week, inhaling and exhaling the heavy cloud of noxious fumes, and while he doubted he would get used to it, he had learned to live with it.

King's Sake. Get used to it? He'd been ready to leave the moment they'd arrived. Thinking how long it would take to become used to the suffocating odor—and being there that long—sent an uncomfortable tremor through his body. He felt his lips bow like he really was going to get sick.

He closed his eyes, taking short, shallow breaths through his nose, then opened his eyes again and looked out over the field and the road that used to cut through it. While he'd been ready to leave the moment they'd arrived, the massed army of Dark Kind beyond the walls hadn't been amenable to allowing their small party through.

The Dark Kinds' numbers changed as the vile creatures were killed and more arrived, but the ranger estimated there were a thousand narjags out there now, organized into two regiments, if masses of Dark Kind could be considered to be organized. There were a hundred ayres that loped restlessly around the outskirts of the narjag groupings. He and the others on the wall had spotted two valaan, which were enforcing loose order on their fellows.

Each day, one of the regiments of narjags would assault the fortress, and so far, each day, the men and women guarding the walls would throw them back.

The fortress straddled a highway that led from Carff to Mordenhold. In places, the highway wound sinuously, looking like a snake, sliding along waterways, mountains, and forests. At the fortified town of Valstock, the road was straight. It thrust northward until it disappeared over the horizon.

Clustering around that road, sprawled out on either side of it like a drunk laying down his head, was a sort of encampment for the Dark Kind. It wasn't like a human army's camp with rigid structure, clusters of tents around cook fires, latrines dug off to the sides, and provisions arranged where they were protected and accessible. No, the Dark Kind slept where they lay. They ate what they could get their teeth into—which sometimes meant each other—and they certainly hadn't taken time to dig latrines.

It was a squalid mess, a roiling kettle of filth that would have had a human army sick and dying within days, but the Dark Kind, if they even got sick, were showing no signs of it. They didn't look bothered by the smell, either. They wallowed it in, like pigs in mud.

Rew scrunched his nose. He wanted to turn away, to find some place he could avoid the awful stench, but there was nowhere in Valstock that could be done. The odor was like a coat of paint that had been layered across the entire place. There was no escaping it unless one left, headed south. In the last few days that had gotten near impossible as well.

When they'd arrived, the Dark Kind were bunched to the north, but in time, the narjags had spread and surrounded Valstock in a loose embrace. Their lines weren't solid. From where he stood, Rew could see half a dozen gaps that a man or horse might slip through, but then they would have the ayres snapping at their heels. A good rider on an excellent horse would have a chance, and since Rew and the party had been there, some had ridden out, carrying urgent pleas from the Baron of Valstock to anyone who would listen.

Rew had told the baron it would be fruitless. There was no one left to listen. The princes were dead, the remaining nobility frantic and confused. There was no one around to command Vaeldon's armies except the king himself, and from what Rew could tell, Vaisius Morden wasn't lifting a finger to confront the Dark Kind that seemed to be overrunning his kingdom.

The king was distracted, Alsayer had claimed. It wasn't the Investiture. That was over. The king had called Rew to come to Mordenhold to face him. Rew had been dutifully complying until they'd gotten trapped in Valstock, so if it wasn't the Dark Kind which had captured the king's attention, and it wasn't Rew's approach, then what was it? What calamity could distract a two-hundred-year-old necromancer beyond those threats?

Shaking his head, Rew studied the Dark Kind, which were massing several hundred paces away. Deal with one problem at a time, he told himself. Fight the battles that are in front of you. Don't go making up dangers which may or may not exist. There were plenty of those already. Telling himself those things worked, some days.

"More of them than yesterday?" wondered Zaine, standing beside him, an arrow held loosely on her bow.

There was no reason to pull back the string yet. She would wait until the last moment to unleash her shaft, when she couldn't possibly miss. Valstock's archers had wreaked havoc amongst the

Dark Kind, felling a thousand of them, if not more, but they were running out of arrows. Another day, two? Then, they'd have none.

The day before, a sortie had issued from the gates, rushing out to collect arrows that had been fired, to try and refill the archers' quivers. Rew had accompanied Valstock's swordsmen, and he'd nearly been trapped out there with the rest of them. They'd been set upon by ayres, and when they turned to race back toward the gates of the fortress, they'd found scores of narjags rising from the field, trying to block their path.

The Dark Kind—defying everything Rew had ever known or thought about the creatures—had played dead, waiting in ambush. Even with valaan directing them, it'd been a cunning and well-conceived plan, and it had nearly worked. It likely would have, if Rew and Raif hadn't charged directly into the midst of the narjags, crashing through like a rampant tempest, forcing the creatures back so Valstock's soldiers could return to the cover of the walls.

Raif had taken a severe beating, but by now, he was used to it, and Anne had been unsurprised when they'd carried the wounded fighter to receive her care.

Valstock's soldiers and Baron Phren had considered the adventure a smashing success, as only three men were lost, and several bushels containing hundreds of usable arrows had been recovered. But Rew understood that had a handful more of narjags been in place, had the ayres been closer when the party ventured out, or had a valaan accompanied its minions, things could have gone very differently. He'd refused Baron Phren's request to conduct the operation again the next day, and Phren's captains had grown suddenly nervous about attempting the maneuver without Rew and Raif accompanying them.

"Hour, hour and a half," assessed Zaine, looking at the Dark Kind as they assembled well out of bow shot. "I think there are more of them. Every day, we cut them down. Every day, more show up. We can't win like this, Ranger. I'm not a military tactician, but even I can tell that. We weaken. They gain strength.

Won't be today, I don't think, but sooner or later, they're going to get over these walls in force and storm down into the city."

Rew nodded and didn't respond.

"A dozen of them made it down yesterday," continued Zaine, her head still turned toward the field, but Rew could feel her eyes on him as she glanced to the side.

"He knows we're coming," mentioned Cinda, standing on the opposite side of him. "I don't know why he doesn't save himself the time and show up in the middle of the night through a portal to take you—and me—but for whatever reason, he hasn't done it. I don't think he will."

Rew still did not respond.

"Ranger, there will be more Dark Kind elsewhere in Vaeldon. This... fraemoth, as Alsayer called it, is building them into an army. Blessed Mother, look out there. They already are an army. We can't face that alone, so we have to consider—"

"I know what you're going to say, Cinda, and I have been considering," interjected Rew.

"Was worried you'd lost the ability to talk," remarked Zaine.

"I can talk well enough," said Rew, crossing his arms over his chest. "The problem is, I don't know what to say."

"We're running out of time for choices," replied Cinda. "Another day or two, and Zaine is right, they're going to break through and get into the town. It'll be easier to hunt them down and kill them in small groups that way, I suppose, but what's the point of defending this wall if we lose the people behind it? I don't think we have a choice, at this point, unless you're willing to sacrifice the entire town so we can slip around. That's not... that's not what you're thinking about, is it?"

"No." Rew dropped his arms and put his hands on the stone of the battlement. "We're not running out of time to make a choice. What I've been considering is that we never had a choice to begin with. Could we slip away without trying everything at our disposal? I don't think any of us would want to live with that. Since we arrived, it's been about when, not if."

"All right then," cracked Zaine. "We fight, nice and simple."

"We fight," agreed Rew, "though it's anything but simple. Think about it. Why has it come to this? Cinda is right. The king could be here in a blink, either destroying the Dark Kind himself or snatching up Cinda and I. I know my father, and against him in a fair fight, I wouldn't stand a chance. Neither would Cinda. He's got two hundred years' experience on her, after all, so what is he waiting for?"

Zaine shrugged.

"And where is his black legion? Even if the man himself isn't leaving Mordenhold for whatever distraction is holding him there, why not send out the army to face the Dark Kind? Mordenhold's garrison is fifty thousand men strong. They're well-equipped, well-trained, and they've more veterans in their ranks than any other force in this kingdom. They have spellcasters as well, a coterie of five or six of them per regiment. There are even a few invokers capable of opening large enough portals to move several companies of the legion across the kingdom in hours. If they sent a few regiments to each province, they could make short work of the Dark Kind."

"Why have an army if you're not going to use it?" muttered Cinda.

"Exactly."

"The king, ah, do you think he's worried about us?" wondered Zaine.

Rew smirked at the thief. "The king is a good judge of his own abilities. He doesn't need an army and a company of spellcasters to deal with us. Pfah. He doesn't even want to deal with us—not like that, anyway. He needs me alive. It's not the black legion we should worry about when we get to Mordenhold, but... is he really that confident we can overcome this? Why gamble with our lives when, as Cinda says, he could be here at any moment?"

"Aye, there's no certainty we can make it past here, much less whatever else is on the road," agreed Zaine.

"We will," declared Cinda. "Today, I'll join the fight, and we'll get through."

The thief grunted.

Rew met Cinda's defiant gaze. He nodded to the young necromancer. "Today, you join the fight."

The three of them looked out at the massing Dark Kind.

Cinda whispered, "If the king isn't keeping his army close because of us, and he's not using them to battle the Dark Kind, then what? What possible reason could he have for keeping the legion nearby?"

"That, lass, is what worries me."

AN HOUR LATER, THE JUMBLED RANKS OF NARJAGS BEGAN TO MARCH forward. They were arrayed in lines one hundred creatures across, five deep. If Baron Phren's forces had catapults, that formation would have limited the damage they could cause, but Baron Phren's family hadn't needed to defend their city in generations. In a peaceful land, they had relied on the sheer mass of the fortress to do the trick and didn't pay for artillery or other defenses that a town along the border or the coast might employ.

They'd been under the rule of the Mordens for two hundred years and had no intention of rebellion. So deep into the interior of Vaeldon, they should have had assistance from Carff or Mordenhold when faced with an attack by Dark Kind. What use was a kingdom if it did not rally to defend itself?

But Valchon was dead, and the king wasn't there. A mercy for Rew and his companions, but it was pressing Baron Phren and his men to the point of breaking. Already, scores of soldiers and citizens had fallen beneath the teeth and claws of the narjags, and as the scrawny, gray-skinned creatures marched closer, long, roughly fashioned ladders on their shoulders, Rew guessed that an awful lot more of Phren's people were going to die today.

If Cinda did nothing about it, that was.

The necromancer had stayed back from the fight, letting Rew, Raif, and Zaine assist over the last week as their skills allowed. For a time, they'd been nervous about drawing Vaisius Morden's attention. A significant burst of necromancy might be sensed by a powerful talent like the king, but as the days had passed, it had become obvious the king wasn't coming. He didn't care about the deaths of his people, and eventually, they decided he wouldn't care about Cinda unleashing her power.

The king had spoken through the corpse of one of Valchon's simulacrum in the ruins of Havmark. He'd known where they were. If he wanted to face them before Mordenhold, he could have.

They all hated putting faith in the idea the king was simply too distracted or lazy to come to them, and they'd scurried north with as much stealth as they could muster, but with Baron Phren's forces on the verge of collapse and the entire town in danger, they'd agreed now was the time.

Rew stood to Cinda's side, and Raif took her other side. Zaine was on the battlements as well, but Anne remained back in the city, tending to the throngs of wounded who were carried down from the wall. If what Cinda tried went wrong, it wasn't Anne's healing she was going to need.

"When we get out of here, I'm going to need to bathe for days to wash off this stink," complained Zaine.

"Shush," warned Raif. "Let her concentrate."

Shaking her head, her face blank, Cinda responded, "No, it's all right. Maybe it's better to not think too much about what I'm doing."

"Are you worried you won't be able to..." murmured Rew.

"This place pulses with power. I've been drawing on it since we got here. I have the strength. I can do this, and with Alsayer's tutelage, I can maintain control. The unknown is how the narjags and valaan will react."

Rew grunted and did not respond.

Zaine raised her bow but did not draw back the string. Along the wall, other archers saw the signal and copied her motion. They would wait until she fired, then they'd unleash, spending valuable arrows, but it would be worth it if it worked. They wanted the narjags distracted, looking up instead of down.

Cinda stepped to the battlement, her hands raised, palms out toward the field of battle.

Rew hissed, "There, see it? In the middle of the formation is the valaan."

Turning her head, Cinda looked to where he pointed, but she didn't speak. She'd begun.

In the stories, battles were always preceded by the stomp of heavy boots and the clash of steel swords against shields. Perhaps throaty singing and chants would stir the blood of the approaching army, whipping them into a frenzy so they would throw their bodies at the enemy, knowing that sharp-tipped arrows, heavy rocks and debris, and boiling oil might be flung their way. Some of them were going to die no matter how the battle ended, and it took a certain type of courage or madness to march directly into that danger.

But the narjags wore no shoes, and while they had an assortment of crude weapons they'd fashioned or better ones they'd scavenged from their victims, not a one of them held a shield. They did snarl and cry out, not in a coordinated song, but from their own hunger and anger. Barely audible beneath the clamor the beasts caused were low hoots that emanated from the largest of the narjags—the shamans.

They were communicating on some base level with their charges, keeping them in line, more or less. The valaan stood at the center, but if it issued commands, they weren't audible to Rew and the others. Instead, the dark creature kept order through its very presence. Around it, they could see the closest narjags cringing in terror. They were more afraid of the valaan than anything the people on the walls were going to do to them.

Why was that? Rew wondered. What special power did the valaan hold over their fellow Dark Kind? An unfamiliar magic?

Because, whatever injuries the valaan were going to cause to the narjags, they had to know the people intended just as much. Hundreds of the beasts, maybe a thousand, lay dead in front of the fortress like a slimy carpet. For a week, they'd been wasting their lives, struggling to fight their way up a wall and failing day after day.

Human captains would have set a siege and waited out those inside. If they didn't have the resources to wait long, they would at least build up their forces until they had overwhelming superiority and they could overrun the walls in one great surge. The Dark Kind just kept coming with what they had that day, throwing more and more narjags at the wall like conscripted shock troops from another nobleman's territory.

They showed a smidgeon of discipline and a little bit of strategy. They'd bothered to build the ladders. They'd set an ambush, but it hadn't been enough. The lackadaisical strategy was getting them killed in droves. It was like the valaan were as happy for the narjags to die as it was for the humans to die.

Rew frowned. Did that mean something?

He would have pondered it, worked the idea over, examined it from all sides, but the Dark Kind were drawing close, and a bitter chill was seeping out from Cinda.

Before, her magic had been cast spontaneously. She'd flung it with little idea of what she was doing, and in Jabaan, when it'd been at its peak, she'd had no control over what was happening at all. Now, she cast her spells with purpose.

Amidst the approaching ranks of narjags, the dead began to rise.

Chapter Two

The Dark Kind moved with wanton fervor, and amidst the chaos of their lines, it was difficult to tell when the creatures noticed something was amiss. From the walls, Rew and the others could see that Cinda had managed to raise her corpses behind the bulk of the Dark Kind, trapping them between the stone barricade and the undead.

The undead were vastly outnumbered by the Dark Kind, as Cinda could only animate bodies of those who'd fallen outside of the walls, but her corpses had an advantage in that they couldn't be killed.

Zaine waited until the first score rose to their feet. Then, she drew back her arrow and fired. A blink later, another wave of arrows lofted into the sky, arcing from the wall then falling down into the massed crowd of narjags.

The creatures were unarmored, and their flesh was soft and vulnerable. When a score of arrows pelted down into them, followed by another and another, the front rank became angry and charged. Many on the back ranks had seen the dead rising behind them, and they rushed at the animated corpses.

Cinda's minions crashed into the scrambling horde of narjags. Clumsily swung swords and spears met ferocious claws and teeth. The narjags' organization splintered and they fought as individuals. Cinda, with only a passing acquaintance with weapons skills and the difficult layer of passing instructions to the dead, had her charges hack and slash.

It was a churning, violent confrontation, where narjags tore bloodless hunks of meat from the undead, but the undead kept fighting, their gory blades rising and falling in an unrelenting rain of blows.

Several of the corpses were swarmed, thrown down and piled upon by dozens of narjags. Beneath the writhing heaps, they would be ripped and broken until they no longer had sufficient mass to continue the fight, but in most other cases, the narjags didn't seem to understand what they were facing. They struck like they would against a living opponent then suffered when the dead struck back.

Zaine and the other archers focused their fire on the wave of narjags that had broken loose and were racing toward the walls. It looked like only half of the creatures had remembered to bring their ladders along. Without the protection of numbers, they suffered brutal losses, but there were only so many archers, and they had only so many arrows.

"This is going to get interesting," remarked Raif. He pointed past the churning froth of the battle.

Out beyond the line of narjags and Cinda's corpses, the other company of Dark Kind were approaching. Five hundred more of them.

"And that," added Rew, gesturing toward the center of the confrontation, where around the valaan, it appeared the narjags were still organized. They'd formed into a tight cluster, keeping the undead from the valaan, and while Rew watched, they turned and began heading toward the wall, toward Rew and his companions.

The ranger grunted. "They've spotted Cinda, and the valaan understands what she's doing."

"I've got it," said Zaine, turning and releasing an arrow

toward the approaching cluster of Dark Kind and the valaan at its center.

Her arrow flew a dozen yards wide. Rew and the others started shouting down the wall for everyone to aim at the valaan. If the leader of the Dark Kind could be felled, the rest would dissolve into a chaotic jumble. Without the valaan stoking them, driving them forward, it was unlikely they would breach the wall. More arrows flashed toward the valaan, but it seemed to shrivel, and soon, they couldn't even see it amongst the narjags.

Cinda's corpses were carving horrific chunks through the main party of narjags, but unlike human opponents, the Dark Kind didn't show fear. They didn't turn and run. They grew ever more enraged and fought harder. The creatures were throwing themselves on the undead, tearing into them with frenzied abandon. Rew supposed the Dark Kind didn't much care if their meat had been dead for a few days, rotting out in the warm spring sun.

He guessed there were two score of the animated corpses. They were easily outnumbered, but the advantage of already being dead was a great one. They fought as ferociously as the Dark Kind, and as the breaths passed, it appeared the undead were holding their own, at least until the second company of Dark Kind joined the fray.

Lead by another valaan, scores of ayres and five hundred fresh narjags came storming into the back of the undead. The valaan must have learned something from witnessing the initial attack because the ayres rushed in, biting arms and legs, trying to immobilize the corpses. The narjags came flying after, leaping onto the things and forcing them to the ground where more narjags piled on, tearing and gnawing at the undead, demolishing them piece by piece with brute violence.

"This isn't working," snapped Cinda, clearly surprised and exasperated. "I've lost half the bindings. Half of them that remain are already on their backs, buried under those creatures."

Rew grunted. The Dark Kind, in the space of the short engagement, had learned about their enemy then adjusted their tactics to compensate. A valaan could learn and then share the information with five hundred of its minions? Cinda was right. It wasn't working, and it was in danger of becoming far worse. The initial wave of narjags had reached the base of the fortress wall, and their makeshift ladders were clacking against the stone.

They'd lost many of those ladders during their charge, but it didn't make much of a difference because most of them had been killed on the way in. In a horrible coincidence, it seemed the survivors had retained just as many ladders as they needed.

The ranger looked down the wall and saw defenders pushing out with stout poles, tipping the ladders over. It was a good tactic, but the walls of Valstock weren't as high as those of Carff or Mordenhold. A fall from that height wasn't likely to kill a narjag, particularly if it fell down atop one of its peers that had been coming behind. A few might break bones in the fall, and some of the ladders would be damaged, but for the most part, tipping the ladders would only delay the attack, not stop it.

Rew drew his longsword. There was only one way to stop the creatures from clambering over the wall.

"Any other tricks?" demanded Zaine. She cursed as another of her arrows landed amongst the narjag cluster protecting the valaan but missed her target.

"Not until someone dies," barked Cinda. "I raised forty of those things! I thought... Pfah. I raised forty corpses. That'd be enough to send a human army—"

If Cinda had more to her story, it was lost when the end of a ladder clattered down directly next to her. She leapt back, and Rew stepped calmly forward.

In moments, a narjag's snarling face appeared, climbing up the ladder. Rew stabbed down its throat. The narjag fell away, and in the space of a few breaths, another poked above the battlement. Working methodically, Rew laid his longsword across his opposite arm for support and thrust at each snarling face. He punched holes in the creatures as they ascended to the top of the wall, but more kept coming. Like the tide rolling in and eroding the base of a sandcastle, the Dark Kind kept climbing the wall.

Down the battlement from Rew's party, Baron Phren's men fought with less aplomb, and it cost them. Instead of waiting for the Dark Kind to appear and striking them before they cleared the crenellations of the battlement, they leaned down, fighting too aggressively, or they were fixated on using the poles to push back the ladders, and that allowed the narjags to scramble off the ladders and clutch onto the stone of the wall. Or worse, the soldiers were frightened, and they backed away, giving the narjags room to get onto the walkway.

First one, then two positions on the wall surrendered footholds to the narjags, and with the valaan directing from below, ladders began to smack down, taking advantage of the space the Dark Kind were clearing of defenders.

Rew watched, frustrated and disconcerted, but he wasn't in charge of those men, and it wasn't he who needed to put some steel into their spines. Where were... He saw Baron Phren's commanders moving to more secure positions, and he cursed.

Cinda's corpses had done good work. The Dark Kind were down to seven hundred narjags, give or take, but they'd fully committed now. Both units, and both valaan, were in the fight. Evidently, the creatures had decided it was now or never, and as the mass of them crawled closer to the wall, Rew saw they were going to take the town or die trying.

Baron Phren's men had the advantage of the wall, but they were outnumbered five to one. They were already withering in several spots, petrified by terror. Their leaders were failing them. The baron himself was nowhere to be seen. Likely, he was locked within his keep back inside of the town. His soldiers would know that, and even the dullest ones would understand what it meant.

There were townspeople back in the city, and they would fight when the Dark Kind swarmed over, but they wouldn't match the ferocity of the narjags. King's Sake. Even if the defenders managed to hunt the narjags through the streets and kill every one of them, the fight would still be a loss. Too many souls were going to be freed the moment the narjags got loose with no armor and steel between them and the citizenry.

"There are too many," growled Rew, looking in dismay as another of Cinda's corpses fell beneath a wiggling mass of narjags. "With the valaan commanding them, there are too many."

"What do you suggest we do about that, Ranger?" snapped Cinda. "I can't… When they get over the wall, I'll have more strength, more bodies to work with. Until then, I've done what I can."

There was despair in her voice, despair that she wasn't strong enough now, despair at what had to happen for her to gain more strength. It was a terrible tradeoff, but what was there to do but to take it?

Rew shook himself. What was there to do?

He spun and shouted, "Raif, protect your sister at all costs! Zaine, draw your daggers and take Cinda's other flank."

"What are you doing?" demanded the thief.

"We can't face them all if they're commanded by the valaan, so I'm going to go hunt down a pair of valaan."

"What? That's madness!" cried Raif, gesturing with his greatsword at the surging mass of narjags beyond the wall.

Rew shrugged but didn't respond. It was madness, but so was letting the creatures into the city. He put a hand on the battlement and hopped up into a crenellation, peering down below, trying to pick his spot.

"Ranger, you can't!" pleaded Raif.

Zaine chased after him, threatening, "I'm going to tell Anne."

Rew smirked at her then leapt off the wall.

HE LANDED ATOP THE HEAD OF A NARJAG, AND THE SMALL CREATURE buckled beneath his weight. Others beside it staggered back, surprised a person was suddenly in their midst.

Rew took advantage of the space, twirled his enchanted longsword, and lashed it back and forth through the closest Dark Kind like he was mowing wheat. The blade had lost the potency of Erasmus Morden, and it no longer tugged at his soul, seeking blood as it once had, but it was the finest steel the craftsmen of the era could forge, and it'd been bolstered by ancient, powerful enchantments. It was a weapon forged to hold the soul of the most powerful high magician of the age, and it'd worked. It'd stood the test of time. Even without the fuel Erasmus Morden's rage had provided, the steel was wickedly sharp, and the blade sang as Rew wielded it.

He'd spent much of his life hunting narjags in the wilderness, and he was good at what he did. He struck with precision, not over-extending. He made each blow, each movement, count. Of course, he'd never been alone in a field with seven hundred of them before.

The moment the initial shock of his arrival wore off, he felt it like a thunderstorm changing direction. The narjags flew at him, slavering mouths, clutching claws. He chopped into them, working his longsword and his hunting knife like he was butchering game.

Arrows flew down around him, either Zaine ignoring his commands and using her bow still or other archers seeing what he was doing and helping how they could. Twenty paces in front of him was the valaan. If he could reach it, if he could kill it, the narjags just might dissolve into an unorganized, self-destructive, chaotic mess.

If he could reach it.

Dozens of narjags stood in his way.

Rew's longsword cleaved into the skull of one, and he felt his tough leather armor get pricked around his lower back. Hot blood dripped down his skin. He twisted and wove, using constant motion to evade blows rather than turning and fighting. He knew he might suffer more injuries from behind, but there were only a few narjags that could fit between him and the wall, and if he was going to survive this bold foray, it would be because he faced the valaan. He had to get to it. He had to confront it before hundreds of narjags swarmed and surrounded him, isolating him from the fortress and any help.

He took two running steps and jumped, a boot taking one narjag in the side of the head, kneeing another in the face. He crashed down on top of them, smoothly slicing his longsword through two more of the beasts, catching a stabbing spear and deflecting it with his hunting knife then ripping the blade across the neck of the narjag who held the spear.

A weak slash cut him in the back of his calf, and he started to regret this plan. It'd made a lot more sense atop the wall, but he hadn't really taken time to consider it.

The valaan moved toward him, flowing like smoke drawn toward a chimney, and the narjags evaporated from its path, clearing a space between Rew and the valaan.

He glanced around to be certain, but yes, they were allowing the valaan to face him. He'd gambled they would, and it seemed he would live at least a few more moments to enjoy being right.

Dark Kind, even in small packs of four or five, were ruled by strength and by fear. The biggest and meanest of the lot directed the others. In the decades that Rew had fought them, he'd learned the most dangerous of the creatures would never stay back from a fight. They commanded the pack through violence, and it was only violence that would keep them there. He'd been fairly sure it was the same with valaan. There had to be some way they kept the lesser creatures in line. If the leaders looked afraid, they would lose control.

A narjag lunged at him, and he twisted, slamming his hunting knife up under its chin, killing the beast. The valaan attacked in a blink, rippling like liquid. Rew flung the dead narjag in between himself and the valaan, but the dark-skinned monster leapt over it, streaking toward Rew with claws outstretched.

He tried to catch it in the air, thrusting with his longsword, but the valaan wriggled like a cat, contorting its body out of the way and swiping a clawed hand at his head. Rew ducked, spun away, and then crashed into a narjag which had sprang at him from behind.

The narjag went flying back from the force of the collision, and Rew cursed. If the narjags were going to be at his back every time the valaan pressed him, this was going to be an ugly, unfortunate fight.

Sensing danger, he hurled himself to the side, rolling over his shoulder across the squelching dead bodies of fallen narjags and springing back to his feet. The valaan was right behind him, chasing closely, but it was surprised at how quickly he'd recovered and earned itself a wicked cut across its abdomen before retreating. Vivid orange blood spilled down the front of the thing, and it hissed at Rew.

An arrow thudded into its shoulder, and the valaan was rocked by the impact. Rew jumped forward, lashing his longsword across its face, but it leaned back in time to avoid decapitation, and as it leaned, it kicked.

Rew caught the blow in his stomach and was lifted off his feet by the force of the strike. The air exploded from his gut, and he was stunned and breathless for a moment. Valaan kicked people? Reacting on pure instinct, he wrapped his arm around the leg while its foot was still buried in his belly.

The creature pulled, trying to free its appendage, and Rew chopped down with his longsword, severing the leg. The valaan fell back, and Rew dropped the leg like it had burned him. Scrambling backward, working toward a wall of narjags, the valaan tried to escape.

Rew pursued recklessly. There were scores of narjags surrounding him now, and fighting his way back toward the fortress wall might be impossible. It would definitely be impossible if the valaan commanded its minions to cut him off, to keep him trapped outside. Narjags swarmed toward him, but he barreled through them, not bothering to fight the creatures, just trying to reach the valaan.

It shrieked at him, trying to crawl to safety, the stump of its leg flapping as if it hadn't realized the extent of the injury. He lunged, slamming his longsword down its gullet, pinning the thing's head to the ground before ripping the sword away.

A clawed hand gripped his arm, and Rew felt hot breath on his neck. He ducked, spilling the narjag over the top of him, and he tried to spin, swinging his sword wide to clear space, but the weapon snagged in a body.

More narjags pressed close, and Rew was trapped.

An icy wind washed over him, and Rew immediately drew a lungful of air and steeled himself. The brief warning saved his life. The wind turned to a gale, and the breath of death poured down from the wall, filling the space around Rew with a freezing fog, choking the narjags to death.

A small eddy of clear air bubbled around him, but he could still feel the caustic fog stinging his skin, his eyes, and his lungs. It was worth it. Around him, scores of Dark Kind dropped dead. They fell, clawing at their necks and their eyes, choking pitifully.

Rew blinked his own eyes and tried to hold his breath as the fog of Cinda's spell billowed out farther from the wall, washing over the narjags, killing scores of them in the time it took them to draw breath.

The air around him cleared as the fog moved past, and the heat of the day and the stench of the dead wafted back to replace it. Tears streaming down his cheeks, Rew turned and began running toward the wall of the fortress, looking for where one of the Dark Kinds' ladders was still propped against the barrier.

Cinda must have killed fifty of the narjags with that spell. He was impressed. Her animated corpses might have taken down another three hundred earlier. It was incredible destruction she wrought, but against a thousand Dark Kind, would it be enough?

Rew paused with one foot on the ladder. Cinda had said that animating the corpses had taken all the power she'd been able to muster. She'd said more people would have to die before she would be able to cast another spell.

Climbing higher, his heart sinking, Rew ascended to the top of the wall and looked down it, where narjags were swarming over the barrier one hundred paces away, spilling like water from a burst dam into the city beyond.

"We've got a problem," declared Zaine, coming to stand beside him.

Cinda stood at the battlement, her eyes narrowed to slits, her hands raised as she drew power from the carnage that was happening in the town and casting it back at the Dark Kind. Raif was clutching his greatsword, shifting on his feet nervously. The giant blade was fouled with the dark blood of narjags, but so far, the lad appeared uninjured.

Rew frowned, looking down the wall where several dozen of Baron Phren's soldiers tried to force the narjags back, but they were too few to cut through the stream of creatures coming over the wall, and if they did, they were too few to defend its length. Hundreds of Dark Kind had been killed, but with the second group of them joining the battle, there were still hundreds left. Too many. They were loose in the city now. They were heading toward...

Rew spun, a hoarse curse bursting from his lips.

Anne.

Chapter Three

The roiling fog of Cinda's death breath spell spread forth like morning dew, clinging to bodies of narjags already dead and those soon to be. The necromancer stood still as stone, awful power radiating from her. Rew gaped at the energy she was casting.

"Cinda!" cried Raif. "The town, they're in the town! Can you direct it down—"

"I don't have that kind of precision," snapped the necromancer, the swell of her spell slowing as she growled back at him through gritted teeth. "If I turn this on the town, there's no telling how many people I'll kill with it. My funeral flame will be worse. Even cold fire will burn timber. No. This way, I can do real damage to them."

Raif spun, looking down into Valstock, where scores of narjags were already racing through the streets, leaping onto soldiers and those who'd been giving support to the soldiers. They could see doors that had been shattered, only wails of terror rising to give clues of what was happening within. Blood stained the streets where narjags had torn apart their victims. Blocks into the city, already they could see individual narjags racing ahead of the packs, looking for easier meat.

AC COBBLE

The fighter stammered. "W-We have to..."

"I have a chance to destroy the bulk of their army," growled Cinda, her body tensing, the fog of death's breath swirling out before them again. "A little longer, and I'll kill every single one of those monsters still in the field."

"You'll kill them, but others will rampage through Valstock," argued Raif.

Cinda ignored her brother, pouring her concentration and her strength into her spell.

Rew glanced down the wall. There were still two dozen soldiers between them and the bulk of the Dark Kind that were passing over. The narjags did not look interested in contesting with the armed men and were passing quickly to find easier meat. The two dozen soldiers didn't look interested in throwing their lives away against hundreds of Dark Kind.

In front of Cinda, there was nothing but the dead. Clouds of death's breath still shrouded much of the battlefield for a hundred paces in front of them, and she was working to push it farther. Their position on the wall was relatively safe.

Was she right? Was it best to direct her power out into the field and cause indiscriminate death, or did she have the talent to weave the spells through the streets. Was she worried she'd inadvertently kill people in the city, or was she worried they'd live?

Either way, they didn't have time for debate. Anne didn't have time for him to stand there stupidly while the narjags closed in on her.

He instructed the others, "Raif, Zaine, stay here and guard Cinda."

He trotted toward the nearest stairs that led from the battlement down into the city and found Raif and Zaine right behind him.

"Stay with her!" he barked.

"You can't fight them all alone," retorted Raif.

"You'll leave your sister alone instead?"

Shrugging, the big fighter replied. "I think she can take care of herself."

"Not if they come up behind her."

Raif glanced at Zaine.

She nodded curtly. "I'll watch her back."

"We're a team, Ranger," insisted Raif. "We work together."

Rew began jogging again, not willing to waste time on the argument when the Dark Kind were ranging ahead of them, hunting, and Anne was unprotected.

"If we see the valaan, stay—"

"Stay behind you. I've heard it before."

———

HUNDREDS OF DARK KIND HAD BEEN SLAIN OUTSIDE OF THE CITY walls, but hundreds more had gotten inside. They roamed uncontrolled down the streets of Valstock, crashing against doors, chasing down people who hadn't had the sense to hide or who were making honorable and foolish efforts to defend the town.

As Rew and Raif made it into the streets, they surprised several narjags and drew others by their presence. Had the creatures been massed together like they'd been outside, within the narrow confines of the cobblestone streets, the two men wouldn't have gotten far, but once inside the walls, whatever control the valaan had over the creatures was lost, and the narjags raced in all directions.

When they saw Rew and Raif, the narjags attacked.

Rew gestured for Raif to take the lead and ignored the big lad's silly grin at being in the front. The fighter was adorned in plate and chain armor, and he carried a giant sword. Against small parties of narjags, Raif would sweep his blade through them and then hammer against them with his heavy, armored body. Rew followed behind and, using more finesse, finishing the narjags Raif hadn't killed.

They both knew where to go. Ten blocks from the walls—far

enough away it was supposed to be safe, but close enough the wounded could get there—was the hospital Anne had been stationed in since they had arrived.

She'd begun by providing small empathy, nudges here and there to keep someone alive until mundane care could save them or improving the condition of others to help them heal fully and quickly. Over time, she'd dropped the pretense of being a knowledgeable medicine woman and was conducting full empathy on those who were wounded on the wall.

There were dozens of them every day, but with Anne's care, most who made it to the hospital survived, and most who hadn't been grievously wounded were back on their feet in days, rather than weeks and months.

Her work had earned Anne the respect of the entire city, but it came at a cost. She'd spent the days wallowing in the pain and agony of others, hardly able to draw more into herself but unable to allow others to suffer. It'd worried the children, thinking she might permanently damage herself, but Rew knew better. She would carry the hurt, as she'd carried it before. It would stay with her and only fade in time, but it pained Anne more to see others in agony. It was other people suffering that she couldn't live with.

Following each shift on the wall, Rew went to her and forced her away from the beds, the cots, and the blankets on the floor where the wounded were stacked up like loaves for an oven. He had to almost physically drag her away and sit with her while she slept to make sure she actually did sleep. He would force her to eat, to rest, and then accompany her back.

It meant he'd had little sleep for himself, just quick naps atop the wall when it was quiet, or he would doze off while he watched over Anne. It was wearing on him, but he was used to long periods with little rest. He had the stamina for it, and in his way, it was a mirror to Anne's empathy. He couldn't draw the pain from her, but he could be with her when she needed him.

And now, she needed him.

The hospital was filled with soldiers, but they were all

wounded. Anyone who could walk and hold a blade was sent back to the wall after a good night's sleep and a hot meal. Baron Phren was hopelessly outnumbered, and he couldn't spare trained soldiers to haul the dead and the wounded back from the front lines, much less assign men to guard a hospital. The walls of the city were their one and only line of defense before the baron's own keep.

Worse yet, from the walls to the hospital was a distinct path marked in drips and puddles of blood. The route the wounded were carried on stretchers reeked of sharp copper and offal. Every day, dozens or scores of people would make that journey, blood dripping from damaged bodies, and the narjags knew that scent like Rew knew the smell of freshly poured ale.

The Dark Kind would attack anyone they saw, and some would burst into homes or shops that were only lightly protected, but many of them would follow the scent of blood straight to the unprotected hospital.

A group of four narjags careened in front of Rew, staggering from a building like town drunks. Crimson stained their maws, and their eyes lit at the sight of the ranger and the fighter. Raif swung a backhand blow, clearing two of the narjags with the strike then he kept running, smashing his armored elbow into the face of a third. The fourth creature slowed, and Rew dragged his longsword across its neck and kept charging down the street after Raif.

Ahead of them, he could see the backs of narjags as they smashed open the doors of the hospital building. Rew and Raif were still three blocks away. They were helpless as the creatures began to stream inside.

———

THE FLOOR OF THE ENTRANCE TO THE HOSPITAL WAS THAT OF A charnel house. Blood and bits of broken bone coated the closely set stones like fresh paint, and even the walls were splattered with grisly chunks. The entry hall was a triage area, where newly arrived wounded were assessed to determine if they just needed some stitches, surgery, Anne's empathy, or if they were beyond the care that could be provided. Everyone who had been in the room was beyond hope now.

Doors leading deeper into the building were open, and Rew could hear screams as narjags must have found bedridden soldiers and the women who tended to them. Anne worked two floors above.

Rew tore his eyes from the hallway that led to the largest room in the place and headed for the stairs. Raif came behind him, clattering in his armor, wordless. There were people who needed their help, people who were dying in the adjacent rooms, but they ran upstairs.

Streaks of crimson marred the walls, but the stairwell didn't have the bodies that the first floor did. Anyone healthy enough to be walking on the stairs was healthy enough to run when they realized the wall had been overrun or when the door to the hospital had been shattered.

They reached the landing and surprised a pair of narjags crouching over the prone figure of one of the hospital attendants. Her dress had been torn away by grasping, clawed hands, and the flesh on her arm, left shoulder, and her face had been eaten away.

Rew hacked down with more force than was necessary, taking the head off one of the narjags. He kicked the other beneath the chin, knocking it back. He lunged forward to stab it in the chest and finish it.

Raif sprinted past him, taking to the next flight of stairs, chasing higher to where Anne's ward was located.

They arrived in a pile at the next landing and found a dead narjag and the bodies of two men, wounded soldiers who had managed to rise from their beds. One held a scalpel, the other a leg from a broken chair. Even without proper weapons, they'd tried to defend Anne and those she cared for.

Rew and Raif kept running. They passed through a hall then

into a room outside of Anne's chambers where the wounded who needed regular but not intensive care were bedded, mostly patients Anne had seen in the days before who were still recovering.

The beds were soaked through with blood, and half a dozen pairs of beady narjag eyes snapped up when the ranger and the fighter ran into the room. The door on the opposite side of the room, leading to where Anne performed most of her treatments, had been knocked open, the door hanging on one damaged hinge.

Rew saw a shape duck into that door, and he ran after it.

The six narjags in the ward leapt at him, but he ignored them. He ran like a breeze, whipping between them before they could react. Like a flash of lightning, he streaked across the room to the doorway.

Anne was in the corner, flinging everything she could reach at a dark figure that was halfway across the room. Without thought, Rew tossed his hunting knife underhanded at the back of the creature. The valaan spun, smacking aside the blade before it sank into its flesh, taking a nick on its arm but sparing itself serious injury.

Rew followed with his longsword, lunging at the valaan. It snarled, catching his second attack with its other hand, strong fingers grasping the blade of the longsword and yanking on it. Startled, Rew was pulled forward.

He had to let go of his longsword with one hand and raise his arm to absorb a blow on his bracer. The valaan held onto the blade of his sword and kept pulling him, its mouth open, a stuttering cough bursting from its throat. Laughter? Did valaan laugh?

Rew let go of his longsword with his second hand and punched the thing in the face as hard as he could. The valaan's head snapped back. Then, the erratic coughing began again. It was definitely laughing at him. It slashed at him with its free hand, and Rew stepped back, avoiding the blow. It swung the hilt of his own longsword at him, still holding it by the blade. Orange blood leaked down the steel, and the hilt struck him on his raised arm.

Rew backpedaled again, cursing and shaking the numbness from his limb. Behind him, he could hear Raif dealing with the six narjags that had been in the other room. The lad was bellowing curses and, from the racket, still fighting hard. Anne was in the corner, holding a roll of linen bandages in one hand and a loaf of bread in the other. Neither one was going to do much good thrown at the back of the valaan.

With a clawed hand still wrapped around the blade of the longsword, the valaan raised the weapon, and stalked toward Rew.

He stared at it uncomfortably. Narjags stole weapons whenever they could, but he'd never heard of a valaan using one. Now, he faced his own enchanted blade, and his hunting knife had been knocked toward the far side of the room somewhere. He had two daggers stuck into the tops of his boots, but he would have to crouch to draw them, and he didn't fancy ducking his head in front of a valaan with a sword.

The creature continued its low, horrifying chuckle and glanced between Rew and Anne. Had it come to her by plan? Was it hunting the empath?

Rew launched himself forward before the valaan moved. He dove halfway between it and Anne. The valaan spun, taking two blazingly fast steps, but Rew caught it. He slammed into the awful creature, ramming his shoulder into its side, wrapping his arms around its legs, and tackling it.

The valaan fell, but it twisted in his grip, raking its claws along his back before they both crashed onto the floor.

Rew swung an arm, knocking the longsword away, and hammered down on the valaan's head with his other fist. Rather than defending itself, it slashed its clawed hand across Rew's face, drawing four parallel lacerations that cut him to the bone. He hammered it again. Then, the valaan kicked up, and Rew was sent flopping over its head, falling hard on his back.

The valaan spun and rose, raising his longsword above its head and holding it by the hilt this time, prepared to smite him.

Rew spun as well, moving like a child's top, sweeping his legs into the legs of the valaan. His shins bounced off the valaan's knee ineffectually. The ranger grunted, and the valaan kept laughing. He rolled to the side before it began its downstroke and got clipped on the shoulder, the enchanted steel of his own sword gouging a painful cut into his muscle. He kept rolling and narrowly avoided another strike.

The valaan jumped after him, trying to land on his legs to pin him in place. Rew drew his legs back and yanked his daggers from his boots. Thrusting down at him again, the valaan stabbed the longsword into the floor.

Anticipating the blow, Rew had rolled out of the way then sliced his dagger across the back of the valaan's ankle. It was only after he'd made the cut that he wondered whether the things had the same tendon that men did, in the same place.

He kept rolling, and the valaan staggered toward him, its leg going out from under it. Hopping on one foot, it kept coming, and Rew kept rolling, bumping over the hilt of his fallen hunting knife. He neared the wall and flopped onto his back. Flinging it backhanded, he tossed one of his throwing daggers at the valaan.

The creature twisted in the air, but the blade sank into its chest with a sickening squelch. It landed awkwardly, fell to a knee, and then dragged itself forward with its free hand, the other still clutching Rew's sword.

The dagger had buried deep, but it had missed the creature's heart. Muttering under his breath, Rew slapped his hand down on the bone hilt of his hunting knife and rose. He held the knife in one hand, his second throwing dagger in the other.

The valaan eyed him coldly. It reared back, raising his longsword as if to throw it at him. Then, it turned.

Rew hurled himself at the creature, shouting for Anne to duck.

Orange and dark blood spun away as the valaan threw the longsword toward her. Rew reached the creature a breath later, slamming his throwing dagger into its ribs then tearing his hunting knife across its neck. Orange blood erupted, but Rew's attention was on Anne.

The empath had yanked an empty cot in front of her to block the sword, but the blade had slid easily through the thin mattress. The wooden hilt stood out straight, and nothing moved.

Rew cried in alarm and ran to the cot. He placed his hands on it gently then peered over the edge, afraid he would cause Anne worse injury by moving his weapon before he saw the damage.

On the other side of the bed, Anne was looking up at him with astonished eyes. A finger-width from the side of her head, Rew's longsword had punched through the mattress and stabbed into the wall. A fistful of Anne's hair was pinned by the weapon, and the empath was speechless.

"Blessed Mother's Grace," whispered Rew.

"If you can free my hair…" mumbled Anne.

Rew grasped the hilt of his longsword and pulled on it. It was stuck in the wall. He grunted and tugged harder, finally freeing the weapon. He tossed the cot aside, and Anne sat, her hand unconsciously touching various parts of her body, as if to make sure she hadn't been injured.

Rew smiled then cursed and spun, looking for Raif. Sounds from the next room came crashing in, and Rew ran out of Anne's chamber.

Raif was standing before the opposite doorway, his greatsword held in front of him, and he was thrashing it with short, stilted movements. Around him, half a dozen narjags lay dead. There were more of them in the stairwell, trying to come in.

"Raif, I'm here," said Rew.

He took Raif's side and allowed the fighter to back away.

The hallway outside was crowded with narjags, kept at bay by Raif's presence and the creature's hatred of each other. They clawed and gnawed at their fellows and had taken deep cuts from Raif, but they hadn't fought their way inside. Rew saw immediately the fighter hadn't been able to finish them because he'd had no room to swing his giant sword. Gouges marred the walls where he'd tried.

Methodically, Rew began stabbing Dark Kind, clearing the hallway of them, while the realization set in that the city was still overrun. Anne was safe, but many others were not.

Chapter Four

They descended the floors of the hospital, clearing it of narjags as they went, witnessing the horrific toll that had been paid. Bodies were mutilated and ravaged. Men, wounded and unarmed—many of them bed-bound—had no chance as the narjags swept through.

The Dark Kind stood almost as little chance against Rew and Raif as they hunted down the foul creatures. Rew's longsword and hunting knife dripped rancid blood by the time they finished clearing the building. Raif took Rew's advice and stopped trying to swing his greatsword in the tight confines of the hallways. He'd sheathed the big weapon, found a hatchet in the hands of a dead narjag, and had been using it to hack and chop his way behind the ranger.

Anne followed cautiously, checking on her charges as the warriors cleared each room. At each bed, with each patient, her face grew darker. Once they'd exited her own chamber, they'd found no one alive. The narjags, perhaps at the direction of the valaan or maybe operating on their own instinct, had dispersed throughout the building, finding every room, killing everyone there.

Two score of them, by Rew's count. The creatures were fat

from feasting on human flesh and were slow to defend themselves. The ranger and the fighter made quick work of them.
When they finally approached the main door to the hospital, Rew
did so with trepidation. They'd faced forty narjags, which had
been easy enough to kill, but only because of the slaughter the
creatures had already conducted. Would the rest of the city be the
same?

The day was bright, the sky cloudless. The sunshine bathed
Valstock in comfortable warmth. That made it worse. The streets
were splattered with vivid blood.

Any people who'd been nearby were in hiding or dead. In the
distance, they saw a party of a dozen soldiers peering into alleyways then stalking across the street to check a building, looking
for narjags still on the loose. That meant the fight at the wall must
be over, one way or the other.

Rew heard a crackle, like shattering ice, and led Raif and Anne
a street over. In the center of a market square, standing over half a
dozen wounded women and children was Cinda, with Zaine
watching her back. They had several soldiers with them as well,
though half of those men still clutched clean steel, untainted by
the blood of narjags.

Cinda's eyes blazed with green light, and around her hands,
ghastly fire danced. She saw them but did not react to their
arrival. Her eyes were scanning the edges of the market, looking
for targets.

A narjag riding an ayre came loping into view, and Cinda
thrust a hand toward the pair. A jet of cold funeral fire arced
across the open space to catch the ayre and narjag mid-leap,
igniting them like a pitch-covered torch. She cut off her flame
before any of the grasping green and white tongues of funeral fire
licked against the wooden buildings nearby.

The necromancer radiated power. She was drawing it in great
gulps from the surge of dying people, but unlike in Jabaan, she
was tightly controlling the flow. The funeral fire she cast was
narrowly aimed and proportional to the damage she wanted to

cause. Despite her earlier concern, none of the buildings nearby had yet caught fire, but Rew thought perhaps from atop the wall, she wouldn't have been able to direct her attacks so neatly. He desperately wanted that to be the case.

The fire crackled and died on the bodies of the Dark Kind, and Rew grimaced at the thought of what could happen if Cinda's funeral fire blasted out of control. The city on fire, in the midst of an attack, would be a terrible tragedy, but he wouldn't tell her to stop. They had to fight on, no matter the risk. Giving up would be worse. Maybe she thought the same. He hoped so.

As more Dark Kind surfaced, Cinda incinerated them, but soon it was obvious the Dark Kind were learning to avoid that market square. The party left the soldiers to guard the wounded and began stalking through the streets of the city.

Rew ranged ahead, moving quietly about a block from the rest of them. He was listening for Dark Kind and trying to track them, though in the chaotic scene in the streets, following any particular signs was nearly impossible.

But the narjags and ayres did little to hide their presence, so time and time again, Rew led the group to them. If there was one or two, he would strike on his own. If there was a pack of them, he would gesture for the others.

Cinda took point, her flames crackling menacingly around her. Anne followed in the middle, darting to the wounded when they found someone alive, but more often, scowling in impotent anger at the dead. Zaine and Raif flanked the others, protecting the rear. The thief had discarded her bow and empty quiver and was holding the two bloody poignards she'd gotten from Valchon's spymaster. Raif had his greatsword out again. Even the narjags caught in their fervor were hesitant to approach the big fighter.

For hours, they stalked through Valstock, encountering groups of soldiers but few citizens. The soldiers eyed them gratefully and nervously. Those men and women rarely spoke, and none offered to join the party. It was clear they understood Cinda and the rest of them were doing more to face the Dark Kind than anyone else in the city, but no sane person was comfortable while a necromancer was practicing their power.

By evening, when the sun was beginning to set, the party was exhausted. They'd been fighting, and in a state of extreme tension, since dawn. Rew's arms felt like warm jelly, and he could see by the way Raif was moving that the fighter was one or two more encounters from slumping down, unable to continue. Zaine looked the liveliest, but she hadn't been the one to bear the brunt of the fighting. Anne's eyes were hollow, and the last victim of the narjags they'd seen lying wounded on the cobblestones, she'd merely looked and shaken her head.

"He won't make it."

Rew cringed. The man's wounds were brutal, but with Anne's skill... The empath drew some of the man's pain to make his passing comfortable, but she did not attempt to heal him. She couldn't. Even Anne had her limits.

Cinda carried on implacably. She did not speak to the rest of them, but Rew could feel the surge of her power had ebbed. She wasn't drawing it as rapidly as she had, but she hadn't used all she'd collected earlier. Street by street, she marched steadily, destroying the Dark Kind they saw, ignoring all else.

Until she looked up at the sky and then back at the rest of them. "Raif?"

The fighter grunted but had no words.

"Can you continue?"

Shrugging his armored shoulders, the big lad nodded.

Cinda's lips twisted, her pale skin and green eyes making her appear haunted. She shook her head. "You look like you can't even make it to the end of this block."

"I can," mumbled Raif, shifting his greatsword in his hands, allowing the tip of the giant blade to rest on the street.

"How many more do you think there are?" wondered Zaine. The sharp yips of an ayre echoed from across the city, and she winced. The thief rolled her head on her shoulders, cracking her neck, and said, "A few more, I suppose."

"We'll have found the bulk of them by now," replied Rew, turning a slow circle, listening to the cries of the wounded and the snarls and distant clashes of battle. "The problem is, those Dark Kind that are remaining will have split up. Individuals, pairs of them, they could have broken into shops or homes or scattered down alleyways and the other overlooked holes in this city. There'll be less than a hundred left, I'd guess. Finding them will take all night, but if we don't find them…"

"They'll find someone else," finished Raif. He lifted his sword, propping it on his shoulder. "We keep going, then."

"There's another way," offered Cinda.

Rew frowned. "The dead? You have strength for it still?"

The necromancer nodded.

"It's not going to make you popular amongst these people. No matter how certain you are of the risk to your life, no one likes seeing their bloody relatives rising from the dead. No one wants a loved one animated like a puppet."

"I'm not trying to be popular."

"There have been times when people have turned on necromancers. A day or two after a battle… They start thinking, remembering. Blessed Mother, lass, you can imagine what it'd be like to see someone you love come back, but they're still dead. That's a moment they'll never forget. Outside the walls, the soldiers were far enough away that it wasn't as… visceral. This isn't a good idea."

"I wasn't planning on staying here long, Ranger. These people may dislike seeing their dead friends walking about, but that's better than them being dead themselves, isn't it?"

Rew grimaced.

"You don't have to approve, but it doesn't matter, it's not your choice," remarked Cinda. "I have the ability to stop the Dark Kind, so I will. I don't much care what it makes people think."

"Or feel."

Cinda shrugged. "For months, we've known I'm not the hero of this tale. It's not I who needs to win the favor of the people.

They'll blame it on me, Ranger, and with luck, remember you as the one who led the defense. For them to fall in behind your banner, they need to be alive."

"That's not what—"

"I know," interrupted Cinda. "I know that's not what you want. None of this is what any of us wants, but we live in the world we have, not the one we desire."

Rew had no response, and Cinda closed her eyes.

The rest of the party tensed. Rew could feel the swirl of Cinda's magic, and he guessed Anne could feel it as well. Maybe Raif, too. It was his blood right as well Cinda's. Zaine, whether or not she felt anything, knew what it meant when half a block from them, there was a loud scrape, and a soldier clumsily rose to his feet. A crude, broken spear jutted from his gut, and slowly and steadily, the soldier pulled it free.

"Now, they hunt," said Cinda. She watched through heavily lidded eyes as the soldier turned and began shambling down the street. Cinda glanced at Rew. "I tried to only raise soldiers, those who had been in the fight. Maybe that will help everyone's… feelings. I can't be completely precise, though, when casting across the entire city. Hopefully, these people remember it is a war that we are in, us against the dark. And if not, hopefully, they see what I can do and avoid me. Either way, we should have peace for tonight. You all can rest."

Rew nodded and grasped Anne's hand. He led her and the others back to the inn where they'd taken rooms. The party followed behind him with the same grace that Cinda's corpses had. He'd thought to rebuke Cinda, to tell her there'd been another way, that if they stopped caring, they were lost, but she'd been right. Without her necromancy, people were going to die. The Dark Kind had to be hunted, and it would take him hours to find them all. It was a war they fought, a war that would decide the fate of Vaeldon and, perhaps, all of mankind.

AT DAWN THE NEXT MORNING, THE PARTY SHUFFLED FROM THE OPEN gates of the city like they'd been amongst the wounded that spread across the market square stuffed together as neatly as vendor kiosks. Others were crammed into the hospital, but most of the aides who'd worked there were dead, and it was friends and family who were giving care to their loved ones. That was, if any friends and family had survived.

The baron, for what it'd been worth, had been inconsolable. He, and most of his advisors, had survived locked within the keep at the center of the city. The Dark Kind had raged around that squat block of stone, finding easier meat amongst the populace. He'd ordered the few household guards he'd kept close to use their crossbows on the raging Dark Kind, but it'd been far too late to turn the tide of the battle. Most of his men had been stationed on the city wall. Late into the evening, before Cinda's corpses had finished the Dark Kind, the baron had toured the city, surrounded by lantern light and a dozen soldiers.

Rew had spoken to the man later and saw he was truly grieving, but then, everyone was. By rote, some of the citizens and soldiers who'd survived worked out of simple habit or to distract themselves from what was all around them. Others sat in quiet places, staring at the walls or the floor.

While the rest of the party slept, Rew had spoken to the baron and his senior advisors before catching a few hours of slumber. Cinda, her eyes glowing like green embers, had watched him collapse into the bed, and she'd woken him an hour before dawn. He looked up and saw her hovering, blank-faced. She'd changed her battle-stained robes, but her expression was identical to the one he'd seen the day before. He wanted to curse at her, to shake her, to make her feel what the rest of the city was feeling, but he couldn't. She wouldn't.

They all agreed on one thing, though. They had to get moving. Until Vaisius Morden was torn from the throne, until someone else took control of the black legion and spellcasters, there was no one to face the Dark Kind. It felt wrong to leave the city, the wounded and the needy, but their way was forward. They had to face the king if they wanted to stop it all.

The weight of the losses dragged behind them like a sledge as they stepped out of the gates. Someone, some captain or sergeant left in command of the wall through the night, had tried to clear the highway that led north toward Mordenhold. They'd done the best they could in the dark and undermanned. Near a thousand narjags and ayres had died outside Valstock, and their bodies lay piled in small heaps beside the narrow path that had been opened and then their bodies were like mown hay for hundreds of paces beyond. Their stench rose, and already, the flies were clustering thick, drawn to the smell of the rotting meat.

Carrion birds flapped nearby, but they did not descend on the field. The foul flesh of narjags would poison them. Instead, the birds scavenged along the walls and in the city when they found an exposed and unguarded body of a person. Rats scurried in the early morning gloom, skittering away at the footfalls of the party.

Rew called to the guards on the wall. They would need to clear the bodies and burn them before disease set in. The Dark Kind always carried something nasty, and the rats would spread it to the city. Of course, there were hundreds of dead narjags within the walls, as well. Sighing at the guards' numb acknowledgement, Rew turned and began walking.

On the wall, the guards watched them go.

Chapter Five

R ew sat in front of the campfire, his legs folded beneath him, his sword balancing on his fingertips. The sky was a purple bruise, the last streaks of pink and gold having faded a quarter hour earlier. The fire cast an ominous hue on the sharp edge of the sword, but to Rew, it felt comfortable. For years, he'd sat with the sword out in the wilderness, just looking at it.

He'd learned of the presence of a soul magically entombed within the blade while he'd still been in Mordenhold. There, on a quiet evening in his father's castle, he'd learned that soul was his ancestor, Erasmus Morden. Even then, Rew had known the ancient ghost was dangerous, that Erasmus yearned for his freedom, and that there'd been a damned good reason he'd been locked inside the blade in the first place. To Rew, the presence of Erasmus had always felt like that of a bared blade, poised to strike.

But Erasmus Morden had answers. He'd been there during the cataclysmic war against the Dark Kind two hundred years earlier, when his son had risen to power on the backs of countless dead. Erasmus had seen hundreds of thousands of soldiers fall in battle. He'd seen Vaisius draw the power from their departing souls, and he'd seen his son gather the people that would go on to form Vaeldon, and had even seen Vaisius lead them against the greatest threat mankind had ever faced.

They'd won that war, father and son, though even then Vaisius Morden had taken most of the credit. He had earned it, supposed Rew. Though the grim hints the ranger had sensed in Erasmus Morden's thoughts had spoken a horrible truth about how Vaisius had earned it. Necromancers were worthless without death.

The father's opinion was heavily clouded by the son's betrayal. Toward the end of the war with the Dark Kind, while father and son were consolidating the various factions and territories and forging them into a kingdom, Vaisius had tricked his father and drawn his power into the longsword, sealing it and the older man's soul away for the last two hundred years.

Rew hoped releasing that ancient spirit to shatter the maelstrom had been the right decision. It'd saved Carff, he had no doubt about that, but the cast off of the remaining storms had meant the deaths of thousands of innocent people along the coast. Better than the million within the city, and maybe worse, had Erasmus managed to spin the storm into something even greater. Of course, Erasmus wouldn't have had a chance to do that without Rew opening the tomb.

Tilting the blade so that the light of the fire danced like the real thing along the edge, Rew pondered what it meant that Erasmus Morden was gone, finally sent to the beyond—whatever that was.

Did Erasmus feel the embrace of the Blessed Mother, as Anne believed? Surely she didn't think Erasmus Morden had earned such a place, though did that matter? Did the Mother judge the dead for their sins in life? Rew had never paid attention to such things when Anne had told him, and he'd certainly never paid attention when one of the priestesses of the Mother had espoused their views.

Was Erasmus now within the domain of the Cursed Father—Vaisius Morden? Could the king summon and control the spirit of his father like he did others? It felt frightening, but Rew couldn't put a finger on why. The king didn't need any additional knowledge or power he might draw from Erasmus. If he did, Rew never would have been allowed to carry the sword.

The ranger wondered what Vaisius Morden believed was beyond this world they existed within. The man's soul had survived for two centuries, and he'd drawn his fingers through the beyond countless times. He'd raised the dead, and he'd communed with shades. He had to know something, didn't he? There was… something beyond. Rew had seen with his own eyes that souls could be recalled from death. He'd spoken to some of them.

Did Vaisius know the truth about what happened after life?

Even when Rew had been younger, living in Mordenhold in the creche, and after, when he was living in Mordenhold and was old enough he should have known better than to be there, Rew had never asked his father. Had anyone? Did Vaisius Morden know a grand secret that he held alone? He implied he did, but no one pressed the king on such things. Was it a secret held by one awful man, or was it a lie, told by the man to bolster the mystery of his power?

Was the genesis of the Cursed Father, a false deity, a lie the king told the kingdom, all so he could siphon the power of death like a drunk spilling cold ale down his throat. Was death knowable? Should it be known?

Probably not. The ranger had learned enough in his time that he understood somethings were best left unknown. Ignorance could be a blessing, though ignorance certainly wasn't helping him solve their current problems.

The ranger sighed and turned the sword again, flipping it to the other side and studying the gleaming steel. Two hundred years old. The blade was a veteran of thousands of fights, and the metal looked as fresh as if it'd just been sharpened by the blacksmith's hand, still lit by the fires of his forge. It was a work of sublime, perfect skill.

Vaisius Morden had been a necromancer. Since the founding of the kingdom, he'd obtained further powers, and he was exceptionally skilled at each talent of high magic, but he hadn't been two hundred years before, so who had crafted such a perfect weapon? Who had enchanted it to be a tomb?

Across the fire from him, Cinda chopped vegetables with stubborn tenacity. Potatoes, carrots, onions, and herbs all minced then fed into Anne's bubbling soup pot. The young necromancer wasn't a skilled cook, but she took Anne's instruction and was a willing set of hands. Every night, when they weren't staying in a hostel or during the week in the city, Cinda had helped in the evenings.

It was a dogged effort to hold onto something normal. Food fueled life. Good food brought joy. It was the opposite of what Cinda did when she released her powers. It was her way of trying to find balance, trying to prove that necromancy was not who she was, or simply, that it wasn't who she had to be. She needed to have a choice in the matter.

Rew wished deeply that he'd had a real choice and had remained a ranger and nothing more. He ached for that simple life, hiking the wilderness and comfortable evenings in Anne's inn. He'd been the eyes of the kingdom and had been content. It was all he'd needed, all he'd wanted once he'd grown enough to know such a thing.

But things change.

"You've been staring at that sword for half an hour, Rew," remarked Anne.

His gaze rose to meet her look. He shrugged and did not respond.

"Does it feel different?"

He frowned and nodded. "Aye, a little. Before, I could feel Erasmus. He felt... strange. It was something like communion, but as if he was reaching to me instead of me to him. It put me on edge, to be honest, because over the years, I came to understand his intentions were not benign, but I knew there were answers there. I knew that if I undertook the risk, I could learn. Now, there's nothing. It's empty. He's gone. His answers are gone."

"Then why do you keep looking at the sword?"

"Habit?"

"Is it?"

"I can't help feeling this tugging suspicion that maybe there are answers still. Not in the blade itself. Erasmus is truly gone, I can feel that, but... what if there's something in his thoughts, in his memory, that could help us? There's a reason for all of this; a reason I killed my brothers, a reason Alsayer led us by the nose, city to city, up until the confrontation with Valchon. There's a reason I held this blade, and I was able to release my ultimate ancestor and scatter that maelstrom. They knew the answers but died holding them. We should know enough to figure it out, don't you think?"

"Alsayer managed to get his head chopped off by your brother," mentioned Cinda, her belt knife working along the length of a stubby carrot. "I'm not convinced he'd figured anything out at all, but whatever his plans, they didn't work out the way he intended. Maybe that's why you don't have answers, because you're asking the wrong questions? Alsayer thought he'd set himself up as second to the king, or maybe he figured there was a way he'd take the throne himself after you tossed your father off it. I don't know, but I do know it wasn't our best interests he had at heart. His answers may not be your answers."

"What would he have gained by betraying us?" questioned Rew. "There was no benefit to him if Valchon killed us. What would the destruction of Carff earn Alsayer? I know you think he was a cold bastard, and maybe he didn't care about those lives, but he cared about his own, right? How did that help him? What did he think was going to happen if he and Valchon portaled away and all the rest of us died? He knew Vaisius Morden's soul would take Valchon. He knew the king would remember that Alsayer lied to him, so why do all of it?"

Cinda stopped her chopping and looked Rew in the eye. "Snakes bite. It's what they do."

Sighing, Rew finally put down the sword.

"You say you're searching for answers," said Anne slowly. "You've gotten them before from the sword? From Erasmus?"

Rew nodded.

"Tell us what they were," suggested Anne. "It's time, don't you think, as we approach the end, for us all to see clearly? How are you planning for Cinda to defeat the king? What secrets did Erasmus share with you?"

Rew grimaced and glanced at Cinda. The young necromancer's eyes were down, and she was working hard again on cutting the carrot. She knew. They both understood what was necessary, and they'd come to terms with it, though the burden wasn't resting comfortably. Anne wasn't going like what they were planning.

"What? You think we can get all the way to Mordenhold without you two saying anything? You think my own imagination isn't conjuring ideas that are worse and worse? Your plans can't be worse than the most terrible thing I can think of."

Rew fiddled with the wooden hilt of his sword then mumbled, "Maybe not."

Anne pointed at him with her soup spoon. "Rew, tell me."

"Your brothers are dead," said Cinda. "There's nothing left but the king. I don't think there's any point hiding from it now. She won't like it, but so what? You and I don't like it, either, but it's what we have to do."

"Well?" demanded Anne, thrusting her spoon back into the pot and threatening to spill the contents with the force of her stirring.

Rew set his longsword to the side and explained, "We can't kill Vaisius Morden. He has the power of eight generations of Mordens, the most talented spellcasters of their time, proven by the Investiture. He's been building his strength for centuries, and that strength is phenomenal. I've seen it, Anne. It's impossible for us to overcome. Pfah, even if we did manage to play some trick and stab him in the back with a knife or blast him with a well-cast spell, it'd be no good. He's... How can I put it?"

"We do not contend with a man but with a spirit," offered Cinda, her eyes still down on the half-chopped carrot. "He's bound to the body, and it lives and breathes, but it's quite possible that when it no longer breathes, he'll still be bound to it. Like the dead that I've raised, he'll be tied to the flesh, and separating him from it is going to be far more difficult than merely killing him. The king is both man and ghost. He cannot simply be killed."

"B-But…" stammered Anne. "The crypts. What if we destroy the crypts? He won't have power then, will he? He won't be able to maintain the binding, right?"

Rew nodded. "That's what Heindaw believed, and I think it's true, but Cinda read in her books there are forty crypts, and they're scattered all across this kingdom. Maybe we injured him, removing Jabaan, Iyre, and Carff from the playing board, but who's to say? Even if that destroyed a measure of his power, how can we finish the job? The remaining crypts are scattered from one end of the kingdom to the other."

"We can try," retorted Anne. "If it works…"

"No matter what we do, his grandest crypt is in Mordenhold. Untold power will be stored there, and when we get there, Cinda would have to vie with him for that strength. I have faith in the lass, but he has two hundred times more experience. Sorry, Cinda. No offense."

Cinda shrugged. "It's true. No matter the potential in my blood, I am a novice at this art which Vaisius Morden more or less invented. We can fight with courage and valor, but we should not be stupid and pretend the odds are different than they are."

"If we could portal, we might be able to attempt destroying more crypts, but we can't portal, and I don't think we're going to stumble across many spellcasters who are willing to assist us. We're not even sure that would work. If we undermine the king's base of power, how quickly can he replenish it? There are thousands of people dying every day to the north. Is he absorbing that power? If we undermine his base, he may just kill more people. He won't hesitate to destroy Mordenhold itself, Anne."

Anne's lips twisted. "I don't understand. If this quest is impossible, what are we doing?"

"It's impossible to defeat the king in his current form," remarked Rew, "but he's not always in that form. Every generation, he changes bodies."

"So, when he…" said Anne, shaking her head. "It doesn't make sense. How would you have any more ability to stop him than your father or all of the Mordens before you?"

"I wouldn't," agreed Rew. "I'm no necromancer."

Anne turned slowly toward Cinda.

"Yes," whispered the girl. "Vaisius Morden is a ghost, and I know how to deal with ghosts. I'll draw his soul into my body, but once he's there, I must be destroyed. Our plan is that when I pass to the beyond, I'll take him with me."

Chapter Six

A nne was rather upset with the plan, and Rew reminding her that was why they hadn't told her in the first place did not help. Cinda's assurances it was the only way, that she'd done the research, that she'd spoken to Alsayer, and that it was on her and this was the way it had to be, also did not help.

Attempting to enlist allies, Anne had called Raif and Zaine to the fire, and she'd fervently explained the plan to them. Both of the children cried, something Anne was too enraged to do. They'd hugged Cinda, and they'd denied it was the only way. They'd been angry as well, but in the face of Cinda's certainty, they crumbled. Anne continued ranting, refusing to accept it was the correct path, but time and time again, Rew asked her if she had better idea.

"Anne, I know my father, and I know that we cannot defeat the man. He's been building power for two hundred years. His physical body is nearly impervious to harm, but even if we harmed it, it would not matter! He's faced down who knows how many of my ancestors and easily defeated them all. I assure you he has no fear of us whatsoever. He doesn't need to fear us. There's nothing I can do to him. I could stab him in the heart. I could chop off his head, and that won't stop him!"

"We could… destroy him," retorted Anne. "We can smash him to pulp. That will stop him, won't it?"

"That would destroy most animated corpses, but Anne, my father knows how to hop into a new body. If we somehow concocted a crazy scheme that allowed us to completely annihilate his body, I don't know if we can prevent him from jumping to a new one. That's why he wants us in Mordenhold, to take over my flesh."

"There has to be a way to prevent that," argued Anne.

"It's the blood," said Cinda. "Vaisius Morden uses the connection to ease his passage. I don't think he could take over just anyone, but he can take Rew, and he can take me."

"All right, then without either of you two, we could, ah…"

The rest of the party sat silent, looking at Anne. The idea the fighter, the thief, and the empath would somehow face the world's greatest necromancer, the man with all of the resources of Vaeldon, and crush him to the point he was nothing more than a blood smear, was laughable.

Raif cleared his throat. "It's rash, even for me, but is it impossible? What if we drew him out and buried him under a rockslide or something? Or… what about my sword? If the king is a ghost, would my blade banish him like it did the wraiths and undead? It won't be easy, I acknowledge that, but if it's not impossible, we have to consider our options."

"He's a living man, as well as a dead one," said Rew, smiling wanly. "I thought about that when we found the properties of your blade. Would a blow from your sword end his mortal life and sever his spiritual one? I don't think it would. It's not the shades themselves which your sword is enchanted to destroy, it's the bindings. You cut the binding, and he may not be tied to the corpse, but that doesn't mean he'll be banished. I think it's likely he'd be similar to one of the wraiths we've faced, and perhaps even more dangerous. Is it even a binding he has upon my father's body, or something else? None of us know enough about the enchantment on your sword or Vaisius Morden's necromancy."

"Oh," said Raif, his face downcast. Then, his eyes brightened. "You said 'think,' so it's possible it might work?"

"Your greatsword exists, and Vaisius Morden hasn't destroyed it. Why would a man like the king allow an artifact to survive which has the unique power to defeat him? If he was afraid of the properties in your blade, he would have taken it or destroyed it long ago. The properties of the greatsword are not a secret, but even if they were, Vaisius Morden has the skill of the kingdom's greatest enchanters. He's seen that weapon, Raif. He knows what it can do better than anyone."

"Maybe, but you still don't know. It could work."

"I know my father," retorted Rew, "and he wouldn't allow a threat like that to exist outside of his hands. It won't work, Raif, and when it doesn't, you and anyone near you is going to get killed."

"You're fine with Cinda dying but not me?"

"Her sacrifice will buy us victory. Yours gets us nothing."

Raif cracked his knuckles, his eyes darting between Cinda and Rew, but what could he say? They all knew the lad would offer himself to spare his sister, but even he could see the foolishness of doing so when it wasn't going to work. The king of Vaeldon wasn't going to be brought down by a boy with a sword.

Rew and Cinda hadn't come to the same plan because it was pleasant. It was because they couldn't conceive of anything else. They had to defeat the king. The cost, if it worked, was inconsequential.

"Did you glean this plan from Erasmus Morden's memories?" queried Anne. "His thoughts were twisted, Rew. All he knew was hate. If he conceived this…"

"It did not come from him," said Rew. He rubbed his face in his hands then admitted, "Though, experiencing his thoughts led me to the idea. Erasmus was frantic to escape, and he thirsted for revenge. He worried taking my body, or that of one of my ancestors, would make him vulnerable. He was right in the end. He's gone because of how he leapt from his prison to me."

"Then, the king…"

Rew shook his head. "Erasmus was a deranged madman. He'd been locked in a steel tomb for centuries. He'd lost everything except his rage. Vaisius Morden is at the full height of his faculties and his power. You know we've thought this through, Anne. Cinda and I reached the conclusion separately, and in the end, we've both decided it's the only way."

"I won't accept that," declared the empath.

Rew shrugged and did not respond.

"I won't accept it either!" bellowed Raif. He clutched his greatsword like a comfort blanket. "We'll find a way, Cinda. We'll find a way."

"I can't have you fighting me all the way to Mordenhold," said the girl. Her cold, green eyes turned to study each of them in turn. "Maybe you think you'll save me, but I don't want to—I can't— do this alone. I need your help."

"Our help to kill yourself?" scoffed Anne.

Raif put a hand on the empath's shoulder and spoke to his sister. "I will always support you. If you need my help, I will be there. Never fear that you are alone. Whatever you need, whatever it takes, I am there for you. That's why—I hope you understand—while I'll be behind you every step from here to the capital, I'm going to keep thinking. I know I'm not the smartest, the wisest, but if I can come up with a solution, I will. I'm with you, Cinda, helping in every way that I can, including ways you don't want. If it… if it comes to doing it your way, I will be there with you."

"Thank you," whispered Cinda.

"Well, of course we'll be there with you," snapped Anne. "I just… It's not…"

"It took me awhile to accept this course as well," replied the necromancer. "Think of ideas all you want. It's what Rew and I have been doing since we understood this journey, but when it's time…"

Anne looked away.

Zaine cleared her throat, and the party turned to her. "I, ah, I feel like this is normally when I make some off-color jest, but I'm with you, Cinda. We are like a family, and families stick together. They help each other, even when it's hard."

"Especially when it's hard," agreed Rew.

ANNE HELD A GRUDGE, AND IT WAS EVIDENT THE NEXT EVENING WHEN they stopped at a small roadside tavern. As Rew opened his mouth to order an ale, Anne interrupted and requested water for him. Zaine thought it hilarious until Anne made sure the serving woman knew she meant water for all of them.

He wasn't sulking about the ale, no matter what anyone said. He just needed some air, so Rew led the children outside that evening for sparring. In the light of two lanterns they'd borrowed from the innkeeper, he had them try weapons of different sizes, including his longsword, and discussed the different tactics they would need to use with different blades.

None of them crossed swords with each other, and Cinda spent the time silently observing, not casting any of her magic to join the fun like she had earlier. After their recent discussions, facing off against each other didn't seem right. They worked until it was late, a light sheen of sweat glistening on their brows in the lantern light, and then returned to the common room.

Rew drew a deep breath and let it slowly slip out when he saw Anne sitting there with half a mug of wine in front of her. He sat down across from her and pointedly did not order himself an ale. He regretted that, and wasn't entirely sure what point he was trying to make, but nonetheless, that was what he did.

Around them, the air was thick with people discussing the Dark Kind. The army accosting Baron Phren's city to the south had been defeated, but evidently, loose packs of narjags and ayres were running rampant in the countryside. They didn't have the numbers to overrun a town and weren't showing the organization they had outside Valstock, but even a group of ten narjags was dangerous. Farmers, woodsmen, and travelers were all susceptible to attacks. Even merchant caravans with plentiful guards were at risk on the roads. Those hired swords had to sleep sometime, and for those with no plans to leave the village, narjags were still terrifying. Their presence was bringing all trade in the area to a standstill, which eventually meant necessary supplies weren't going to come. That was a different kind of fear, a kind you could not fight with a sword.

After listening for a moment, Rew cleared his throat and began offering advice to the inn's other patrons. Raif joined him, and by the time they were ready to retire, they'd spent an hour coaching the locals and the travelers on how best to survive an encounter with the Dark Kind.

The people thanked them effusively, and as they ascended to their rooms above, Rew complained, "It's not enough."

"No, but it's something," replied Raif. "Look, we can't make them all rangers in a night, but we can make them a little more prepared. Might not save all of them, but if one person lives because of the conversation we had, it was worth it."

"Sounds like something I'd say," responded Rew with a grunt. He opened the door and entered their room. "There is wisdom in those words, but it still doesn't seem enough."

"I know," agreed Raif, kicking off his boots and disdainfully feeling the straw stuffed into his mattress. "This isn't very fresh."

"Who's going to mow hay when the Dark Kind are out there?"

"Good point," muttered the fighter.

Raif sat on the narrow bed, methodically stretching his legs. He stripped off his shirt, preparing to wash it in the basin between their beds but paused to touch a long, pink scar on his ribs that hadn't fully healed despite Anne's attention. She'd been worn to the bone following Valstock, and all of her energy had been spent on critical cases in the moments before they had left. Since then, she'd recovered and given Raif what empathy she had, but it'd been too late, and she still wasn't herself.

"Are you all right?" asked Rew.

"I'm fine," replied the lad, "and a scar will make me more interesting to women, if you listen to Zaine. It's not sore, really, just... I guess I've gotten used to getting injured with no consequence. That's a foolish thought, isn't it? The danger is real. We could get hurt, or even killed."

Rew shrugged. Could... or would. What was there to say.

The lad studied his back for a long moment then asked, "Do you think Anne will be all right?"

"She'll recover," assured Rew. "She'll recover from Baron Phren's city, that is. I don't know what it will do to her when we see through this quest. She's the one being vocal, but I know it won't be easy on you, either. It's a brave thing you're doing, continuing on when you know the cost."

"You will try to think of another plan, won't you?" asked the fighter. "I'll do as my sister asks, I always have, but it's going to ruin me. If she asks me to... I don't know if I could do it, no matter what she says."

"Trying to come up with a better plan is what I've been doing for months," replied Rew. He slipped off his boots and propped his longsword against his bed. "I won't offer you any shallow words and false hope, but I will try to think of an alternative. Until I can't any longer, I'll try."

Raif nodded. He splashed water on his face, scrubbing it over the wash basin, then asked, "Ah, do you think they've any towels?"

Water dripped from the fighter's chin, and Rew grinned at him. He walked to their wardrobe and pulled it open. A man, wearing a dark cloth mask and holding a dagger, was standing inside.

"What the—"

The man thrust at Rew with his dagger, but it wasn't a clean strike because his arms had been awkwardly crossed so he could fit inside of the wardrobe.

Rew turned a breath before the dagger plunged into him and caught the man's arm as it stuck past him. He elbowed his assailant in the face, and bone cracked from the blow. He elbowed him again for good measure, mercilessly striking the broken bone. Then, he swept the man's feet from beneath him and slammed him onto the floor. Leaning a knee onto the man's arm, Rew trapped the dagger out of the way then punched the man a few more times in the face to keep him still.

Raif peered over Rew's shoulder at the prone body pinned to the floor. "That was weird."

Rew grunted and did not reply. Instead, he grabbed the man's cloth mask and ripped it free. "Recognize him?"

"No."

"Neither do I," muttered the ranger.

The man had dark hair and dark eyes, and his face was already discolored and swelling where Rew had broken his jaw. Blood ran freely from his nose and speckled his lips. He'd lost a tooth, though Rew didn't remember knocking it out. If the man had distinguishing features, they were hidden beneath the damage Rew had done to him.

The man tried to speak, but it came out like he was chewing on wool.

"Shouldn't have broken his jaw. We'll be lucky to understand anything he says now," chided Raif.

"I didn't... The man was hiding in our wardrobe with a knife! He jumped out and tried to stab me. Sorry I didn't think to keep his jawbone intact."

Raif bent and plucked the knife from the man's fingers. "In the stories, they'd be able to tell what city this blade was forged in."

"Aye, and a professional assassin would be carrying a weapon from his own city? One that could be easily identified? I suppose they'd also etch their name into the hilt, in case it got lost, or perhaps some contact information so we could return it to whoever hired him?"

"I said in the stories…" complained Raif. "An assassin, you're sure?"

"He wasn't here to rob us," said Rew, "which means—Pfah, go check on the women!"

Raif gasped then raced out the door, his socked feet stomping like he still wore his heavy boots. Rew could hear him running down the hall and could hear his voice like a bullfrog's inquiring about the women then eagerly explaining they'd caught an assassin. Other doors in the hallway banged open, and a lively discussion broke out in the hall. If there were others lying in wait, they had plenty of warning now.

Rew glanced back down at his captive. "So, who would you be, and more importantly, who hired you?"

The man stared back at him balefully.

"I know it hurts to speak, but I imagine it doesn't hurt nearly as much as me pounding on that broken jaw some more. No comment? Should we find out?"

The man's lips opened, his jaw scraping awfully, and he croaked out, "Barnaus."

Rew blinked. "The baron of Olsoth?"

The man nodded.

"How long ago?"

The assassin held up two fingers with his free hand.

"Two weeks ago?"

Again, the man nodded.

"Where?" questioned Rew. "Where did you receive the commission? Was Barnaus there in person? Carff. It must have been. The baron was in Carff?"

Tears welling in his eyes, the assassin nodded again.

Frowning down at the man, Rew asked, "Why?"

The assassin shook his head.

He didn't know why. Rew believed that. This man was no special talent. He was a head basher, taking a commission that was past his skill set. The baron wasn't going to explain his reasoning to a man like that. Barnaus had probably thought the assassin was too thick to identify him.

Or maybe it wasn't Baron Barnaus. Maybe someone had claimed to be the baron and had hired this man expecting him to fail and reveal the wrong name.

"What to do with you?" wondered Rew with a sigh.

The assassin looked quite worried about what the answer might be.

"Send him back to Barnaus," suggested Cinda.

The assassin turned, and his eyes bulged.

"Recognize my robes?"

The man froze.

"Why would I send him to Barnaus?" asked Rew. "This man tried to kill me."

"Don't send him with cakes and a card. Send him back with his knife," advised Cinda. "The baron paid this man to kill you. Return the favor."

Rew scratched his beard, keeping his knees firmly on the injured man beneath him.

"Ranger, if the baron was in Carff, he knew you defeated your brother. He knew you'd won the Investiture and that you would become king, one way or the other."

If possible, the man beneath Rew grew even more nervous.

"It is illegal to assassinate a king, is it not? Surely even the heir apparent is off limits. Baron Barnaus betrayed you personally, and he is a traitor to Vaeldon. He deserves what's coming to him."

"Aye, he did betray me," murmured Rew. "If it was him, that is."

"Well?"

"He might have done this in fear we'd go to Mordenhold and fail, and the king would have the chance to interrogate our spirits."

"Does that make a difference? The world needs us to be hard, Ranger. We have to make the difficult choices."

"I suppose it doesn't make a difference why the baron did it, but I'd like to know. We've still got a long way to go, and if these fools are going to be hounding our every step…" He looked at Cinda. "Where are the others?"

"My brother is frantically banging around the room, searching for more assassins. What are you going to do with this man? When my brother can't find any others, he's going to come back here looking to work off some of his excitement. He's not going to be in favor of letting the man go. We can kill him—he'd deserve it —but we shouldn't waste our resources. Make use of him. Send him back to kill the baron before my brother gets a say."

"This man is a coward. If we let him go, he's more likely to flee than to attempt the baron, and we have no way to ensure he does as we ask."

The man, wide-eyed, tried to shake his head.

"Killing him is justice," murmured Rew, "but information is invaluable. I'm not sure he knows why the baron really hired him, but perhaps we can figure out what he does know."

"You want me to call his spirit?"

"It's worth a try."

Cinda pushed back the sleeves of her robes and flexed her fingers. "I'm surprised you're suggesting it, Ranger, but I agree this is a good use of a potential resource, and Alsayer did say I needed practice. Let's act before Anne comes to check on you. She won't appreciate this."

Rew reached down and grabbed the back of the man's head and his chin. "Sorry, Friend, but you really shouldn't have gotten into the business of killing people."

The man's free hand gripped Rew's wrist, and he began to thrash around, but Rew had all of the leverage, and he twisted the man's head violently, turning it at a sharp angle and pushing until he heard the man's neck snap.

Kneeling beside the dead man, Cinda put her hands on his body.

Chapter Seven

T he city of Yonn was a rambling, unconcerned affair. Rew
imagined that from above, with a bird's eye view, it looked
like dozens of smaller villages smashed in together rather than a
proper town. It had few protections and fewer pretensions. Yonn
was the breadbasket of central Vaeldon. It lounged in a broad
river valley, spreading like the arms and legs of a grotesquely
obese man, its outskirts a hard day's travel from the keep that
sprouted incongruously warlike in the center.

As the party approached, fields of agriculture stood in manicured rows. In some places, there were long mounds of freshly
tilled dirt. In others, ranks of new growth sprouted from dark soil.
Some fields had mature vegetation, and laborers moved relent-
lessly along the rows, plucking the harvest off stalks or vines.

The people were of the simple sort, but they looked healthy,
and their clothing was in good repair. Yonn was a prosperous city,
if not wealthy like the trading capitals on the coast. It was a
wealth rooted in the earth, and it swelled and retreated with the
cycles of nature. When the harvest was good, life in Yonn was
very good. Just as often, there were lean years, and the farmers
and the laborers relied on each other to scrape through.

The condition of the men and women in the field was a good

sign that despite the chaos of the Investiture, it was a good year. It wasn't uncommon for workers to be as thin as sticks and adorned in garments more thread than clothing. There was little recourse for the peasants if their lord leaned upon them heavily, and the ranger had always found the condition of a man's people spoke toward his character more so than any other signs. The people they passed appeared to be well taken care of.

Clustered amongst the fields around Yonn were collections of buildings, villages really, though they were sparse on general good stores, inns, and, unfortunately, decent taverns. Instead, they were mostly homes, though some of the largest clusters did have ramshackle taverns where during the day, meats were grilled and stuffed in bread for the laborers to carry into the fields for their midday break. In the evenings, ales were poured to salve the ache of labor, and chickens were roasted to take back to families. Those little places did not look welcoming to strangers. Fortunately, the city of Yonn itself was like a jolly uncle with arms spread wide.

The highway between Carff and Mordenhold ran through Yonn, and the central thoroughfare in the city was lined with the inns and taverns that were missing elsewhere. A block back, shops crowded the narrower streets, with brightly painted signs sticking from above doorways like flags, trying to catch the eyes of passersby.

Zaine whistled appreciatively at some the more creative images and shop names.

"Didn't really think of using a riding crop like that," she drawled, "but now I can't stop thinking about it."

Raif laughed and told her, "You ought to look the other way and see how they believe a person should be using a candle. Not sure I'd enjoy that. A sensitive area and all."

Zaine leaned back, peering down an alley they'd just passed. She grinned at Raif. "Never know until you try."

The fighter's face reddened.

Anne noisily cleared her throat. The empath told them, "Neither of you have any more experience with these things than I do conjuring imps, and as long as you're in my company, it's going to stay that way."

Winking, the thief responded, "Aye, not much experience, but we've got good imaginations, don't we, Raif?"

Raif looked like he was regretting mentioning the candle shop.

"I'm incorrigible," declared Zaine. "The Ranger told me."

"That you are," agreed Rew, putting his arm over the shoulder of the thief. "Now, why don't you make use of those nefarious skills you have, and try to keep an eye on the person following us? No, don't turn and look, lass. Try to be subtle. If they realize we saw them, they'll slip away, and we'll be itching for an assassin's knife in our back for days. They're about twenty paces behind, left side of the street. The girl with her hood pulled up even though it's spring. Blond hair, almost white."

Rew let go of her, and Zaine pointed to another sign they were passing, remarking on it to Raif loudly. The fighter kept blushing, but Zaine turned, still gesturing toward the sign and peeking at their tail.

"I can see why you noticed her, Ranger," jested the thief, stepping back beside him as they moved down the street. "She's striking."

"She's following us," reminded Rew, "and just two days ago, I found an assassin in my wardrobe. I'm not worried about which of us is going to buy her an ale. I'm worried about whether she'll slash my throat the moment I fall asleep."

"She doesn't look like the violent type," argued Zaine.

Rew shrugged. "Neither do you. Been more than one person surprised by that, hasn't there? For whatever reason, she's following us, and I'd like to know why."

Zaine grinned at what she apparently took as a compliment and kept a subtle eye on their tail.

They walked deeper into Yonn, heading toward Duke Findley's square stone keep in the center. The woman stayed behind them, clearly following them now that they were aware of her, but she wasn't coming closer. Rew trusted Zaine to let him know if things changed, and he turned his attention to the keep.

It looked like a great block of fieldstone, though the ranger knew from previous experience it was not one solid formation as it appeared from afar. The joints between the stones that built the structure were hair thin, and the exterior was smooth as fresh paper. He suspected it was all native rock, piled up from the fields in the valley then fashioned into imposing walls. It was a testament to the skill of the craftsmen that lived in Yonn.

Duke Findley was a match to his town—large, comfortable, and seemingly having occupied his seat since the beginning of time. He had children, many of them by now, along with a horde of grandchildren, but the duke had never deigned to step aside for one of them to assume the throne. Maybe he didn't think they were worthy, or more likely, administering Yonn wasn't a difficult task, and it was always better to be the one on the throne than the forgotten father who had no value left to offer the duchy.

It'd been years since Rew had seen Duke Findley, but he believed the old man would recognize him. They had history. Rew needed to lean on that history now because he had something to ask of Findley. Ever since discovering Baron Barnaus's assassin, Rew had realized that from there until Mordenhold, they would have knives at their backs. The cowled woman stalking them through the streets was evidence enough his hunch had been correct.

Despite what the king had told Rew, there'd been no official word, no proclamations that Rew was going to ascend the throne. The king, and his advisors, hadn't said anything at all. There'd been no comment on the death of his three sons, and Carff, Jabaan, and Iyre all remained ungoverned. The lack of official recognition meant that Rew was fair game for the nobles who were willing to take great risks for great reward.

Many nobles might believe he was the son of the king, the heir to the throne, but if the king didn't acknowledge it, it wasn't official, and the nobility thrived by operating in the gray area between what was permitted and what was not. For now, until the king said the word or until Rew actually took the throne, killing him was an option.

For an ambitious soul like Baron Barnaus, perhaps he thought by eliminating Rew, he would clear a path to greater power for himself, or maybe he worried about what he'd told Rew and what the king would find out if Rew failed. There could be dozens of reasons a noble might eliminate a claimant to the throne, as long as they thought they could get away with it. It was what they did —what they were bred to do—and the king encouraged it.

Rew couldn't rely on his father to finally make an announcement, so he decided they would take matters into their own hands, and that was why he needed Duke Findley.

From the battlement of the duke's keep, Rew planned to make an announcement. He would tell how he'd killed his brothers and how he was going to kill the king. He would speak of the Dark Kind, the threat they posed, and how the king was failing to protect the kingdom. Rew would tell the people that once he unseated Vaisius Morden, he would turn to pushing back the Dark Kind and bringing peace to Vaeldon. He'd considered asking for help, but he guessed no one would join him, so rather than face that embarrassment, they would simply carry on. He told himself that would send a bolder message to the nobles and common people. He wasn't asking them to risk their lives. He was risking his life for them.

Rew wanted it to be nothing more than a warning for those behind him, a declaration to scare off additional assassins. If they believed he'd killed all three princes, not even the highest paid assassin would attempt to face him, and their employers wouldn't want to risk crossing a potential future king of Vaeldon.

They didn't know the king was the same man who had ruled them for two hundred years. For all they knew, Rew was claiming he would face his own father, and the child was always stronger than the parent. If it wasn't for the army and the company of spellcasters around Mordenhold, they might even give Rew decent odds of success, but if they didn't think he was the stronger, they would know he had the loyalty of his fellow rangers, and that counted for a lot.

It didn't much matter if the nobility thought he'd succeed. What mattered was that they considered him a Morden, and Vaeldon's nobility had long survived by avoiding angering the Mordens.

As they had approached Yonn, Rew had begun to second-guess the rationale of announcing himself. It likely would buy them passage to Mordenhold, but if everyone knew who he was, they would expect him to assume the throne once he killed his father. He was committing to a decision he wasn't sure he was ready to make, but none of the others were sympathetic.

"Make the speech, or don't make the speech," Cinda finally shouted at him, "but stop moping about it. Blessed Mother, Ranger, when this is all done, you're going to take the throne. What other choice is there?"

He stared at the girl, blinking slowly.

The others fell silent around them, holding their breath.

"I'm marching to my death," continued Cinda, now speaking quietly, "because it's the only way forward. We cannot continue the lives we had, you in the forest, me in Falvar. We cannot continue any sort of life until this is done. Would you even want to? The king has bred us and raised us as his playthings. We're no better than Valchon's simulacrum, false people with no purpose but to grovel and fight for the king's scraps, to serve as a barrier between him and the world. Can you do anything but fight?"

Rew looked away.

Cinda stepped toward him and put a hand on his arm. "You can't. I know you, and I know you can't turn away. You'll fight, and we have to prepare to win. If we do… what then? Don't cheapen my sacrifice by pretending you'll run away again and hide."

"Cinda—I wouldn't."

"Then don't."

He turned back to her. "I won't make a good king."

"Who will make a better one?"

Rew frowned. "Plenty of people, I imagine."

"Then find them, train them, put the support they need around them, and let them take the throne," replied Cinda. "Maybe one day, you could return to the wilderness, but you've work to do first. In other times, you could nominate this Duke Findley or some other noble, though I've no idea which one you'd trust. Over time, with the help of the army and the spellcasters, they could consolidate their power and rule a peaceful kingdom, but not now. The Dark Kind are rampaging across this land. The nobles are falling upon each other. This kingdom has never known anything other than a Morden's rule. Without that, how will they come together to face the Dark Kind? We have to give them a Morden, and you're the only one left."

"Refusing to take the throne does seem like you're putting your personal comfort over the good of the kingdom," remarked Zaine, "but also worth considering, would you be able to live a normal life if you did find someone acceptable to take over? First thing I'd do if I was on the throne would be to send assassins after you. You are a Morden, which means you'd always be a threat to their rule."

Rew turned slowly to look at the thief.

"Well, not me, I mean. I wouldn't have you killed—probably. Doesn't matter. I'm not going to be king. I meant some power-hungry noble who could be. How would they rule when you're still out there? Any time there is dissent, they'd suspect it was you or someone trying to use you. If we survive this, you will be the one who killed the king and all three princes. If you're not the king, you're a permanent threat to the king."

Rew grunted.

Cinda, her sparkling green eyes on Zaine, remarked, "We'll make a noblewoman of you yet. Well said, Zaine."

The thief blushed.

"Nobility is a right and a responsibility," claimed Raif. "Even the most well-intentioned nobles glean comfort and support from the wealth and privilege their roles provide, but in exchange, they work for the people. They protect against threats, invest in the land, and negotiate opportunities for coin to flow through the pockets of their subjects. It goes both ways. You're the rightful heir to the throne, which means you owe a debt to Vaeldon whether or not you want to."

Rew looked to Anne, and the empath smiled at him. He asked her, "Nothing from you?"

She shrugged. "They seem to have laid it out pretty plainly, don't you think?"

"It's not just about me. It's about a Morden on the throne," complained Rew. "The people expect it, but it's because they don't realize there's another way. I hear your arguments, and they make sense, but mine does as well."

"Then make sure there's not a Morden on the throne for long," retorted Cinda. "Take the throne and do the work to find someone to replace you. If you're king, it's up to you if you want to abdicate, and none of us will argue if you do it as soon as you can with a clear conscience."

"The king gets to drink as much ale as he wants," added Zaine. They laughed, and she grinned. "Who's going to tell him no?"

"Very well," said Rew, carefully not looking at Anne. Again under his breath, he repeated, "Very well."

Chapter Eight

When they arrived at Duke Findley's keep, the gate was shut.

"We're here to see the duke," Rew called loudly to a guard atop the sturdy stone and steel construction.

The man peered down at them curiously through a crenellation. The soldier waited a moment, as if anticipating more. He asked, "You're expected?"

"No."

The soldier rubbed his jaw and responded, "Don't work like that, mate."

"How does it work, then?"

"If you're expected, my sergeant tells me, and I know to open the gate. If you're not expected, you stay outside."

"Well, what if I told you that I was the son of the king, and I'm on my way to Mordenhold from Carff, and I require an audience with Duke Findley."

The soldier eyed them placidly then responded, "If you were to say that, then I wouldn't believe it."

"It's the truth."

Standing straighter, the soldier made some remark to someone out of view then looked back down at Rew. "If you was the son of the king, you'd be a prince, and if you was a prince, you'd portal to Mordenhold. I don't know much about high magic, but I know that much. You don't walk when you can portal. Pfah. You don't even have a horse. What kind of prince doesn't have a horse?"

"I'm an estranged son of the king," muttered Rew. He rubbed the top of his head. "Can we see your sergeant?"

"He expecting you?"

Rew threw up his hands in frustration.

Cinda called, "Do you know what my robes mean, Soldier?"

The man eyed her. "No."

"They mean I can do this," she said. Then, she sent a jet of ice-cold green flame in a tight spear that exploded a pace to the right of the soldier, searing the stone with a dark scorch mark and a sprawl of fractal ice.

The man leapt away and began shouting to people inside.

"Sorry," said Cinda, "I thought this might be quicker."

"We'll see. I'm pretty sure he didn't run off to open the gate," remarked Rew.

They heard the clatter of men running, and soon, the battlement above filled with soldiers holding bows, all of them with arrows nocked, strings taut, aimed at Cinda.

She frowned.

Rew whispered to her, "Could be worse. They could be aiming at me."

"I am Raif Fedgley, baron of Falvar," boomed Raif. "You are threatening my sister."

"Baron of where?" demanded a gruff voice. A heavyset man with a collection of gold tassels hanging from his shoulder appeared in the middle of the soldiers. "Never heard of Falvar."

"Well, that's just rude," complained Raif quietly.

"You're one of Duke Findley's brood," said Rew. "Take us to see your father."

The big man shuffled then asked, "How'd you know who I am?"

"I know your father. You have his look. Let us in to see him."

Rapping his knuckles against the battlement, the man replied, "You attacked us!"

"Aye, the lass is a necromancer. She directed a bit of her funeral fire up there. Do you think she missed your man because she can't aim or because she can?" Frowning, the other man opened his mouth to respond, but Rew continued, "In either case, it's mighty foolish to be standing out in the open, isn't it?"

The man looked slightly discomfited by that idea, but he wasn't yet willing to bend. "How do I know you know my father and haven't just seen a likeness of him or heard a description?"

"He's a big fat slob who looks like he ate everything your farmers have harvested in the last two seasons, along with the lot of you. Somehow, he's managed to have more children than there are people I know, and last I heard, he was still at it, though that was a few years back. He's on his fifth wife, and I won't tell you how two of them died because it's not fit for mixed company. He was last in Mordenhold a decade ago, and that's when I first met him. Go fetch him and tell him I'm here."

"You said you're a prince? Only princes I know of are dead."

Sighing, Rew replied, "Tell him Rew, the King's Ranger, is here. He knows who I am."

DUKE FINDLEY SPRAWLED LIKE AN OVERRIPE FRUIT, LOOSE AND sagging, and a bit mushy. His son, the one who'd escorted them inside and who evidently only rated commanding the guards at a closed gate, was quickly waved out of the room.

"I don't need protection from you, do I?"

"I'm not sure he'd do you much good if it came to that, m'lord."

"Will it come to that, Senior Ranger? Or is it Prince, now?"

Rew grunted.

"It's been a long time since I've seen you. Pfah, it'd been years since I'd even heard of you, until recently."

"Last time we saw each other was in Mordenhold, wasn't it? Over a decade ago."

"Over a decade ago, aye, but not in Mordenhold, and that last encounter isn't going to earn you any favors in this court."

Shifting uncomfortably, Rew forced himself to keep his eyes on the duke and to avoid looking at Anne. There'd been some times in his past, before he'd become a ranger, that he'd done things he wasn't proud of. She knew, more or less. No reason to dig into the details.

"Seems you've come a long way since then," continued Duke Findley. "I'm not sure if the trajectory is up or down. Look, you're a Morden, so we both know I can't throw you out, but if the king's acknowledged you, he hasn't done so to me, so let's cut to it. You're headed to Mordenhold?"

Rew nodded.

"Why hasn't he named you his heir?"

"You'd have to ask him that, but you must be aware, there's no one else. For what it's worth, my concern isn't the throne, but for Vaeldon. There are grave threats to this kingdom someone must face. My father has failed to do so."

"You mean to face him and take the throne? You have come a long way. If you defeat him, you'll have to take the throne, you know, whether or not you want it. With your brothers dead, my fellow nobles won't kneel before anyone else. It would plunge this land into even more chaos than it's in, without a king. I'll confess I didn't think you'd do it. Rumor was, you didn't want the throne."

"Where have you heard that?"

Duke Findley cocked his head and smirked.

"I don't want to be king, but I have to face my father. You know what's happening in the lands around here. It must be done. And… you're right. There's no one else who can rule this kingdom."

"What about me?" inquired the duke, a coy smile curling his sausage-like lips. "It's never been my aspiration either, but I wouldn't refuse it."

"Aye, and how long before they rebelled and overthrew you? You'd have assassins lurking behind you before you even got the crown settled upon your head."

"There is that," admitted the duke. "Perhaps I am best in Yonn, then, holding my ancestral lands, supporting the king as I always have."

Rew crossed his arms over his chest.

"You aren't the king. Not yet," continued the duke. "I hope you don't expect me to send my army with you on your journey to Mordenhold. My men are... Well, there aren't very many of them, and I'm not sure they drill very often. They do good work monitoring my fields, keeping order within the city and surrounding area, but they're no match for the black legion."

Rew shook his head. "I don't want your army. My contest is between my father and myself. I'd prefer no one else involve themselves, in fact. I just need a platform to say my piece, so we can continue on—"

"You'll fight your way through the Dark Kind?"

"We faced a thousand of them south of here, at Valstock. You heard?"

"Word traveled ahead of you," replied the duke. He nodded toward Cinda. "It's nice to have powerful allies, but the king would have stomped them out in a tenth of the time, and he wouldn't have lost half the city doing it."

"The king is still in Mordenhold."

Duke Findley fidgeted with a ring that had somehow been forced onto one of his thick fingers. He mentioned, "There are two more armies of Dark Kind harassing my people. My men... Well, I said they aren't the black legion. If you're headed north anyway, we could use your help."

"You want us to help you fight the Dark Kind?"

"Isn't that what you're asking of me?" questioned the duke. "You're not my liege. Not even a noble, formally. You ask a favor of me, but would not return the same one? I took it you meant to be a different sort of leader than your father..."

"I am not your liege, yet. If my father commanded it, would you not bend over backward to meet his request?"

"I'd march that day. He'd have my head if I didn't. But that is his way. What is your way?"

Rew grunted. "You walk on thin ice, Findley."

The duke leaned back in his chair, seeming to seek a non-threatening pose. "Do I?"

Frowning at the man, Rew sighed. "You've been asking around about me, then? You're right. I'm not my father."

"Good," replied the duke. He smiled. "Don't tell your father I said that, of course. He is a cruel man, and I'd never disparage him where I thought he'd find out, but the man has an army, and right now, that's what I need. I hope you understand. Perhaps that's what you sought here? An army? I'm afraid my people are more farmers than they are soldiers."

Rew's lips twisted, and he nodded. Two more armies of Dark Kind. He had not expected to hear that. It'd make travel to Mordenhold difficult, if it was even possible.

There was a knock on the door, and the duke's son poked his head in. "Father, the refreshments are laid out in your solar."

"Help me up?" asked the duke.

Rolling his eyes, Rew strode forward and offered the corpulent duke a hand. "You definitely wouldn't ask my father to help pull you to your feet."

"And he wouldn't do it if I did," agreed the duke. Then, he nearly pulled Rew down as the tugged on the ranger's arm, struggling upright.

"How many children do you have, now?" asked Rew.

Duke Findley waved a hand. "Too many to count."

"Are any better looking than that one?"

"They're my children. It's not all about looks, Ranger. It's our brains that have kept my family in power nearly as long as yours."

Rew laughed and said, "That I can respect, but humor me, will you? I'd like to see your most attractive children, those that are of age but not so old and so single they've gotten a queer reputation. Have them join us in your solar, please."

"You're going to marry one of my children? That will be a first for the Mordens."

"It's not for me," assured Rew, "but you seek more soldiers, and I know of another prestigious man who seeks suitable marriages for his children. Perhaps we can make an accommodation. I don't suppose you have an invoker with the talent to open a portal to the Western Province?"

Duke Findley wiggled his fingers as he tottered toward the door and to his solar where the promised refreshments awaited. "Many of my children are as worthless as rain on a river, but they aren't all such wastes. I have to say, Ranger, you surprise me. I don't believe I've ever negotiated with a Morden before. Your father, his father, your brother, they always made their demands and expected immediate compliance. It makes me nervous about what you're really after."

"The only thing I ask of you I believe you'll give me freely."

Duke Findley cackled and said, "Now that is spoken like a king. I don't believe a word of it, but what can I say? Come then, and I'll send for my children."

"One other thing," said Rew.

The duke rolled his eyes dramatically.

"There was a girl following us through your streets," continued Rew. "I wouldn't think anything of it, but there have been assassins on the road…"

"I'll have a talk with her," huffed Findley. "She wasn't supposed to be seen."

Rew frowned at the duke.

Findley grinned back. "If you're worried about assassins, Ranger, then you're entering the wrong profession."

THE AIR RIPPLED, AND A GOLD AND PURPLE VORTEX BEGAN TO SPIN. IT churned ponderously then faster until the swirls of color spun apart and framed a window in the air that looked across Vaeldon. They were staring into a dark bedroom, though it would be nearly midday in that part of the world.

A man sat up and glared at them. Then, his eyes widened, and he complained, "I won't like this, will I?"

"You might, Duke Vincent," replied Rew. He cleared his throat. "Care to come through and join us in conversation, or ah, we can come through to Shavroe?"

Duke Vincent glanced down at a lumpy form covered by thick blankets lying beside him and smiled. "Perhaps I should come to you."

The duke slipped elegantly out of his bed, his bare chest rippling in the room's candlelight. He picked up a silken dressing robe and tied it around his waist, covering his voluminous lounging trousers.

"You can get dressed first," offered Rew.

"A formal occasion?" asked Vincent, looking past Rew to where Duke Findley sat on his wide, wooden throne. "Not that formal."

"We have a proposal, Vincent," called Findley. "Put some trousers on. I'll hold the portal until you're dressed."

Vincent moved out of view of the portal, and they were left staring at the bed.

"Is that one person in there or two?" questioned Zaine.

Anne shushed her, and they all fell silent. They could hear soft noises from the other side of the opening as Duke Vincent dressed, but the shape in the bed was still.

"I'll bet you five silver it's a man," said Zaine. She leaned toward the portal, pursing her lips, then added, "Two men. I think it's two men."

"Of course it's a man," barked Raif. "I'll bet you five silver it's just one—"

"Shush," snapped Anne.

They waited longer.

"Five silver. I win if it's two men," whispered Zaine. "You do if it's one."

"How will we find out? It's awkward to ask the duke, don't you think?"

Grinning at the pair of them, Rew cried, "You, in the bed!"

Abruptly, two blond heads popped up. They both had long, curly locks and wore artful pouts on full, red lips. One was a woman. One was a man.

"Well, Blessed Mother's Grace," said Raif. "I guess neither of us is the winner."

"I think Duke Vincent is the winner." Zaine cackled.

Duke Vincent's bald head came into view. He saw where they were looking and glanced back at the bed. He snapped for the pair of people to cover themselves, shaking his head ruefully.

He stepped through the portal, still tugging his clothing into place. He was no longer wearing the billowing white silk shirt and snug dark trousers they'd last seen him in. A bellwether for fashion, Rew figured, and Valchon's style was out now that he was dead. Instead, Vincent was wearing a simple but well-tailored cotton tunic and dark trousers that could have been worn by anyone in a dozen professions, though they were still unusually snug. What message was the man trying to send with such plain attire?

"If you peer unasked into a man's bedchamber, it's not his fault what you find," purred Duke Vincent.

"I opened the portal to you," mentioned Findley. "Who knew you'd still be abed at this hour. Does your wife—"

Grinning and shrugging, Vincent replied, "I've been married to the same woman for thirty years, Findley. What are you on, number five? You could learn a thing or two from me."

"It's not like that. We didn't leave each—"

Vincent waved a hand dismissively. "I know what happened to your past wives. Does the current one?"

Flushing, Findley fell silent.

Rew shifted. This wasn't a good start to their alliance.

"You mentioned a proposal?" asked Vincent, sauntering over to Duke Findley's sideboard, which was filled with pastries, cuts of cold meat, jams, and butter. There was a pitcher of ale and one of water. "No wine?"

"We specialize in ale in Yonn, and one partakes of one's own bounty."

Rolling his eyes, Vincent poured himself an ale. "That's one way to do it." He glanced at Rew. "I told you I wouldn't support you directly when you faced the king. You're a better man than he, and you've gotten farther than anyone would have thought, but he is still my liege."

"He's your liege. That's why you support him?"

Vincent sipped his ale, licked his lips, and said, "Aye, that's the way it's supposed to be, right? That, and he's got an army at his back, has more spellcasters than Findley here has children, and he's a master of necromancy, where you are a master of hiding in the woods. No offense."

Rew stared at the duke.

"I said no offense," protested Vincent. "In truth, Ranger, I wish you luck, but I cannot openly support you against the king. The odds, frankly, are not in your favor. I'm a family man, and I won't risk the lives of my children on a gamble which I wouldn't risk five silver coins on. It's nothing personal, but family first. Besides, if I show no loyalty to your father now, how could you think me loyal if you manage to defeat him?"

"What if I don't ask for your help against the king?"

Vincent frowned. "Why have you brought me here?"

"There are small armies of the Dark Kind roaming the Duchy of Yonn. Findley needs men and spellcasters. You have them."

"I have my own people to look after. The river is restless after the death of Calb. Won't be long before we've pirates on the coast as well. I have men, true, but for a reason."

"You've more than enough resources to deal with a few pirates. What of the Dark Kind?"

"There have been reports that they're massing north of us."

"Days away, then. If they were able to make it through the swamps that surround Shavroe, you could portal your men home before you're in danger."

"My men are my people, and while I wish no ill to Findley and his, I don't see what's in it for me. Spending my men's lives costs more than your goodwill because I expect you'll dead weeks from now. Promised favors are a currency I've learned not to accept."

"You have children who seek advantageous matches. Findley has children he needs to get rid of. Vaeldon's agricultural capital, paired with one of its largest ports, there are possibilities there, m'lords."

Vincent grunted. "Findley has wealth, aye, but he also has a plethora of heirs to spread it amongst. While it's true Shavroe could use an influx of products to ship, Carff is closer, and there's a well-trod highway leading straight to it. I might be greedy, but I'm not foolish. By the time Findley's yams reach Shavroe traveling the twisted network of roads between us, they'll be spoiled. I see where you are going, Ranger, but this marriage proposal isn't enough to buy the blood of my men."

"Don't dismiss it so quickly," suggested Findley. He glanced at Rew. "Even without the Ranger's involvement, it could make sense. You're right. Transporting my bulk products across the entire kingdom is impractical, but what of information? What of coordination? How would you like to be the first to know the price of wheat each fall? Or to hear what Carff's buyers are seeking? An alliance could benefit us both, even more so if there's no obvious commerce between our capitals."

"I appreciate the value of information as much as any wise man," allowed Vincent. He scowled, tapping his lips with a finger. "Though, I don't know which of my own brood would be willing to, ah... You and your people are of the land. My line is not. It's not a farmer my daughters want tilling their soil, you understand?"

"Surely not all of your children are so shallow as to seek a union based only on looks? There are other practical considerations."

Vincent shrugged. "I made a practical choice, but I won't say it resulted in a happy marriage."

"Weren't you offering me marital advice a moment ago?"

"I've had a successful marriage," huffed Vincent, "which is not always the same as a happy one. I'd like my children to have both."

"We want many things for our children, don't we?" replied Findley. He tilted his head. "My grandmother once said that given the choice between the two, it's just as easy to love a rich man as a poor man. The lands around Yonn are fertile and productive. In these trying times, our bounty will be more valuable than ever. Perhaps, if given the opportunity, your children may learn to appreciate that. Hrm. You come from a line of enchanters, do you not?"

Vincent nodded slowly. "And you are an invoker."

"My second wife's family is of good enchanting stock."

Vincent arched one of his carefully manicured eyebrows.

"A Delwebb of Mordenhold. You're familiar with them?"

"I am, but are they in the king's service?"

"Not this branch," rumbled Findley. "My wife's grandfather was. He performed some act for the king and was granted a title. He made good matches, and let me tell you, she cost me a fortune to buy away from those sycophants around the capital. It's been worth it. You've already alluded to how many children I have."

"How many are hers, and how many have her talent?"

"Seven children, four with her skills. I've older children skilled in invoking, if they'd be more appealing. My first wife was an invoker whose talent rivaled my own. That is the question that's plagued us for generations, isn't it? What to do—strengthen the power of your core talent or diversify into other magics? My children could help you do either. Thanks to our friend the ranger and his fight with his brothers, magical talent is becoming a precious resource, Duke Vincent. As he proceeds toward Mordenhold, I think it likely magical talent may become even more... scarce."

Rew coughed at that but did not interrupt.

"What percentage of your offspring develop talent?" questioned Vincent.

"Half," boasted Findley. "Like I said, fertile soil."

"That's a good ratio," murmured Vincent. "The enchanters, born of your second wife, how many are female?"

"Three."

"Unfortunate it's not all," remarked Vincent.

"And your sons?"

"Just one with true talent. I've been... reluctant to sire more of them."

"Your line grows thin," warned Findley. "Your lifestyle comes at a steep price. You need more branches on the family tree, Vincent."

Duke Vincent kept tapping his lips with a slender finger and did not respond. These men were not friends, but Rew suspected they'd been introduced several times throughout the years. The dukes of Vaeldon were always aware of each other, assessing their peers for potential allies and enemies. With the generational bloodbath of the Investiture, it was critical to keep an eye on both populations. How often during those meetings did conversations like this happen behind closed doors? Two old men bargaining their children like they were trading hunting dogs.

"None of the girls are betrothed?" inquired Vincent. "They're not spoken for?"

"None of them are betrothed to the son of a duke. All three are available to wed. Your son may choose a wife with my blessing. The other two would make fine mistresses, if I can be sure their homeland is protected."

"Putting all of your eggs into one basket?" asked Vincent with a laugh. "I thought you farmers warned against that."

"I need your men," replied Findley with a reluctant sigh.

"Three regiments for the three girls. Eight-week term. You provide quality armaments and material. I'll provide the food."

Vincent grunted. "I was thinking one regiment for one girl and a four-week term."

"Meet in the middle at two regiments, six-week term?"

"That'd take two girls," warned Vincent. He began pacing the room. "Who commands? I won't have my men thrown away by you. How can I be certain you're not wasting them to keep your own soldiers from harm?"

"The ranger will command. Is he neutral enough for you?"

Rew choked, trying to protest quickly. "What?"

"A third party we have equal trust in," murmured Vincent. He rubbed his bare chin then said, "I find that agreeable. Two regiments fully kitted for six weeks under the command of the ranger. I ask that you send one daughter to Shavroe with me now, the other when my men return."

"You have a deal."

"I must say, Findley, I'm surprised you're so willing to offer all of your daughters from this line. I won't come to regret this, will I? They are as talented as you've implied? None are barren, are they?"

"I have no reason to think so. Their mother was not," responded Findley. He drew a deep breath then released it. "The truth is, the Dark Kind threaten us. Yonn is so close to Mordenhold that my ancestors never built our military presence, and I followed their lead. We relied on the king to watch over these lands, and your guess is as good as mine as to where he is or what he's doing. Without your men, I may no longer have a duchy. If that comes to pass, my daughters are more mouths I cannot feed."

"Will two regiments be sufficient, then? I have four in fighting condition, but I don't need more than two daughters. What else can you offer me?"

"Two regiments ought to do it," replied Findley. "The ranger comes with a necromancer of impressive skill. They should be sufficient."

Vincent shrugged.

"I haven't agreed to this," barked Rew.

"You won't fight the Dark Kind?" asked Findley. "Isn't this what you wanted from us?"

Rew scowled at the man.

"Killing your brothers earned you respect for your strength," said the duke. "If you want to be different than your father, if you want the love of the people, you have to protect them. Vaisius turns us against each other to keep his control, but you have an opportunity to bring us together."

Rew's eyes narrowed. "Thought about that, have you?"

Duke Findley held up his big hands. "If you'd been seeking power, you've gone about it in a terribly roundabout way. No, ever since I heard what happened in Jabaan, I've wondered what your goal was, and now that I've met you, I know."

Beside them, Duke Vincent nodded slowly. "He has a point."

Rew grunted then sighed. It took an army to face an army. Now, he had one. No sense complaining about it. And if Findley's information about what was between them and Mordenhold was accurate, he was going to need them.

He glanced between the two dukes then said, "Very well. When can we be ready to march?"

Chapter Nine

Two regiments of Duke Vincent's men streamed through the open portals at a trot. Portals allowed travel from one end of Vaeldon to the other in a matter of heartbeats, but it required substantial talent to open one big enough for more than two people to walk abreast, and keeping it open long enough for thousands of men to make it through was a skill that only the most elite invokers could manage.

Findley and Vincent had cobbled together as many invokers as they could, including Findley himself. They were rushing ranks of men to the north of Findley's city from Shavroe, but even at a trot, it would take two days for all of the soldiers to get through. When they got there, they would join a regiment of Findley's own, and there would be near three thousand men encamped, ready to march to war against the Dark Kind.

Rew oversaw the burgeoning army with a scowl on his face. He preferred to be alone, and in the midst of the sprawling mess of tents and swearing men, he definitely was not. If he had the choice, he would be ranging ahead, scouting the armies of the Dark Kind, counting their number, making note of the terrain, and planning the action from the ground.

Instead, at Findley's and Vincent's insistence, he was trapped in the camp, trying to sort through a collection of attachés and captains and bring order to the two groups of armed men.

Findley's sort carried a little extra heft from spending most of their days guarding farmland, which, a week from Mordenhold, had never been under threat, even fifty years before when the Dark Kind had last attacked the kingdom en masse. Vincent's men were leaner and had a dangerous look to them. Their task was guarding the coast and the river. They were a few years older on average, and they were used to skirmishes with pirates and bandits who plagued the shipping lanes along the water.

Eyeing some of the men as they walked past, Rew wondered how many had actually been pirates and bandits before joining Vincent's service. The duke was a practical man, and if someone knew the use of a sword and could trim a sail, he would use them. Those men would be good in a scrap, and with the might of Duke Vincent behind them, they would be quite brave. Against more equal odds and non-human opponents, Rew would find out.

Ideally, he would have been given time to recruit and train the men. Even a few weeks of drills together could improve their formations, communications, and chances of survival by orders of magnitude, but taking a few weeks to train wasn't a choice.

He only had the army for six weeks, for one. Though if pressed, he didn't know if Vincent would truly draw his men back from battle. In addition, while the soldiers assembled, the Dark Kind rampaged. Reports were coming frequently about towns north of Findley's that were being overrun. Traffic from Mordenhold had ground to a stop.

There were small groups of the creatures scattered around the heartland of Vaeldon, but from what intelligence they'd gathered, the bulk of the problem was two units of Dark Kind. They didn't know the exact numbers, but it was enough to call them an army. The Dark Kind had to be led by valaan, but Rew could only guess at how many of those were required to master so many narjags. In his lifetime, it hadn't been done.

What little information they knew had been difficult to come by and was a source of constant frustration for Rew. He knew he could go off alone and learn what he needed to, but if he did, who would command the armies? Findley and Vincent had already deferred to him, and Rew had no idea if any of their captains were competent. Even if they were, what sort of message would that send to the men, the commander disappearing before the army even arrived?

No, as much as it chaffed him, he had to be visible, and he had to be seen in command. When it came to his issuing orders on the battlefield, the men needed to know him and respect him, or if he didn't have time to earn their respect, he hoped to instill a healthy fear. He'd killed his three brothers, the princes of Vaeldon's provinces. He let that be known.

Rew didn't tell the men that he was going on to face his father, and he'd sworn the dukes and their closest advisors to secrecy. He thought that behind his back, they might send word to the king, but he didn't think they would tell their men. Vaeldon's nobility had strange notions of loyalty when it came to matters like that. Fortunately, the king already knew Rew was approaching, and as he'd yet to confront them, Rew was confident that Vaisius Morden wouldn't bother until they reached Mordenhold itself.

That confidence was dangerous, but that didn't mean it was undeserved. If the king had wanted to face Rew sooner, he could have portaled to Havmark just as easily as he'd animated the corpses of Valchon's spawn.

Another group of Duke Vincent's finest, looking even more like pirates than the last bunch, streamed past. At their head was a wiry man, tanned like a hide, who looked as battered as the dice in the dingiest gambling hall.

"You!" barked Rew.

The man paused then glanced at the ranger with an eyebrow raised. Around him, his men stepped out of the way so others could exit the portal then they clustered in a loose formation, like they expected a street brawl.

Rew sighed.

"Do I know you?" queried the man. "More importantly, do we got a problem? Word is, we're marching to fight some storybook creatures. Dark Kind or whatever. Duke is convinced it's the real thing. Means I gotta be looking ahead, so if we got a problem, let's have it out here and now."

Shaking his head, Rew responded, "I'm your new commander. You a captain?"

"Aye," said the man with a grin. "Been a captain. Still a captain."

"How many more of Vincent's captains are left in Shavroe?"

The captain scratched his arm. "Two or three, I'd venture. Six or seven have come through."

"There's a large tent at the center of this camp. Gather your fellow captains and meet me there two hours before sunset."

"How do I know you're who you say you are?"

"You know," said Rew with a tight smile.

The captain puffed himself up, studied Rew and the rest of the party around him, and then nodded curtly.

"Like two dogs sniffing each other's butts," whispered Zaine.

Ignoring her, Rew told the captain, "There will be ale."

The captain granted the ranger a shallow bow and declared, "In that case, we'll all be there. Maybe even a little bit early!"

The bluster was for the benefit of the captain's men, and they were grinning and slapping each other on the backs as they rejoined the stream of soldiers appearing through the portal. Rew let them have it. Through the years, commanders had tried all sorts of tactics to win the loyalty of their men or, if unable to do that, the discipline to follow simple orders. Some ways were more effective than others. Most took time, which Rew didn't have, so he would settle for moving fast and not giving the captains and their subordinates time to consider what he was going to tell them. A bit of ale to lubricate the discussion made consideration even less likely.

Facing the Dark Kind was difficult, even for those with experience. Doing so without training, limited intelligence, and uncoordinated forces wouldn't help, but that was their situation, and the only thing that would make it worse was people second-guessing his orders. Rew wouldn't allow that.

He turned to Zaine. "I don't like you going out there."

She shrugged. "None of these men will have even seen a narjag, Ranger. You can't spare your invokers because that will delay the movement of the troops, and even if you could break them away, it'd be a risk to send them out into the unknown. If you want to know what the Dark Kind are doing, one of us has to go. It makes sense for it to be me."

Rew grunted. Zaine had insisted on accompanying the scouts. It did make sense, but that didn't mean he had to like it. There would be ayres out there, and they could smell a person coming from leagues away. On foot, if they came after her, she would have no chance but to turn and fight.

"I'll take care of her," offered a gruff voice.

It was Ranger Adro, a solid man that Rew did not know well. He'd been lurking around the outskirts of Yonn, and by chance, Rew had thought to check with the drop points Ang and Vurcell had set. He would have done it more often on the journey north, but he'd forgotten most of them, and he'd hoped the twins would have collected the stragglers by now. Luckily, they'd connected with Adro, and the man agreed to help.

He would go with Zaine, along with a dozen of Findley's best trackers. It was only Adro's presence that convinced Anne it was a plan worth considering. Even so, she likely would have fought harder, but already a steady flow of wounded was coming down the road. Some were Duke Findley's people, living and farming on the outskirts of his duchy. Others were from farther north, technically under the dominion of Mordenhold itself. That none of them fled toward the capital was concerning.

Anne had settled herself overseeing the temporary hospital that had been set up for the injured, and Rew had tasked her with discovering why everyone came south instead of moving toward the security of the kingdom's capital. She'd fallen into both tasks, and he hadn't seen her for a day.

Rew clapped Adro on the shoulder and in a low voice so only the man could hear, said, "Think of her like my daughter. That means you don't come back without her, you understand?"

The man blinked and nodded.

Turning to Zaine, Rew asked her, "Will you see Anne before you leave?"

Pursing her lips, the thief shook her head. "She's distracted. Let's keep her that way. I'll be back in a few days."

"I'm still willing to go with you," offered Raif.

Zaine grinned. "Why? To make sure they hear us? You're the loudest person I know, Raif. You're a lot of things, but not a scout."

The big fighter flushed.

"I will miss you, though."

Raif's cheeks grew redder, and Rew let out an audible groan. Raif seemed to be struggling to speak, and with a wink for them both, Zaine turned and flounced off. Ranger Adro gave Rew a quick bow then followed.

It was only after Adro had left that Rew considered the import of the man's gesture. A bow. The rangers were an independent bunch. They prized skill and rarely gave deference to anyone. Even their own commandant rated nothing more than a curt nod and a slightly lower volume of cursing. But Adro had bowed.

Rew rubbed his face in his hands then quickly forced them back down by his side. In front of them, a constant stream of soldiers jogged by. Every one of those men glanced up surreptitiously at their new commander then quickly looked away. This was going to take some getting used to.

"Come on," Rew told Raif. "Let's get to the tent and prepare for the captains."

"Prepare? How so."

"Cracking open that ale barrel, for one."

For the meeting, Rew had requested Duke Findley and Duke Vincent not appear. There'd been an argument to having them there. It was always good for a soldier to personally see their liege listening to a new commander, and had they been marching on Mordenhold, Rew would have wanted to bolster his authority that way. But against the Dark Kind, he wanted to lean on experience. He didn't want these men listening to him because they'd been asked to. He wanted them listening because he knew more about Dark Kind than anyone they'd ever met. When it came to the heat of battle, he hoped they would recall that and that they still listened.

The captains arrived close enough together that Rew suspected they'd already been meeting and had decided to trickle in one after the other. When they came into the large command tent, Findley's and Vincent's men clearly did not know each other well, but they were united in not knowing Rew, and the company of their fellow soldiers was evidently more comfortable than that of a man who'd claimed to have killed the princes who'd controlled their respective provinces.

The soldiers might have doubted it, but Findley and Vincent had confirmed it, and the men would take it as fact now. It meant they wouldn't openly defy Rew because they would be afraid of him, but military men had numerous ways of silent insubordination. At the meeting, Rew hoped to end that before it started.

He allowed the men to dip themselves a mug of ale from a barrel he'd placed in the corner and then sipped his own mug before clearing his throat and standing from behind a large table. It was the sort of table commanders would layer with maps of the surrounding terrain, marking where the enemy was and where their own units were, but while Rew had acquired some maps, they had little information about what they faced.

Still, he had placed the maps on the table in front of him. Vincent's men needed some knowledge of the terrain they'd venture into. Truth be told, so did Rew. He'd traveled the highway between Yonn and Mordenhold before, but when he'd lived in the capital, most of his journeys had been by portal stone, and he'd never had reason to visit the smaller towns that were scattered a day or two from the main road. Unfortunately, those were the places the Dark Kind were targeting.

Several of the villages and towns had been overrun, and those had been marked on the maps. From the pattern of destruction, Rew made his best guess at where the Dark Kind might be now, but it was only a guess, and the circles he'd marked were uncomfortably broad.

"Captains, I appreciate your attendance," began Rew. Absent-mindedly, he rubbed a hand over his freshly shaven head. "You'll hear soon enough that I'm not a commander of men. The units I've overseen numbered half a dozen, and half of them knew more about their business than I did. In some regards, that hasn't changed. You know your men, and you know how they are most effective, but I know the Dark Kind, and we're going to need that knowledge to finish this campaign alive."

The fifteen captains—ten from Vincent's forces, five from Findley's—stared back at Rew silently.

"Has anyone faced narjags, ayres, or valaan?"

One of Vincent's captains snickered in disbelief until two of Findley's men raised their hands. The first, a dour man with a shock of dark hair, a lean muscular body, and hands and face scared from a lifetime as a soldier, spoke up.

"We've fought the narjags. Didn't know what they were at the time, but the duke has an arcanist, and they match the descriptions in his books. I seen some of the ayres but from a distance. Narjags were riding them. Scouts, I suppose, though these things using scouts wasn't in the books. Don't think anyone has seen a valaan. Least, no one's lived to say it."

Rew nodded. "Aye, that's the way it is, more often than not. South of here, at Valstock, there were two valaan. They marshaled about five hundred narjags each. I believe we'll be dealing with more of them this time, and we cannot protect Yonn and all of the communities around here if we hide behind Findley's walls."

The faces of Findley's men were dark. Those of Vincent's were confused.

"Captain," asked Rew, looking at the man who spoke, "can you give our friends from the west an update on Valstock?"

The man nodded, turned to his counterparts, and told them about the consequences of failure.

Chapter Ten

The captain, a practical-seeming man named Eddla, once he succinctly described the situation in Valstock, was promoted to colonel. Rew had no knowledge of any of the men or their capabilities, but he figured the one who had actually seen Dark Kind before and had the courage to speak in front of the others was a safe enough bet. Two other captains, one from each of the duke's forces, were arbitrarily selected as lieutenant colonels, and the rest were left commanding the men they already had.

"We'll need three new captains promoted to take your old roles," said Rew. He glanced at the colonel and the lieutenant colonels. "I trust you have some men in mind?"

All three nodded.

Gesturing to Raif, Rew continued, "This man is my attaché. Consider any word from him to have the same authority as if it came from me."

The captains turned as a group and studied Raif skeptically. He could have been younger than some of their children. Rew had warned the lad it would happen, and Raif was ready.

"My name is Raif Fedgley, Baron of Falvar, which I don't expect you to care about. What matters is that I've faced the Dark

Kind a dozen times, and I've personally killed hundreds. Like the ranger, I respect your experience and wisdom, and I'll listen when you speak. Grant me the same respect, and we'll get along well."

"Where's a young man like you been finding so many Dark Kind?" questioned one of the captains from the back of the pack.

"Here and there," said Raif. "They attacked my home, and it started us on a journey that's spanned the kingdom. Perhaps you've heard a little bit about it? Everywhere the ranger went—Jabaan, Iyre, and Carff—I was by his side. It hasn't been an easy journey, but we've made it this far."

The captain who'd questioned Raif swallowed uncomfortably. It appeared he'd actually managed to forget what Rew and his companions had been doing, and the reminder was harsh.

The newly promoted Colonel Eddla raised a hand tentatively. "M'lords, I don't know you, and you don't know me, so I hope you don't take this as insubordination, but as you've selected me to lead this motley group, I'll ask the question we're all wondering."

Rew nodded. "You'll learn I don't have much use for protocol, and we don't have time for politeness. You can call me Rew, and go ahead, ask your question."

"We were told you killed the princes. I heard Duke Vincent himself say it, which is good enough for me, but there have been other rumors... stories... about what happened. Jabaan, for example. We were told, ah, is there any truth to those rumors?"

"The lad's sister," said Rew, turning his head slowly, meeting each man's gaze, "she's a necromancer of profound power. Yes, it was her work in Jabaan. It was her as well in Valstock. She's learning her strength, learning control. She's more skilled than she was in Jabaan. That was raw power, nothing more. For those of you who take comfort in shadowing beneath a powerful spellcaster, rest assured, she has power that's unmatched outside of Mordenhold. For those who are nervous about such things, I advise we do our job, so you don't have to see her do hers."

The colonel grunted.

"We're at war," continued Rew, "mankind against the Dark Kind. It will be as bad as it was for your grandfathers fifty years ago. Likely worse, I believe. Back then, the king acted. The princes fought. Now, they've failed you. All of them only made the situation worse, if they did anything at all. It's on us."

"We were told six weeks," muttered a man from within the crowd of Vincent's captains.

"Six weeks on this campaign," agreed Rew. "We ought to be able to finish these armies before then, and I won't hold you longer than I need you, but like the lad said, he and I have traveled from one end of the kingdom to the other. When this is done, go home, kiss your wives, hug your children, and prepare. War is upon us. We'll need every sword we can muster, and if that frightens you, look at your wives, your children. You do it for them. You do it for your mothers and fathers. Your neighbors. The girl you make eyes at. The friend you share an ale with. People you don't know. This war isn't one we sought, but it's started, and we will finish it."

―――――

"THAT WAS A GOOD SPEECH," SAID RAIF SHORTLY AFTER THE CAPTAINS had left, heading back to their sections of the camp to settle their men and begin organizing them into a cohesive army.

Rew grunted and did not respond. He was looking down at the maps, wondering where Ranger Adro and Zaine were now and how quickly they would return.

Two days north of their current position was the last town which had been overrun by Dark Kind. Within ten leagues of it, there were several more towns that hadn't yet felt the hunger of the narjags. On the opposite side of the highway, a day away, was another town that had fallen. They assumed it meant two units of Dark Kind, but was it possible it was one?

He was walking off distances with his fingers, estimating travel times for the narjags. Raif had dipped himself another ale and meandered over to watch. The fighter knew how to read a map, but when it came to figuring the times and distances, anything he added would be pure guesswork. Raif had been trained to review accounts for the barony, but in truth, he had only a passing familiarity with mathematics.

"You're going to have to find a tutor, lad," murmured Rew, working out in his head that the two latest sites of the Dark Kind attacks were a day and a half apart, even at a forced march, and they'd been discovered and estimated to have occurred just one day apart. It had to be two armies. Or three? He didn't think so, but that was a possibility. He drummed his fingers on the table then readjusted his notations of where those armies could be now.

"A tutor?" exclaimed Raif. "What are you talking about?"

"You won't always have a life on the road, living on your skill with a greatsword."

Raif looked down at the maps, chewing on his lip. He replied, "My father never took it down. Did you know? An enchanted blade made to face the shades of the departed. It's true, he didn't need it himself. He could banish the shades easily, but he didn't allow a champion to carry it into the barrowlands, either. How many lives could have been saved had this sword been wielded by a strong arm? Dozens, hundreds over the years?"

Rew glanced up. "You don't believe there'll be a time you can set that blade down?"

Raif shrugged.

"What if instead of Duke Eeron, there'd been a duke who cared for his people? Someone who worked with the barons instead of against them? It wouldn't be a dozen lives saved, it'd be thousands. Tens of thousands just this year. You're getting good with that sword, Raif, but you're more than that."

"It takes two to make peace."

"Good men finish necessary fights. Great men avoid them in the first place. Perhaps you can be the sort of ruler who shows 'em your sword then doesn't have to use it."

Raif snorted.

Rew grinned.

The fighter sipped his ale and was silent for a moment. Then, he sat the mug down and asked, "I've been thinking. Why did Alsayer do it? He forced us out of Falvar. Sometimes, it felt like he was leading us around the kingdom by the nose. He betrayed all three of your brothers, us, and even your father. I hate the man for what he did to my family, but I can also acknowledge he was a master backstabber. Did he truly not predict your brother would turn on him or that the maelstrom would be cast?"

"I've struggled with that as well," admitted Rew.

"What was the point of it all? The man was a cold-hearted wretch, but he had goals. What did he gain from us facing Valchon in Carff? He set us up, us and the entire city, a million souls, including ours and his. He can't have gone through everything he did, everything he put us through, just for us to die along with everyone within ten leagues of us. He had easier ways to kill us."

Rew drummed his fingers on the map table. Finally, he responded, "It's been churning in my mind like a storm on the horizon, lad. He shook us from the Eastern Territory, as you said, then directed us at Calb and stood aside when we moved against Heindaw. He set us up in Carff, but here's what's bothering me; up until Carff, his plans worked. He was a step ahead of everyone. He knew the entire time Valchon was going to want to kill him. King's Sake, he was the one who told my brother we were coming the night of the fete, so how did Valchon surprise him? Or... did Valchon surprise him? We keep assuming Alsayer fell for an obvious betrayal, but what if he didn't? What if, like all of his convoluted plans, this one worked?"

"You're suggesting he wanted Valchon to cast the maelstrom and he wanted us to defeat it? That he wanted to get himself killed in the process?"

"Maybe he didn't plan on getting killed, but could he have wanted us to face the maelstrom and break it?"

Raif crossed his arms and frowned. "Bit of a gamble with one million lives on the line. So he was either insane, or... I don't know. Not much else makes sense, does it?"

"When Cinda raised Alsayer's ghost, he told us where Valchon fled to," continued Rew, scratching his beard and peering at the maps, knowing there were no answers there. "She said he was willing. He slipped away once he'd related that information."

"He didn't think Valchon could kill us. Maybe he thought he'd survive as well, or maybe the crazy bastard was willing to sacrifice himself."

"He wanted me to use this sword," murmured Rew. "He gave me the hint right before he died. He knew I could use Erasmus Morden's knowledge to defeat the maelstrom. That has to be it. He risked the entire city on the hope I would release Erasmus Morden and destroy the spell."

"I'm glad I never played that man in cards," said Raif with a whistle.

Rew drew his longsword and placed it on the table in front of them. "He knew I could do it, but why? Why force it? To prove I could face the maelstrom? So that I released Erasmus? But if he hadn't told Valchon we were coming, there wouldn't have been a maelstrom in the first place. He must have wanted our ancestor released from this blade. How does that help anyone? Such an enormous gamble, the reward doesn't seem worth it, does it?"

"There's more to it which we don't understand yet."

"Aye," said Rew, frowning down at the blade, "and now that Alsayer is dead, I'm not sure we will understand until it's too late."

"Things were simple before your family came into my life," groused Raif. He tapped his empty mug on the table. "Another?"

Rew laughed then nodded.

THEIR ARMY BEGAN ITS MARCH, AND SCOUTING REPORTS BEGAN TO arrive. The early indications were that the towns near Findley's city were so far untouched, but more and more often, they encountered refugees from farther afield, people who had been lucky to be away when the Dark Kind attacked or who lived on small farms some distance from the settlements. There were very few reports of survivors after an attack.

Hundreds of Dark Kind, thousands, would overwhelm a small town in no time at all, and it was almost impossible to hide from the creatures. Narjags had sensitive noses, and they would make sure to root through every building, sniffing for more victims. Ayres had even sharper senses, and one could only guess what the valaan were capable of.

Each step, each league they traveled north, steeled Rew's resolve. He hadn't wanted to take command of an army. He'd wanted to get to Mordenhold as quickly as he could, to bring a conclusion to his father's mad game, but he came to understand that while facing his father was his path, the path had a turn in it.

He needed to do this, for Vaeldon and for himself. The duchies had been abandoned by the Mordens. The dukes, if they had survived the Investiture, had been left to fend for themselves. Some would fight for their people. Some would not. They definitely weren't going to go fighting for someone else's people, and that was why they needed a king.

Vaeldon's duchies weren't strong enough alone to face the threat of the Dark Kind. They needed to work together, to fight as a whole. If the kingdom fractured, they would fall under the black tide of narjags and their valaan commanders, the fraemoth, too, whatever that was.

Was that what was distracting Vaisius Morden? Was the king facing the gravest threat? Or did the empty tomb within Rew's sword have something to do with the creature? Rew wasn't sure why, but he didn't think so. Alsayer had told him that the king had killed a fraemoth fifty years prior. If he could do it then, he could do it now. In theory, he was even more powerful, which wasn't a comforting thought.

Under a swirling cloud of worry and confusion, they marched.

Three thousand men and a supply chain of one hundred wagons stretched out behind them. Near the head of the column rode their cavalry, three hundred mounted soldiers, lightly armored, sitting on snorting, stomping war horses. The beasts must have sensed something of their masters' emotions, and they appeared eager. Of course, they hadn't faced Dark Kind before.

In squads of ten, Rew sent the cavalry out ranging, watching the way ahead, riding swiftly on the flanks, making sure there was no looming mass of Dark Kind waiting in ambush. A year ago, he would have thought anyone suggesting such a thing to be mad, but that was before he'd been ambushed.

The Dark Kind, whether because of the valaan or the influence of the fraemoth, had learned tactics. Rew expected that soon, they would begin to encounter ayres with narjag riders scouting for the opposition. The blue-skinned canines couldn't outrun a horse over the course of hours, but in quick bursts, they were faster.

He'd warned their scouts to watch out for them. He'd instructed them on the best way to face the creatures, but he wasn't surprised when the first squad of riders failed to return. Ten men on horseback could move several times faster than three thousand on foot. They'd established specific intervals the closest scouts would be out, and two hours after sunset, it was clear the unit had found trouble.

Colonel Eddla stood across the map table from Rew in his command tent. The grim-faced colonel murmured, "There's still no word from them."

Rew nodded, his finger tracing the line of a ridge the scouts had been assigned to move along. From the vantage, they would have had leagues of visibility, enough distance to escape a pack of ayres, though it was possible they could have been run down or driven into more danger. A valaan might have caught them. A straight ambush seemed most likely. They could have inadvertently come close to a defile on the ridge or a stand of trees large enough to conceal a war party of narjags and ayres and hadn't made it away in time.

The scouts had been instructed about those dangers, but for men used to guarding empty fields and keeping farmers from feuding with each other, combat against the Dark Kind was more dangerous than they would anticipate. Even when you expected it, seeing the narjags gnashing teeth and the ayres muscular bodies bounding toward you could shatter a strong man's nerves beneath the weight of abject terror. The Dark Kind didn't want to beat you in a fight. They wanted to consume you.

"Tomorrow, I want six units to roll out along the base of the ridge, spaced evenly a league apart from each other," instructed Rew. "Our fastest riders, lightly armed. They'll survive by escaping, not fighting. Make sure they know they're looking for the remains of the missing party."

"You're sending them into danger," mentioned Colonel Eddla. "If the first group wasn't able to escape..."

Rew nodded, glancing at the man.

The colonel blanched. "I suppose that's what must be done."

"If a second party goes missing, we'll have a better idea where the Dark Kind are, and we can react with force. These men have lives, families, I know, but so do all of the other men. It's the unknown which is our greatest threat."

"I'll see to it," agreed Eddla. The man snapped off a salute which was sharper than usual and departed.

When they were alone, Cinda emerged from the shadows at the far corner of the tent. Rew had sensed her there, though he was unsure if he'd heard her or felt her presence. She was like opening a door to a cellar. Chill and musty, like forgotten relics.

"There's another way," she remarked.

Rew grunted and did not respond.

"You would raise the fallen men?" asked Raif.

Cinda stood straight-backed, her face blank. "If I'm directed to by our commander."

"How far is your reach?" asked Rew.

The young necromancer frowned. "In terms of leagues... I'm not sure. In Jabaan, I reached across most of the city, but I was riding on a wave of power from within the crypt. In Valstock, I was able to extend hundreds of paces with little trouble. A quarter league, perhaps, but there was a surge of power from the departing souls there as well. My reach won't be as great with just ten men missing."

She stood over the table, looking at the coins Rew had placed to represent their forces and the missing squad of cavalry. Those men were notations on the map to her and nothing more. Rew winced. Did Colonel Eddla believe Rew thought the same way? He was using the men as callously as Cinda, wasn't he?

"That is… ten leagues from here?" she asked. "I did not even feel the deaths at such a distance. Here, maybe? Is this a peak on the ridge? It should grant good visibility, and I think I might be able to feel the site of the ambush from there. Unless you're wrong about where it occurred, or these maps are no good."

"Those are possibilities. But regardless, I won't put you at risk when we have common soldiers," hissed Rew, glancing back at the open flap of his command tent to ensure they were alone. "We need you, Cinda. Only you can face the king."

The girl's lips twisted into a mocking smile. "The King's Ranger, weighing the value of each of our lives. I didn't think I'd see the day."

Rew glared at her. "What would you have me do?"

Cinda paused then shook herself. "I don't know. I… I'm finding myself becoming less and less attached. To people, to this world. I did not mean to mock you. My skills are available, should we need them, but I understand why I'm not suited for this task."

"Cinda…" murmured Raif.

Rew watched the girl and did not speak. It was her battle. There was nothing he could say. He had his own war to fight against the Dark Kind, against himself.

After a long moment of silence, the necromancer drifted out the door, and Raif followed. Rew glanced at the maps but knew there was nothing there to see which he didn't already know. He growled to himself then left to find Anne.

Chapter Eleven

Rew trotted comfortably at the front of one hundred and fifty horsemen. It was half of the men and the beasts that he had available. The rest of them were working steady patrols around the main force of the army.

The men behind him were lightly armored, carrying a mix of horse bows, long spears, and wickedly curved scimitars. They were a motley collection, assembled from a variety of units that Findley employed scouting the fringes of his realm. From Duke Vincent, they'd received no cavalry support. Shavroe, wedged between the sea and the swamp, had no use of horses and the men who rode them.

The loose organization of Findley's men meant Rew's cavalry wasn't used to working together as a large group, and they weren't used to pitched battles. They'd already demonstrated they didn't ride in formation well, and he worried what their beasts were going to do when they were first assailed by ayres. Would the dumb animals panic, causing chaos, or would they be able to hold a charge, allowing the spear wielders to plunge their lances into the Dark Kind while the bowmen covered their retreat?

The ranger had no faith in horses, but one of their patrols had spotted a group of one hundred Dark Kind, and his plodding footmen stood no chance chasing them down. The Dark Kind, displaying a frightening grasp of tactics, were evidently moving in units similar to the size of a company, constantly changing positions then coming together in larger groupings to attack a town. Rew's maps were a mess of sightings and conjecture.

He still didn't know how many of the creatures they faced or what their purpose was, but he knew a group of one hundred of them could be overwhelmed by his cavalry, and that would be one hundred fewer they would have to fight later.

And it would be good for the army to have some action under their belts. Whether it went well or poorly, it would give them a chance to learn their capabilities, and the survivors could share their experiences around the campfire with their fellows.

Rew glanced back. The horses were trotting in a loose pack, Colonel Eddla at their head. Beside him was a giant beast, ridden by one of their best riders, with Raif clinging onto the side of the thing, his feet wedged into an extra pair of stirrups.

The horse was a proud animal, and Rew had to admit it was impressive seeing the animal move with a rider on its back and Raif on its side. It was an old breed, no longer common in Vaeldon, its ancestors dating from a time when war on horseback was common in these lands. There was a bannerman to Duke Findley, Rew had been told, who still raised the things as a hobby. Few others bothered. With spellcasters and portaling, the advantage of horses in combat was minimal.

But they didn't have spellcasters, so it was coming in use now.

Along with Raif, they had another fifty footmen who were riding on the sides of the largest of the animals. The cavalrymen told Rew the other beasts weren't strong enough to support a second rider at speed over a distance. The ranger had shrugged and taken what they'd offered.

He alone was on foot. He alone could keep up with the rigorous pace they were traveling at.

Ranger Adro might have kept up as well, but the man and Zaine were still afield. None of the soldiers in the dukes' employ, used to life in the barracks or onboard a ship, could cover the ten leagues they traveled in less than a day. Eddla had wanted more men for their first clash of significance with the Dark Kind, but Rew had insisted on speed.

His instincts were, whatever the Dark Kind were attempting, it would not benefit the men to sit on their haunches waiting for it. Not to mention, he only had four weeks left with Vincent's soldiers. After that, the duke had promised to return them to Shavroe.

Turning his eyes ahead, Rew studied the innocuous ridge that crawled along their right flank. It had a gentle slope, only the occasional boulder or bare shoulder of rock attesting to the stone in its spine. Thick, summer grass covered the rest of it. It was bare of trees, though there were patches of thick brush. Down at the base, the land was verdant and fertile. Trees grew, though in most places they'd been tamed through the ages by men, and none had the stature of the old grandfathers Rew was used to walking beneath in the wilds.

It was little cover for a group of one hundred Dark Kind, yet the creatures had taken two of his scouting parties. Had the narjags hidden in ambush? Had the scouts been careless? Was Rew being careless?

Ahead of his men where they could not see him, he allowed an uncertain frown on his lips. On the run, he jumped atop a rock that split the green grass and leapt off. Behind him, the horses spread around the rock, trotting like a stream.

If he'd been alone, he would proceed cautiously, locate the Dark Kind, and then plan an attack. But with one hundred fifty horses pounding across the land behind him, there was no chance of stealth. The Dark Kind would know they were approaching. How best to use that? Or did they use that? Was it better to announce their presence and force a straight battle?

All his life, Rew had trained for combat. He'd learned in the creche to fight and kill, preparing for the confrontation with his brothers. He'd used those skills as an assassin, doing his father's bidding. Then, he'd battled in the wilderness, fighting for himself and Eastwatch as a ranger. He knew his business, but somehow through all of it, he'd never been tasked with commanding large parties of men. His father—his family—had generals for that.

Their role was to call upon high magic and to command loyalty, to muster resources. The details of formations, of how best to use a mixed assortment of soldiers, was not their specialty. Rew had been taught how to win the loyalty of a general through rewards or threats, but a Morden didn't pay any more attention to the details of troop movements than they did the details of their kitchens baking bread.

But now, Rew was thrust into command of three thousand men, and he had no choice except to wrestle with how to deploy them, how to make them an effective force against the Dark Kind, and how to keep them alive.

Muttering to himself, he kept running, his eyes roving restlessly across the terrain ahead of them. The Dark Kind had taken two of his patrols, but one had escaped. They had to know Rew and the others were coming. They would be waiting.

REW SQUATTED ON A LOW SHELF OF ROCK THAT JUTTED OUT FROM THE side of the ridge. Beneath him, his men milled about, tending to their horses, cinching straps, and adjusting their arms and armor. Beside him, Colonel Eddla and Raif stared ahead, hands held over their eyes in nearly identical poses, but it wasn't the sun preventing them from seeing ahead. It was that there was nothing to look at.

"You're sure they're ahead, m'lord?"

Standing, stretching his legs to loosen them from the hours of running he'd done so far that morning, Rew nodded. "Aye, I'm sure."

Slowly, Eddla pointed out, "I don't see anything, m'lord."

"I'm not a nobleman. I'm a ranger, and when a ranger tells you something is there, believe it."

Colonel Eddla appeared as if he did not agree, but he was professional enough—and had enough experience as a soldier—that he kept his mouth shut. In Vaeldon, talking back to a superior could get you killed as often as rushing over a rise without properly scouting it.

Rew sighed then told the man, "You're right to question my judgement. I'm new to command, and you do not know me, but I spent a decade in the wilderness hunting these things, Colonel. I know when they're out there." Rew pointed toward the grass in front of them. "It's difficult to see, but there's a dip there. The ridge folds, and it'd be easy enough to hide a hundred bodies within it. And there, five hundred paces down the slope, that stand of trees could hold one hundred more. The side of the ridge is steep, here. A man on foot could ascend it with some trouble, but a man on horseback would be hard pressed to do so. If you're not paying attention, it'd be easy to crest the fold in the land near the base, see the Dark Kind, and by the time you turn to run, more of them are streaming out of the trees. It's a good place to box in one of our patrols."

Scratching his head, Eddla bobbed his head. "What you say makes sense, but I don't have the skill of reading the land like you do."

Rew handed the man his spyglass. "Look down there, by the little creek. Does the ground appear disturbed?"

The colonel did as instructed then offered, "Maybe."

"My thought as well. I believe that's where the scouting party was caught."

"What do we do, then?" asked Raif. "As you say, the slope of the ridge is too steep for our horses. Trying to skirt up the ridge then charging down will get half their legs broken. Circling the other side of the ridge and coming back might improve our position a bit, but a human commander would place sentries to prevent us charging at their backs. If we approach those in the woods, our cavalry will be useless. Narjags and ayres will be able to weave through the trees and nip at our heels while we spin around helplessly trying to maneuver the lances and find a clear shot with a bow."

"We've got to charge right down their throats," declared Rew.

"And if they've built fortifications? A nest of stakes?" questioned Eddla. "I don't like charging blind. There's too much risk."

"Risk is unavoidable in war. Prepare the men."

The colonel handed back the spyglass then made to climb down the spit of rock they'd been looking from.

"Colonel," called Rew, "you recall the description of a valaan? Spread the word. If you see it, avoid it. Leave that for me."

Eddla blinked then asked, "You'll be with us? I thought... I assumed you'd stay behind."

Rew gave the man a grim smile. "I wouldn't ask you to do something I wouldn't do myself. Stay clear of the valaan. It's death if anyone else crosses its path."

THE PARTY BEGAN TO RIDE, AND REW RAN AHEAD, ANGLING UP THE slope, past where it would be safe for the horses.

Raif and Colonel Eddla were in the front of two contingents of horsemen. Raif's group, those on the larger animals with footmen hanging from the side, would swing wide, running between the gorge they approached and the trees five hundred paces away. Eddla's men would track slightly higher over the hump of the ridge, and they would strike first.

If there was a problem, Eddla's men would feint a charge, giving the other group weighed down by the extra passengers time to turn and flee. Once Raif's men were on the ground, it would be almost impossible to disentangle them, but with them on the ground, they could provide support to prevent the Dark Kind from encircling the cavalry, and they could serve as a bulwark against the narjags Rew believed would appear from the trees. The cavalry would be a fast-moving, mobile component, while Raif's unit played anchor and kept the battle where they wanted it.

Rew was operating alone, hoping to get visibility before the clash began and to locate the valaan he was certain was with the Dark Kind. It would take one of those creatures to set up an ambush like this. Even with direction, the narjag shamans wouldn't have been careful enough to obscure the site of their previous attack. They wouldn't have waited in place, knowing there would be more men coming to investigate.

He was confident the cavalry could face three or four times their number of narjags and take the day with acceptable casualties, but a valaan could disrupt the entire plan. The creature would be almost impossible for the common soldiers to kill unless they were able to surround it, which would be difficult amidst the battle with the rest of the Dark Kind. And if they couldn't kill it, the thing would wreak havoc on a party their size. A dozen, two dozen men down, and how long would they hold? How long until they turned and fled? In battle, losing oneself to fear got men killed, and there was nothing so fearsome as a valaan.

Facing a valaan was best done by the spellcasters, of which they had none, but they had a ranger.

Long, easy strides propelled Rew up the side of the ridge. He'd already drawn his longsword, and he looked down to see the parallel columns of his cavalry peeling away from each other. Raif was down there, clutching onto the side of his mount, his greatsword on his back. Another hundred paces, and his rider should slow, allowing the fighter to leap to the side, clear of the men behind.

There was no movement yet from the trees and no sound from beyond the ridge. Rew gulped, momentarily worried there would be nothing there, and all of this fuss was a waste of time, but he could feel it. He knew they would find something on the other side. In heartbeats, he crested the ridge and looked down at a knot of what must be close to one hundred narjags.

Speckled amongst them were larger specimens, clutching staffs adorned with feathers and colorful rocks. All of the creatures were armed with a motley assortment of swords, axes, and spears, better equipment than what they would carry in the wilderness. Rew didn't have time to look closely, but he guessed some of those arms came from the two parties of scouts he'd lost.

Rew paused a breath at the top of the hill, looking for the valaan, but he saw none. He began to descend to the other side as the first wave of horsemen broke around the swell in the ground, seeing the Dark Kind for the first time.

From the trees, a chorus of excited yips broke out, and ayres began to bound from within the confines of the trees. They did not move at a coordinated pace like the men, but there were dozens of them, and they had narjag riders on their backs. In total, it was more than the one hundred they expected to face, but the odds were still in their favor.

Rew lost sight of the creatures coming from the stand of trees as he plunged down the side of the ridge, heading for the first group of narjags.

Colonel Eddla's horse slowed, and his men fanned around him, those with lances lowering them, those with bows beginning to release their arrows, arcing shots close above the heads of their fellows.

There were no commands given, no attempt to maximize the impact of a massed release. The Dark Kind wouldn't wilt under a hail of missiles like people would. With their shaman and possibly a valaan to stiffen their courage with greater fear, they wouldn't run. They would just get mad, and they would attack.

The first arrows landed, striking sickly gray flesh. The narjags were impossible to miss, clumped together as they were, and few of them wore armor, but the horse bows didn't have the power of a longbow, and a fatal shot loosed while on the run, aiming over the backs of the lancers, was more a matter of luck than of skill.

Still, the narjags squealed and screeched, some of them falling, others taking painful wounds. It broke the direct command the shamans had, and the narjags charged, racing straight at the thicket of lances that Colonel Eddla's men aimed at them.

In front of horsemen, the narjags dissolved into a mess of howling beasts. Then, Eddla's column hit them.

Narjags were flung before the chests of the heavy animals, their small, unprotected bodies crushed by the weight of the attack. Spears—some aimed well, some not—skewered the creatures or smacked against their sides, spinning them into the face of another attack.

Eddla kept his men moving, dropping his own lance then drawing his scimitar. The colonel had fifty horsemen with him, and they plowed over the narjags, only a few pockets escaping the mass of muscle and bone that had descended upon them.

In one area, two of the horses had gone down, and a cluster of narjags had sheltered behind them. Rew raced in behind the cavalry and vaulted the dead horses and their dying riders. He wheeled his longsword around, taking the head from one narjag then grabbing the neck of a shaman.

The shaman swung its staff at Rew, but he easily batted the blow aside. Then, he drew the edge of his longsword across its throat, releasing a waterfall of foul blood. A third narjag came at him, and Rew dodged then struck, plunging his longsword into its chest.

All three of the creatures fell, and Rew stood over the shaman's body. He was looking for one of the mysterious crystals he'd found outside Arhold, but the shaman appeared to have nothing. Rew frowned. Did that mean a valaan was lurking nearby or that it wasn't?

He looked around and saw Eddla and his men tangled with the remaining narjags. Two of the Dark Kind who'd somehow avoided being trampled headed toward Rew.

Raising his longsword, the ranger moved to meet the creatures, but one of Eddla's men appeared behind them and leaned over, swinging down with his scimitar at an unsuspecting narjag's head. Rew sprang at the other one, finishing it quickly.

"Well done, sir," said the man, looking in surprise at the narjags Rew had killed and the dark blood staining his longsword.

"Clean this up," instructed Rew, pointing at where Eddla was still engaged. Then, he looked back, searching for Raif and the others.

Their heavy horse hadn't joined the conflict in the gully. Rew could see them swirling, locked in battle, and beside them, the footmen were scattered, engaged in individual fights, clawing and scratching in a bloody brawl.

"King's Sake," growled Rew. Then, he began running toward the fight.

Chapter Twelve

Raif was laying about with his greatsword, tearing huge holes in the wave of narjags that threatened to overwhelm him. He was throwing back an entire pack of them by sheer force of his will. Then, he had to stay a blow as a man stumbled into his reach. A narjag lunged at Raif, and he brought an armored knee up, catching the creature on the chin, crunching bone. He pounded the pommel of his greatsword down upon its head.

A pair of men fought in front of the fighter, and in moments, they were cut down as a wave of blackness seemed to blow between them. Cursing, Rew poured on speed. Raif had no choice but to engage the valaan.

The big fighter struck quickly, slashing his greatsword at shoulder height, hoping to make contact, trusting the bulk of the weapon to do sufficient damage if he did. The valaan ducked, gliding around the blade, then swept forward and slashed at Raif, screeching across the lad's breastplate then snagging on the chain-mail covering his ribs and popping links and tearing flesh. Raif bellowed in pain and attacked feverishly.

Rew was a dozen paces away, but he slowed. The big lad had gone completely berserk. He was twirling his greatsword like it was half its size, and Rew couldn't work around him to meet the valaan.

Raif forced it back, but as Rew watched in horror, it kept ducking in, drawing its claws across the lad's armor. Sparks flew as the valaan's hard claws met steel. Blood trickled from where it found gaps in the sturdy plate. Raif kept pressing, and around them, narjags and men backed away, stunned by the ferocity of the fight.

"Raif!" cried Rew. "Out of the way!"

The fighter didn't listen, or he didn't hear.

Raif crashed after the valaan, forcing it to retreat, but he took dozens of small wounds as he did. Individually, they wouldn't slow him, but together, they would kill him. Rew wondered if Raif didn't feel the pain. Maybe he didn't know the damage he was taking. Maybe in his state of madness, he didn't care.

Snarling, Rew lunged forward, caught the edge of Raif's back-plate with his open hand, and flung the fighter out of the way. The valaan paused, as if surprised. Then, it struck. Rew raised his sword and kicked, slamming his boot into the valaan's chest and knocking it back.

It came again, but this time, he was ready and yanked his hunting knife from his belt. He lunged, thrusting with his longsword, trying to meet the valaan's charge, and when it slipped past the tip of his blade, he slashed with his hunting knife.

The valaan stepped back, tilting its head at the ranger.

He didn't give it time to consider him, to wonder who he was. He kept pressing, striking with the longsword, waiting for the valaan's counterattack and meeting it with his knife. He scored a strike on the side of its head, opening a bright, bloody gash. It sliced a deep laceration on his forearm.

Rew grinned, letting his glee show on his face as he came forward. He was trying to goad the creature into overextending.

In the immediate vicinity around them, the battle had stilled, but farther away, the fighting was ferocious, and then Eddla's men began to join the skirmish. Leaning down from their horses with their scimitars, they carved chunks of narjags away. In pairs, the men started chasing the ayres, the riders with bows stopping to fire arrows at the racing, blue-skinned canines.

The tide of the battle was turning. Eddla's initial charge had demolished the first narjag force, and now that they were in the thick of the second scrum, the men had the numbers and the strength of arms.

The valaan's head swung, taking it in with one quick sweep. Then, it threw itself at Rew.

He'd been waiting for the attack, the moment it decided to no longer play with him, but even then, he was surprised at how quickly it came. The valaan was a blur, moving as fast as his eye could track, but he had anticipated it, and when it came, it sacrificed grace for speed.

Rew missed with his longsword but buried his hunting knife in the valaan's gut. Without pause, he ripped it upward, tearing a hole in its stomach larger than his hand.

The valaan clawed at him, ripping a deep gash on his shoulder, but Rew hammered his fist with the hunting knife into its face, knocking it away. Then, he stabbed it in the chest, punching his longsword deep for a killing blow.

The valaan wailed, and the small control it had still held over the narjags vanished. They devolved into screeching, thrashing, individual combatants, and against the more numerous, better-armed, and organized men, they were slaughtered.

Seeing the way the fight was going, Rew staggered to Raif. The fighter was lying on his back, his teeth gritted, bloody rents marring his armor in half a dozen places. "You alive, lad?"

"For the moment."

"Anne will kill me if you die," mentioned Rew, glancing around to see they were in the clear then kneeling beside Raif. "And then your sister will bring me back so that she can kill me, too. Hold still. Let me get a look at this."

He began slicing the leather straps of Raif's armor away, pulling off the ruined breastplate. Around them, the sounds of fighting faded. It was replaced with the sounds of men crying in pain or shouting wordlessly at the thrill of victory.

Rew had left his pack tied to the rear of one of their pack horses that was stationed half a league away, but he was a ranger, and rangers were prepared. He removed a pouch from the back of his belt. "I hope there's enough."

Tearing Raif's tunic away, Rew began daubing a paste he'd mixed that morning on the worst of the fighter's wounds. Behind him, he heard the heavy steps of a horse.

"M'lord," said Colonel Eddla, "we have the field."

Nodding, not looking up, Rew told the other man, "See to the rest of them, Colonel. We'll need tents for the wounded, water, bandages, and I believe there was a surgeon traveling with our supplies. Anne—my healer—will have provided him with herbs he'll need to stave off infection. That's our greatest worry, if the injuries aren't immediately fatal. The Dark Kind are foul beasts, and fever will set within half a day of a wound from their claws and faster from a bite."

"Shall I send someone to tend—"

"I've got this one," interrupted Rew. "Hurry now. The others won't be used to dealing with these sorts of injuries."

The colonel clicked his tongue at his horse and began to move away, rising in his stirrups to shout orders.

"Did we win?" rasped Raif. He struggled to sit up, but Rew held him down. "Blessed Mother, did you see that thing? I... I don't remember much, but it was fast as blazes. Is it dead?"

"Aye," said Rew, smearing more paste on an ugly-looking cut across Raif's ribs.

"Thank you, then," mumbled the fighter. His head fell back, and his jaw was tight with the hurt of his wounds.

Shaking his head, Rew kept smearing the poultice until it was gone then grimaced at the remaining injuries. They were shallow, more annoyances than anything, but even shallow wounds from the Dark Kind were prone to infection. He laid Raif's greatsword across the lad's body and bent to pick him up. The ranger's back cracked with the strain, and he grunted. The things he did for those children.

"I'M TOLD THE LAD HELD HIS OWN," REMARKED COLONEL EDDLA several hours later when he was conferring with Rew, tallying their losses. "He'll live?"

"Aye, he'll live," said Rew, "though we need to get him and the others back to the bulk of our army as quickly as we can."

Eddla nodded. "Our riders, if they're unharassed, should be back to the main force already. An hour after dark, the wagons should be here, and before dawn, the wounded will be in the care of our surgeons and your Anne."

"We have enough wagons?"

Clearing his throat, Eddla remarked, "There weren't as many wounded as we thought. Most, ah, most of those who were injured died."

Rew winced.

Eddla checked his figures. "Last report, seventeen too wounded to ride, twenty-eight dead, and at least forty of our horses will have to be put down. I don't mean to sound careless about our soldiers, but the horses will be more difficult to replace. Findley has more men, but we've already gathered all the suitable war horses in the duchy."

Rew rubbed his head, considering it. It'd been smart to use the cavalry for the engagement, but Eddla was right. Forty horses... Rew hated using the animals, but their speed meant human lives could be saved. If they had a tool, they had to use it. The loss of the horses would be felt in their next engagement.

Sighing, Rew tapped another sheet of parchment that had been dropped by an aide minutes earlier. "One hundred forty narjags, thirteen of them possibly shaman, eleven ayres, and the valaan. Seems most of the ayres fled, and an unknown number of narjags."

Eddla nodded. "Too bad. By the time they started running, we had the field well in hand."

"Dark Kind don't run," remarked Rew. He leaned back and stretched. "Somehow, another valaan took control of them and instructed them to flee. I can only guess how close they'd have to be to do that."

"A second force nearby?"

Rew shrugged and did not respond.

"I heard you ordered us to triple the sentries tonight."

"It'll be another day before we're reunited with the main army," said Rew. "Until then, we have to be vigilant. Will the men complain about the extra duty?"

Eddla shook his head. "We handled the narjags easily enough, but they all lost friends, and most have visited the wounded." He paused. "Many of them saw the valaan. That thing... If it hadn't been for the lad drawing its interest and you facing it, I don't want to think what could have happened. Dozens more of us would have died. Maybe all of us, I don't know. It doesn't wound my pride to admit I wouldn't stand a chance against that thing. I don't know how I'd even try."

Rew smirked. "If it comes to that, my advice is to offer a prayer to the Blessed Mother and just start swinging. Care for an ale?"

"Aye, if we don't stop at just the one."

"I knew you were the right man for this job."

THE COLUMN TRUDGED WEARILY NORTH, WALKING ALONG THE highway between Findley's city and Mordenhold. Vaeldon's capital was still a week away if they had an open road, and Rew had three weeks with his army. They'd made progress, finding and destroying half a dozen companies of Dark Kind and scores of smaller bands, but they'd been wounded as well. Hundreds of men had died in the fighting, and hundreds more had been sent home, packed in slow-moving wagons.

Rew had twenty-five hundred men left in his command, but he still didn't know how many Dark Kind he was facing. Some. He knew that much.

For three days now, they'd been constantly harried. Day and night, ayres would come racing out of hiding, raking alongside the column, usually getting killed as they did, but sometimes retreating back out of sight. They'd followed them, at first, but found ambushes set by narjags hidden amongst the hills and trees.

Rew had led expeditions of men off the flanks, surprising some of the ambushes, slaying the narjags, but there were always more. The creatures were like mushrooms in early autumn, sprouting under every stone and rotten log.

The day before, Rew had thrown up his hands and given up trying to take the fight to the narjags and instead had the men remain ready for attack. Constant vigilance had saved lives, but it was a strain on the army. There was only so long you could study the side of the highway, looking for an ambush, only so many times you would wake up in the middle of the night and hear the sentries—your friends—battling for their lives.

But the Dark Kind, whether by plan or some evil fortune, did not mass into large groups any longer. There wasn't a big group of them Rew could crush. Instead, it was like a constant swarm of biting insects. You could swat them when they came near enough, but you couldn't catch them all, and each time they approached, you were going to get bit. Annoying the first time, frustrating the second and third, but by now, it was absolutely maddening.

Looking ahead, he hoped that would change. Zaine and Ranger Adro had returned and reported a new fortification sprawling across the highway. It was a network of earthen bulwarks hedged by sharpened stakes. They'd said men were working constantly to expand it, and hundreds of soldiers were sheltering inside. The rising barricades were attracting Dark Kind like jackals to a fresh kill. If there was to be a pitched battle, it would be there.

Rew didn't know what to make of the news.

As the fortification came into view, he was even more confused. There was nothing there. No city. No town. It had been an empty stretch of highway the last time he'd walked by, years earlier. There wasn't even a way station or small tavern in this place.

But now, it was a hive of activity. He rubbed his eyes with his fists, feeling like he was striding through a dream. He wanted to speed up but couldn't without leaving the army behind. He glanced at the others and saw they were just as apprehensive as he was. There was no reason for the fortification that anyone could see.

Still walking, Rew dug out his spyglass and held it to his eye to get a better view of what they were coming across. Fresh earth was mounded as high as his head and half again. Stakes—some slender, some as thick as his leg—were studded around the recently raised hills. Freshly cut wood shone pale in the sunlight where it wasn't marred by dark stains. The Dark Kind had already been testing the defenses.

"They've raised another hundred paces of wall since I was here last," said Zaine, pointing to the far end where Rew could see scores of men with wheelbarrows and shovels and scores more with bows and swords standing guard. "What is this, a quarter league long?"

"Aye," agreed Rew. "Why would anyone build this? Why here?"

"I was hoping you'd be able to answer that."

Shaking his head, Rew lowered the spyglass. They were getting closer, and he didn't need it. Then, he raised it again, pointing toward what looked to be a wooden gate bound with thick ropes, placed where the road had once run through. Flanking the gate, sitting atop two raised platforms, were a pair of imps.

"King's Sake," muttered Rew. "This is… I don't know. A warlord, trying to claim a hunk of land maybe, but why build the thing so expansive? It's far more than one would need to squat on the highway and charge merchants a toll. Against the Dark Kind, a quarter league long will make it a beast to defend unless they've got a lot more men inside there than the smoke implies. For sustained defense with a small force, you build a fortress up, not wide. It'd take two thousand men to line both sides of the enclosure."

"Those stakes they've placed will slow the Dark Kind," added Raif, "but they won't stop them. A valaan could direct his ayres to leap over in some places, and in others, they'd swarm and rip them out if the stakes are not buried a pace or two deep. But if not for the Dark Kind, what else are they defending against? There's no water here. None of the necessary resources to build a settlement, but surely no one is bold enough to try and block commerce just a week from Mordenhold. Not even a greed-blind warlord would choose to stake a claim within the king's own lands."

"Aye, you're right," agreed Rew. "This is temporary, meant for the Dark Kind, but who would build it? Not the king himself, obviously, and we've got most of Duke Findley's army marching behind us."

"Only one way to find out," remarked Zaine.

Rew nodded, and still walking, he turned. "You and you," he said, pointing to Zaine and Raif. He raised his voice and added, "and Colonel Eddla, one of the lieutenant colonels, and ten good men, come with me. We're going to go ahead to find out what is going on. Tell the others to stop and rest at least five hundred paces from the gates. I want them out of bowshot. Keep an eye on those imps."

Eddla began addressing his bugler, who rode beside him, giving instructions then pausing as the lad tooted out the signals to the marching column of men.

There was a wave of pleased groans at the opportunity for rest and curious questions about what the strange fortification ahead of them was. Some of the men in Findley's service would have traveled north before. They would know that a month ago, there wasn't a fort there.

"Tell them to keep watch to the south as well," instructed Rew. "It's been a few hours since we've been attacked, but Zaine and Adro said the Dark Kind were gathering nearby. Something is odd here, and I want the men ready. It feels like we're dreaming, doesn't it? Let's not get complacent. Have a tenth share stay on their feet on the perimeter. Give them half an hour then swap."

Eddla continued calling out orders, and Rew and his companions trudged ahead. Cinda and Anne emerged from the column, studying the fort just as everyone else was.

"Anne," warned Rew, "we're not sure what we'll find in there. Perhaps it's best if you stay behind with the men?"

The empath shook her head. "You don't know what you'll find, which is why I want to go. We're in this together."

Rew glanced at Cinda.

The necromancer smiled. "What she said."

Rolling his eyes, Rew waited for another moment until Eddla joined them with his selected men. They began walking toward the fort. The work on the fringes of it didn't stop at their approach. It seemed everyone was ignoring them, except for the imps beside the gate.

"Never seen anything like that," muttered Eddla. "Duke Findley's an invoker. Just portals and such. I suppose he could cast some combat spells if he had reason. Those things... Never seen one so big."

"Controlling an imp requires the attention of the spellcaster," said Rew, studying the two in front of them. "Two of them that size is no small feat. Whoever summoned them must have a decent level of talent and knowledge. They'll be experienced. To hold onto them long enough for something as simple as guard duty... I don't think I've seen that, either. When a spellcaster calls an imp, it's for a purpose."

"You think they'll try to stop us?" asked Zaine, clearly evaluating the distance to wall, trying to guess when they would be within bowshot. "Should we have brought a few more men with us?"

"I'll protect you," said Raif, a grin on his lips.

"Pfah," retorted Zaine. "Three days ago, I was having to dip an ale for you because you said you couldn't walk."

"Maybe I just liked watching you bend over to do it," suggested Raif.

Zaine leaned toward him and cuffed him aside the head like he was a naughty puppy. Apparently, she'd learned to avoid striking his body, which was covered in steel plates and links of chain. Colonel Eddla watched, a small smile on his lips. The younglings' banter was one of the only entertainments they had on the march, and it seemed to amuse the entire army that the long-suffering Raif was constantly getting the worse of it. The men had taken a liking to the lad, and he'd earned their honest respect, but he was still a baron, and to any common man, watching a noble get slapped upside the head was worthy entertainment.

"Focus," warned Rew as they drew within fifty yards of the gate.

The imps hadn't moved much, just shifting their stance to follow the newcomers' approach. They were big, twice the mass of a man, with curling horns spiraling up from broad, hard heads, and tusks protruding from lipless mouths. Their eyes were solid black lumps, but Rew could feel their gaze upon him. He couldn't see their hands or their feet, but he imagined large, curved claws there. In a fight, he was confident he could take them, but they were impressive specimens, and he reevaluated his assumption of the conjurer who'd summoned them. There would only be a dozen spellcasters in the kingdom who could summon one such creature, fewer still who could call two of them and maintain control for very long.

Rew touched his longsword and then his hunting knife, making sure his cloak was pushed back and the weapons were accessible. Now that Calb was dead, were there any spellcasters who could manage two imps as impressive as these for more than a few minutes?

"Ho, the fort!" called Rew, keeping his hand casually resting on his longsword.

A small, round head popped up beside one of the imps. "Took you long enough."

Rew blinked at the man.

The man stared back.

"Ah, are you the conjurer who summoned these imps?"

The man shook his head, his over-large ears almost flapping with the motion. "Nah, not a spellcaster. These creatures serve Brian of the Brambles."

"Is he here?"

"Aye," said the little man, his head bobbing agreeably, "and he'll want to meet you, he will. Been waiting for days for you to finally arrive."

"Brian of the Brambles," whispered Zaine. "My ma told me stories of him. One of the first things I remember. Seems like a dream now. Ah, wasn't he a rabbit?"

"In the stories," agreed Raif. He frowned. "You think there's a big rabbit in there?"

"No, but…"

Rew ignored them and shifted his feet, waiting, but when the little man atop the wall didn't continue, Rew asked, "Are you in there alone?"

"No, of course not! We've a whole army here. I'm the only one who'll come near the imps, though. The rest are waiting down below to open the gate."

Rew scratched his beard. "And will they be doing it soon?"

Owlishly, the little man blinked then bellowed, "Quite right you are!" He spun and began shouting down into the fort.

Moments later, the gate cracked open. A dozen swearing men seemed to be lifting it by hand, and with great effort, they shifted it out of the way. Rew supposed that out in the middle of nowhere, they didn't have the metal or a forge to fashion hinges.

"The thing is heavier than it looks," apologized the gatekeeper, his own hands tucked safely behind his back. The fellow stood distressingly close to one of the imps, which seemed to share his interested look. "You'll be wanting a guide to Brian, then?"

Rew nodded impatiently.

"Your men coming along?" asked the little man, peering back behind Rew and the others at where the army had settled.

"Not yet."

"Cautious. Wise," tittered the little man. Then, he disappeared, and in a flash, he was standing in the center of the open gate. "After me. You think we ought to leave the gate open? Brian didn't give me any instructions on that. With your men out there, don't think the Dark Kind will get through, eh? We've big problems if they do."

Rew and the others followed the little man in the gate. The men who'd opened the gate stood around mutely. They were an odd assortment, dressed like it was a feast day, or they were peddlers garbed brightly to attract a curious eye. None of them were armed.

"How is this getting weirder?" asked Zaine, watching their little guide scamper ahead into a vast encampment that was almost entirely empty.

Chapter Thirteen

Most of the enclosure was open, flat dirt, except for the far end, which was full of men working. They were building the mound of dirt higher and farther. They were sharpening stakes, and they were carting supplies on makeshift sledges. Closer, there was a long tent, which might have served as a mess hall, and others, which could have been lodging. It was housing for hundreds of men, though the fort was large enough for thousands.

They were led to a circular tent made of silk that was tattered and stained from long use. A streamer hung limply in the still air, banded with different colors, where a noble might hang his coat of arms, but the streamer wasn't of a style Rew was familiar with.

He glanced at Anne and saw her eyebrow raised. Both of them had traveled from one end of Vaeldon to the other, and Rew had been trained to recognize the signs of nobility from birth, but he didn't recognize this one.

It wasn't until they were almost to the entrance of the tent that he saw a knee-high imp standing attendance outside of the tent flap. The little creature squeaked at their approach then ducked inside.

The small, bald man who was their guide stopped outside of

the tent and waited, seeming to bounce on his feet, until the little imp reappeared and held open the bottom corner of the tent flap. Their guide took it and opened it wide for Rew and the others to enter.

Rew looked back at Colonel Eddla and instructed, "Stay out here, and stay alert."

The colonel nodded.

In other circumstances, a military leader might have demanded to accompany his liege into a meeting with unknown and mysterious forces, but Eddla had seen enough of what Rew, Raif, and Cinda could do that he didn't bother to mention it. If they couldn't handle themselves inside, what was he going to do?

Rew entered first, blinking his eyes to adjust to the gloom and breathing shallowly. Small, copper burners were placed around the tent, and thin tendrils of fragrant smoke curled up from them. It was a heady scent, cut by the tang of the hot copper. The smoke hung, stirred in slow eddies around their heads as they walked deeper into the tent. Another of the little imps lounged on a mound of silk pillows, and a man was sitting cross-legged on a layered pile of rugs.

Rew rubbed his face. The scene was so strange it felt like a dream.

The man's eyes were closed, and he was old. Not the withered age of Commandant Eckvar. The former ranger commandant was like brittle paper. This man was old like tarnished brass. His wrinkled face showed the passage of years, but his frame was solid, and he sat with a straight back, and his knees were folded beneath him like a younger man or a man who'd been doing it so long his joints had finally given up protesting. The man had an impressive beard that hung in a narrow white curtain that reached down to his waist.

He was dressed in the green robes of a conjurer, but the cut was different from what Rew had seen before. It looked like around his legs the robes had been tailored into baggy trousers as if for riding, and they were cinched at the waist by a broad, black leather belt. As strange as his clothing, his face had a familiar look. A friend of a parent who used to come around but had not been seen since childhood, except Rew's father had never had friends, and any conjurer with strength to summon the imps outside would have been noteworthy in Mordenhold's court.

Leaning against the table was a heavy, steel-headed maul, and at a glance, Rew saw the weapon had seen use. A spellcaster with a war hammer? He'd think it was someone else's, but there was no one else in the room, and the space had the esoteric feel of a spellcaster's lair or the fuzzy specificity of a dream.

The man rose silently to his feet, his eyes snapping open as he did. His voice was a rich baritone, still strong after his evident years. "Apologies, visitors, for not greeting you at the gate. I was dreaming. I find as I age, I need more contemplative periods than I used to. It's difficult to stay within this world without slipping to the other." The spellcaster's gaze moved over them then settled on Cinda. "Well, well. This is a surprise."

Rew cleared his throat and asked, "I don't mean to sound rude, but who are you? I believe I would know any conjurer of your skill, and your attire and tent aren't of a familiar style."

The man nodded. "My name is Brian of the Brambles."

"Like the rabbit?" whispered Zaine. "Doesn't look like one."

"I am not from this kingdom," continued the old man, evidently not hearing Zaine. "Let me assure you your customs are as strange to me as mine are to you."

Rew crossed his arms over his chest, frowning and unsure of what to say to that.

The old man gave the ranger a closer looked then said, "Why have you not developed your talent, lad? Is this common? But I see you're a warrior. Your hands... that longsword. It's enchanted. I've seen the like once before. It is empty now?"

"You've seen a sword like this?"

"Old work. Weapons like that travel, don't they? It's as if they seek conflict. As if they're alive." Brian of the Brambles stopped speaking abruptly and looked at Rew as if he was waiting for something.

"Yes, the sword is old," muttered Rew. "It's seen battle. Many of them and many more to come it seems. I do not mean to be blunt, but who are you, and what are you doing here? I should know you, but I do not. I do know there was nothing here until you erected this earthen fort. Why?"

"The fort is to defend against the Dark Kind, what else?" offered the spellcaster. "And we began building it here precisely because it's in the middle of nowhere. I did not believe I would receive a friendly reception if I built a barricade squarely within one of your nobles' lands, but my companions and I needed what protection we could find against the Dark Kind."

"I see," said Rew, though he did not see.

"You're right. The nobles may have objected to a fort being built upon their lands, but ah, why are you here at all?" questioned Raif. "You said you are not from these lands..."

The spellcaster smiled at the fighter. "Your weapon is enchanted as well. A boon to you, given your quest. Are enchanted weapons more common now than I expected?"

"I don't know what you expected to find here in Vaeldon, but no, they are not common."

"Good, good. I've always found uncommon allies are the best allies."

"Allies?" Rew coughed.

"I've gotten reports that your army battles the Dark Kind. That is why I came here. My enemy's foe is my friend. Do you know that saying?"

"Something like it."

"Then, we are allies, or something like it," said the old man, a smile on his lips, the skin around his eyes crinkling. He glanced again at their weapons and then at Cinda. "Necromancy. Uncommon indeed. A dead art. Ha. Do you get it?"

Cinda stared back at him blankly.

"A new talent but your blood smells old. I recognize it. Interesting. I have questions, if you have time to answer, and certainly, you must have questions for me. If we're to be allies, then let us get to know each other."

"Yes, we do have questions. Our men…"

"Bring them inside," offered Brian of the Brambles. "We've been expanding the fort the last week in anticipation of your arrival. Soon, the fraemoth will be upon us, and you'll appreciate the work we've done, though I'm afraid it will be horribly inadequate. Still, we must try, mustn't we? And do not worry. Your men far outnumber my own. That should give your soldiers comfort they are not walking into a trap. Men at arms are always paranoid about such things, I've found. But if a trap I set, your men have the might to fight their way out of it."

Rew looked around the group of his friends, and all he saw in their eyes was confusion. Did the man just admit… No. He was trying to reassure them he meant well, Rew thought.

The ranger dropped his hands and said, "Raif, tell Eddla to bring the men in and find them places to establish a camp. See that they're getting settled then return to us here."

Raif nodded, still eying the spellcaster curiously before he ducked outside.

The spellcaster steepled his fingers and asked them, "This land is bubbling with rumors. I'd like to know, are they true?"

"People call me Brian of the Brambles," said the spellcaster, sitting comfortably on the stacked rugs. He shifted, and beside him, his small imp mimicked the motion flawlessly. The spellcaster didn't seem to notice, but Rew couldn't ignore the tiny beast and its bizarre parody of its master. "I styled myself that some time ago. It's from a dream, from when I was a child. It's of my mother reading me a story. For brevity, I suggest you call me Brian."

Rew nodded then cleared his throat, pulling his gaze from the imp back to the spellcaster. "My name is Rew. This is Cinda, Zaine, Anne, and Raif is the big lad who left to fetch the others."

"Rew," murmured the spellcaster. "Brevity indeed. We have much in common, don't we? May I know your surname, Rew?"

"Morden. It's been many years since I've used it."

"The rumors are true. Pfah, more than that. They are accurate. Isn't that strange? It's a shame we don't have time to learn more of each other. I have so many questions, but answers may only bring more of them."

"I know that feeling," grumbled Rew. "You said you came from across the sea?"

The spellcaster let out a long, slow sigh. "I am not of this land. I must tell you more than that, mustn't I? You want to know of me as I want to know of you. Much in common. So much."

Rew shifted, finding the man's piled carpets rather uncomfortable, but there were no chairs in the room, and Brian of the Brambles had not offered them anything to drink. Maybe that was for the best. A spellcaster offering freely to share information? This man was foreign in more ways than one.

"I hail from the city of Stafford, the capital of the land of... I could spend all day sharing those details. My background and history might interest you, some other day, but I would spend more time explaining my home than I would explaining myself. For our purposes, and I will try not to be too long winded, as you appreciate brevity as much as myself, you should know that I was called to face the Dark Kind. The fraemoth, in particular. The creature is a manifestation of a deep fear, and it is terribly dangerous to these lands."

Rew eyed the man, not responding.

"You have heard of it?"

"Little. Very little."

"Of course. I understand it's been fifty years since a fraemoth plagued this place. A long time, but it seems only a moment since I last had this dream."

"What can you tell us of the fraemoth? Do you know how to defeat it?"

"With your sword, lad. Stab it, or do whatever you warriors do. A fraemoth can be slain easier than some fears, but such a victory is ephemeral until you destroy the source of the fear itself. North of Mordenhold, there is a fortress. Do you know it?"

"Not well," said Rew, frowning. "Northguard. I have been there but once and did not stay long. It's an uncomfortable place."

"Yes, yes, it is," agreed the spellcaster. "A cold, dead place. A prison like no other. I know. But within that prison, there is a weakness, a fear that is bubbling and spilling over. It is there that the fraemoth was conjured. It is there you must go to stop it from happening again. Or perhaps... Yes, of course. You must go to Northguard. You must bring your sword and finish it."

"I don't understand."

"You will, at the end, when the view is clear."

Shaking his head, Rew whispered, "We go to Mordenhold to face the king."

"You must kill him. All else is a waste if you do not. Perhaps he can be brought to Northguard, and all will be resolved there."

Rew scratched his beard. "I'm afraid I don't understand what you're talking about."

"You will."

"What does this have to do with the fraemoth?" wondered Cinda. "It's standing between us and both Mordenhold and Northguard. Can you tell us more of it? Why isn't Vaisius Morden destroying it himself? It's our understanding he did fifty years ago when the last one was... conjured, did you say?"

"Vaisius Morden had different goals fifty years ago than he does today. He's gotten bored, I suppose. That is dangerous for us all. Yes, indeed, he looks beyond the old boundaries. He seeks new horizons and challenges. Pfah, if I'd known not even the frae-moth would interest him... Well, what is done is done. The frae-moth is conjured, and someone has to deal with it."

"Conjured?"

The spellcaster gestured to the small imp beside him. "Of course you're familiar with imps?"

Rew nodded.

"It is common belief they are conjured from a plane beyond our world, some place they have their own society, their own cities, I suppose. How anyone could think that... But it's not entirely false. Imps do come from another plane, another piece of existence. They come from dreams—or perhaps I should say, nightmares."

"Wait. Imps aren't real?" barked Cinda.

"We make them real." Brian of the Brambles poked the small creature beside him, grinning at its squawk of protest. "You can see it, feel it, touch it. It is real, but it is also a piece of my dream which I've made manifest in this, the waking world."

"You dreamed that thing up, and then just—" Zaine snapped her fingers.

"Exactly."

"So they're not from another plane? Then..."

"They are," corrected Brian. "The plane we inhabit when we dream."

"Where do the Dark Kind come from, then?" pressed Cinda. "Are those from our dreams as well? Are they conjured just like an imp?"

"Dark Kind are conjured but not by the men and women who practice the art in this kingdom. The Dark Kind are the nightmares of a people before. A necromancer, yes, with the smell of old blood, you're familiar with the barrowlands? You must have lived near there. Am I right?"

"I'm familiar with the barrowlands," whispered Cinda.

"The shades of these ancient people still exist there but as ghosts," said Brian. "They are creatures of the plane of death, stuck in this one, but from their dreams, issue the Dark Kind."

"The wraiths in the barrowlands conjure Dark Kind?" asked Rew, sitting forward, his throat feeling tight.

"You've seen a wraith from there?"

"I… I can call to them," said Cinda.

"Interesting," replied Brian of the Brambles, his eyes twinkling. "The wraiths you would have seen cannot conjure Dark Kind, but their people can. Their conjurers."

"They still live?"

Brian shook his head. "Only one."

"Vaisius Morden. He… conjured the Dark Kind?"

"No, not like you are thinking. Shall we say his brother? He's entombed, but he lives, and he dreams, and the Dark Kind spill forth."

Rew gaped at the spellcaster.

"That is why you must travel to Northguard. You must shatter the barrow and destroy the last of the Mordens. It is your blood, lad. Spill the blood of family. End it. If you do, the Dark Kind will no longer threaten this kingdom."

"The king has a brother," said Rew, choking out the words.

"Brother is not an entirely accurate term, but for our purposes, yes."

"I've never heard of this."

"He's been locked away over two hundred years," mentioned Brian.

"But he can still touch this world?" questioned Cinda.

"He can. His prison is… imperfect. He can escape his dream and wake in this world from time to time, though he cannot remain long. But while he dreams, he's prolific. The Dark Kind and their issue have long plagued these lands. He must be destroyed or placed somewhere secure, or this will never end."

Both Brian and Rew glanced down at his sword.

"A prison?"

Brian nodded. "That sword was crafted by three… brothers, to continue using the term and avoid a proper explanation, which we do not have time for. The blade was fashioned to contain the soul of their father. Each brother, in their own way, meant to use him. You lass, you understand, souls have power. The three brothers meant to betray each other as well. It turned out Vaisius

Morden was the most cunning, or at least the quickest to act. He sealed his two brothers away, thinking he'd done so like their father, but alone, his work was not complete. There are holes in the prison, and they are growing larger."

"King's Sake, Ranger, your family is messed up," declared Zaine.

Rew gave her a wan smile then turned back to Brian. "That is why there are more Dark Kind now?"

The spellcaster nodded.

"Why does the king not destroy his brothers himself? If we're capable of it, then surely he is as well."

"For the same reason the king did not use that sword. He is a powerful man, but he is not an omnipotent one. He could not control Erasmus. He cannot control his brothers, not completely. Sealing them away was the best he could do, but that weakness is why his prisons are failing. First, the one to the world of dreams, which will release a flood of Dark Kind like you cannot imagine. Then, the one to death will fail as well, and you'll wish for the Dark Kind. Vaisius is trapped, afraid of his own creations, and desperate for more. That's why he needs you."

"Us?" barked Cinda.

Brian glanced at Rew.

"But why me?" demanded the ranger. "I have no high magic. I have no talent which he needs."

"You're assuming high magic is what he needs. Think, lad. The king could not control the power within that sword, but you could. You have skills beyond his. Old magic, ancient magic, the magic of the world and all of the wild places. He has been severed from his original, mortal body for a very long time now. His connections to the ancient magic, the natural world, are thin. Yours are stronger than steel."

"Blessed Mother," declared Anne. "All this time, he's been breeding invokers, enchanters, and conjurers, but he needed a ranger."

Brian bowed his head to the empath.

Everyone in the tent fell silent, Rew studying the longsword in front of him, the others pretending to do so while all surreptitiously looking at the ranger. It made sense. Vaisius Morden the Eighth had allowed his son to find his own path, one far afield of the well-trodden roads their ancestors had journeyed along. He needed... communion. A connection to life, to the vibrancy of the world. A world Vaisius Morden had long ignored.

Two brothers? The king had brothers? Rew's head was spinning. It was an awful truth, but he could feel it. It was the truth of a sort—three brothers, locked in combat, the strongest surviving. Vaisius Morden had forged a kingdom and a legacy that mimicked his own rise, a monument to all he'd done and where he'd come from. He supped on the power of his family as he always had. It was all a sick game, the millions of deaths, for nothing more than one man's ego, one man's bloody ode to himself and the betrayal that had fed his rise.

They had to stop it.

Long moments passed, and then Raif quietly entered the tent. The big fighter glanced around at his companions, frowning at their silence. He shifted on his feet and cleared his throat. He asked, "Well, what'd I miss?"

Chapter Fourteen

R ew felt like he was running downhill, thoughts flashing by like tree trunks, his legs pounding, his body flailing out of control, every moment another chance to crash, tumbling and skidding or smashing into one of those ideas, stopping him dead.

His father had brothers? They'd fought each other?

The twisted logic behind three brothers fighting for the throne, the uncomfortable echoes between his life and Vaisius Morden's... And those brothers' prisons were weakening. It was like a bucket of cold water poured over his head. That was why the king hadn't come to them, why he gave them only the smallest sliver of his attention. Vaisius Morden had his own brothers to contend with.

It was crazy, wild, and over and over, Rew declared loudly they had no evidence, no reason to believe any of it was true. But the old, ancient magic thrummed, and he felt it. They'd stumbled across a truth. Brian of the Brambles, a strange man of stranger habits, had told them something no one ought to know.

Rew had questioned the man, tried to press him on where he'd gotten his information, where he'd come from. The old man claimed to have dreamed it. When Rew accused him of telling them false stories, the spellcaster merely looked the ranger in the eye and asked if he thought it was false.

There were more questions than answers, just like Brian had said when they'd first begun talking to him. Rew kept asking until he was reminded, in their immediate future, it mattered very little what he believed or did not believe. Whoever had done it, someone had summoned a fraemoth. Alsayer had claimed it. Brian of the Brambles confirmed it.

Rew didn't trust either man, but the evidence was there for anyone to see. As Colonel Eddla had led Duke Findley's and Duke Vincent's men into the earthen compound, on the other side of it, to the north, there'd been more and more sightings of Dark Kind. Narjags were riding on the backs of ayres, darting out of cover, racing across the length of the bulwark, but not coming within bow range. The creatures were scouting, assessing how many people were within the newly risen fort and how progress was coming on completing it.

Some Dark Kind general had assigned them to scout. They were reporting to something. There was a power out there with authority to command even the valaan. With his own eyes, Rew had seen narjag shamans using magic. It was unprecedented. It had to be the influence of the fraemoth.

Brian of the Brambles had tasked the bulk of his men with finishing their work on the earthen barrier, piling barrow after barrow of soil into a head-high mound then adding several more layers. They had stacks of branches to be sharpened and placed outside. Rew assigned some of Findley's men to help. They were from farming stock, and they knew the secrets of moving soil. The ranger knew they had little time, so he convinced Brian that instead of expanding the compound, they seal off what wasn't finished.

Rew also directed Ranger Adro to scout in the woods, to see what they were up against. But it wasn't long before that became too dangerous. Not even rangers could outrun an ayre, and the Dark Kind had been waiting. Ranger Adro managed to escape, but half a dozen of his scouts were caught too far from the walls. They stopped trying to scout after that.

Cinda tried her hand at intelligence gathering. Standing atop the earthen barricade on the north face of the enclosure, she raised the corpses of the scouts who had fallen back within the trees, and she sent them shuffling deeper into the woods, searching for Dark Kind, trying to learn how many more there were, but her minions did not last long.

Whether because the Dark Kind believed they were living men or whether they understood what she was doing, they quickly fell on the animated corpses. The undead were resilient, already being dead, but they were not fast or stealthy. Within several hundred paces, Cinda's minions were set upon, and they were torn apart until there was nothing left for the souls to bind to.

Cinda shrugged and quietly whispered to Rew. "If more men die out there, I can give it another try. I could bind a corpse then leave it where it lays. Maybe they won't notice if it's lying still, and I can see what is passing by."

Wincing at her suggestion, Rew shook his head. "We're not going to sacrifice men to implant a... a dead spy, out in the woods."

She shrugged. "Knowledge wins battles, Ranger."

"We know enough," he told her. He gestured expansively, covering the road and the terrain beside it. "Nothing along that entire front is getting more than a couple of hundred paces before being attacked by a score of narjags or ayres. Do the math. How many must they have lurking to jump on us so quickly?"

Cinda pursed her lips. "Several companies of them spaced evenly. Presumably more behind that which we aren't reaching. We should assume they have thousands."

Rew nodded. "Not to mention the valaan that must be coordinating them and this fraemoth, whatever it is capable of. We need to speak to Brian again, find out what else he knows."

"He's over there. Dreaming, he says."

Rew grunted and led Cinda to the spellcaster's side.

His eyes opened, and he gave them a sour look. "I was trying to do the lass one up and send my imps over the wall to see what's out there. I can't look through their eyes, but I can feel them. One by one, they were caught and destroyed. Didn't make it four hundred paces beyond the wall."

Cinda laughed, her mirth startling given the circumstances. "My corpses didn't make it beyond three hundred. They're harder to bring down but slower moving, I guess."

"You saw what they saw?"

She nodded.

Standing slowly to his feet, the old man shook himself, loosening stiff joints. "If we survive this, I will have many questions for you. Necromancy is a new talent, and when I became familiar with it, it was too late. I'd like to learn more of it, if I can."

"And when did you become familiar—" began Rew.

Brian held up a hand to stall him. "You're curious. That is good, but for the moment, may I suggest we direct your curiosity to the fraemoth. If we cannot defeat it, then the rest of this idle chitchat will be for naught."

Cracking his knuckles in frustration that the spellcaster continued to elude his questions, but admitting to himself the man was right, Rew nodded.

"Imps are the product of our imaginations, our fears," explained Brian. "These days, they all have a similar look, follow similar patterns, because while they stem from our dreams, people are not particularly imaginative creatures. We expect a thing, and it is. As children, we're told stories with sharp teeth and big claws, so that is what we still fear as adults. When a conjurer begins their study, they are shown live examples or depictions of imps others have conjured. In their dreams, those old fears are given flesh, and the nature of their conjuring is set. Thusly, all conjurers summon some version of the same imp."

"Some imps are bigger than others," remarked Cinda.

"Some fears are greater than others," retorted Brian. "It is not the specific image that the conjurer summons but the idea. The imp is simply giving shape to the conjurer's fear."

"I understand, sort of."

"The Dark Kind are a different kind of fear, felt by a different kind of people," continued Brian. "They have claws and sharp teeth as well because some fears are universal amongst our peoples, but beyond that, the Dark Kind have a hunger. They seek to take from us, populate our lands, and eventually replace us. The fraemoth is the epitome of that fear. It hungers, like they all do, but it's intelligent. It has self-restraint, which means it can plan and plot, though its goal is always the same as the others."

Rew frowned at the man.

"Worse than that," said Brian, "the fraemoth can become us. It can take what makes us... us, and adapt that to its own needs. Our power is its power. A true replacement, you understand, and when it supplants us, we will be forgotten. The fear of the ancient people was a deep one and, it turns out, a valid one. You have replaced them. Even on the outskirts of the barrowlands, no one of this kingdom remembers what was here before."

"A fraemoth was conjured fifty years ago?" asked Rew.

Brian of the Brambles nodded.

"And the king killed it?"

Again, Brian nodded.

"Why would he not kill it now?"

"He's busy, I suppose."

"But he could?"

"Oh, I am sure Vaisius Morden has the power to destroy a fraemoth. They're terrifically dangerous creatures, but he... Well, you know more of his current might than I do. Yes, he could face it if he wanted."

Rew crossed his arms over his chest. "What does he gain from letting it roam freely?"

"Power," said Cinda. "Every person that the fraemoth slaughters is another soul to fill Vaisius Morden's cup. He'll sacrifice his people to gain strength. We've known that this entire time."

"Aye," responded Rew, "but power for what? He doesn't need it to face us. Brian, does he need that strength to reseal the tombs?"

"Perhaps, if that's his goal."

Rew gaped at the spellcaster. "It's not?"

Shrugging, Brian of the Brambles responded, "I won't claim to know the mind of Vaisius Morden, but I do know this. He seeks control. It's what he's always desired. That's why he imprisoned his father, his brothers, why he rules this kingdom two hundred years after founding it. What does that mean... you will have to find out."

Rew and Cinda shared a look.

Zaine cleared her throat and then too loudly asked, "This frae-moth, it's like... a giant moth? A really big one?"

The spellcaster laughed and offered her a patient smile, like a grandfather whose grandchild had yet to learn the ways of the world. "No, lass, it's not a moth. Not like you're thinking. If you see it, it could be you. It could be your friends. It is your greatest fear. It is drawn to that fear like a... pfah, like a moth to flame. It hungers to become you, to replace you, and it will seek your greatest weakness."

Zaine frowned and whistled softly. "You have to fight your-self? Creepy."

"Perhaps, if that is your greatest fear."

"What sorts of abilities do they exhibit?" asked Rew.

"They're fast. They're strong, highly intelligent," answered the spellcaster. "You've fought valaan? Like that and more. They coordinate their minions across distance. Most dangerously, they can cast spells and filter their own talent through their minions. There are stories of them displaying the ability to invoke, to enchant, and even practice necromancy. If they conjure, it's never been recorded, but my guess is that they cannot. What would the fears of our own fear look like? That's a twisted tunnel I will not go down. Ah, and one more thing, it will be impervious to magic."

"King's Sake," barked Cinda. "You're sure that's all? A crea-ture that may take our own faces. It's faster than a valaan, and Grace of the Blessed Mother, it can cast spells at us, but we can't do the same in return?"

"Yes, I believe that's an adequate summary of what you'll face."

Rew felt sour. He recalled Alsayer returning from a clash with the fraemoth. Was that why the spellcaster had been unable to kill it? It was immune to his magic? How had the king... Rew grimaced.

"What?" asked Anne.

"I know how the king killed the last one and why he hasn't killed this one," muttered Rew. He put a hand on the hilt of his longsword. "Fifty years ago, Erasmus Morden was still trapped within the tomb of this sword. It was in Vaisius Morden's possession then, but now, I have the blade, and my father's magic is useless against the fraemoth. He's waiting on us to kill the damned thing for him."

Zaine threw up her hands. "Your family, Ranger! Blessed Mother, they're an awful bunch."

"No arguments there," admitted Rew.

"Simple enough, then," said Raif. "If Vaisius Morden could kill the thing with the sword, then so can you. Unless, is he a better swordsman? I guess if he's been alive for two hundred years, maybe he's been practicing. He's old, though. Not old like you but really old."

"Thanks, Raif," drawled Rew. He shook his head. "Vaisius Morden is not much of a swordsman, as far as I know, but he had Erasmus. He could activate the power within this blade, but that is gone now."

"Oh," responded Raif. "That's not good. Faster than a valaan, eh, and stronger? Hmm. Ah, Ranger... Is that... do you think..."

"We need help," admitted Rew. "I need to call to the rangers, but we told them when the call comes to go to Mordenhold or to disperse. I can't explain the situation to them through the trees. The only information I can relay is simple, not even words. Thoughts and feelings is all."

"A fast rider on a good horse could make it to Mordenhold in days," mentioned Zaine.

"Aye, except the fraemoth and its army is between us and there. Cinda's undead and Brian's imps can't even get five hundred paces beyond these walls."

"We could go around," suggested Zaine. "Go wide enough, and... I wonder how wide? A few leagues, a day's ride?"

"Across rough country," said Rew. "They'd move half the speed they would on the road, not even accounting for the need to avoid the Dark Kind, and we've no idea how far to the sides the creatures might extend or how far north, either. Valaan or this fraemoth could have ayres patrolling their flanks for days around the bulk of their army. Assuming someone could make it around, it'd take a week or more to get to Mordenhold, not days. Getting back would be just as difficult. That'd be two weeks before assistance arrives, which I'm afraid could be too long. Wherever the fraemoth is, it's closer than that."

"We need an invoker who can portal," surmised Anne.

"Duke Findley, back in Yonn," grumbled Rew.

He rubbed his hands over his head, thinking furiously, but it was no use. If the fraemoth couldn't be damaged by magic, the only hope was to fell it with a blade. He would do his best, but if it was both faster and stronger than a valaan, and it came with an army of Dark Kind at its back, he was self-aware enough to admit his odds were not great. His best might not be good enough this time. He'd barely survived the encounters with valaan that he'd already faced. He needed help.

"I'll tell Eddla to send his fastest men south," said Rew. "I'll instruct—no, ask—Findley and Vincent for their help. Ranger Adro can accompany the riders. He's still a king's ranger, for whatever they believe that's worth. Once they're gone, we'll be cut off. We won't know if help is coming until a portal opens within the compound—or until it doesn't."

"Great," said Zaine. "Sounds like a plan."

Rew scowled at her.

She grinned. "I mean it. Sending to the other rangers for help, buckling down to hold on until it gets here, it's about the most sensible plan I've ever heard you utter."

"She's got a point," said Raif. "We've clambered across the bottoms of bridges hundreds of paces above the rocks below. We've summoned entire crypts of undead. Blessed Mother, we faced a maelstrom. Guarding the walls of a fort, even a dirt one, is downright sensible compared to the other madness you've dragged us through."

Looking around, the ranger saw the rest of the party staring back at him, fighting to keep grins off their faces. He threw up his hands.

"I suppose we ought to get to it, then," suggested Anne.

"Aye," replied Rew. Then, he glanced at Brian. "If your imps cannot harm the fraemoth, what were you doing here, building this enclosure and trapping your men and yourself within it?"

"In my dream, I sought guidance from the Blessed Mother," replied the spellcaster. "When I heard about you, what you'd done in Carff and the approach of this army, it seemed like divine intervention."

"You think we are the answer to your prayers?" scoffed Rew.

"Trusting in you seems better than giving up and allowing Vaisius Morden to rule the kingdom and perhaps the world someday as an immortal necromancer."

"Right," said Rew. He closed his eyes and rubbed them with a finger and his thumb. "Right. All right, then. Like Anne said, let's get to it."

Chapter Fifteen

✤✤✤

Colonel Eddla conferred with his captains, and they identified the twelve fastest riders in the cavalry. Along with Ranger Adro, the men were dispatched south with stern instructions to ride until they were ready to drop and then to keep going. They had to reach Findley's city, and they had to implore the man to portal to the quiet glade where Rew had sent Ang and Vurcell. They needed the duke to portal the rangers into their makeshift fort because by the time word got to anyone who could help, Rew thought they would be under attack, likely surrounded.

There were no better swordsmen in the kingdom than the King's Rangers, and against the fraemoth, Rew was going to need them.

Atop the earthen walls, Brian of the Brambles and Cinda stood side by side and began casting their magic. Brian summoned more imps and sent them scampering into the trees. Cinda swirled death's breath and sent it billowing outward.

The imps wouldn't do more than get killed, and Cinda's death's breath wouldn't do more than irritate any targets at such a distance with little potency, but they hoped it would serve as a distraction. The valaan and the fraemoth were intelligent, and they might guess it was a ploy, but they would still have to react to it.

While the spellcasters were unleashing their magic, Rew accompanied the riders a league to the south, making sure they got away cleanly. They could hear the excited barking of ayres as they rode out, but it was north, on the other side of the fortification and out of sight. If the Dark Kind had thought far enough ahead that they'd sealed the road farther to the south to prevent messages from getting out, they were done for anyway. They had to trust that the riders would get through and that Findley would agree to help.

But to find out if that trust was well-placed, they would have to wait another week. The riders were the best they had, but Yonn was far away. It would take the duke time to absorb what he was being told, and even traveling by portal, it would take more time to find the rangers and bring them to the fort.

"Six days," Ranger Adro had claimed.

Rew had grunted, grasped the man's forearm. He'd pumped it once. "Luck out there."

The other ranger had nodded then clambered up onto a horse and disappeared south without further word. They both knew Adro wasn't the one who was going to need luck.

Rew returned to the earthen enclosure and found Brian of the Brambles and Cinda. He asked them, "Learn anything?"

Cinda shook her head then offered, "I learned there's an awful lot of them out there."

"We saw a valaan," added Brian. "Just one, but I'm certain there are more lurking out of sight. I didn't see or sense the fraemoth yet. That's something."

Rew rubbed the stubble on his head. "Where would it be, do you think?"

"It was coming from the far north."

"Northguard."

The spellcaster nodded. "It will have originated there, but by now, it should be south of Mordenhold. It's hard to stay."

"Where's it going, I wonder."

Brian tugged on his beard then suggested, "To you."

"Me?" scoffed Rew.

"If Vaisius Morden needs you in Mordenhold... wouldn't his enemy benefit from stopping you?"

"Oh," murmured Rew. He frowned. "Oh."

"I wonder what it's like having so many people wanting to kill you," quipped Zaine.

Rew glared at her and shook his head.

"Can we use that somehow?" asked Raif, who had joined when he saw them conferring. "There's a lot we don't know about the fraemoth, but if we know its motivation, that's something. We've got to think about our angle."

"What are you suggesting? That I act as bait?"

"It has worked before," reminded Cinda.

Rew walked from the others and climbed the earthen wall, looking north toward the forest. Bait? It had worked before, but when they'd done it, there'd been someone ready to spring the trap. Brian's and Cinda's spellcasting wouldn't phase the fraemoth. If it was stronger and faster than a valaan, he didn't think Raif or Zaine would have much luck against it either. But they had an army. Could the soldiers surround it? Use their numbers to overwhelm the thing?

He turned, looking over the length of the camp. Colonel Eddla had the men settled in neat rows, their supply dumps protected, the lanes clear in case they needed to rush from their bedrolls to defense. Brian's men, just five hundred of them, were arranged in similar formations, though not quite as sharp as Eddla kept his forces. Three thousand men, all told. If they caught the fraemoth, that had to be enough, didn't it?

But for Rew to be bait, they needed to allow the fraemoth into their fortifications. Could they do so without bringing in hundreds of other Dark Kind as well? That would be risky. Too risky, the more he thought about it. Dangling himself outside the walls was even worse, though. He wasn't afraid of putting himself in danger, but he wouldn't expose the entire army like that, and for a trap to work, the men would have to be out there, too. He jumped down and rejoined the others.

"The problem," he told them, "is that we don't know what to expect. I have no clue what this fraemoth is capable of. We've faced similar circumstances before, but each time, we were the aggressor. We snuck up on my brothers and on the simulacra. Now, it's the fraemoth coming for us. That puts us at a disadvantage."

"Do you think we go to it, then?" asked Raif. "We try to surprise it before it gets to the rest of the Dark Kind?"

Rew rolled his shoulders, and replied, "I would, but we don't know where the thing is, exactly. Somewhere between here and Mordenhold is a lot of ground to cover. Too much ground. Not to mention, if we venture out looking for it, we'll be harried by the ayres and narjags that are near the fort. We've got enough men to fight through them maybe, but then what?" Gripping the hilt of his longsword, Rew continued, "Brian has done good work building this fortification. I think our best bet is to make use of it. We deploy our men as sensibly as we can, knowing at least what to expect from the narjags, ayres, and valaan. We'll defend this place until we learn more about the fraemoth. Maybe then, an opportunity will present itself. Maybe by then, the other rangers will have arrived. With them at our sides, I'd feel more comfortable venturing out, but without them, this enclosure is the only advantage we have."

"The other rangers could turn the tide of a battle," acknowledged Cinda. "Knowing I can't hurt this fraemoth..."

Rew nodded. "You can't hurt it, but you can hurt the rest of them. Let's find Colonel Eddla. Brian, gather your captains, and we'll start planning our defense."

THEY HAD A LONG WALL OF HEAD-AND-A-HALF-HIGH MOUNDED earth studded with sharpened stakes. When they'd arrived, most of it had been completed, except for a fringe Brian's men were trying to expand. Rew had assigned Eddla to provide protection, and the final piece was completed with minimal harassment by the Dark Kind.

It was evident there were hundreds of narjags and ayres nearby, along with a few valaan, but not enough to seriously press the men now that both forces were combined. Rew suspected the Dark Kind were waiting for more support, or maybe they were waiting for the fraemoth.

Outside Valstock, the creatures had been reckless. Unfortunately, it seemed they'd learned from that encounter. Rew toured their fortifications, hoping it was enough, knowing if he spotted a weakness, it was too late to do anything about it.

The stakes and the wall meant any rush by the Dark Kind would be slowed, and it would give the men time to respond. Because of that, Rew stationed plenty of watchers along the top of the berm and instructed them to work in hour-long shifts. That would prevent the men from getting bored and complacent. Flying units were assigned to stand on duty for two-hour stretches, always prepared to run toward one of the sentries' calls. They were in groups of twenty, and they'd been placed throughout the encampment.

The rest of the army was allowed to rest, though none of them would stray far from their weapons and armor. Eventually, they all knew, the Dark Kind were going to press them, and it would require every man on the wall to hold them off.

The cavalry might be of little use. They only had one gate in the wall, and it faced south, opposite of where the Dark Kind were massing. Rew thought they might be able to use the cavalry as flankers, running out and slicing the edges of attacking Dark Kind or chasing stragglers down and thinning them out, but it would be a long ride around the edge of the fort, and with ayres in the mix, it would be dangerous. Colonel Eddla had suggested erecting another gate in the northern wall, but they didn't have materials to do it, and Rew was reluctant to open a breach in the wall without the ability to quickly close it.

They had some archers, and Rew sorely regretted not having more. The ranged attacks would be extremely effective against the narjags, who didn't use bows and rarely wore substantial armor. A well-timed flight of arrows could shred a charge before it even reached the stakes, and the damage they could do before the narjags got to the walls would save lives.

But while the sharpened stakes would slow incoming attacks, they didn't have spearmen, which meant they couldn't strike from a distance while the narjags were weaving between the initial barricades. There was nothing to do about that, though. There were no settlements of any size near where Brian of the Brambles had elected to make his stand, which meant there was no hope of reaching an armory and returning with thousands of spears.

They would have to count on the swordsmen, which made up the bulk of their forces, to meet the Dark Kind after they'd wiggled or stampeded their way through the thicket of sharpened wood. It would be a brutal, vicious battle atop the earthen walls, and there was little hope of conducting it without serious losses.

Raif would lead a group of fifty swordsmen, and he would follow behind the flying companies to the hottest, deadliest engagements. After the encounters they'd had on the highway coming north, Raif and his greatsword inspired confidence in the men around him. Something about a giant fighter going berserk allowed others to think they were invulnerable as well.

Rew would float. He would join the engagements where he was needed, but more than anything, he would be on the lookout for valaan and select the opportunities to deploy their spellcasters.

Brian could summon up to four of the giant imps they'd seen guarding the gates when they'd arrived or a dozen smaller ones. Rew had instructed him to focus on the larger variety, the creatures that would cause the most devastation against the Dark Kind. The huge imps should be able to tear through scores of the awful creatures before the imps were swarmed and taken down. They were going to get killed, but Brian seemed unconcerned.

"I can summon four at once," he'd told them, "but it might be best if I stick to two. I can maintain those for some time then quickly conjure two more when they fall. After that, it will take some effort to work my rituals, to manipulate the power and draw them forth. I told you they were of my dreams, but it still takes substantial magic to make them manifest."

Rew nodded. He was impressed the man could master four of the huge summonings, and he had questions about who Brian was and where he came from, but the spellcaster seemed to adroitly turn the conversation every time Rew asked, and when they weren't in council, the man was ferociously difficult to find, though the two tiny imps he kept were constantly underfoot.

Cinda was their backup. Brian understood, Rew thought, but they did not discuss her talent much in front of the soldiers. They were far from the population centers, far from what she called the power of ambient death. Out there, for her to be a significant part of their defense, someone was going to have to die. The imps and the Dark Kind were worthless to her when they fell. It was only when their own soldiers began dying that the necromancer would be able to make a serious contribution.

Rew instructed her to hold back, to wait until the Dark Kind were swarming over the barrier, and then she would raise their companions who had fallen. The undead would be safer to their own men than death's breath or funeral fire.

Cinda had mentioned wraiths, but Rew shook his head. The risk of her losing control was too great. If battle was fully engaged, the wraiths would be as close to their own men as the Dark Kind, and it was the blood of men that the wraiths hungered for.

The undead would serve them well, they'd both eventually agreed, though it soured Rew's stomach, and he knew the effect it would have on the rest of the soldiers when they saw their fallen peers rise again.

Chapter Sixteen

Ayres thundered across the front of the earthen berm, narjags clinging to their backs like fleas on a dog. There were a hundred of the pairs, and they passed a score of paces in front of the forest of stakes Brian of the Brambles' men had erected.

The blue-skinned canines leapt and bounded. At the height of their jumps, the narjags rose and flung crude javelins toward the men guarding the enclosure.

Some of the weapons had iron or steel tips, but most were rough spears sharpened by the narjags. The narjags couldn't put much force into their throws, but they were assisted by the speed of their mounts, and while the missiles were poor quality, there were a lot of them. The javelins rained in an erratic storm, most falling short, in no danger of hitting a target, but a few pierced flesh, and men went down screaming and wailing.

The day before, Anne had realized the narjags had done more than just sharpen their missiles. They'd smeared excrement on them, and any wound meant infection was certain. Some of the men's cries were more in disgust than pain.

Duke Vincent's and Duke Findley's men huddled beneath the onslaught, hiding behind makeshift shields or crouching, presenting as small a target as possible. Rew looked on the scant protection grimly. They hadn't brought shields, knowing they could move faster without the extra weight. He hadn't thought they would need them. As far as he knew, this was the first time in history the Dark Kind had used ranged weapons. It was another sign the creatures, or the fiend that was directing them, were learning and adapting. He was sickened at the implications.

The onslaught progressed, and Rew's frustration bubbled. They'd tried sending the men down below, behind the protection of their walls, but then the ayres would spring at the forest of stakes, attempting to jump over the barriers so they could race along the top of the wall before jumping down at a weak point inside the camp. Only a handful of ayres had made it to the top of the walls, but it was enough that they couldn't afford to leave those walls unguarded.

A jagged shaft of wood flew at him, and around the ranger's feet, men crouched and leaned away. He swung his longsword, catching the spear on the side, knocking it away where it fell harmlessly on the mounded dirt of the berm.

Behind him, a call rang out, and a fleet of arrows flew up from behind the wall, arcing toward the narjags and ayres. The archers were hidden behind the fortification and firing blindly. Rew looked back, trying to keep half an eye on the Dark Kind, watching for more javelins coming his direction.

"Who ordered that?" he bellowed. "Who said to fire?"

One of his captains was storming over to the company of archers who'd loosed their shafts and was already haranguing a man who must have called for the others to start shooting.

Rew turned back to the Dark Kind, letting the captain handle it. The officers understood. It rubbed them all raw, standing before the Dark Kind, taking the javelins, and watching the ayres speed away, but it was all they could do.

The Dark Kind weren't coming to try and kill the occasional man with each one of their sweeping attacks. No, they were coming to draw fire from the archers. Rew could sense it. Another lesson they'd learned from Valstock? The idea was uncomfortable, but it was what he would do if he didn't care about whether or not his men lived or died.

The ayres were mobile, difficult targets. The archers were firing blindly. Only one in twenty arrows might find a mark, and even then, only a few of the strikes would be fatal. The valaan would gladly sacrifice a handful of narjags and ayres if it meant depleting the stockpile of arrows that Rew's forces had.

He had one hundred horse archers and another two hundred bowmen. Each one had come with two quivers of twenty arrows. Six thousand arrows total, less what they'd used on the march north. The company of archers had just fired off one hundred of their remaining stockpile, and Rew looked glumly at the three Dark Kind they'd managed to cripple.

A portion of their precious arrows, and just three Dark Kind injured. He closed his eyes, forced himself to breathe deep and slow, then reopened his eyes.

The first wave of Dark Kind had drawn a stiff response, and Rew and the other leaders had ordered for them to be taken down. Then, he'd realized the danger, and they'd told the archers to stop firing. But it was hard, almost impossible, to sit still and watch your friends get struck by infected spears and not retaliate. It went against everything these men knew.

How many arrows had been fired in the last two days? Half of all they had?

The Dark Kind had finished their run, and the ayres and narjags disappeared into the trees that bounded the road five hundred paces north of the wall.

Rew looked up and down from his position, noting that two men had been injured. Neither appeared to be a fatal wound, and with Anne stationed at the hospital tent to provide her empathy and ward off infection, the men could be back on their feet in a day.

Two men wounded, three Dark Kind that would likely die, but one hundred arrows lost. The awful math of war was a bitter draught, but they had to swallow it. They had to think strategically and conserve their resources to outlast the Dark Kind.

A chorus of howls preceded the next wave of ayres and narjags. Another hundred or so of them, riding in pairs, raced toward the walls.

"Incoming," cried the scouts up and down the wall.

Scores of men stood on watch, crouching near the crude shields they'd managed to fashion. Hundreds more gathered close, still behind the berm. They had to be ready in case the Dark Kind turned to a full attack, but they only left enough men atop the wall to communicate what was happening and guard against ayres trying to come up. It was a delicate balance, deciding how many men to put at risk.

"Hold your fire!" shouted Rew. "No one fire!"

He crouched and collected the javelin he'd knocked down on the Dark Kind's last pass. It was a short stick, the length of his arm, and the end had been hacked into a dull point. There was a deep gouge where he'd struck it with his sword, but it still stood straight enough. It was smeared with something foul, and as he hefted the weapon, he found it poorly balanced and lighter than he would have liked.

The captains moved behind the wall, excoriating the men to be ready but to hold their fire.

Rew waited, watching the Dark Kind come closer, the narjags raising their spears, the ayres bounding, fat pink tongues hanging from blue mouths, yellow eyes glowing. He cocked back the javelin he'd recovered then flung it at a narjag before the creature could launch its own weapon.

The short shaft of wood whistled through the air and smacked into the narjag, flipping it off the back of its ayre, where it disappeared beneath the rest of the charging pack.

Dark Kind javelins flew at the men, and they ducked or tried to block them. To Rew's right, a javelin shattered on a shield that someone had cobbled together from pieces of the supply wagons. To his left, a man let out a sharp scream which was quickly cut off. None of the javelins threatened Rew. Then, the Dark Kind were off, running back to the forest.

An individual narjag stood up from the path the others had taken then scampered away, blood streaming from its nose, its arm hanging at an odd angle. Rew wasn't sure if it was the one he'd hit, and the trash weapon hadn't managed to even pierce the thing's skin, or if it was another narjag that had somehow fallen off its mount in the excitement. Either way, with no medical care, the creature was probably going to die. Would it come back and fight, or were its fellows going to slaughter it for food when it got into the forest?

Sighing, the ranger looked to the man who'd been hit, and his heart fell. Two soldiers were dragging him away, the broken shaft of a javelin still sticking from the man's neck. The missile had struck the soft skin right above the man's chest, and blood welled freely around the wound. If the man still lived, he wouldn't for long. The wound was too deep and too serious for Anne to spend her energy on it. Maybe if he'd been the only one she had to care for, but even then... One of their men was dead, and a narjag had gotten a broken arm.

Rew drew his longsword from the dirt where he'd stuck it to throw the javelin and hopped down into the enclosure, looking for Colonel Eddla, Brian of the Brambles, and Raif. Something had to change.

REW STOOD ATOP THE WALL, PEERING DOWN AT THE NEST OF STAKES below him. They'd been placed in erratic patterns, most about as wide apart as his shoulders. It wouldn't be difficult to weave between them moving down from the head-and-a-half-high earthen wall. The difficulty was coming back up if you were in a hurry.

AC COBBLE

"Everyone is in place," Zaine told him.

Giving one last look at the forest several hundred paces north, Rew raised his hand then chopped it down. It was bright daylight. The forest looked quiet. They weren't going to get a better chance.

Rew, Zaine, and a score of archers who'd volunteered for the assignment began moving down the slope. Behind them, on the other side of the compound, the gate would be opening, and one hundred horsemen would be trotting out.

Raif, Cinda, and Brian of the Brambles stood atop the earthen wall down from where Rew and Zaine were descending. They were all watching the forest nervously, waiting for the Dark Kind to appear. Rew reached the bottom of the stakes and hurried ahead, his longsword already drawn, his gaze roving restlessly.

A narjag, one that had been wounded and fallen earlier that morning, stirred. The ranger hurried and stabbed it with his longsword, silencing it. He was nervous the Dark Kind would try the same trick they had outside Valstock and suddenly rise from where they'd been laying in ambush.

Around him, archers were spreading out, plucking arrows from the turf, taking some from the bodies of the Dark Kind they'd managed to kill, but finding most lying on the ground. A distressing number of those looked to have been stomped on by the charging ayres. The ones that had stuck in bodies could have damaged heads. Rew had told the archers to ignore those, to only gather arrows which hadn't struck anything and looked sound, but he wouldn't correct them now. It was more important they stay quiet and work quickly. The Dark Kind likely had watchers in the trees, but if they didn't, he wouldn't give themselves away by causing a ruckus.

One by one, the archers filled empty quivers with the used arrows. Rew let a smile curl his lips. This was working. There was no ambush. They would resupply their quivers and slip back into the compound with minimal risk.

At the forest line, the ayres came bursting out of hiding, hundreds of them giving none of the yips and howls that were customary of their kind before a charge. Some had narjag riders. Most were alone.

"Back!" shouted Rew, and the archers immediately turned and began running toward the enclosure.

The ayres were tearing across several hundred paces of open ground. There was the long wail of a horn, and then the cavalry came racing around the end of the enclosure. They had lances, and they lowered them, aiming toward the ayres.

The blue-skinned canines saw the approaching men on horse, and some turned, but some did not. That was good. Against the full pack of ayres, the cavalry would be outnumbered and at risk, but against some of them, the weight of the horses and the reach of the lances ought to win the day.

A bestial roar crashed over the noise of the charging forces, and two big imps jumped over the walls of stakes and began a loping run toward the ayres, moving on their knuckles and feet like overgrown, terrifying apes. The imps were heavily muscled, twice Rew's bulk, and they had long claws and sharp teeth that put the narjags' to shame. What sort of fears was Brian of the Brambles dreaming of to have conjured those things?

The ranger could see Brian was holding the imps back, allowing them to move toward the pack of ayres that was curling toward the archers and ignoring the group that was racing to meet the cavalry.

Rew reached the wall of stakes and paused, urging the archers to pass through before him. They moved carefully. At walking speed, the sharp ends weren't going to kill you if you bumped into them, but they would still hurt. Turning, Rew cursed. Two of the archers were still scrambling about, bending and collecting more arrows.

Rew yelled at them, "Back, now!"

The pair of men looked up at him then started trotting his way.

The cavalry, lances lowered, smashed into the charging pack of ayres. Wood splintered, horses screamed. Ayres barked in excitement and pain. The lances had punched a hole in the midst of the ayres, and the crush of the horses and their pounding hooves were smashing scores of the blue-skinned monsters into the ground. Some of the ayres had avoided the lance tips, and they leapt at their tormenters, clamping down on men's legs or on those of the horses. The riders dropped their lances and drew their swords, stalling as they tried to mop up the remaining ayres.

"Retreat!" screamed Rew, shoving the laggard archers in front of him. He raised his voice, bellowing at the cavalry, "Fall back!"

The men on horseback didn't hear him, and their bugler who was supposed to be signaling their withdrawal appeared to have lost his head. Rew saw the young man rise in his stirrups, a sword held high, the bugle still slung over his shoulder.

The two archers made it into the small protection of the rows of stakes. Rew watched, outside the enclosure still, as the cavalry got mired in the pack of ayres. Given time, they would annihilate them. The canines were fierce and terrible foes to a man on foot, but against men on horses and outnumbered, the ayres stood little chance. Unless—

There was a terrific roar, and Brian of the Brambles' two imps tore into the pack of ayres in front of them. They were four or five times the size of the ayres and many times stronger. They smashed clawed hands into the massed flesh of the Dark Kind, lurching forward and snapping powerful jaws on unprotected skin and bone.

An ayre jumped, making an impressive leap over the backs of its foes, trying to lock teeth on an imp's neck, but the imp caught it with one hand and squeezed. Even from fifty paces away, Rew heard the ayre yelp in agony. Then, it fell silent, and the imp flung the broken body away.

The two imps were carving parallel tracks of blood and gore through the pack of ayres, but they were vastly outnumbered. The ayres in front of them were torn to shreds, but others of the Dark Kind closed behind the imps and began to dart at the summonings' backs with biting mouths and raking claws.

Rew, sickened and fascinated by the tussle between the two conjured sets of monsters, began to move through the stakes and up the slope of the earthen berm. He wanted to engage, to help the imps, but there were too many ayres in the field. It was a suicide mission the imps had undertaken. Brian had sent them, knowing they wouldn't return but thinking they would buy time for the archers and men on horseback to return to safety.

It was working, and as Rew climbed the final pace to the top of the earthen wall, he spun and saw one of the imps was down, a thrashing pile of ayres on top of it. The other still stood, somehow, but gapping rents in its skin spilled blood like water from a pitcher. Under Brian's command, it would fight until the end, but that wouldn't be long now. Around the imps, an impressive swathe of ayres had been obliterated. A score of them. Two? It was impressive but gruesome.

Down the wall, a bugler was furiously tooting the signal to retreat, and Rew's heart fell. The cavalry had decimated most of the ayres they'd faced, but hundreds of narjags were pouring from the forest. The horsemen could have trampled the things if they'd had time to set a charge and still had their lances, but moving from an engagement with wounded men and horses and no lances, they couldn't be effective.

Someone had been sharp enough to see the cavalry's own bugler had lost his presence in the madness of battle and had gotten the one in the fort to start sounding retreat.

Several of the cavalry heard the distant call. They told others, and many of them began walking their horses back, still swinging swords, fending off the few remaining ayres they'd been tussling with. Others stayed engaged, either unable to break away or uninterested in retreat. To the men in the field, it must have felt like they were enacting a legendary victory. They'd thoroughly crushed a column of ayres and would cover the retreat of the men on foot so the archers didn't lose a single soul, but did they not see the approaching mass of narjags?

More and more of the horsemen were freeing themselves of

their fight, and their captain looked to be regaining order following the fervor of the battle. Their bugler finally put his sword away and put his instrument to his lips.

"They've got time. They'll be away in moments," declared Raif, coming to stand beside Rew. "Ranger, the plan is working—"

"King's Sake!" snarled Rew.

Behind the horsemen, four valaan had materialized as if from thin air, though Rew guessed they'd merely approached close to the ground, allowing the chaos of the battle to distract everyone from their presence. The Dark Kind had not pulled the same trick they did in Valstock. Not exactly. They'd learned and adapted. Instead of surprising the archers and facing Rew, they were going after the horses.

Rew and his captains could always put a bow into another man's hands, but they weren't going to get any more horses. The valaan knew that. They'd changed tactics again and were cutting the men where they couldn't afford to bleed.

The first of the cavalrymen saw the valaan, spun his horse, and then died. The Dark Kind were like shadows, flickering amongst the horses, leaving blood in their wake. They were killing the men they could reach, but from afar, it was obvious their goal was to cripple the horses.

"Fire on the valaan!" cried Rew. "Archers, fire on the valaan!"

A few arrows were released, but only a few. Rew turned wildly, seeing men with arrows nocked, but they weren't releasing.

"They'll hit our own men if they loose," warned Raif.

"Our men are dead if the archers can't hit those things," retorted Rew coldly. He drew his longsword and prepared to run into battle. "Better we accidentally hit a few of our own men than letting them all die out there."

Raif grabbed his arm. "You can't go."

"Without help, every one of those men is dead!"

"You can't."

Rew tugged his arm free from Raif, but he didn't head back down through the stakes. Raif was right. There was nothing he could do. The archers… If they didn't trust their aim, then Rew shouldn't trust it either, and if he charged out to assist the cavalry, there would be no escaping the hundreds of narjags who were running toward the fight. There were too many of them, even for him.

Cinda quietly approached. Her face was blank, but her eyes glittered. He understood. Power was rushing into her. Rew met her gaze then nodded curtly.

They might not be able to save their men, but that didn't mean they would let the valaan get away. The Dark Kind had wounded them, but it would come at a cost.

The necromancer closed her eyes, and the fallen cavalrymen began to rise again. The valaan were ready. They struck at Cinda's undead, moving far faster than her minions could react, but destroying the dead required work, and the valaan were surrounded by both living and dead soldiers.

Cinda's minions closed, getting torn to pieces by the valaan, but others swung, uncaring if they hit their fellows, and landed clumsy blows. More living men died, and more undead rose. The narjags arrived in a disorganized wave, crashing into the horse-men, jumping onto the surviving horses and men, clinging to the undead, claws and teeth ripping furiously.

Cinda kept her eyes closed while the battle raged, and then she opened them. The Dark Kind were retreating, leaving piles of dead ayres behind them, along with several score of narjags.

"I killed two of the valaan and wounded a third," said Cinda quietly. "I don't think it will survive long. There were a few more men I hadn't touched, but I've exhausted myself. That took all of the power from their deaths and all of my reserves. I'm getting better at commanding them, but I'm not good enough. Not yet. I need practice."

Rew grunted and did not respond.

"Three valaan," replied Cinda. "It may have cost half our

remaining cavalry, but three valaan. You could argue that's a win."

They stood quietly, looking out over the field of battle, at the dead bodies of the Dark Kind and of their own people.

"None of this is a win," declared Raif.

Chapter Seventeen

A narjag scrambled up a pile of its brethren, using their bodies like a ramp. Behind it, a horde of gray-skinned monsters swarmed, pressing against the earthen berm and the sharpened stakes that studded it like the quills of a porcupine. In front of Rew, the pack was thick enough and pushing hard enough that the first wave of the creatures had been impaled on the wooden shafts, creating a route for the others to climb.

Again, they were learning. The crude ladders they'd used in Valstock would be worthless in climbing over the stakes studding the walls of the enclosure, but their own bodies were getting the job done.

The narjags below, skewered on the sharp points, had squirmed and thrashed, but as more and more narjags climbed up the pile of bodies, they forced the ones below farther onto the points, killing them. More came behind in a swarm, crushing ever more bodies beneath them. Without spears to keep the creatures back, the soldiers could do nothing to prevent the Dark Kind's suicidal frenzy.

Rew stood atop the earthen wall, longsword in hand, meeting the scrambling horde. A narjag crested the top of the wall and lunged at him. He thrust with his longsword, taking the thing in the chest. Then, he kicked it, sending it toppling back down the pile, crashing into its fellows. The others tore at it, ripping the body apart and snarling as they forced their way higher.

Rew's longsword dripped with thick, dark blood, and his arms and shoulders burned from exertion. For hours, he'd been standing in the gap the narjags had forced, killing them and throwing them back from the earthen barrier. He'd lost track of the rest of the battle, lost in the stab and the chop, but he could sense there were other gaps and other teams of men holding the wall.

Zaine had been serving as a messenger, darting amongst the swirling troops, taking orders, and updating him on how the battle was going. It'd been an hour since he'd seen her last. He didn't know if that meant she'd been injured or if they were being pressed harder elsewhere.

Another narjag clawed its way to the top of the macabre pile of bodies, and Rew swung, decapitating the thing before it could get its bearings. Grasping hands caught it from behind, and it was torn away, clearing the space for more to climb and attack.

Beside Rew, a squad of soldiers were holding his flanks, leaping in front of any narjags that came at his sides or when more than one of the creatures appeared at once. Before, Rew had been cycling back and resting while the others held the line, but half of them were dead now, and the ranger was reluctant to put the soldiers at more risk than he had to.

Elsewhere, the men wouldn't have the help of a swordsman like Rew, but over the course of the last hour, it'd become apparent that the ranger was drawing the worst of the violence. Narjags, ayres, and even two valaan had assaulted his position. They were coming for him. He could feel it.

Brian of the Brambles had been right. The fraemoth wanted Rew. Uttering an unceasing string of curses, he kept killing narjags. He lost track of time, but eventually, Zaine returned, calling loudly to be heard over the battle.

"Ranger," she said, taking his side, the two poignards she'd received from Valchon's spymaster held low and ready in front of her. "We've got four places now where our defenses are under serious strain, though none are as hard pressed as here."

Two narjags came bolting up the pile, and Rew shouted, "I have right."

Zaine didn't reply, but she darted forward, feinting with one poignard then easily sliding the second into the narjag's neck. It crumpled immediately. Rew dispatched his as well, and he and the thief stepped back.

There was a heap of narjags twice the height of the earthen wall, now. Even with the creatures hauling their dead back into the pack, there were so many they were being crushed, pulped beneath the weight of their fellows who kept coming, kept climbing.

Zaine flicked her poignard, flinging away the narjag blood.

"Have you been using those?" questioned Rew. "I thought... We talked about this. The old man said there was a cost."

Zaine snorted and gestured around them with the narrow point of her blade. "Seemed to me that today, the price was worth it."

"Can you feel anything?"

The thief shrugged.

"How are our reserves?" questioned Rew, nodding for the soldiers beside them to step forward and take over while he finished getting Zaine's report. He wiped the back of his hand across his brow, trying to smear the sweat away from his eyes, but he felt the tacky damp of blood. His hands and forearms were covered in splattered narjag blood up to his elbows. His chest and the front of his trousers weren't any better.

"That's gross," remarked Zaine. She shook herself and looked back to his eyes. "The reserves are thin, and I don't think there's a man or woman in this enclosure who hasn't seen combat today."

"The wounded?"

"Anne is working on them, though she's making some hard choices about who is receiving her empathy and who is on their own. The hospital tent was almost overrun half an hour ago, but Raif made it in time and helped retake the wall. The interior is secure, for now."

"He's not overdoing it, is he?"

"You know Raif."

Rew grunted, half an eye on the pile of narjags next to them. The squad of soldiers were working well together, alternating attacks, letting each other pull back after each strike. They were exhausted, though, and as Rew watched, a man stumbled, tripping over the arm of a dead narjag, and one of the living creatures latched onto him. Rew surged to the man's defense, smashing the tip of his longsword into the narjag's skull, but as it was knocked away, it took a mouthful of the soldier's flesh with it, and a geyser of blood erupted from the unfortunate man's neck.

"Get him back!" cried Rew to the rest of the squad as he and Zaine moved in to protect the retreat.

The soldiers grabbed the arms of their fellow, and one of them said, "M'lord…"

"Get him back," repeated Rew. "We don't leave our own here no matter what, you understand?"

The soldiers nodded and hauled the dying man away.

Zaine danced up the pile of narjags, stooping and stabbing as she went. She peeked over at the field beyond then returned to Rew's side.

"There are more of them," she reported.

He grunted. There were more. Hundreds more. He'd been watching them all day, though some time ago, he'd given up trying to count. Recently, he hadn't bothered to look. He could hear them. There were more, but they weren't coming as quickly, he didn't think. Could the narjags be worn out, tired from screeching and shoving on their peers? Had some of the valaan fallen and weren't exhorting the creatures as hard? Or was it something else, something bad?

From their position on the pile of dead narjags, they had a good view of the rest of the compound. Rew turned, scanning for concerns. There were plenty, but none that were unexpected. Bodies of the wounded were piling up outside the tent Anne and the surgeons occupied. Tired men looked harried and close to defeat at several places along the walls, but there were still others armed and resting within the compound who would soon rush to replace the weakest points of the defense.

He saw Raif leading his flying company, charging toward an opening where the Dark Kind had finally pounded their way through the field of sharpened stakes and into a thin line of defenders. It was a dangerous surge, but Raif and the forty men with him ought to be enough to seal the breach and give the other defenders a chance to rally and reestablish their lines. The soldiers of Brian of the Brambles, Duke Findley, and Duke Vincent were being tested, but they were holding up.

Rew glanced skyward and frowned. With a grimace, he climbed to stand beside Zaine at the top of the largest pile of dead narjags. Hundreds of them swirled below at the base of the heap. Rew could see a thousand milling around the fringe of the enclosure. Ayres, he didn't bother to count how many, barked and raced excited circuits outside of the narjags. He saw several whorls of activity and guessed that was where the valaan were moving. If the fraemoth was there, Rew couldn't tell. Above, the sun beat down, the heat of the afternoon rising. Another three hours of daylight. They could hold out, but what then?

The Dark Kind could see better in the dark than people. When in battle, they fell into a frenzy. They were relentless and uncaring of their losses. Could the men defeat a thousand Dark Kind at night? They could, Rew thought. They would hold because they had to, and they still had the advantage in numbers, but how many hundreds would they lose when the sun fell and their visibility along with it?

He cursed. At night, the valaan could stalk the encampment like assassins. They were as stealthy as a ranger and naturally more difficult to see in darkness. How many valaan were out there? They could have their narjags continue to press against the sides of the enclosure, and under the cover of night, several of them could slip in unnoticed. None of these soldiers had the training to face a valaan. Without rangers, without vastly superior numbers and the ability to surround the valaan, the common soldiers would be butchered.

Rew turned, studying the mass of Dark Kind, trying to count the valaan, and wondering if that had been the plan all along when they'd attacked that day. It didn't matter. Whether the Dark Kind planned it or not, he couldn't risk the bulk of their men fighting on the wall at night while valaan roamed unguarded at their backs. With the men committed, with so many Dark Kind so close, there would be no chance to stop them getting inside.

Rew instructed Zaine, "Tell Cinda she has half an hour. Then, we hit them hard. They can't get more concentrated than this, and I don't want to wait until she can draw more power."

The thief grunted. "Brian of the Brambles?"

"We'll keep his imps in reserve for tonight."

Nodding curtly, Zaine scampered off.

Rew rejoined the squad of men who were frantically defending against two narjags and an ayre. Half an hour. They could hold out.

A WHITE MIST ROLLED DOWN THE SIDES OF THE COMPOUND LIKE FOAM spilling from a tankard. It washed over the narjags, bathing them in a fog of noxious gas. The creatures shrieked in terror, unsure what was happening, but knowing that breathing the clouds of white air burned.

For a long moment, the Dark Kind stayed pressed against the sharp stakes and the defenders, still trying to break in, to overwhelm the protections on the wall, but as they started to drop dead, they panicked.

Whether the hold the valaan had over them broke or whether they were silently instructed to retreat, Rew wasn't sure, but soon, hundreds of narjags had turned from the cloud and were fighting their way backward through their own fellows. Claws tore and blood gushed as the closest ranks ripped into the narjags behind them. At the far outskirts, they were still trying to get closer and hadn't seen what the others were turning from.

Beside Rew, Cinda's eyes were closed, her hands raised in front of her, directing the deadly fog. Hundreds of souls had perished in the fighting. Hundreds of men had died, allowing her to call upon terrible power. She'd trained with Alsayer for weeks, forming death's breath, making it dense enough to kill, but no more, spreading it efficiently to cover the largest possible area.

Her training had paid off, and the spell was devastatingly effective against the army of tightly packed narjags. Each man's death paid for the deaths of two or three narjags, though only some of the creatures were killed by the spell itself. At least as many were killed or injured when the front ranks collapsed, and they began a general stampede away from the enclosure.

"Very good," said Rew, letting out a low whistle.

He was watching nervously. Cinda insisted she could control the spell, that it would be safe, but if the wind changed, if she lost her focus, the potential existed for that deadly cloud to turn back onto them. He worried about that, but the breeze held steady, and the lass kept firm control.

Brian of the Brambles was on the other side of the young necromancer, and he nodded as well. He remarked, "I've never seen necromancy, but this is a sound use of the art. It's as effective as anything I've seen an invoker do. Of course, they're able to act without... ah, you know."

"I'm not advocating others learn this," muttered Cinda, "but in times of need, we do what we can."

"So we do," agreed Brian. He looked around her at Rew. "My imps?"

"Hold them in reserve. Do you have any varieties that can see well in the dark?"

The old man shook his head. "No better than a man and worse

in most cases. They make poor nighttime sentries, if that's what you are thinking."

"That's what I was hoping," admitted Rew.

"I've exhausted nearly all of the strength I gathered today," said Cinda, her eyes still closed, her lips barely moving. "If you'd asked, I could have animated some corpses, set them at key points. They can see well enough in the dark, and best of all, they don't need sleep."

Rew shook his head. "No, forcing the Dark Kind back was the most valuable use of your powers. Look, see? They're falling away all around us. Without pressure on all sides, they know they can't fight their way in. The narjags are too small, too weak compared to a well-trained and fully equipped man. They're effective when they can outnumber an opponent or surprise it. You've bought us another day."

"If that does us any good," complained Cinda. She opened her eyes and pointed toward the forest line where fleeing narjags were disappearing. In the trees, they could see others who had been watching and hadn't joined the fight yet. "More come each day, Ranger. They don't care about their losses. Tomorrow, the day after, they'll break through. When they do, we have nowhere to run, nowhere to hide. We need reinforcements."

Rew grunted. "The men found your... use of the cavalry disconcerting. It was effective, Cinda, but we have to think about the morale of the men as well as the easiest ways to kill narjags. The men are strained to the point of breaking already. Having their dead friends standing watch over them while they try to sleep might be the thing that shatters them. I know what your corpses can do to the narjags, but we have to think of what they'll do to our own men."

"I could call—"

"No, no wraiths," interrupted Rew. "It's too dangerous."

The necromancer eyed him dispassionately. They'd had that argument before, when discussing her casting death's breath. She asked him, "Can you talk to the rangers like we did in Iyre?"

"In Iyre, they knew to come to us. My last instructions were to meet us in Mordenhold or to flee. Neither of those helps us now."

Cinda scowled. They'd had this discussion before as well. She could guess what he would say, but she was trying to plant the seeds, so that in time, he would unleash her fully. Her magic could be devastating to foes, but it was dangerous to allies as well. She listened to him, for now, but neither of them seemed sure how long that would last.

They needed another army to shatter the mass of Dark Kind, or they needed the rangers. He worried that instead, they would get the fraemoth.

THAT NIGHT, AS THEY SAT IN THE COMMAND TENT, REW STRUGGLED to keep his eyes open. Next to him, Anne had already fallen into a deep slumber. She'd been healing from dawn until well past dusk, taking the pain from a hundred soldiers, their agony wracking her body, but Rew knew there was no use telling her to stop, to take a break. The hurt of letting those men die would have been worse for her.

Cinda stood quietly at the wall of the tent where they'd rolled up the flap to try and entice a breeze to stir the stale, foul air. The stench of hundreds of dead narjags suffused the enclosure like water in a pot. It was horrible, but Rew and the other commanders were at a loss for solutions.

Sending out crews to clear away the dead narjags and ideally burn them wasn't practical in the midst of a battle. When men fought men, there would be a chance to parlay, to request time to clear the dead, but the Dark Kind didn't respect their own fallen, and the people were nothing more than rotting food to them.

Zaine was seated at their map table, poring over the documents there, but Rew couldn't fathom what she was looking at. The Dark Kind had the entire place surrounded. They weren't going anywhere that required directions and a map.

Raif was out in the encampment, checking on the sentries, conversing with the captains, and ensuring everyone was doing what they were supposed to be doing and had what they needed —or had what they could have, at least. They had food for days still and water, but bandages, herbs, and other necessary supplies could be out by the next day. Raif and Colonel Eddla were rationing those critical supplies as best they were able.

Rew had made his rounds earlier, but he'd entrusted the details of the logistics and provisions to others. Raif and Eddla understood the ranger was not a normal commander. He was a fighter, and he'd spent the day with a sword in his hand. For hours, he'd faced the worst the narjags could throw at them, and he would do it again the next day.

Shockingly, Raif was proving highly competent at commanding the attention of the regular soldiers and directing them to their tasks. He didn't always know what those tasks should be, but he was accumulating captains who offered sound advice, which—even more surprising to Rew—Raif listened to.

His authority with the men might have something to do with the huge, enchanted greatsword he carried with him everywhere. It was an impressive weapon, and enough of the men had seen him use it that they gave him the respect a warrior was due. It was more than that, though. Raif had matured since Eastwatch. He was no longer a child but a grown man who knew the import of what they attempted.

Rew blinked, a yawn cracking his jaw. Had he been asleep?

Anne was still beside him, breathing deeply. Zaine was still at the map table, but when he looked closer, he saw the girl's head was cradled in a hand, and her hair had fallen down over her face. Cinda was gone.

Blessed Mother, he had been asleep.

Moving slowly as to not disturb Anne, Rew stood and stretched.

His muscles were tight, like he'd been petrified. He grunted. He wasn't that old. He worked through some motions, forcing the blood to pump through his body, to loosen his arms and his legs and his hips, which were terrifically sore. He bent and collected a pillow then gently put it beneath Zaine's head and moved her hand, propping her head on the pillow and saving her an awful crick in her neck when she awoke.

He stood up, his back protesting, and he scowled. Maybe she wouldn't have a sore neck. Had he gotten sore when he'd been her age? He didn't remember feeling like this, even after the toughest days Mordenhold's weapons masters could throw at him.

On the corner of the table was a wooden plate with a hard, stale biscuit and a half-eaten piece of salted beef. He frowned. Had Zaine been eating that or Cinda? There was an empty ale mug beside it, flecked with dried foam. Zaine, then.

He picked up the mug and glanced around, looking for an ale barrel, but there wasn't one in the command tent. Would anyone be awake at the quartermaster's depot? Would they care if they saw the commander dipping himself an ale in the middle of the night? Rew decided that if they did care, it would be worth it. He walked out of the tent into the warm night air.

It stank.

Disease could spread on the air. Anne had told them, warned them strenuously about it, though she didn't know if it was possible to catch an illness like that from the Dark Kind. Their claws and teeth would give you a nasty infection if they got into you, but was that because of the foul carrion they ate or something in their alien blood? It didn't much matter. There were a thousand Dark Kind dead lying outside of their compound, and Rew wasn't going to put the entire army at risk trying to clean them up. The most he'd been willing to risk was removing some of the fallen creatures from where they'd been impaled on the sharpened stakes that ringed the compound. They couldn't get rid of them all, but they could get rid of the ones that had been pounded into crude, bloody ramps.

Looking around, he couldn't tell if that work had been done

yet or not. The earthen walls of the enclosure were dark. He could see some silhouettes of men walking on patrol, but if they were working through the night on cleanup, they were doing so with no lights.

The camp was almost entirely dark. What wood they had they turned to defense. Depending on the piece of wood, they used them for makeshift shields or more stakes to plant outside the berm. It was only when the cooks were stewing meals or boiling bandages that anyone used fires. It was warm enough they didn't need them for heat, and they had to conserve all of the resources that they could.

King's Sake, it would have been a boon to have enough fuel to burn the bodies of the Dark Kind. It smelled something awful when their disgusting flesh roasted, but that smell would pass. Now, it was going to be a lingering blanket until they managed to get out of there. Rew sighed. Another day, two? How long would it take for Duke Findley to portal the rangers into the compound? Would he even do it at all?

Rew began walking toward the quartermaster's depot. He wondered if they would have an extra mug there. He would get two ales, if they did, or maybe something stronger. The quartermasters must have some spirits hidden away. He was the commander. They would turn it over to him if they did.

Clouds swept across the sky, but the wind was high and barely stirred the air over their fortress. It was an hour past midnight. He yawned. He'd gotten three hours of rest, he figured. He could use more, but it would be good to be seen up and about by the men.

Halfway to the quartermaster's depot, Rew saw Cinda standing beside a wagon. It was parked behind the hospital tent and was used to carry the unfortunates who hadn't survived to a shallow pit where they were burying the dead each morning. There was no chance of a proper burial or even a funeral pyre, which was the custom amongst some parts of Vaeldon. All they could do was put the bodies in the ground then layer a thin shroud of dirt across them.

Rew hadn't asked, and Cinda hadn't mentioned, but she was seeing to the bodies before they were buried. Was she somehow drawing more power from them or placing a binding on their forms? Were the corpses going to burst out of the ground some moment like bears returning from hibernation? He didn't want to know.

They'd agreed that for as long as possible, she wouldn't animate any more corpses within the compound. It creeped everyone out, and stuck in the tight enclosure, surrounded by the Dark Kind, they did not need to raise the level of tension past what it already was.

The men and women working the hospital tent and the soldiers walking patrols throughout the night must have seen her. They must suspect what the crimson-robbed girl was doing beside a wagonful of dead bodies, but they'd also seen what her power could achieve earlier that day. She'd sent death's breath billowing over the army of the Dark Kind, killing hundreds of them, ending the fighting and buying them a break. That sort of thing bought a little leeway with the common soldiers, though in time they might turn on her. Necromancers were rarely popular people.

"Cinda," called Rew.

The young necromancer turned at his voice, her eyes sparkling green in the darkness.

"Were you looking for me?"

"No," he replied, raising the empty ale mug.

A half-smile formed on her lips. "Sorry I left you all there. It appeared you needed the sleep."

"I did," conceded Rew. "That was good work today. You saved lives. Maybe a lot of them. How are you holding up?"

"I've been worse," said Cinda. "Casting so much power is exhausting, but not... It's not sleep that I need."

"Can I help?"

She shook her head.

"Join me for a drink?"

Cinda laughed and responded, "I'll watch you drink. It'll be like old—"

The night seemed to leap into physical form, and Rew lunged at it, swinging his wooden mug.

A valaan twisted out of the path of his strike, and the mug clipped Cinda on the side of the head, sending her spinning and falling to crash against the side of the wagon. The valaan hissed and lashed out at Rew.

He stumbled back, already pulling his hunting knife with his off hand, barely getting it up in time to deflect the valaan's sharp claws. The impact knocked the blade from his hand, and the knife went spinning away. Still reeling backward, he flung his empty mug at the valaan and drew his longsword but then had to throw himself into an awkward roll to avoid the valaan's next attack. The valaan pursued him, and he retreated until he saw another of the jet-black creatures emerging to stand over Cinda.

"No!" bellowed Rew.

The girl was unconscious from the blow he'd accidentally given her. The valaan in front of him pressed, and Rew could barely see its dark arms and legs, his senses as a ranger the only thing allowing him to move his blade to meet the valaan's strikes. Arm cocked back, the second one prepared to strike the defense-less necromancer.

Steel gleamed, and the blade of a giant greatsword whipped into the second valaan, catching it in the torso, nearly cleaving the creature in two.

Rew's valaan charged him, and he lunged, moving his sword to where the Dark Kind was going and slamming the blade into its chest. His longsword plunged deep, the hilt thumping against its cold flesh. Swinging the blade to the side, Rew let the valaan slide off his sword. He started toward Raif and Cinda then saw another shape atop the wagon.

"Raif, above!"

The fighter spun, swinging his sword before he looked.

The valaan leapt, clearing his head and landing lightly behind him, poised to pounce on the big man's back. Rew caught it just in time, bringing his blade around and chopping into the side of the valaan's skull.

Shouts echoed throughout the camp, and there was at least one furious fight happening out of sight. Precious torches were lit as captains emerged from their tents, trying to figure out what was going on, how serious was the attack.

"'Ware the walls!" cried Rew. "Valaan in the camp, but ware the walls!"

Raif stood with his back toward Cinda, his greatsword out and ready to defend her again. The fighting spilled closer to them, and Raif shouted, "Go! I'll watch her."

Rew nodded then sprinted toward where a dozen soldiers were getting torn to shreds by another valaan. He crashed into the back of the fight, charging directly at it.

The creature sensed him and spun to meet his attack, but the men around it struck, three swords hacking into the valaan at once. The monster wailed, thrashing at its attackers.

Rew struck, taking off a hand. Another man rammed his sword into its leg. Then, a soldier plunged his blade into its back, the steel bursting in a shower of orange gore from its chest. The men kept hacking at it, and Rew stepped away. That one was done, but he would let them exercise their frustration on it.

Torchlight had sprung up in two dozen places, and men were racing about the camp. Rew saw a captain descending from the earthen bulwark. He called to the man, "Anything?"

"It's quiet out there," said the captain. He glanced at where the soldiers were still chopping up the ruined remains of the valaan. "I'll double the guard and get men searching every bit of this camp, but I don't think we'll face the full brunt of an attack tonight. These look like assassins to me. We're lucky we broke their attack earlier, aye? Would have been a mess if we were tangled up and these slipped in behind."

Rew nodded. "Yes, that'd be a mess."

Chapter Eighteen

The next morning, when the light of the sun shone down, the Dark Kind began marching out of the forest in rigid ranks. Calls of alarm were raised, and Rew, his friends, and the other commanders in the army rushed atop the wall to see what they faced.

"Well, that is unexpected," commented Raif.

"Even fifty years ago, there weren't reports of the Dark Kind marching like this," said Rew. He gripped the wooden hilt of his longsword. "I think we're going to see the fraemoth today."

"Why are they in formation?" wondered Zaine. "Why do men walk like that, just so they don't step on each other's heels? Or is it so they can all set spears together or something like that?"

"So they can set spears together," replied Raif. After a moment, he added, "And so they don't step on each other's heels."

"They don't have any spears," mentioned the thief.

"The fraemoth sent the valaan after Cinda last night because it was worried she could disrupt their ranks," said Rew. He scratched his beard. "It had seen what she could do when they were packed close together."

Raif glanced around. "Is she out of the hospital tent yet? We could use her talents now. Strike while the iron is hot, right? They're packed as close as they were yesterday."

"She'll need to gain more power to attack. Until we start dying…"

"Will the knock to her head harm her ability to cast?" worried Zaine. "Anne healed her, but spellcasting is a delicate art, isn't it?"

Rew shook his head. "Anne's empathy ought to be enough to get her on her feet."

"She was lucky you were there," said Raif. "Do you think the valaan knocked her out because it planned to take her? I was up half the night worrying what it meant if they were trying to capture her alive."

"Ah, I think it was just part of the attack," mumbled Rew, looking steadily out at the ranks of narjags. "She and I saw it coming before it struck her, and it must have just missed. That can happen, you know. You're putting too much thought into this."

"What's wrong?" asked Zaine, stepping toward the ranger. "You seem strange."

"No, just worried about Cinda is all."

"I'm worried about all of us," said Raif, turning to look at the approaching Dark Kind. "Today is the first day we might expect the rangers, right?"

"Yesterday, if everyone had moved fast enough," replied Rew.

Raif grimaced.

"Ranger Adro and the riders could have been delayed, or maybe Findley needed time to… He could have taken a day or two to locate Ang and Vurcell. My directions weren't that specific. A lot of things might have happened that aren't catastrophes. They could still be coming."

"Might not be a catastrophe if we can hold out today," remarked Raif. He shifted, his armor rustling. "I'm not sure we can."

"You did well yesterday, lad. Just do it again."

The big fighter grunted and turned to join his flying company, which was assembling under the direction of the captains and sergeants in the compound behind them. Rew looked up and down the wall and saw that the other leaders in the army were directing their men as well, falling into the pattern they'd established days ago.

The ranger found himself with very little to do. He'd been roving, helping where he could, and had no one under his direct control. His task had been to sense the flow of the battle and utilize the spellcasters and other specialty units when they would be most effective. Because he had no one to order about, he was the only commander who could focus his entire attention on what the Dark Kind were doing.

He frowned. Watching what they were doing and figuring out what they were doing were evidently two different things. The narjags were in ranks, ten by ten, forming blocks of around a hundred of them. It was eerily similar to the way men organized an army, except there was no particular reason for them to be arranged in that fashion. Even men, when assaulting a fortification, didn't march in close units like that. It made them vulnerable to siege machinery and ranged weapons.

There was a reason the Dark Kind were doing it, though. There had to be.

He saw ten of the narjag companies then twenty. Then, he stopped counting. There were as many of them out there as there were men within the enclosure. He studied the companies, looking for valaan. After they'd killed the creatures the night before, how many could there be left?

He spotted a few but determined each company was not led by a valaan. There were shamans there, clustered in groups of three to five, and they seemed to stand a dozen paces in front of each of their companies. Narjag captains preparing to lead the charge? If there was a fraemoth on the field, he didn't see it, but he supposed he didn't know what he was looking for, so maybe it was there. Brian of the Brambles had said the creatures took on the aspect of your greatest fear. Rew didn't think the spellcaster meant small spaces or heights.

With so many out there, if the Dark Kind came hard, they had a decent chance of bursting a breach in the defenses. The men would benefit from their walls, their better armaments, and their size advantage over the narjags, but Rew dreaded every death in his army, and the Dark Kind didn't care. The men needed to do more than just win. They had to win decisively.

They would use all of their arrows today, decided Rew. As long as the narjags were clustered in formation, the shots would be effective. If they thinned the narjags out on the approach, Rew's army could win a pitched battle against two thousand of the Dark Kind, though nothing so far had felt like victory.

He gripped his longsword, trying to ignore his doubts. Those thoughts were nothing more than distractions because they couldn't change their plans. They were stuck within the earthen fort. They had no way to gather more resources. If they tried to flee, they would be run down from behind by the ayres. All that was left was to fight.

Rew blinked. Where were the ayres?

He drew his spyglass and began peering along the ranks of the narjags and at the dense forest behind them. A twinkling light caught his eye, and Rew saw something sparkling at the midst of one of the groups of shamans. No, within the groups of all of the shamans. He adjusted the brass-bound glass, focusing on the closest cluster of them. The shamans were clutching a crystal between them, each of them touching it with a grimy hand. The crystal was shimmering with incandescent light.

Communication to the fraemoth or…

Rew snarled and spun to grab a soldier to serve as a messenger then gave up and began running. Brian of the Brambles was standing amongst a group of his men, evidently giving them encouragement for the coming battle.

"Imps!" cried Rew from fifty paces away. "We need imps."

Brian blinked at him. "For, ah…"

"The narjag shamans are about to cast a spell," said Rew, skidding to a halt. "I don't know what it will do, but—"

"Narjag spellcasting?" asked Brian doubtfully. He saw Rew's face then croaked, "Narjag spellcasting!"

Rew grabbed the conjurer's arm and began dragging him toward the wall.

FOUR OF BRIAN'S LARGEST IMPS JUMPED IN SPECTACULAR ARCS, FLYING over the thicket of sharpened stakes and landing with heavy crunches on the bodies and wreckage beyond. In great bounds, they began running toward the narjag shamans.

Four imps. There were eight clusters of shamans holding the sparkling crystals. The narjags saw the imps coming, but the ones standing in the ranks did not rush forward to defend the shamans. Instead, they stayed back, huddling together and falling out of their orderly rows.

"King's Sake, we're about to get hit with something," growled Rew. He began shouting down the line for the men to take cover.

Some heard him. Some did not.

The shamans Brian was targeting scrambled back, trying to fall behind their minions, who also began falling back, but none of them had the speed of a full-size imp. The hugely muscled monstrosities were on the narjags in a dozen breaths, and they tore into the shamans with relish.

"We might—" began Brian.

The lights in the midst of the shamans who hadn't been targeted by the imps pulsed, and there was an enormous crack.

Rew grabbed the spellcaster's robe and flung him down the hill back into the fort. At the top of his lungs, he yelled, "Duck!"

The ranger leapt from the embankment, and behind him, he heard a terrible roar, like thunder but several times faster, and the dirt barrier he'd been standing on exploded. He crashed into the ground hard, the air blasting from his lungs with the impact. He curled into a ball. Dirt, rocks, and splintered wood pelted him and kept coming down like a rain shower.

He lay face down on the inside of the compound, his mouth gritty with dirt. Rew spit then rolled over. Between his toes, he could see blue-skinned ayres running. Running toward him. Where was the earthen wall they'd been defending the last several days? Sitting up, he saw a huge hole had been blown through it. Fifteen paces wide. A flattened path of soil led from the Dark Kind directly to him.

Rew struggled to his feet, his body protesting at being so mistreated. To the sides, he saw more identical gaps in the wall. That was not good. The ayres were racing, frothing at their mouths, streaming between the orderly companies of narjags, already halfway to the wall. Really not good.

Brian's imps must have killed some of the shamans, but they hadn't killed them all. Rew shook himself and found the spellcaster lying where he'd landed. The old man was laying on his side, clutching his arm and cursing in a language Rew did not know.

"You all right?"

"No," responded the spellcaster through clenched teeth.

"Broken arm? Sorry to say this, but you'd better get up. We're in trouble."

"Trouble?" gasped the spellcaster. He tried to sit. "What kind of trouble?"

Rew began walking toward the gap in the wall. He called over his shoulder, "Get it together, man. We're going to need you."

Around him, soldiers stood stunned and dismayed. For days, they'd been risking their lives, dying on the earthen walls. The day before, the walls and the wooden stakes had been the only thing that had given the men an advantage, the only thing that had kept them alive. Now there were giant, gaping holes smashed through that they had no way to repair.

Rew took the gap and glanced over his shoulder. He saw Raif thirty paces away.

"Lad!" he bellowed. "Take three companies, rotate them, and hold one of the breaches. Assign Colonel Eddla to another. Throw something into the last opening to absorb the initial wave, and tell Cinda that one is hers."

Zaine appeared by his side then gasped as she saw the rushing wave of ayres.

"Get Brian of the Brambles to Anne. I think he broke his arm. We're going to need more of his imps if we're to survive today."

"What about you?"

"I'll hold until his imps get here."

"Rew, you can't!"

"You're wasting time, lass."

The thief ran toward the fallen spellcaster, and Rew turned to face the approaching horde of ayres.

The pack had run between the companies of narjags and then reformed into four distinct streams charging toward the four breaches in the earthen wall. Beyond the leaping, racing canine-like Dark Kind, Rew could see Brian's imps still ravaging the narjag shamans. Legions of gray-skinned Dark Kind leapt and struck around the imps, but the giant summonings were tearing through the lesser beasts with stunning violence. Eventually, the small wounds the narjags were inflicting would take their toll, but it appeared Brian's imps might be able to fell the shamans before they were lost beneath a scrambling pile of Dark Kind.

It was too late.

Without the added height and protections of the wall, injured and exhausted, the soldiers were going to have hell defending their encampment. If the ayres got inside, if they were able to use their incredible speed to move behind the men, attacking from any angle...

Rew set his feet in the breach of the wall, his longsword held lightly in his hands, his face grim. One hundred fifty ayres were coming directly at him. Too many. Even for him, it was too many. But he had to try.

Fifty paces out then thirty then—

Colonel Eddla, leading a ragtag assortment of all that

remained of the cavalry, circled the edge of the encampment and charged.

The bugler rode beside the colonel, blowing frantically on his horn, though what signal he was trying to send was lost in the madness of the day. Behind him and the colonel, the cavalry fanned out, the men lashing and kicking at their horses, driving the terrified beasts into certain death.

The ayres were surging, almost to Rew, when the cavalry crashed into their flank. Some of the men had lances. Others swung gleaming scimitars. The charge was disorganized and didn't have the heft of when the unit all impacted at the same moment, but the men plowed through the line of ayres and kept going, heading for the next column of the Dark Kind.

Spinning, leaping, and snapping at the men on horseback, the ayres' attack on the breach Rew was guarding faltered. The ranger bellowed a war cry and ran forward. He bounced over the bodies of dead narjags, like walking on a soft, slimy rugs. They'd been trampled for days, ground into the soil, so there was little risk of tripping, but it was slippery and foul.

The first of the ayres had been ahead of the cavalry charge, and Rew met them. Three of the blue-skinned monsters—their eyes rolling back at the chaos behind them—were distracted from the ranger plunging into their midst.

Rew stabbed his longsword into the side of one of the ayres, and a second leapt at him. He reached up, his hand darting beneath its open mouth, and caught it around the neck. Yanking his longsword free, he slammed the second ayre down on its back and stomped on its head with his boot while spinning his longsword then bringing it down on the top of the third ayre's skull.

He jumped over the falling bodies, approaching two more ayres that had escaped the cavalry charge. He pulled his hunting knife and met the ayre's yawning teeth with a fang of steel.

More ayres came at him, and he angled his blades toward their mouths and heads. The things had long, powerful nails which could tear skin, but those wouldn't sink deep. It was the ayre's jaws that would kill you. They had thick necks, corded with muscle. Ayres were built for clamping down and then twisting and tearing away raw flesh. If one sunk teeth into you, even killing it would mean losing a hunk of skin and muscle.

But Rew had spent years in the wilderness fighting these monsters, and he knew how to avoid their bites. He danced amongst them, taking raking blows from their feet but deftly avoiding their slavering jaws.

His longsword and hunting knife flickered, plunging into blue-skinned bodies but more often slicing across the skin, opening their necks or clipping them on the backs of their hind legs. Twenty paces from the wall of the enclosure, a crippled ayre was as good as a dead one. Even if its companions didn't feast on its body, it was out of the fight, far enough away from the other men that it couldn't cause any harm.

He felled a dozen of the creatures then spared a momentary look at where the cavalry had gone. They'd burst through the second line of attacking ayres and approached the third, and there, they'd stalled. Farther than Rew would have given them credit for but now they were surrounded by hundreds of ayres. Rew could see Colonel Eddla, standing up in his stirrups, his scimitar, dripping dark blood, raised above his head as he called to his men.

The colonel was trying to form them into a whirling circle, constantly moving, their horses at a gallop, scimitars out forming a ring of stamping hooves and swinging steel, but there were too many ayres and not enough space for the formation to take shape. Whether the motley collection of cavalry could have pulled off the maneuver, they would never know. In the breaths Rew watched, he saw the ayres breaking into the ring, running at the legs of the horses, powerful jaws snapping at them, causing them to stumble and spill their riders.

The men behind had to either swerve their own mounts

around the fallen or jump over them. The formation collapsed chaotically, and Rew didn't need to watch the rest.

From the moment he had ridden out of the enclosure, Colonel Eddla must have known it was a suicide mission. There'd been no chance to smash through all four lines of attacking ayres and then escape back to the safety of the fort. They'd been outnumbered five to one. There was a marching army of narjags two hundred paces away. It'd been hopeless, but their sacrifice gave hope to the others.

Rew killed two more ayres then fell back. A dozen soldiers had joined him, and he called for them to retreat as well. The initial attack by the ayres had faltered. They'd survived the quick strike on the breaches the narjags shamans had opened with their magic. Now, they just had to survive two thousand narjags with four gaping holes in their walls. There was no time to shore up the fortifications. No time to plan. Only time to fight.

Chapter Nineteen

❧❧❧

Shouting at the top of his lungs, Rew began organizing the nearby soldiers into a coherent defense. Colonel Eddla was dead. Rew had no idea where the man's captains were, but the soldiers around the ranger reacted as quickly and as efficiently as could be expected. It didn't take a tactician to look out at what they were facing and understand they were in trouble.

The only way to survive the day was to work together, for the men to stand shoulder to shoulder, to protect their fellows, and to expect their own sides and backs would be watched in turn. Quickly sizing up the available men, Rew began putting them in place.

A man, a captain Rew thought, though he couldn't be sure as the man's clothing was as torn and blood-stained as anyone's, caught his sleeve. "M'lord, Colonel Eddla was supposed to hold the breach in the middle."

Rew cursed.

"I can take this position," stated the soldier calmly. "Look out there. The bulk of the narjags are going to hit the middle. M'lord, they're going to need you."

Turning from the men, Rew saw the narjags approaching, a mere hundred paces away. A spear was forming in their lines, the tip pointed at the center gap in the earthen wall. A spear tipped by dark bodies. Valaan.

"Go," said the captain.

Rew scrambled up the side of the destroyed dirt wall then began sprinting across the top of it. He couldn't spare time to see how many, but the valaan were leading the attack. They would cut through the common soldiers like a scythe through spring grass. Where were Brian's imps? Where was Cinda?

Rew jumped off the wall, landing in the gap a score of paces ahead of the valaan. The men there were trying to form lines, trying to arrange themselves, but their terror was palpable. They were good men. Brave men. They'd been prepared to hold the line against the narjags, even hundreds of them, but valaan? There was brave, and there was stupid. They hadn't fled, but they knew they couldn't face the captains of the Dark Kind. The valaan were too fast, too strong.

The men needed arrows raining down in a storm. They needed weapons masters on the line, backed by spearmen who could reach past them to keep the valaan cautious with sharp tips of steel. But they had the ranger.

"Don't let them get behind me," instructed Rew, raising his voice so everyone in the breach could hear him. He stood before the line, facing the six approaching valaan. He didn't bother to count the narjags behind them. There were more than he could see. A legion of them.

The valaan were a dozen paces away when Raif shoved through the line. The lad's eyes burned bright, and he didn't seem to notice Rew. His gaze was fixed ahead, his chest and shoulders heaving with excited breaths. The fighter raised his greatsword, and without pause, he charged.

Cursing, Rew leapt after him.

Raif chased into the midst of the valaan like a dog after geese. The dark figures melted away in front of his greatsword, but the lad kept swinging. He clipped one of them, and the valaan went spinning, bright orange blood trailing behind it.

Another slid in behind Raif's sword and tore its claws across his back, rending the steel armor, carving bloody gashes in his shoulder. The fighter swung over his head with the greatsword and caught that valaan with a strike, though it jumped back, not seriously harmed.

Raif's greatsword moved faster, a blur, and Rew watched in awe as the lad landed more strikes but took twice as many cuts from the valaan. He was moving with such force, such raw energy, the creatures couldn't land a fatal blow, though he couldn't seem to land a killing blow on them, either.

The rest of the battle was lost to Raif. His entire focus, his entire presence, was on the fight with the six valaan. He was fully berserk, and it was a terrifying thing to see. The valaan, deadlier fighters than Raif, appeared shocked at his ferocity.

Rew took advantage and snuck up behind two of them. He struck quickly and efficiently while they were distracted. He killed two, and then the other four saw him. A pair of them peeled off, leaving him and Raif both outnumbered against the valaan.

The ranger lost sight of the fighter when the two valaan converged on him. The creatures hissed and then struck. One lunged at Rew's legs. The other came high. They were both faster than him, but he'd anticipated the strategy.

Rew stuck his longsword point down, the razor-sharp edge facing the valaan. The tip stabbed into the detritus of dead narjags and into the soil a heartbeat before the valaan got there. Diving toward Rew's legs, it met steel instead, and the force of its movement drove it hard onto the edge of the blade.

Letting go of the hilt of his longsword, Rew stepped into the other valaan, surprising it as well, and rammed his hunting knife up, taking the valaan in the gut then ripping across its belly, gouging a hole in its stomach and spilling its entrails like slop from a bucket.

The valaan kept after him, and Rew got his free hand up in time to punch it on the side of the head, knocking its teeth away from his neck. It stumbled, its guts tangling in its feet, seeming to not know it was dead.

The ranger grasped the wooden hilt of his enchanted longsword and drew it from the earth, sliding the blood-slick steel from the body of the first valaan. The second fell before he needed to use the sword on it.

Beyond, Raif was screaming in rage, charging the remaining valaan. It ducked his blow, came inside his guard, and slashed its talons along his side. The fighter headbutted the thing.

Rew gaped in surprise.

Raif dropped his greatsword, grabbed the valaan, and lifted the Dark Kind above his head. The creature twisted in his grip like a weasel, but the fighter's hands were clasped on the valaan like steel manacles. He roared then brought it down onto his raised, armor-plated knee.

The valaan's muscular body slammed into Raif's leg, and the creature buckled. A man's back would have snapped cleanly, but valaan were no men. It was bent into a u-shape. Then, it seemed to flip, its legs kicking up and smashing into Raif's face.

The fighter stumbled back, the force of the blow staggering, even in his berserk state. His greatsword was half a dozen paces away, and the valaan landed cat-like, rising slowly to its feet. It held itself crooked, as if Raif's knee had shattered bones, but it stood, and it was between the young fighter and his weapon. Raif flexed his hands, his fingers held out like the valaan's claws.

"Didn't I tell you to stay behind me, lad," instructed Rew, stepping around the boy and thrusting his longsword into the wounded valaan. Rew wrenched his blade free then put a toe beneath Raif's greatsword and kicked it up so the fighter could grasp the hilt.

Raif raised the blade with one hand and touched his forehead with the other. Blood was leaking down his face where he'd split his scalp headbutting the valaan. "What happened?"

"You didn't listen to my advice, as usual."

The fighter grunted then pointed with his greatsword over

Rew's shoulder. The ranger turned and saw a wall of narjags descending on their position.

"King's Sake," rasped Rew.

He raised his longsword and prepared to fight.

A SOLDIER, HIS HELMET TORN AWAY, A BLOODY LACERATION COATING half his head in crimson, stepped beside Rew. His arm trembled, but he held his sword high. "Looks like you could use some help."

Rew nodded, giving the man a grim smile. Fifty paces in front of them, the narjags were racing forward, all pretense at organization and restraint dropped when the last of the valaan fell. The narjags clawed and snapped at each other, but it didn't matter. There were thousands of them. More than Rew could see.

Raif took Rew's other side. "If this be the end, Ranger, then I wish I'd never gotten out of that jail cell in Eastwatch."

Rew laughed and clapped the fighter on the shoulder with his fist. Next to the first soldier who had joined him, another claimed a place in the line and then another. Behind them, Rew could hear men shuffling into position. A dozen of them? Two dozen? He looked back. The men were resolute. Serious. But they weren't enough.

He'd hoped with the other rangers... but they were not there. Had Duke Findley betrayed them? Had he tried to reach Ang and Vurcell but failed? Blessed Mother, maybe the riders never made it to Yonn. Maybe there'd never been a chance. These men would fight, and they would fight well, but they weren't enough.

Rew turned back. The leading narjags were a score of paces away. Their eyes gleamed with the madness of battle. Berserk, like Raif. Their mouths were open. Spittle flew as they salivated at the thought of the men. Rew twisted his foot, trying to find sturdy ground amidst the carpet of dead narjags. He would die, but he wouldn't die easy.

The first of the narjags smashed into them, and Rew cut the thing down easily. After facing the valaan, killing the narjags was a breeze, or it would have been, if there weren't a thousand more of them still coming. The faster, more rabid of the creatures pelted into the lines of the men, but it was the press of them which would overrun their line.

More soldiers filled the gap, giving Rew and Raif space, forming a bristling wall of swords. The man who'd joined first, a captain evidently, was shouting orders, though Rew couldn't hear a word of what he said. Blood dribbled down the man's cheek, dripping off his chin, staining his chainmail and tabard. There was so much blood on his clothing Rew couldn't tell if the man was one of Findley's or Vincent's, but he was there. He was prepared to fight.

Rew reared back and kicked a narjag in the chest, pounding the creature back. He slashed his sword across the face of another. He stabbed a third. In moments, he would have to fall back. There were too many. They were already pressing against the line of men. The sheer weight of them would overwhelm the formation, and they would be trampled beneath the mass of creatures. It wasn't a fight of skill. It was about brute strength and raw numbers, and the narjags had the numbers.

A man half a dozen paces to Rew's right went down silently. To the left, another man screamed. Then another. Rew roared at the narjags. Hack and slash, his blade rose and fell.

Screams were erupting from the camp. Ten. Twenty. A hundred men shouting in terror. Blessed Mother, had the narjags encircled them already? Had ayres snuck over the southern wall while they faced the valaan to the north? Had they failed to hold one of the other breaches, or was the fraemoth joining the battle?

"I'll cover you. See what's behind us," called Rew to the blood-soaked captain beside him.

The man moved behind Rew's shoulder, craning his neck to peer back into the camp. "There's nothing, M'lord. But the men..."

They're... Something is attacking them. They're dying, but I can't see what is killing them."

The fraemoth. It had finally joined the fight.

"What do we do?" cried Raif, sweeping his greatsword in front of him, dragging the enchanted steel through three narjags, and forcing back half a dozen others.

Rew gritted his teeth and fought. Five narjags. Ten. It was never going to be enough.

"It's coming closer!" warned the captain.

The fraemoth would want Rew. It would come for him. It'd been sent for him, to stop him from reaching Mordenhold. The ranger killed another narjag then fell back, letting others take his place. They did so without complaint or need of instruction. They understood. He was the King's Ranger. They could face the narjags, but only he could face the fraemoth.

Rew moved back through the lines of men, and they parted for him, some sense telling them they could not face what was killing their friends within the camp. A cold, bitter chill washed over them all. Frowning, Rew shivered. A cold chill. The fraemoth's presence?

Fifty paces from him, a man's scream was cut off in a wet, gurgling choke. Blood spurted from his ruined neck, and he fell to the side. Then, a dozen paces west of Rew, another man was decapitated, his head removed in a horrific, wrenching twist. And then a third fountain of blood burst near the earthen wall as a man appeared to be torn in two.

Rew swallowed. Fraemoths? Three of them? Or...

"Raif! I need you," cried Rew.

Frantically, he spun. The fighter was hammering forward into the narjags, lost again in the berserk. Rew could see from his back, the way his shoulders were set, his lack of defense.

"Raif! I need your sword!"

More men within the camp were torn apart in sickening showers of gore. The soldiers were panicked, but they didn't know where to run. Behind them was invisible death. In front of them were two thousand narjags pressing against the berm of the enclosure.

"Raif!" screamed Raw. Then, he stepped forward.

It had to be stopped. The things had to be stopped.

He couldn't see Cinda anywhere, but she was close. These were her wraiths. Chill terror swept the soldiers, and the line against the narjags began to crumble as men grew afraid of what was at their backs. The wraiths were unnatural, a grasping hand from the beyond. The men might not see them, but they would feel them. They knew something was terribly wrong.

The men on the walls and in the breaches were dying, their will sapped by the spectral presence of the wraiths. The creatures fed on life. They began draining their victims before they got close. Exposed to them long enough, and the bravest warrior would turn into a blubbering wretch. Unable to master their fear, facing an overwhelming attack by the narjags, men were dying.

One of the wraiths drifted across the earthen berm, headed to the other side and the Dark Kind. A second wraith was coming closer, though, headed right through the gap the thin line of men were trying to hold.

Calling for Raif frantically, trying to recall everything his tutors had told him decades before, Rew put himself in front of the wraith. It slowed, sensing his resolve. The creatures were shades, specters long dead. They feasted on the invisible force that drove all life and blood. Steel could not harm them. Magic could, if cast properly, but Rew had no high magic. It wasn't easy, but he'd been told that without magic, warm flesh could stop a wraith as well. They were the antithesis of life. You could harm them with its force.

Striking a wraith was said to be like striking a pane of glass. You could break it, and it would shatter around your hand, cutting you deep, but unlike glass, wraiths were not of the world. They were meant for the one beyond. Until they were sent there, they could reform into their ghostly shapes. Rew had been told it was possible to do enough damage to destroy the things, but possible and likely were not the same.

These wraiths were ancient, from a time before. Called down from the barrowlands. They'd been haunting the world for longer than the kingdom had existed. They were steeped in power. Rew sheathed his longsword and raised his fists.

Most of the men had the sense to run. Those who were too slow paid with their lives. One of the wraiths floated toward Rew, and with a constant litany of curses streaming beneath his breath, the ranger jumped forward and punched what he figured was the thing's face. The wraith let out a spectral wail as his warm flesh passed through its incorporeal body. It felt like every bone in his hand had shattered, but the wraith was knocked back, and as he shook his hand, he found his bones intact. So far.

His hand throbbed with incredible pain, but he'd done it. He'd shown he could harm them. Whether the wraith harmed him more in the process…

The wraith flowed back toward him, evidently drawn to his resistance. He swung at it again, a clumsy blow, because he could barely see what he was swinging at.

His arm tensed, and the wraith retracted. He tried to grab it, but it was like grabbing fog, bitterly cold fog, colder than the coldest night in the wilderness. His hand felt like it was getting rolled under a wagon wheel, but he'd caught… something.

He held it with one hand and struck with his fist, hammering the wraith. It deflated beneath his attacks, scattered and unable to counterattack, but the pain to the ranger was enormous.

Rew lost track of what was happening around them. Not lost in a berserk, but in agony. His senses were roiled, hurt blanketing him, but he kept hammering the wraith, kept swinging his balled fist into the space that it occupied.

He felt another one coming.

He closed his eyes, pounding at the one he held.

A man roared, and Rew's eyes flicked open. The blood-soaked captain charged, swinging his broadsword at thin air, like a child pretending to be a soldier. His steel sailed through the wraith, not harming it. Then, the shade tore the man from groin to chin. His insides were outside, and the captain's hot blood splattered Rew.

The ranger kept flailing at the wraith, his numb fist clutching the ephemeral form of the ghost, his other thrashing through the air.

The second wraith came at him.

Raif hurtled into view, his huge, enchanted greatsword cleaving the cold air then plunging through the awful chill of the wraith. There was a crackle and a wail, and Rew's head rang like a bell. The fighter stumbled through where the wraith had been, his enchanted greatsword having banished it. He spun.

"Raif, the other…" stammered Rew, slumping to his knees.

"Where?" demanded the fighter.

"Here…" rasped Rew, but he trailed off. Confused. The wraith was gone. His hand was empty. King's Sake, he'd beat a wraith to death?

"I don't understand," muttered Raif, turning to look around them. "Did the king send these?"

Rew tried to rise but stumbled and fell back to his knees. He shifted. The men of the line were going to fail. They were going to…

The narjags had fallen back. No, not fallen back, not in retreat. The wraith that had passed over the wall was amongst the narjags now. From the sound of things, there were others as well. They were sawing through those creatures with the tenacity of a beaver gnawing through a log. From his knees, looking around the men on the line, Rew could see dark blood spraying. He could see the narjags panicking, not understanding what they now faced.

The fraemoth had learned how to face men, but evidently, it hadn't learned to deal with a wraith yet.

"T-The king is attacking us!" yelled Raif, only a slight stutter betraying his confusion and doubt.

It wasn't the king attacking them. Rew growled to the fighter, "Help me up, we need to find your sister."

"Cinda! Of course. She'll know what to do," said Raif, leaning forward to haul Rew to his feet. He turned, his head swiveling between the dead men in the compound and the carnage outside of their walls. "I don't... Did the king..."

The wraiths were tearing through the narjags, but across the camp, they heard another high-pitched shriek of pain. Not all the wraiths had attacked the Dark Kind. Some of them had gotten distracted and had turned on the men and women of their camp.

"We need to find Cinda," instructed Rew. "Now. We need to find her now."

Chapter Twenty

Rew shouted at Cinda.

The necromancer looked back at him, her face flat, her jaw set like stone. She wasn't calm, but she wasn't cowering before his anger either. She was disinterested.

A small part of Rew noted her demeanor and wondered what it meant, but mostly, it made him mad. Anne had briefly tried to calm him, to reason with him, until she'd understood. Raif just stared dumbfounded, as if he'd wanted to defend his sister, to scream back at Rew, but he was grasping for an explanation, a reason that wasn't there.

Zaine had disappeared. Rew had seen her. He knew she was alive, but she wasn't in the command tent. Green-faced and trembling, she'd left, and now, it was just the four of them.

Raif lay sprawled in the corner, dozens of wounds marring his flesh. Anne crouched beside him, quietly employing her empathy. Rew stormed about the center of the room, feeling like a kettle fit to explode. Occasionally, he pointed a finger at Cinda, snapping off sharp questions then pacing again, glaring at her.

Cinda stared back at him, watching, waiting for him to exhaust himself.

"You won't even try to defend yourself, to reason with this... this madness?"

"Defending myself is what got you so angry in the first place," replied the necromancer, her tone droll, her face unmoving except her lips and the sparkling emerald green glow in her eyes.

"You killed hundreds of our men!"

"Her wraiths..." muttered Raif loudly. "Her wraiths did it. Cinda, you must have lost control. It was an accident, right? Tell him. Tell him what happened."

"No," replied the girl, a hint of sorrow bleeding into her voice. She kept her eyes on Rew and would not look at her brother. "I did not lose control, not entirely. I sent the wraiths on the most expedient route to the Dark Kind. It's unfortunate there were men in the way."

"Of course there were men in the way," snarled Rew. "You called the things right through the center of our camp."

"That was the quickest path."

Rew scowled at her, seething.

"I called a dozen of them," said Cinda. "My control was in place, but it was... loose. I would have stopped them from killing our people if I could, but when they passed so close, it was easier to let them take a life and then move on. I could herd them, not fight them. I knew a few lives did not matter when considering the magnitude of the war we're in. We lost some men. That's unfortunate, but it happens in war. It's no different than when you sent out the scouts. Besides, if it wasn't for my wraiths throwing back the Dark Kind, all of those men were going to die anyway."

"Not by your hand."

She shrugged.

"Cinda..."

"We are at war with the king—and his brother, if what Brian of the Brambles claims is true. Two of history's most powerful high magicians, men whose souls have somehow survived two centuries apiece. We will not win this fight without taking losses.

Terrible losses. I will die for this cause, and if my death alone was enough, I'd be glad, but it's not. We cannot protect everyone."

"Protect them? You didn't even try."

"I did what I did. I would do it again. I killed a thousand Dark Kind with those wraiths. I won the battle so that we may still fight the war. I regret that sacrifices were made, but it doesn't change what I had to do."

Rew looked away.

"We should leave at dawn," advised Cinda. "The Dark Kind are shattered. The remaining narjags will be running for days after that." The necromancer turned to her brother and Anne. "Will he be able to travel?"

Raif shifted, wincing at the tug on his wounds.

Her voice resigned, Anne allowed, "He'll be able to walk. It's taking me some time to heal him. I'm… drawn thin, but by dawn, he'll be able to travel, if not fight."

"Good," replied Cinda. "We leave at dawn."

The young necromancer moved to the map table and sat down, pretending to study the terrain sketched there. Rew knew it was an act. He would be the one to guide them the rest of the way to Mordenhold. She was acting busy for their benefit while absorbing the power in the air, the strength released from the hundreds of men who had died that day. The hundreds of men she had killed with her wraiths.

He knew she hadn't directed those ancient spirits to take the life of any man, but she hadn't stopped them either. Loose control, she'd said? Herding them? She could have summoned fewer. She could have… He grimaced and walked outside of the tent.

Zaine was lurking there, looking crestfallen.

"You heard?"

She nodded. She cleared her throat and said, "I sent the guards outside of the tent to the walls. Told them they might be needed there, though I haven't seen any of the Dark Kind since… Pfah, I figured the men didn't need to hear what you were discussing.

There are rumors already that it was an attack by the king, his wraiths, and that Cinda redirected them."

"Rumors you started?"

"She... She wasn't always like this. We've got to help her hold on to what she was, regardless of what she thinks she must become."

Rew nodded, too tired, too disappointed, to respond. He continued, walking deeper into the night, Zaine falling in at his side. Evidently, the thief wanted nothing to do with the mood inside of the tent, or perhaps she wondered whether Cinda had heard them and didn't want to face the necromancer just yet. Rew could understand that.

Walking slowly, feeling the weight of the battle with each step, he began an inspection of the encampment. The captains were doing what they could to restore some semblance of order, but so far, they hadn't progressed past dragging the dead narjags and ayres away from the cook fires and their tents. Rew thought about giving instructions, but there was only one that really mattered. He had told them at dawn to bury their dead and then to go home.

As he and Zaine made a circuit of the camp, the thief was quiet until they passed the hospital tent where Anne had spent most of the last week. The empath had left to tend to Raif and the rest of them. In the tent, men were dying. Rew had never seen Anne turn from such need. He didn't know what it meant, what she was thinking. He worried how deep her own pain was, if she wasn't able to face this. Had Cinda done that to her, or was it the weight of the empathy she'd already conducted?

Behind the tent, stacked in disorderly rows, were half of the forces they'd brought north. Over a thousand dead men, butchered by the Dark Kind—and by Cinda.

"I guess she was right," murmured Zaine. "She's not the hero."

REW DID NOT SLEEP THAT NIGHT. FOR SAFETY, THEY'D ALL BEEN bedding down in the command tent, except that night, Cinda was there, and she did not sleep either. She sat quietly beside the map table, her green eyes glowing dimly. The ranger could feel her watching him, but when he would roll over, she was looking away.

Raif slept like a man at the end of a three-day bender. He'd been battered and beaten and fought himself beyond exhaustion in the throes of his berserk. Anne as well. The empath had healed Raif as best she was able, though she'd been drained tremendously over the last week from tending to the soldiers. She'd finished and tried to go back to the hospital tent. Rew had stopped her, and she'd acquiesced. That, more than anything, was a sign of just how tired she was.

She'd murmured something about healing the ranger's wounds, and he'd shaken his head. He'd told her, "I'll suffer."

Snorting, she'd asked, "Is that meant to be a jest?"

He'd scratched his beard and sighed. "I don't know. Not a good one."

"It's too close to home," she'd told him. Then, she'd retreated to her bedroll near Raif's and had fallen asleep.

Zaine had bounced around for hours, making rounds outside in the dark then loitering inside the tent. She didn't go near Cinda. Finally, she'd joined Raif and Anne and was quickly snoring. Her hand was outstretched, nearly touching the lad's.

Shaking his head, Rew stepped outside, trying to ignore Cinda's blank stare. He'd thought about it, when he was tossing and turning, trying to sleep. The girl had knowingly put lives at risk. King's Sake, she might as well have directed her wraiths to kill those men. He knew what she would say if he accused her of it. She would tell him that he was the one who'd raised the army, and he'd sent men to the line and off to scout dangerous terrain. He'd done so knowing many of those men would die. She'd done the same. It was war. Men died in war.

But it wasn't the same.

He'd raised the army to protect the villages that were under attack. Duke Findley had as much a hand in it as Rew. They were the duke's people. The soldiers had to hold the line to save their fellows, to save everyone behind them. The scouts had to put themselves in danger to gather intelligence that could be the difference between victory and abysmal failure. Cinda's wraiths could have circled the encampment, or she could have summoned fewer and held tighter control. She could have…

But she didn't.

Cinda had been willing to let those men die so that her wraiths could get to the Dark Kind quicker. She'd known what she was doing. She was a smart lass and had worked out the odds. She'd known and done it anyway. Did the mathematics make sense? Another ten minutes, would they have held? Trying another spell or calling fewer wraiths, would either have been as effective?

Three months ago, it wouldn't have mattered. They would have done everything they could, no matter the odds. They'd prevailed making wild gambles and leaps of faith. They'd trusted each other and those around them. In his gut, Rew knew there'd been another way.

What did it matter?

Cinda was broken. She'd lost her connection to others. She cared only for getting to Mordenhold, for facing Vaisius Morden. She would die there. She knew it, and he knew it. Was that excuse enough? Did that absolve her from sacrificing others as she would be sacrificed?

Rew kicked a battered helmet and watched it roll dully and unevenly across the hard-packed, blood-stained ground.

They were going to Mordenhold. Cinda would die there, one way or the other. Did it matter how he judged her? He knew she wouldn't care, but he needed her—all of Vaeldon needed her, even if it didn't know it—so in his despair, Rew acknowledged there was nothing he was going to do. He couldn't arrest the girl, couldn't set her on trial for putting the lives of hundreds of their soldiers at risk. She would sacrifice anything to make it to the king. Isn't that what he was asking of her? Isn't that what he was doing as well?

In the end, his choices were his own, and he would carry the burden of the sorrow they caused. He might make mistakes, he'd done so plenty of times before, but they were his. He could live with his own cloak of pain because he'd earned it. What hurt him, what cut deep, was watching Cinda earn her own sorrow. He didn't like her choice, and he hated that she'd had to make it.

He saw as he walked that the men were having trouble sleeping as well. The blood-rush of battle was slow to fade. They'd been high for days, and after that subsided, the sleep wouldn't come for other reasons. They would remember the faces of the men they'd marched with, fought with side by side. They would remember those men's deaths. They would remember their own terror at facing the narjags. The unspoken embarrassments that brought all men low.

Grown men, trained for battle, could still wet themselves in fear when they faced death for the first time. Some of them might have ran or hidden while their friends died. They could have allowed others to volunteer to take an extra watch, to line the earthen wall. Other men would have charged into the thick of battle and died for it. Maybe these men came back and fought. It was a piece of redemption, but that wouldn't make them feel any better. Not when they were alone, and it was dark, and they relived those worst moments. They would ask themselves if they could have been braver and would that have saved their dead friends. They would ask themselves if they were cowards. Surviving a battle like the one they fought was its own special kind of guilt, no matter how the men had earned it.

Rew had been there. He knew.

Did Cinda?

He shook himself, scrubbing at his eyes with the heels of his hands. She'd done what she'd done. They were going to Morden-hold. There was nothing else to think about. He swallowed hard, forcing down a lump in his throat and kept walking.

Rew acknowledged the men on duty when he passed them, and they nodded back. No one spoke. The camp was quieter than it'd been since the moment they'd arrived. Frowning, Rew wondered if anyone had located Brian of the Brambles and his men. Zaine had taken the man to the hospital tent. Rew had been told that later, soldiers had seen more imps join the fight, but no one had seen Brian or any of his people.

Zaine had gone looking. She was certain the spellcaster and his men were gone. The enclosure wasn't that big. Rew trusted her judgement, though the thief could hardly trust herself. It was difficult to believe that someone would just... vanish.

Half the army was dead. Had all of Brian's men perished? Had the spellcaster ventured out from the hospital tent, swung his giant mace, and then fallen somewhere they hadn't yet searched? It felt like they'd all dreamed the spellcaster's presence, but the earthen enclosure was real enough. The devastation the imps had caused had been real. The man's tent was still there. The cold cook fires his soldiers had huddled around... it was all still there. It was just the people who were missing.

Walking a slow circuit of the camp, Rew realized he hadn't spoken to any of Brian's men. Not that he recalled, at least. They must have had captains, but he couldn't remember them, either. They must have had someone he'd given orders to or received a report from. He pinched himself to make sure he wasn't dreaming then kept walking. Brian of the Brambles' disappearance was a mystery they did not have time to investigate, no matter how strange.

Rew stopped at the hospital tent, perhaps feeling some obligation to Anne. The men in there had needs beyond the skills of a ranger, but they were owed his attention, even if he couldn't help them. For an hour, he paced down the crowded rows of wounded, maneuvering around the surgeons and the soldiers who'd been pressed into duty as nurses. It was hard to tell, given the condition of the army as a whole, whether a man was meant to be a patient or a caregiver.

Many of the men were asleep, but plenty were not, kept awake by pain, physical and emotional. The surgeons had run out of the herbs they'd been using to dull the pain, and Anne couldn't take all of these men's suffering. No one could take their sorrow.

Rew helped a young man tie a bandage around the leg of another, showing him how to tuck it away neatly, so it wouldn't snag and pull off if the patient thrashed around. He opened his mouth to suggest changing the linens on another victim but then closed it and moved on without speaking. If there had been clean linens, they would have used them.

No one seemed to be in charge. He supposed Anne had been, or maybe Findley's or Vincent's regiments had arcanist-trained surgeons. If so, they must be resting. They'd earned it, Rew was sure.

People looked at him, not with hope, but with… pride, he thought. They'd faced impossible odds, and they'd survived. Half of them, at least. Some more of those in the tent would not make it, but most would. They'd seen the depths of fear, the worst a man could see. It would scar them, wound their very souls, but they had lived. They would keep living. They would see their families, their homes. There was a victory in that, and they would celebrate it, no matter how much it had cost them.

Pride and pain. They'd know wider joy, and deeper hurt than they had before. They'd be different people when they returned home. But they didn't know that. Not yet.

When he had passed each cot, each pile of filthy blankets, and had met the eyes of every man awake in the tent, Rew stepped outside and drew a deep, shuddering breath. The air was foul, and he couldn't wait to move far from their camp. He looked up. Just another hour until dawn. When had it gotten so late?

He needed sleep, but that time was past. He started toward the tents where the men were sleeping, where the cook fires smoldered. Maybe someone had started coffee already. If so, he would promote them on the spot. A new captain. No, a new duke, if they'd made it strong and in sufficient quantity. Smirking, he spied a fire that was more than just embers. Small flames. A kettle? Yes, he thought that might be a kettle hanging over it.

"Rew."

He blinked and turned.

Anne was there, striding toward him. Her eyes were bright, her shoulders high. He frowned. Had she woken and already dressed? He'd figured he was going to have to wake her soon, roll her off the blankets she'd collapsed upon. Surely she needed more rest than that.

"I found this."

In her hands, she held a sword. It looked like a common blade that any of Findley's or Vincent's men might carry. There was an ugly nick on the steel and a smear of dark blood. It'd seen use, though the hilt looked as fresh as if it'd just come from the forge or off the belt of a soldier who spent more time in the barracks than they did in service. But someone had used it. Someone had accounted themselves well against the Dark Kind.

Anne walked closer.

Rew asked her, "What am I supposed to be seeing?"

The empath didn't respond. Instead, she thrust the blade at his neck.

Her attack was blazingly fast, and Rew only avoided it by twisting to the side, the point of sharp steel breezing by the thin skin of his throat with a finger-width of room to spare. If his eyes hadn't been on the blade the moment it had thrust toward him, he would be dead.

Anne turned the blade and tried to draw it back across his neck.

Rew threw himself into a roll, tumbling past her, over his shoulder, then back to his feet. She was spinning, and a soft-booted foot cracked into the side of his head, knocking him down. He rolled again, coming back into her and tripping her as she lunged forward, plunging the sword down into the ground where he'd fallen.

She fell beside him, and he raised an elbow to crash it down on the back of her head, but he paused and then scrambled away, rising slowly. She rose as well and bent to retrieve the sword.

"Anne?"

She attacked again, and he fell back, reluctantly drawing his longsword.

Steel clanged, resonating in the early morning air.

Anne was quick and strong. Skilled.

Rew cursed. Some trick, like when Valchon had disguised one of his simulacrum as himself? Except... Rew knew Anne. He'd been close to her for most of his adult life. He'd seen her near daily in Eastwatch. He'd spent almost every moment with her the last months. He had a connection to her that ran deeper than recognition. He knew her.

But he also knew she wasn't a skilled swordswoman, and as he backpedaled, frantically defending against her, his fear bubbled like a boiling cauldron.

"It's the empath attacking the ranger!" cried a voice.

She thrust her sword at him, and Rew dodged to the side then leapt inside her guard. He jammed a leg behind her, gripped her shoulder, and shoved her back. She fell, and he landed on top of her, a knee wedged against her sword arm, pinning it down.

"What—"

Her balled fist smashed into his groin. Then, she brought her legs up behind his back and wrapped them around his neck. She slammed him down on the ground. She rose, and he kicked, knocking her back and giving him time to climb to his feet.

She swung at him, and he ducked then slapped her wrists, knocking the sword from her grip. She scowled at him then clipped him across the face with a vicious backhand, her bladed hand striking his cheek and splitting his skin.

He reeled away, blinking in pain and confusion. He'd been slapped before by Anne but not like that. She didn't know how to hit like that. But those were her clothes. He'd seen her buy them. Her hair when he'd landed on top of her smelled like her hair.

The way her jaw was set, the way she bent as she stooped to

collect the short sword again… He'd seen those hands a thousand times. He'd touched them, held them. He knew her. He knew that face, that scent, the way she carried herself.

"Rew, I'm scared. I need you."

He shook himself, trying to dislodge the fear that clutched at his throat, made it difficult to speak. "What is happening, Anne? What are you doing?"

She stepped closer, one hand open, one hand holding the short sword. He raised his longsword warily. Something was wrong. He didn't know what, yet. But this wasn't her.

Anne put a gentle hand on the side of his blade, pushing it aside just enough she could approach. Her lips were trembling. She opened her mouth and closed it, grinding her teeth.

He'd seen her do that a thousand times when she was frustrated or scared.

"You're not thinking straight, Rew."

She was right. He wasn't thinking straight. Watching her… he was so confused. Was this a dream?

"Put down the sword," he told her.

She nodded then dropped it. The steel thumped softly onto the dirt. Anne reached forward, putting a hand lightly on his, just the fingertips. She was hesitant, non-threatening. He felt her warmth, saw her breathe. She stared into his eyes. The rise of her cheeks, the curl of her lips. Freckles speckled her cheeks and the bridge of her nose. He'd spent years looking at that face. This was no trick of makeup or magic. He felt the connection to her. It was her.

Then, she yanked his hunting knife from his belt and tried to stab it into his ribcage.

Rew blocked the blow but not before the blade pierced his skin. He rocked forward, clubbing Anne in the face with his forehead.

The empath staggered back, crying. Blood spurted from her broken nose, pouring down over her familiar lips. She was sobbing. Tears joined the blood dripping from her face.

"Anne, I—"

He dropped his longsword and stepped forward.

She swept his hunting knife up again, aiming for his throat.

Acting on instinct, Rew caught her wrist, chopped a hand into the crook of her elbow, and forced the knife into her chest. The bone hilt stuck out from her, and blood cascaded down, coming in ragged gouts as her failing heart tried to keep beating. She fell back, and Rew caught her, lowering her to the ground.

Opening her mouth, she whispered, "Rew, why…"

He was stunned. Dumbfounded. He'd acted without thought, decades of training, of surviving. The movement had been beaten into him so thoroughly he'd acted before he'd realized what he was doing. He hadn't meant to… Hadn't wanted to stab her. To kill her.

Anne blinked, the blood from her nose slowing, a bubble of it escaping her lips, but no more words. He moved his hands thoughtlessly, trying to staunch the flow of blood from her chest, but he knew it was too late.

He'd killed Anne. Or… Had he? He put a hand on her cheek, smearing the crimson liquid. She was still warm. Her small freckles, mixed now with splattered blood expelled with her dying breath. Long eyelashes. Soft, auburn hair. He saw himself in her eyes, glistening. Her body stilled, but those eyes remained open, staring at him. Accusing him.

She'd been attacking him. Trying to kill him. It couldn't be her. It had to be a trick. But he knew that face. He touched it. There was no makeup, no illusion.

"Rew!"

He looked up.

Anne was running toward him, her hair streaming behind her, unbound, tangled. Her clothing was filthy with blood and sweat, her eyes hollow from exhaustion.

"I heard the shouts. Are you all right? You're covered in—" She came to a skidding stop. "Blessed Mother, what is that? It that… me?"

"It is you," he mumbled, his voice a harsh whisper. "It was you. I thought it was you. I feared... You attacked me."

"You killed me?"

"I—Wait, no. You were trying to kill me. I thought... King's Sake, I thought I'd killed you. I hadn't meant to, but you thrust at me, and... I didn't mean to, but it's not you. I thought it was. I thought I'd just killed you. I'm not making any sense. None of this makes any sense. I was so scared... But it's not you."

Anne walked closer and stopped above her own body. She stared at it uncomfortably.

Rew stood, and they were both speechless for a long moment.

"The fraemoth," she told him. "It found your greatest fear—losing me. It knew the one person you could not fight. How did you overcome... Ah, its eyes. They are brown, and mine are blue. You saw that? Rew, how did you see that even in the dark?"

He stared at the fraemoth and did not reply.

Chapter Twenty-One

"So that was a fraemoth," muttered Zaine. "Even creepier than I'd imagined, but I still think it'd be weird to fight yourself."

"Aye, creepy, that it was," agreed Rew.

"Looked exactly like her, except for the eyes."

Rew didn't respond.

They were hiking an hour north of the encampment, their bodies weary and damaged, their souls worse. Cinda followed behind them like a shadow, present and silent. They did not speak to her. Raif and Zaine could normally be counted on to lighten the mood with their chipper banter, but they were both exhausted, barely stirring themselves to walk, much less putting any energy into their flirting and teasing. The thief wouldn't even look at the necromancer. The shine was off the apple, figured Rew, though he imagined in a day or two, Raif would stir himself. The ardor of a young man was like the rising sun. It might be hidden by storm clouds one day, but you could always count on it to rise again.

Anne and Rew walked close together but didn't know what to say to each other.

He'd killed her. He'd thought so, in those awful moments after plunging the hunting knife into her chest. The soldiers, everyone, had seen her attacking him, and had thought it was actually her. In the moment, no one had been able to tell the difference. Rew had known something was wrong, that it couldn't be her, but he'd thought... He grimaced. He thought he'd killed her, and it'd been the worst thing he'd ever experienced. The fraemoth had chosen its form well, and it'd almost worked.

Meeting his gaze with her bright blue eyes, Anne did not speak. She wouldn't claim to understand what it was like to think you'd killed someone you loved. She acted like he'd known it was not her despite Zaine's loud claims no one could have seen those eyes in the dark. Rew kept his mouth shut, refusing to consider what he'd known or not known. Anne dropped it as well, perhaps also understanding some pots were best left unstirred.

Damn the eyes of the fraemoth. He was going to have to live with that over his head for the rest of his life.

"Another week?" asked Zaine, breaking his reverie.

Glad to have something else to talk about—anything else to think about—Rew confirmed it would be another five or six days and then began telling the thief about every landmark and hillock he could recall between them and Mordenhold. Perhaps sensing he needed the distraction, Zaine let him talk and for once, held her own tongue.

TWO DAYS LATER, A PROFOUNDLY SWEATY, RED-FACED, FRUSTRATED-looking Duke Findley found them. The man was surrounded by twelve armsmen and a single spellcaster. Watching the rotund man waddle down the road would have been amusing, except the duke was obviously in distress.

When they reached him, he rubbed a thick hand across his glistening brow. "Finally, we found you."

"You've been looking?" asked Rew wearily. Three days earlier, they could have used the man.

The corpulent duke nodded then let out an exasperated sigh.

"Your riders found me in Yonn. I immediately set out looking for the rangers, and it didn't take me long to find them."

Rew frowned and gestured for the man to continue.

"Things in Mordenhold are... complicated."

"Figures," muttered Rew.

"The surrounding countryside is under attack by a horde of the Dark Kind. The king is nowhere to be found. Another day or two, and you'd be bumping up against the backs of those gray-skinned monsters. I've been searching non-stop to find you before you find them."

The party shed their weariness like a cloak.

"The king isn't in Mordenhold?" barked Rew.

Duke Findley shrugged. "I was there two days ago. He wasn't there then. Your rangers, Ang and Vurcell, took command of the city. The other rangers are serving as captains. They claimed if they abandoned the defense, the citizenry would lose heart, and Mordenhold would fall. They thought you'd understand, assuming you survived the Dark Kind. Both of them had faith you would."

Rew grunted and did not respond.

"I saw what they faced, and I agreed that without the King's Rangers, Mordenhold could collapse in days. You understand? The king and his legion are gone! Vanished. No one knows where they went."

"Can you take us there?"

Findley nodded. "That's why I came."

THE PURPLE AND GOLD VORTEX SPUN INTO EXISTENCE AND THEN opened a window into Mordenhold's throne room. Rew stepped through cautiously.

It'd been years since he'd walked down the cold slate floors of his father's throne room. Even as senior ranger, he'd strenuously avoided any task that took him to Mordenhold. He would communicate through Vyar Grund, and several times, he'd sent Tate or Blythe with Vyar through a portal when a representative from Eastwatch was required.

He didn't know if other senior rangers were allowed the same flexibility to avoid their superiors, but he was the son of the king. If the king didn't demand he attend, the king's administrators, even Vyar Grund, weren't going to push the matter. But years before, Rew had been a regular in that cold, empty hall. The chill in the room brought a jarring recollection what his home had been like and why he'd left.

The black slate floors were gashed by bright shafts of light that stabbed through the tall windows. The puddles of sunlight were dissected by shadow from iron bars guarding the hall's narrow windows. As a child, Rew had skipped over those thin shadows while he and his brothers and cousins tried to push each other onto them. The gulfs between the light were narrow, but with enough brothers clinging to you, you were always dragged into the darkness sooner or later.

The hall was quiet now. It usually was. Vaisius Morden was not the sort of king who welcomed petitioners. His nobles conducted their business in the provincial capitals, and the smartest ones dreaded the occasion to visit Mordenhold, which didn't mean none came. The hungriest, greediest men always sought power, no matter the danger. The king was not cruel, exactly. He just did not care for anything other than his own particular interests. Those had always been a mystery to Vaeldon's nobility, and they moved carefully lest they upset some plan they did not understand, but Rew understood. Better than anyone in the kingdom, he understood.

Iron sconces, as dark as the floor, studded the walls. They were unlit. The sharp light of day piercing the barred windows was the only illumination. At the end of the hall, the hard stone and iron finally surrendered to a thick, red rug that covered half a dozen steps to a dais, where a large onyx throne squatted. It looked uncomfortable, which was fine because it was rarely used. Behind it, a massive tapestry depicting a map of Vaeldon hung from the ceiling. Even when the hall was crowded, and the sconces were lit, and braziers were brought in for additional illumination if not warmth, it was difficult to take in the entirety of the map. It was fifty paces wide and just as tall. Rarely did the light in the room reveal the northern span of the map, where Mordenhold lay.

Rew peered at the map, straining his eyes, but he could not make out what lay above the capital. Northguard wasn't depicted there, he did not think. What was in that northern fortress? A pair of prisons, like Brian of the Brambles had claimed?

They'd never found the spellcaster, and two days after they'd left the enclosure, the party found they had trouble remembering much about him. He was old, they'd agreed on that, but little else. Raif thought he'd carried an axe. Zaine thought he had no weapon at all. Rew was certain the old man had a giant mace in his tent, but he did not bother arguing with the younglings about it. They all agreed the only combat he'd engaged in was through his imps. Anne did not recall healing the man, but they knew he'd been injured, and at the time Zaine had taken him to the hospital tent, Anne was inside. It was like a shared dream, and with dreams, the details were inconsistent.

It bothered Rew, but it seemed some of the things Brian of the Brambles had implied were truth. Mordenhold's throne room had an air of abandonment. The spellcaster had been right. The king and his legion were gone. Had they gone to Northguard like he'd suggested?

Rew heard the portal snapping shut and turned.

"It appears the king has not returned, but surely someone noticed the black legion leaving? There are over fifty thousand men. My father may have slipped off unnoticed for a time, but you cannot march an army through the gates without people seeing them."

Duke Findley shrugged. "Aye, they were seen leaving. It's just not known where they went. Your rangers asked, and I was told they found no answers. You can question them about it if you like.

My time the last few days was spent looking for you, not your father."

"This is weird," declared Zaine. "All this time, coming to this place, in fear for our lives, and now... No one is here. It's completely empty. Do you think he's dead?"

"He wasn't dead when we were in Carff," reminded Rew.

"If someone killed the king, they'd be here," concluded Raif. He had a hand over his shoulder, grasping the hilt of his greatsword. "Perhaps he did go to Northguard."

Rew nodded.

"Where is that?" asked Findley. "Northguard, it sounds familiar, but—"

A great clanging racket rose, booming peals echoing down the stone hallways of Mordenhold.

"That's the alarm. The city is under attack," said Rew. "Come on."

He led them into the old, familiar halls of the keep. The fortress at the heart of Vaeldon's capital city was nearly as old as the kingdom itself, though the construction was new compared to the provincial capitals. Mordenhold was the first major project Vaisius Morden had undertaken when he'd been crowned king. Rew wasn't sure what the old man had been hoping to accomplish. Some grand design which was sung about by the bards? The keep was not that, but if the king had been going for gargantuan, dark, and unwelcoming, then he'd nailed it.

Granite, untouched through the centuries by damage or decoration, rose in a heap. The hallways felt more like tunnels, and it didn't help that they were rarely lit. Sunlight did stream in during certain times of day through bare windows, but the light was fleeting and moved with the sun. It disappeared hours before full dark behind the mountains that surrounded the city.

The city itself was large and crowded, thick with administrators, diplomats, sycophants, merchants, the black legion, and the even larger army of craftsmen who supported them. It was near in population to Carff, though more subdued. No one moved to Mordenhold because it was pleasant.

There were few good taverns.

Wind ripping across bare rock and the echoes of voices on stone were akin to the sea birds and babble of commerce in the southern cities, but while it felt forlorn, the place was secure. Had it ever been threatened, an invading army would have an awful time getting their way through the granite walls or up the looming battlements. Provided there was food to feed the mouths of the king's immediate staff, the keep would be almost impossible to assail, and if there was no food, portals could solve that problem easy enough. Not that it mattered. The true defense was Vaisius Morden himself.

If an army attacked him, each one of their fallen soldiers would become their enemy. The king could command a legion of the dead. It wasn't the kind of thing that encouraged others to challenge him.

Vaisius Morden could only bind the souls of people, though. He couldn't wrest the spirits of the Dark Kind back into their bodies. Had the king fled before the horde because he feared them? It wasn't his way, and he'd proven he was capable of facing the Dark Kind in the past. While his own magic was stunted against the creatures, he had a crypt full of bodies and power to draw on. Beyond necromancy, he could also invoke, enchant, and conjure. He had a company of spellcasters and an army.

Approaching the city walls, Rew began to get nervous. How many Dark Kind would it take to scare away Vaisius Morden?

The city walls weren't as thick as the keep's, and without the black legion in town, they would be largely unguarded. That wasn't unusual. The arcanists would claim the city had outgrown its original footprint, and that was why some of its citizens had fewer protections. They conveniently ignored that the death of each of those people would make the king more powerful.

It was no secret within the keep that if Mordenhold was ever attacked, the plan was not to try and save everyone. It was not the king's way, though many would have trusted the black legion to make a stand. If they were not on the walls, preparing to face the horde, where had the black legion gone? What use were they except to confront the Dark Kind?

Grimacing then turning and speaking to her for the first time in days, Rew asked Cinda, "What do you feel?"

"No one is dying yet. Today, that is. I can feel an echo. It's been bad here in the last days. Maybe not as bad as what we faced, but they've got a lot more people. Findley was right. They've been pressed. There were villages within a few leagues of here?"

Rew nodded.

"Not anymore."

Rew grunted and began to lead them out the open gates of the keep, into the city, and to the exterior walls that surrounded it.

"It's worse to the north, Ranger. That's where he is."

"We'll worry about that... soon. Not now."

"He's not here. There's no reason for us to be here, either. We should go. Findley can open another portal and—"

Rew spun and stared into her emerald eyes. She met the look, not backing down.

"We're going to the wall, and we will help if we can."

For a long moment, she just looked back at him. A smirk. A touch of insolence. Outright defiance. Acceptance. He would have been happy to see any of those expressions, but her face was blank, dead and emotionless.

Finally, she simply shrugged.

He turned and began walking again. Dead. She still lived and breathed. Her heart beat, but did that make her alive? Was she already gone?

Giant siege machines, placed on the outside walls of Mordenhold, cranked to life. An impressive trebuchet groaned and squealed. Then, there was a heavy smash, and over the rooftops of Mordenhold, Rew could see a giant section of masonry launched into the air, spinning awkwardly before disappearing outside of the city.

So many Dark Kind they were using siege machinery against them? The black legion, evidently all of the spellcasters, and the king himself, gone? King's Sake. Rew shook himself then mouthed, "Blessed Mother."

He scratched his beard and figured he was going to have to learn some new curses.

The ranger led the party through the rigid streets of Mordenhold. The city was laid out on a strict grid, though buildings varied in height, and it wasn't uncommon for bridges to span the alleys and roadways below them. The mountains had been carved away in brutal hunks, though not even the art of the most industrious engineers could completely tame the harsh terrain. The streets were straight but rose and fell on the folds of those mountains. In some areas, buildings appeared to soar along the spines of ridges, and in others, they huddled hidden in the bottoms of valleys.

The majority of construction was dark granite, like the keep where the king ruled. The stone was available and sturdy. The people were just as hard. They might not know the uncomfortable details of how Vaisius Morden had sustained his soul, but they knew what kind of ruler each of the Mordens had been. The king expected complete obedience and gave little in exchange.

Though, the freedom from his demands had allowed certain sectors of the population to thrive. Vaisius Morden's casual brutality brought a certain kind of peace to Vaeldon and a cold justice that prevented most from testing the laws of the land. Up until now, none of the citizens of Mordenhold had to fear an attack.

Normally, the streets were filled with men and women going about their business and the business of the kingdom. Men wearing gray chainmail and the black tabards of the king's legion would be speckled amongst the crowd like pepper in a soup, but the black legion was gone, and the people had either fled or were in hiding.

As they got closer to the exterior walls, Rew saw many of

those people had been conscripted. Men, and not a few women, were arranged in clumps atop the granite barrier. Some of them had chainmail that must have been looted from the legion's armory. All of them were carrying new swords, spears, or axes. One thing about Vaisius Morden, he didn't let his soldiers want for any weapons. Mordenhold's forges were as notorious as its king.

Even at a distance, you could tell if a man knew the use of his weapon. The people on the walls did not, but as they got closer, Rew saw others wearing the dark browns and greens of foresters, rangers who must have gathered with Ang and Vurcell south of the city. They'd come when there was need.

They would be deadly fighters, all, but they were used to combat in small groups, in the wilderness. They weren't trained to hold a wall during a siege. Rangers, bakers, tailors... Rew dreaded what they would face.

He approached the main gate to the city and, without being challenged, climbed a stairwell to the turrets that bracketed the gate. The view was astounding and disheartening.

The mountains around Mordenhold clawed the air in dramatic, beautiful spires. The stone was framed by heavy forest at its base and crowned on the highest peaks with glistening snow which had survived the first months of spring. Brilliant azure sky framed the peaks, a setting which made them sparkle like diamonds.

It was a raw, untamed land that surrounded the city, except for wide roads which had been gouged through the landscape and angular blocks in the deepest valleys where settlements had been established to provide food and resources for the capital. There were dozens of those, perched in narrow gullies or clinging to the sides of the ridges with gentler slopes. Anywhere flat enough to farm or to conduct other industry had been colonized, though in the sharp mountains around Mordenhold, there were few enough of those places.

Most of the food, clothing, and other supplies in the city came down those hard roads from the provincial capitals. Merchants amassed fortunes selling goods and getting paid in the king's gold. It was the only way to manage the impractical city, by the crown financing life in the difficult land, but the practicality of supporting the place wasn't why Vaisius Morden had built his capital there. He'd done so because the mountain passes around Mordenhold were a natural defense that made attacking the city nearly impossible.

Approaching armies would have to pass through narrow defiles which could easily be ravaged by stones thrown from the walls. There was nowhere outside the range of those weapons to gather and muster sufficient strength to make a sustained assault upon the gates. Invaders could not live upon the land, and unless they had extensive supply chains, they couldn't conduct a long siege.

The mountains were a playground for spellcasters. They could topple towering rock formations onto attackers. They could conjure beasts to block the narrow roads. There were enchantments set for leagues around which served as traps, though none of those enchanters seemed to be around at the moment to activate the snares.

Rew gazed out at an approaching horde of Dark Kind, thousands of them coming down the road, some scampering along the rocky ridges. They were poised to take brutal losses.

He looked down the wall at the siege machines, surprised to see that they even worked. In the two hundred years since Mordenhold had been established, he wasn't aware of it ever being attacked. It was suicide to face the black legion on their home terrain, and that was before you factored in Vaisius Morden.

As he watched the Dark Kind, Rew wondered. Was the security of the city and the keep at the heart of the reason Vaisius Morden had selected this place as his capital? Or was it something else, something to the north?

Another of the hulking siege machines cranked to life, and with a rumbling groan, its arm swung forward and then crashed into the frame, launching another giant chunk of granite masonry wobbling through the air. The stone soared high above the rocky ground below then landed with a crash and tumbled across the hewn roadway, smashing through a column of Dark Kind. Scores of them were crushed immediately, dozens more injured from flying debris or their fellows fighting to get out of the way, but the column kept marching.

Valaan flew like cattle dogs along the outskirts, instilling fear and discipline in the approaching narjags. It worked, and the creatures kept marching over their fallen brethren, kept coming toward Mordenhold.

Several more of the siege machines on the walls were being cranked backward to fire, and Rew was sure they would unleash devastating casualties when they launched, but most of the devices were sitting idle. They were either broken, or more likely, they didn't have the engineers available to operate them.

Rew grimaced.

Not just engineers. There weren't enough able-bodied citizens to operate the things even if they knew how. Hundreds of men and women stood on the walls, but the walls around Mordenhold were massive, and the people were scattered in sparse clumps, like shoppers in the market half an hour before it opened.

If all of Mordenhold's siege machines were working, approaching the city would be nearly impossible, but of the dozen Rew could see, he only saw movement on three of the big devices. With a determined opponent that didn't care about its losses, that wasn't enough.

Zaine leaned over the battlement, staring at the approaching Dark Kind. "It feels like we've been under siege this entire journey, doesn't it? Every step since Carff, we've been tested by these things. Each league, we've had to fight our way north. I'm getting rather tired of it."

Rew grunted and did not respond.

"She's got a point," remarked Raif. "It has been one long siege. What does it mean? When does it end?"

"It means we need to find Ang and Vurcell," Rew told them, "and it's going to end when we end it."

———

THE TWIN RANGERS WERE SEVERAL HUNDRED PACES DOWN THE WALL, puzzling over a trebuchet that had a shattered chain.

"Can it be replaced?" they were asking a man who was wearing a thick, leather apron.

The man rubbed his scarred hands together and nodded grimly. "Give me a few hours, and I can replace this broken link. I can see several more that'll shatter under any sort of strain, though. Might be three days to repair them all. You've got to understand, no one keeps chain this thick lying around, unless the black legion has a stockpile stored somewhere that I don't know about."

"Not that we've found," replied Ang with a disgusted grunt. "In three days… Pfah, we don't have that much time."

The man, a blacksmith evidently, worked his lips, as if chewing the inside of his cheek. "I been all over these things as thorough as I could in such short time, but I've never worked on these machines before, and I'm guessing as much as I'm knowing. I'll tell you this. Don't trust the legion's blacksmiths with any work you care about. I—"

"It's not your fault," assured Vurcell, gripping the man's arm. "Blessed Mother, another engine would have made a difference, though. You're sure there's not parts you can scavenge from the others?"

"That's how I got these four—sorry, three—working. I'll look again, but it's been years since anyone's been over this stuff proper. The chains are in bad shape, but the ropes and arms are even worse. Some of these devices'll be more dangerous to us than the Dark Kind if we try to use them."

Shaking his head, Vurcell replied, "No, you're right. Let's not waste the time. I want you between the three we have working and doing your best to keep them that way. Anything you need, let us know, and we'll find... We'll do what we can."

The blacksmith scampered away, headed down the wall toward where a group of men were awkwardly trying to load their trebuchet with another block of stone. They were sweating, swearing, and trying to maneuver the stone with brute force and thick sticks used as levers. Rew couldn't see how they'd gotten the big rock into place to begin with. Had they torn down that building? There had to be an easier method than they were attempting, but evidently, they didn't know it, and neither did he.

Ang glanced at Rew and gave the former senior ranger a weary smile. "I'm glad you made it."

"We could have used your help," remarked Rew, unable to keep his mouth shut. Ang and Vurcell hadn't known how hard he and the others had been pressed. They couldn't know how close of a thing it'd been.

Vurcell scrubbed his lips with the back of his hand. "I know. They needed us here, too. The week before Duke Findley found us, the farming hamlets came under attack. Ang and I, and the others, waited a few days to see if the king would protect his territory. Nothing happened. We sent a messenger to Mordenhold, knowing it might give us away, but Rew, no one was here. The black legion, the spellcasters, they were all gone. At first, we thought they'd withdrawn to the keep and were sequestered there. We know now that wasn't the case. The king abandoned Mordenhold. As the Dark Kind continued to pour into the region, we decided we had to do something, even if it meant exposure. Even if it meant we couldn't come when you called."

Rew grunted.

"The rangers began mustering the hamlets and directing the people to Mordenhold. We knew we had to get as many people behind the walls as we could. Others were too far away, and we sent them from the area. South, though I'm not sure that was wise now. You didn't... I suppose you didn't see any of them?"

"Where did the black legion go?" questioned Rew.

"North," replied Vurcell. "Northguard, I guess, though not even the administrators and courtiers know why."

"I've some idea," muttered Rew.

Another of the huge trebuchets thumped, and another giant hunk of stone went flying over the wall. They all watched its arc until it crashed down amongst the Dark Kind, killing scores, but there were so many more of them.

"This isn't enough."

"We know," acknowledged Vurcell.

"Why would the king abandon his capital?" questioned Raif.

"Because if no one is here to defend it, all of these people will die," answered Cinda. "The king left Mordenhold unguarded for a purpose. If all of the citizens of this city were to die, Vaisius Morden would ride an incredible swell of power that'd be multiples greater than what I felt in Jabaan or Carff. He'd have access to a literal army of bodies he could raise. They'd be fresh, strong. The king... Blessed Mother, he wants Mordenhold to fall."

"Ranger," declared Zaine, "I am beginning to dislike your family."

Chapter Twenty-Two

"We evacuate the city," declared Rew, "through the portal stones and portals if we can find enough spellcasters to open them. We have to get these people out of here."

"These are their homes, Rew," protested Ang. "It won't matter how strenuously we tell them we can't hold the walls. They won't listen, or if they do, it'll be too late. There are, what, three quarters of a million souls here? Some fled, but we brought in more from the hamlets. Mordenhold has the largest collection of portal stones in the kingdom, but it will take days to move so many bodies through them, even if they started lining up right now."

"Two days," instructed Rew. "You've got two days to get them through. Task the rangers with it. They can deputize anyone they need to organize the departure and liaise with whoever is on the other side of the portal. As agents of the king, the rangers have the authority to demand whatever they need from recalcitrant nobles. We'll need their help to receive all of these people, and it'll take too long to ask. Have Duke Findley and Duke Vincent portal to any rangers still in the field. Commandant Eckvar if he's got anyone physically able, Blythe, the recruits, all of them. Bring them here and begin evacuations within the hour. I'll make sure the keep is expecting you and has the way prepared to the portal stones."

"I'll give everyone the good news," said Vurcell. He looked out toward the mountain pass where another giant stone had been lobbed and was smashing into a rocky ridge, bursting a shower of debris that rained a deadly hail down on the Dark Kind below. "Good shot, but we're not going to have a breath to spare. Blessed Mother, there are too many of them."

Rew turned to Raif. "I need you commanding the wall. It's your responsibility to get us the two days."

"Me?" squeaked the fighter. "How am I going to get anyone to—"

"Show them your sword, lad, then tell them what to do. Berserkers don't ask permission."

Raif snorted, but he immediately began looking up and down the wall, assessing his resources, and silently mouthing curses because once the rangers left the walls, he wouldn't have much to work with.

"I'll see to the hospitals," offered Anne.

Rew nodded. The empath knew what to do. Whatever healers were in Mordenhold would immediately recognize the skill and experience she brought.

"I'll help my brother," said Cinda.

Rew shook his head. "No, lass, I've got another idea for you. Vaisius Morden is gone, but his crypt is still here. It's his largest."

Rew didn't know if Cinda could still smile. Her lips didn't move, but the sparkle in her eyes brightened, and she gave him a curt nod.

"The door is probably locked," mentioned Rew.

He glanced at Zaine. The thief was still cold-shouldered toward Cinda, but they were in Mordenhold now, and they didn't have time to be upset with each other, no matter what had happened.

"On it," said Zaine. She drew one of her gleaming silver

poignards and twirled the deadly weapon in her hand then glanced at the necromancer. "Shall we?"

Turning from the swarming Dark Kind, Cinda replied, "Yes. Let's go, there's no time to waste."

They began trotting off, but Zaine stopped. Over her shoulder, she asked, "Ranger, what will you do?"

He lowered his hands to his side. Without realizing it, he'd crossed them over his chest. His heart was hammering, and his breath was coming in shallow draws.

He cleared his throat then answered, "The people of Morden-hold are used to a Morden commanding them from the throne. Since my father is gone, I suppose I ought to go take a seat. I don't like it, but it's the only way to get this evacuation moving."

Zaine's jaw fell to her chest. Anne stumbled where she'd already started down the stairs, and Raif let out a low whistle.

"I want regular reports from everyone," instructed Rew. "Use the rangers when they arrive as messengers, or Zaine. Raif, you have to hold this wall. Get more strong backs from the city if you can find them. Have Ang and Vurcell empty the armory. Do you understand? You have to hold."

The fighter nodded.

"Cinda, there'll be a time…"

"Of course," she said. Then, she and Zaine started off.

"Good luck, Rew," offered Raif.

The ranger looked toward the keep and did not respond. King's Sake.

He supposed that would be His Sake, now.

THE SMOOTH, ONYX THRONE WAS BITTERLY COLD, LIKE A GLASS FILLED with water and left outside in a freeze. He felt the chill through his trousers and moved his hands after resting them uncomfortably on the wide armrests.

There were ranks of braziers holding unlit timber which could be set alight. The fires would burn has high as a man, blazing forth energy and heat, but it would take days to warm the cavernous room, and they didn't have days.

So instead, Rew pulled his cloak tight about himself and avoided touching the throne with his skin. Perhaps it wasn't kingly, but he did not feel like a king. He felt like a child who'd snuck into his father's room, and he sat upon the man's chair, pretending to be him.

He scowled and stood. He wasn't his father, and he didn't want to pretend to be. Vaisius Morden was not the example Rew aspired to. Vaisius Morden was not the king they needed. The ranger strode down the thick carpet that led to the dais and frowned as the audience stepped back, cowering in fear or surprise. Rew didn't know if the assembled notaries expected him to smite them or what, but he needed them, as insufficient as they might be.

Irremon, an invoker who'd been ancient when Rew had been a child in the creche; Hawn, an arcanist who could have been the other man's grandfather; and Vinelle, a stern woman who served as his father's chief steward. She was the only one whose age could be reliably guessed at. She'd been a senior servant when Rew had lived in Mordenhold, though he hardly recalled her. If she'd been as brittle then as she was now, he might have remembered, but it was hard to say. Everyone in Mordenhold was brittle. The harsh mountainous terrain, the cold winds, and the drafty granite keep made for difficult, unpleasant people.

He smirked. He supposed that after two centuries of drawing his hands through the beyond, manipulating the powers of death, Vaisius Morden no longer felt the cold, and his close advisors must have seemed like brilliant stars of life.

"My father has abandoned the city, so I will serve as her king," he told the two men and one woman who represented the rest of the staff. They were the three highest-ranking administrators anyone could find still inside the city. "My first, and perhaps only, instructions are to—"

"You mean to serve as a... temporary king?" questioned Hawn, the man's voice as dry and quiet as two sheets of parchment sliding against each other.

"No."

"Is your father dead?"

Rew shrugged. "He is not here in Mordenhold's time of need. Whether he's dead or not, he's abandoned the city, and Mordenhold and Vaeldon owe him nothing."

The invoker Irremon cleared his throat, and croaking like a dying toad, he rasped, "That's not the way our laws work, ah, M'lord."

Rew eyed the man. He'd been surprised to learn there were any spellcasters remaining in the city. There'd been none on the walls, prepared to defend the place. Evidently, Vaisius Morden had left a few of them who were too old and frail to make the journey to Northguard. Rew would use any spellcaster who could still muster a spark of high magic, particularly the invokers, but he'd also considered the possibility he might need to make some firm examples.

"I defy my father and declare myself king," said Rew quietly. "As he's offering no challenge, here in the throne room of our family, by our laws, I am the king."

"If there's a law like that, I'm unfamiliar—" muttered Irremon.

"It's new. I just made it by royal decree."

The spellcaster stared at him.

"You're his only surviving son," remarked Hawn. "Vaisius Morden will crown you when he returns, but there's a process. There's—"

"So you agree I will be the king, and the only thing we disagree about is the timing. I find it curious, then, you're beginning our new relationship with defiance of my authority," said Rew coldly. "I've been absent from the politics of this kingdom for some time, but one thing I believe you know about me is that I killed my three brothers to become the only surviving son. If I killed the most powerful spellcasters in the kingdom, members of my own family, how do you think I'll deal with traitors?"

Hawn swallowed. "No, you misunderstand. I was just—"

"You have my allegiance," said Vinelle, her voice like the blade of an axe after the old men's crumbling grumbles. "Whether or not your father placed the crown on your brow, we all recall when you lived here. We know who you are, Rew Morden. It's your right, following the Investiture, and I for one, won't wait for the ceremony. Perhaps my colleagues aren't aware of what's outside the city gates?"

Rew nodded in grateful acknowledgement of her pledge.

"You said there was one instruction you'd give?"

"We must evacuate Mordenhold."

"I'd hoped you'd say something like that," replied the chief steward. "The portal stones?"

Rew nodded again then turned to Irremon. "Along with any of your spellcasters still hale enough to open a portal."

"Duke Findley was—"

"He's gathering the rangers. They'll oversee the organization and evacuation of the city proper, along with our reception on the other side of the portals. Vinelle, I need you to prepare these halls and your people to shepherd the refugees to the portal room. Irremon, I need an inventory of our spellcasters and their capabilities. What they can do today, man, not what they once did. The past is dead as far as any of you are concerned. If they can manage a portal, I want them assisting in the evacuation. If they cannot, I want them on the walls. And, Hawn, I have a man, Baron Raif Fedgley, who is charge of the defense. I need your insight on what traps and wards have been layered around Mordenhold and how we can activate them."

The arcanist shuffled, leaning on a short cane which appeared to be equal parts affection and necessary to keep him standing. "If we activate the city's defenses, it will take us weeks to dig the passes back open. Your father and your ancestors never saw reason to—"

"Do you have any idea what is out there?" snapped Rew.

The arcanist shrugged. "A pack of narjags, I'm told. We've faced worse."

"There are thousands of them."

"Thousands of crude beasts that have no craft to breach our walls. They are dangerous, no doubt, but surely—"

"I killed a fraemoth less than a week ago. Have you faced worse than that?"

The arcanist mouthed the word fraemoth and looked stunned.

"Truly?" questioned Irremon. "Little is known of the frae-moths. Their appearance can be deceiving—"

"It looked to be one of my companions, a woman I am very close to. I thought I'd killed her. Even after the fight, I could not tell the difference between the two of them. I only learned it was not her when she appeared at my side and spoke to me. Does that match the descriptions you've heard?"

Slowly, the spellcaster nodded. "M'lord, if there is a fraemoth…"

"There's an army of Dark Kind outside of these walls. Thou-sands of them are already through the pass. They are operating strategically, with all the guise and skill of a human force, except they're willing to sacrifice anything to destroy us. Thousands of them, led by a fraemoth. I believe I'm the only man alive who's even seen one of those creatures alive," growled Rew. "It seems all the spellcasters less than half the age of this fortress are gone, along with every man in the black legion. Our siege machinery is in disrepair, and it's too late to call for help from our banner-men. Our entire defense rests on fewer than one hundred rangers and whatever cooks and cobblers we can recruit from the populace. This is hopeless. The city is lost, and our only chance to save the people is to evacuate. I expect you to get on it immediately."

Vinelle had already turned and was scurrying toward the doors, her voice rising to call to the staff hanging outside like they'd been eavesdropping. It seemed they'd heard enough. Rew could see running figures through the door on the far side of the throne room, not waiting for more specific commands.

The two old men moved with less urgency, but they were so old and their bodies so weak, Rew half-expected them to collapse before they even made it out the door. His orders given, what remained of his staff in motion, Rew wasn't entirely sure what to do next. Was that all there was to being king? Issuing orders, dealing out the occasional threat, and then sitting around and waiting?

Scratching his beard, he wondered what his father would do in these circumstances. He cursed. He knew what his father had done.

EVACUATIONS BEGAN IN FITS AND STARTS. THE HOUSEHOLD STAFF acted with speed and precision. Pathways from the entrance of the keep to the portal stones in the basement were cleared. Signs were put in place, and then people were stationed at various points to direct those who could not read and those who pretended they could not read so that they could sneak off and steal something.

The people of Mordenhold surprised Rew by their willingness to march in somewhat orderly lines toward the keep then disappear into portal stones to locations scattered all across the kingdom. For the common man, once on the other side of the stone, return might be impossible. They weren't going go get access to the portal stones again without royal decree, and the expense of travel to the capital was beyond the means of nearly everyone.

Watching the refugees beginning to trickle into the hallways, Rew had expressed surprise to Vinelle that they'd come so quickly. She'd told him he was a Morden, and the people in the capital had learned that when the king spoke, they didn't wait. Rew supposed that when the king could siphon power from any subjects he executed, there was incentive for him to mete justice ruthlessly, and an incentive for everyone else to jump to obey his law.

The spellcasters and arcanists had offered some resistance initially, as it turned out Irremon and Hawn weren't so much the leaders of the two groups but the oldest, which earned them a sliver of respect and an additional heaping of disregard. Respect for ones' elders no longer made sense when those elders were tottering old men who could barely feed themselves.

Evidently, the spellcasters and arcanists as a group expected the new king to be a spellcaster himself, but Rew was not. Use and knowledge of arcane powers were how those men convinced themselves they were better than everyone else, and Rew heard they were struggling to follow a man who they considered inferior.

Fortunately, when Rew met the first concentrated resistance, he was able to solve the matter by grasping the back of a conjurer's neck, and then smashing the man's face into a stone wall. The conjurer, in a moment of rash defiance, had summoned a very small imp. Without thinking about it, Rew had grabbed the summoning by its ankles and proceeded to beat the conjurer into submission with his own imp.

It wasn't a proud moment necessarily, and Rew was glad the children weren't around to witness it. Such a loss of temper wasn't the example he wanted to set for them or how he wanted to rule the kingdom, but it had worked. Evidently, the conjurer's own spell being turned against him was terrifically frightening to the other spellcasters. They might have thought they would have some room to maneuver with Rew since he had never developed his own talent, but they were wrong, and to their credit, they learned that quickly.

The child was always stronger than the parent. Rew told them that, and they believed him. After witnessing the spectacle of their injured peer being dragged off, the remaining spellcasters fell into line. But none of them were strong in their art, and Irremon's catalogue of their talents was a half-legible disaster. Mordenhold's spellcasters had never been forced to defend their city, and it was obvious.

With the ancient spellcaster at his side, Rew had scoured the older man's notes, and they'd assigned several spellcasters to the city walls, but most of the remaining magicians would be of no use. Rew questioned if that was all of them, and Irremon insisted it was. The king had taken everyone who had any life left in them, it seemed.

Luckily, Raif's defense of the city walls seemed to be progressing well enough even without spellcasters to support him. Rew hadn't found time to visit yet. The reports were terrible and filled with dire predictions of imminent collapse, but the Dark Kind hadn't breached the walls, citizens had taken up arms, and that was the best they could hope for.

Rew didn't know what was occurring deep in the bowels of the palace, in the crypt. Zaine had resurfaced, and she'd informed him with colorful detail how she'd managed to crack the lock and open the massive door which sealed the tomb, and that Cinda was now inside. She didn't give any details of what Cinda was doing in there, and Rew didn't ask. The necromancer had gotten uncomfortable to be around even when she wasn't ensconced inside of a crypt filled with a million dead bodies and hundreds of years of stored power.

The remaining rangers arrived in the city in a steady stream. Most of them made excuses to visit the throne room and pay their respects before joining the fight or shepherding the evacuation. The constant roar of battle outside, and the panicked stream of people coming inside, was enough to convince them not to linger, but the people saw them, and they saw the rangers' deference toward Rew. The rangers had a new king. The message was clear.

"Senior Ranger," said Rew solemnly when Ranger Blythe appeared with several green-looking recruits that Rew did not know. These were the men and women selected to replace Tate, Jon, Ang, Vurcell, and himself?

Blythe approached and clasped his arm, pumping it vigorously.

He asked her, "How fares the station?"

"Finally getting things in order after the disaster of the last Senior Ranger."

Rew snorted. The recruits' eyes boggled, and several courtiers, who were quicker than the others and realized what the comment meant, looked as though their heads might explode. With the last king, the jest might have gotten Blythe executed. Vaisius Morden wasn't known for his sense of humor.

Thinking perhaps he ought to signal a softer side after bashing that conjurer's face into the wall, Rew gave the senior ranger a grin. He scratched his beard, turning from her to the recruits. Had he ever been so young? Surely he'd still been in the creche at their age.

Blythe told him, "Sounds like you've been mucking up the capital nearly as much as you did Eastwatch."

He rolled his eyes. "You'd do better?"

"Couldn't do much worse."

"Talk like that will earn you a promotion. Perhaps to a position where you can have a big influence, like our records keeper? I'm sure the official logs would benefit from your extensive expertise and crisp penmanship."

"Someone said there was an army of narjags nearby?" questioned Blythe. "Where? I'd rather go off and face the lot of them alone than spend my days recording everyone else's notes. Have you seen Ang's handwriting?"

They both broke into smiles, and Rew drew her into a hard embrace. "It's good to see you."

"You as well."

"Unfortunately…"

"There truly is an army of Dark Kind outside of the gates?"

Rew nodded. "We're evacuating the city."

The recruits gasped in surprise. Blythe looked concerned, but she nodded understanding.

"I need you to liaise with the eastern dukes and barons. If they balk at receiving the refugees, if they don't provide for them as I expect, you'll be in charge of dragging the nobles into line."

"Don't keep me from the wall because we're friends," warned Blythe. "I heard what was out there. You need every good blade you can find."

"I need someone who knows the politics in the east and won't bend before what's left of the nobility there. I won't throw the refugees into a worse situation than the one they're in here."

"That'd be awful difficult to do," mentioned Blythe. Then, she shook herself. "Right, I agree. At the moment, the east is run by a hot mess of second and third sons, upstart spellcasters thinking they are warlords, and anyone else who has figured out how to raise a banner. Sorting through it all—"

"You have permission from the king to use your sword if you need help getting the message across."

The Senior Ranger smirked. "As you command, your kingship."

Shaking his head, Rew instructed, "Best get to it. We've already got the first ranks of fleeing citizens entering the portal stones. It won't be long before the people on the other sides figure out what's happening and how many more are coming. A new king, with no decree that I've ascended the throne, and their first knowledge of me is that I've lost Mordenhold…"

"We'll straighten them out," assured Blythe. She snapped her fingers, and her recruits fell in behind her sharply as she turned and began marching toward the portal stones.

Rew watched them go. Blythe, Ang, Vurcell, Jon, they'd never jumped to his commands so readily. He wondered what that meant for his future as the king.

"Rew?" asked Blythe from across the throne room.

He looked to her and raised a hand to still the other hundred or so voices that bubbled in the room as reports were made, questions asked, and the business of defending and evacuating the city was conducted.

"Is it true you beat a conjurer unconscious with his own imp?"

"Well, he didn't, ah, stay unconscious for a long time. Once they dragged him off to the infirmary, he got right back up after they put some smelling salts beneath his nose. I think he needed a little healing as well before he figured out where he was or what had happened. You can imagine the look Anne gave me."

Blythe's gaze rolled slowly across the others in the throne room who were listening avidly. They must have heard some version of the story by now but not from Rew's own lips.

"He deserved the beating?"

Rew shrugged and did not respond. How to judge such a thing?

"Good example for everyone else, then," said Blythe, her voice booming. "I don't suspect you'll have much more trouble with insubordination again, but if you do, I hope you don't mind a little advice from an old friend? If they don't listen to orders, then send 'em to the crypt, not the infirmary. You're the king, and your word is law."

"You've work to do, Senior Ranger."

"As you command, Your Majesty."

Chapter Twenty-Three

I t was the next day when Rew was finally able to revisit the
wall. On the way there, he'd had to pass winding throngs of
Mordenhold's citizens who were pressing in slow-moving,
sinuous lines toward the keep and the portal stones housed
within its bowels. The crowds were anxious, pushing, shoving,
and shouting at each other. The rangers, and anyone else they
could trust with a little authority who wasn't needed on the walls,
were doing their best to keep the peace, but it was a difficult chore
and fraught with small failures every time one's back was turned.

Some citizens had begun lining up as soon as Rew gave the
order, but initially, there'd been a level of resistance by others. As
word spread about the Dark Kind gathering outside, that resistance faded. When it was clear that the defenders on the wall were
going to leave within the next two days, regardless of who was
left in the city, the resistance turned into a rout.

But they couldn't move fast. Mordenhold had two dozen
portal stones, and they exited into a variety of places which
processed refugees at differing speeds. The portal room itself was
large but not huge. The hallways of the keep could fit ten big men
walking abreast, but there were hundreds of thousands in the city
attempting to leave. There were frightened children, the elderly,

and families hauling heaps of possessions on their backs or pushing over-laden carts with the items that had made their life.

Rew had wanted to order everyone to leave all of that behind, to bring only what they could fit into a pack on their backs, but when he'd gone out to observe the process, he decided to remain quiet, even though it slowed the evacuation. How to tell a craftsman to leave the tools behind they'd spent a lifetime earning? How to tell a mother to discard that package of food she'd brought for her children?

On the other side of the portal stones, Rew hoped the receiving nobles and their cities would be generous, but the truth was, he didn't know. Some nobles might force the refugees into lawless camps outside of their cities, or they might require labor or tithe. In time, if he remained king, Rew could straighten it all out, but there was no guarantee he would survive another day. He could give the people a chance to escape, and that was all he could be sure of.

None of the looks he received out in the streets or on the walls suggested anyone understood that difficulty. The Mordens, with all of their flaws, were strong. Evacuating the capital on his first day as king did not bode well.

But once within the keep, people kept relatively peaceful. They had confidence they were going to make it... somewhere. And while they might not like it, stories of how many Dark Kind there were had spread, and Vaisius Morden and his legion were gone. People understood that much. Those lined up outside were not as passive. They could hear the sporadic crash of the siege machines. They could hear the shouts coming from the walls. They could hear the cry of the Dark Kind.

The farther one got from the keep, the more panicked people were. Rew guessed they'd been the last to believe the city would truly fall. They thought Vaisius Morden, or his soldiers, or anyone would arrive and bolster the defenses. Realizing that wasn't going to happen was a harsh awakening.

Rew broke up three fights on his way to the wall, forcing irate citizens away from each other, sometimes out of the line and directing someone to take the offending party to the back. Halfway to the walls, he began to have serious doubts about whether he would be able to make it back inside of the keep himself.

He was the king, more or less, but he wasn't wearing a crown, and he didn't have a company of heavily armed soldiers and dozens of spellcasters around him. These people knew how the king traveled, and it wasn't with only Zaine for company.

When they reached the wall, Rew's heart fell. One of the three siege machines the defenders had been using had broken apart like a loosely tied sheaf of wheat spilled on the floor. Heavy beams and the long, sturdy arm of the thing were lying in a jumble like a game of sticks. There were bodies near it, just as broken.

The two remaining siege engines were still cranking back slowly and offering a steady barrage of masonry and debris to pelt the field of Dark Kind, but it took no more than a glance to see the damage they were doing was like trying to empty the ocean with a tankard. Tens of thousands of Dark Kind swarmed below, pressed against the wall like a restless tide.

"King's Sake," muttered Rew.

Zaine merely shook her head.

It wasn't until later he realized how ridiculous that sounded since he'd taken the throne, and how distraught their situation that Zaine hadn't commented on it.

The swarming narjags were lightly armed. Evidently, they hadn't encountered many victims to scavenge weapons from. They also didn't have proper equipment to attempt an assault on a walled city. The crude ladders they'd used in Valstock wouldn't reach more than a third of the way up these walls, and the narjags didn't have carpenters who could fashion sturdier ones.

Periodically, there would be a flash or an explosion, and magic would burst on the walls. The narjag shamans were casting similar spells to the ones that had destroyed the earthen berm

Brian of the Brambles' men had raised. Fortunately, the walls of Mordenhold were enchanted against such attacks, and so far, the Dark Kind hadn't figured a different spell that could cut through the defenses.

If it'd been a conventional siege, the Dark Kind didn't have the resources to defeat even a token defense, but what they did have were numbers and a cold disregard for their losses. Without ladders, grappling hooks, or tools to build a ramp to the wall, they used their bodies.

Sourly, Rew complained the Dark Kind had learned the tactic from the earlier battle at the earthen fort. He and Zaine's eyes had met, and Rew's heart sank. He realized it was true, and he worried what else the foul creatures had discovered.

Already, Rew could see several ramps of crushed, pulped narjags that had been trampled into a slick, oozing mass like a stairwell. In less than a day of combat, they'd reached the battlement. Raif had his men arranged in strategic pockets where they could defend the tops of the ramps. He was making good use of the black legion's extensive armory, but the fighter was short on bodies and had left long unguarded stretches along wall. A few men roamed those open spaces, working in pairs, facing any narjags that managed to climb the stone. It appeared some had made the difficult ascent but not many.

Where the ramps already reached the top, the fighting was fierce, and when a narjag fell, others hauled the body down and flung it to the side, expanding the width of the rising piles of flesh. An endless sea of narjags waited to fill in whenever one fell. The creatures at the front, whipped into a froth of battle frenzy, didn't seem to realize they were being sacrificed to build a road for their fellows behind them. They thought only of hunger and anger, and they charged up at the men, were summarily killed, and then tossed aside like a grisly paving stone.

When a man fell, there was no one to replace him. Several hundred defenders facing tens of thousands of Dark Kind, it was a wonder the men hadn't turned and fled. Then again, if they did, where would they go?

Sporadically, flashes of light or ragged bolts of heat would splash against the walls, but in a lone incident of good fortune, it seemed the walls had been enchanted to rebuff such attacks, and they exploded several paces away without harming anyone. The Dark Kind had magic, but they couldn't do any more with it than the ancient cadre of spellcasters that had been sent to Raif. Both sides lobbed weak attempts that did little more than illuminate the gray, cloudy day.

It took Rew and Zaine some time, but finally, they found Raif and pulled him from a pack of men who were taking turns standing at the top of a ramp, slaying the narjags that crawled up the unsteady pile.

Raif was covered in equal parts sweat and blood. His armor might have a few extra dents in it, but it had gotten difficult to tell. He hadn't suffered any serious injury yet. The lad stood panting, his eyes glassy as he slowly came down from his battle fever.

Zaine leaned forward and mopped his face with her sleeve, smearing the sweat and the blood but keeping it from dripping into the lad's eyes. She retrieved a ladle from a water barrel that had been placed for the soldiers and tipped it into Raif's mouth. The fighter drank, his chest heaving, his body slowly withdrawing from the madness of a berserk.

Men passed them and gave the lad a nod or a tight salute. He was earning their respect. They didn't look at Rew. He hoped that was because they figured he was just another soldier and not because they knew he was king.

Claimed to be king.

He wasn't comfortable with that situation, but it'd been the cleanest way to force the administrators in Mordenhold to expedite the evacuation, and it backed up the rangers and others who were negotiating with the nobles on the other sides of the portal stones. Someone had to take command to get anything done, and before he'd sat himself upon the throne, he couldn't think of who else might be able to pull it off.

Raif cleared his throat and rubbed at his chin. "How long did you say you needed us to hold?"

"Two days," replied Rew.

Frowning, the fighter shook himself. "And how long has it been?"

"One day," said Zaine, her voice thick with concern. "We, ah, just got here yesterday."

"A bit less than a full day," acknowledged Rew. "We got here yesterday evening."

Raif drew a deep breath and slowly released it. "In the stories, this is where I'd tell you we'd hold, and somehow, we would."

"Aye, in the stories."

"We can make it until evening," said Raif, holding a hand above his eyes and glancing up at the midday sun. "If it's like yesterday, they'll pressure us through the night. I... Pfah, I'm losing track of time. I don't think I've slept since we got here. I wish I could say something else, but the evacuation needs to be complete by sunset. By then, they'll have twice as many of those ramps reaching the battlement, and I simply don't have the men to cover it all."

"What if we got you more men?" asked Zaine.

"Do you have more men?"

"The rangers..." Zaine glanced at Rew. "Could we spare a few?"

"A few, sure. That'll slow the evacuation, though. You both know nobles. If an agent of the king isn't standing there demanding they take the refugees, do you think they'll keep the portals open or close them from the other side and pretend ignorance? Without the rangers strong-arming the nobles, the evacuation might stall completely."

Shaking his head, Raif leaned against a stone crenellation. "It doesn't matter. A few men and women, even if they're rangers, may as well be none. It's a matter of numbers, not of skill. Is there any chance the rangers can shake some soldiers out of those nobles on the other sides of the portals? Spellcasters would be better, just a few of them could buy us time, but I'll take anything I can get. A few companies of fresh bodies may get us through to tomorrow, at least. If spellcasters could blast away these piles of narjags…"

Rew shook his head. "No one is coming."

"Did you even ask?" queried Zaine.

"Ask who? Most of the spellcasters who don't have a title would have pledged loyalty to my brothers. If they managed to survive Jabaan and Iyre, then Carff would have finished them off. Don't you remember? Valchon killed every invoker in the city so no one could flee his maelstrom. There ought to have been scores of the spellcasters in Mordenhold, of course, but my father…"

"Right," muttered Zaine. "The nobles themselves? They're all spellcasters."

"Any noble you bring in will be dangerous," warned Raif. He propped his gore-covered greatsword against the wall beside him and shoved his sweat-damp hair back from his face. "A duke, even a baron, will be dreaming of taking the throne themselves if they see the state we're in. They're as likely to attack us as to help us. Phah, some already have. Remember the assassin Baron Barnaus sent? It's no use. You're right. There's not time to collect anyone, even if we found someone with the skills we need. I'll die on this wall if I have to, but I can't promise to hold until tomorrow. There are simply too many of them and too few of us."

"There's Cinda," said Zaine. "If she called more wraiths… Stop, Rew, I know. I know it didn't go well last time. There's a risk it will happen again, but what choice do we have?"

Raif leaned his forehead against the pommel of his weapon, and speaking into the steel, he said. "If we trust my sister against the king, then we must trust her now as well. I'll talk to her. This time—"

"There isn't a 'this time,'" insisted Rew. "I won't let her do that again."

"What choice is there?" demanded Zaine.

"Calling the wraiths drained her power for days," retorted Rew. "That's power she needs to face the king. What use winning the battle if we lose the war?"

Zaine threw up her hands then pointed out toward the narjags. "We just passed the line of people trying to get to the portal stones. They won't be gone this afternoon. Not by tomorrow, either! It'll take them another two or three days to get out of here. Not to mention the thousands who are still in their homes, barricading the doors or just hoping it all passes over. We've got to do something! If not the wraiths, what about all those corpses down in the crypt? A few regiments of those will buy us time to evacuate."

"The narjag shamans are casting spells at us, which means there ought to be a fraemoth out there somewhere. If there is, Cinda's magic may be of no use. We can't waste the power she's drawing down in the crypt. I want to win this fight as much as anyone, but it's not the true battle. Cinda was right about one thing. Our quest is the king. It's all pointless if we expend ourselves getting to him."

Zaine crossed her arms over her chest. One hundred paces down the wall from them, there was a thump, and another of the Dark Kind's wobbling globes of purple light shattered on the battlement's enchantments. "We have to do something."

"I'm thinking."

"We don't have time for that," growled Raif, standing back up and grasping the hilt of his greatsword.

Rew reached out and grabbed the boy's arm. "Don't be foolish. We can't win this battle by fighting mindlessly. Think! The Dark Kind tried to pin us down days south of here. Why? Why did the fraemoth come there, and why hasn't it shown itself? The narjag shamans are casting spells. There must be another one, right?"

Raif shrugged, his armor scrapping harshly.

"It was all guesses and dreams," replied Zaine. "Most of what we thought we knew came from that spellcaster, Brian of the Brambles, but where is he now?"

"Dead," muttered Raif.

"He can't be. We never found his body," insisted Zaine. "He and his men fled somehow, or maybe they really were a dream. Maybe we imagined it all like these conjurers imagine the imps and the Dark Kind."

"Brian was real enough, and that fraemoth was real enough," said Rew, putting his hands on the battlement and watching the swirling army of narjags below. "But why was he there? Why did the fraemoth come for me?"

"To stop us from getting to Northguard?" guessed Zaine. "You think that's what we should do now? Flee north and face your father?"

"Does it matter?" asked Raif. "We're not going anywhere. The city is surrounded, and… You don't mean to flee through the portal stones, do you?"

"Is there one that connects to Northguard?" questioned Zaine.

"No. Portal stones can't reach that place," said Rew, his gaze fixed on the grim army below. "No portals can reach North-guard's keep at all, actually. The mountains around it are thick with veins of copper. High magic is virtually impossible. It used to be the same here, but they mined out the copper."

"Well, unless you have a good idea, I think it best I get back to it," growled Raif, straightening up and lifting his greatsword to rest it across his shoulders. "The men have been cheered seeing a commander willing to throw himself into the fray. I don't think they witnessed that often around here. It might hearten them to see the new king dirty his blade if you have time. Could stiffen their resolve. Buy us a few more hours."

Rew shook his head. He was drumming his fingers restlessly on the hard stone. They'd mined all of the copper from beneath the city. Perhaps he could use that. Or maybe they were right. Maybe their only choice was to unleash Cinda.

He growled then told the fighter, "I can't now. I need to go see your sister."

An eerie, green-tinged white glow suffused the frosty air of the crypt. Rew saw no source of the light, and the only explanation he could think of for why it was so much colder beyond the looming copper doors of the space was uncomfortable to consider.

At first, he'd thought Cinda was sitting cross-legged atop a carpet, but instead, it was a pile of burial shrouds. When he came beside her, he saw some were ancient, and at least one appeared quite new. It was even less comfortable to think about where she might have gotten that.

The girl had her eyes closed and looked to be meditating. She sensed his approach, though, and murmured, "I haven't felt a sudden wave of death. My brother still holds the wall?"

"He does."

"For how much longer?"

"Not much."

"How much longer until the evacuation is complete?"

Rew shifted then told her, "I don't think it will be complete. Not in the time Raif and the others can realistically hold on. I could put every ranger in the city on the wall, every man with strength to lift a blade, but the rangers are few and the citizens of Mordenhold unskilled. The narjags are like the sea. I don't think there's a scenario where we can hold for much longer."

"Yet you fear to unleash the wraiths."

He nodded. He didn't know if she could sense the movement, but it seemed she understood. He asked her, "If you were to call to them… could you control them better"

"Worse," she admitted. "The wraiths I called were from the barrowlands. If I were to bring wraiths here, they'd be of Mordenhold. I've been… They have a different flavor, you could say. I don't know if it's corruption from your father, or something else, but my commands will have to be brief. They'll still be effective, Ranger. If there are no other choices, then we must do what we must do."

"No," he replied. "No wraiths."

"What shall we do, then?"

"We can't win this fight."

"You don't know that."

"If you use the power you've found here, will you be able to face the king?"

"If you don't come to ask me to fight, then are you here to ask my permission to flee? You're the king, Ranger. That is your decision."

"No. I—"

"You're hoping I have some idea that hasn't occurred to you?"

"I'll listen if you've got one," replied Rew with a grunt. "Have you… learned anything down here? About something other than the wraiths?"

Cinda's eyes opened slowly. "Why does your father want you?"

Rew blinked. "He needs a strong body to continue his life. I defeated my brothers, proving myself. Without me—"

"You are cunning, but Vaisius Morden will smother your personality and intelligence with his own. Beyond that, you know what he attempts, which makes you uniquely dangerous to him. You're capable of high magic, but your talent is undeveloped. He cannot know your strength. For all he knows, you might be like my brother, barren of the talent your blood is supposed to carry. He breeds us, Ranger. Like livestock. Like Eckvar's bear. Vaisius Morden breeds us to encourage the magical talent in our blood. You and your brothers more than anyone, but you're the unknown amongst your family, so why you? Why does he want you and not Valchon, Heindaw, or any of the others?"

"I defeated my brothers…"

"Vaisius Morden made the rules of the Investiture, and I don't doubt he'd break them anytime it's convenient. You proved yourself, but it's still a risk to him. Does your father take risks? There has to be a reason he wants you, and it has to be powerful enough it outweighs the fact you might have little talent for high magic."

Rew frowned and did not reply.

"Why does he want you?" Cinda stood, pushing her hands into the sleeves of her robes. "For hours, I've sat here and pondered that question. I think the answer may steer our course, but I don't know the answer. Anne might say it's because you're stubborn, but in fairness, your brothers were mighty stubborn as well. You're a survivor... but it's not your personality the king is interested in. He'll destroy what makes you, you. What were the others missing? What is it about you that Alsayer saw, that he believed gave you an advantage none of the other rebels in your family have claimed?"

"I don't know," admitted Rew.

"You're a ranger," said Cinda. "It's unique, amongst the princes."

"I don't think Vaisius Morden cares about how effortlessly I stalk through a forest."

"Probably not."

"Communion," said Rew with a hiss. He gripped the hilt of the longsword at his side. "I can communicate with animals—with all life—and my brothers could not. The king has lived for centuries. Brian of the Brambles told us, he's grown distant from life. Communion has to be the answer."

Cinda's eyes flicked down. "Others in your family have tried to use that sword, have they not? But they went mad?"

Rew nodded. "Erasmus corrupted them."

"But not you?"

Rew snorted. "I like to think he did not."

"I couldn't feel him," said Cinda suddenly. "You say his soul was trapped in that blade, but I couldn't feel it. It wasn't necromancy like I know it. I felt something, though. It was like a dream.

The spirit of your ancestor felt like I was in a dream. Did you feel that as well?"

Rew scratched his beard.

"There is a skill you have which I do not, that your brothers did not, a skill we can assume Vaisius Morden does not have as well. I think that something about the way you commune allowed you to wrestle Erasmus Morden when your ancestors could not. That's why your father wants you, why he did not take Valchon's body when he could have. The prince was the strongest in high magic. He was the final surviving heir, the proclaimed ones, that is. Valchon would have been the king's preference if it was about high magic, but it's not. It's about what you can do, and I think it's all starting to slide into place. Vaisius Morden needs your ability to commune to repair the tombs he locked his brothers in."

Rew scratched his beard. "Perhaps. That's a lot of guesswork."

"What else do we have?"

"That's the truth," said Rew. He frowned. "If it's me they are after, it's possible if we fled, the Dark Kind would follow."

"Possible, yes."

"We might save the city that way. It's dangerous, though, if we're wrong."

"That's not my decision, Your Majesty, but I will say this. If the city has no hope with us here, then we're wasting our lives staying and trying to fight. Our battle is at Northguard. Whether the Dark Kind follow us or not is unimportant."

"Your Majesty," Rew said with a snort. "Didn't think I'd ever hear you say that."

Cinda stared at him, and he would have given a finger—a hand even—to see her smile.

Rew crossed his arms over his chest and asked Cinda, "Are you able to tap into the well of power here? The corpses my father has stored…"

She shook her head. "There is no deep well of power here. No bodies, either. He's taken them, Ranger. There's a bit of latent energy I've been collecting. This is a true temple to the Cursed

Father. It seems to… funnel death into this place. There are things I could learn just sitting here and feeling what he's done, but not in time to help us here or against your father. He is the Cursed Father, a true god of death. I am sure of that now."

"There is no Cursed Father," retorted Rew absentmindedly.

Cinda shook her head. "You're wrong."

"So if he took the power from here with him…"

"I cannot face Vaisius Morden strength against strength," stated Cinda. "I have a few months of practice. When I've performed my greatest feats, it was with a fraction of the power he commands. I can feel the echo of what was here. It's like a yawning chasm. The power in Jabaan, Carff, they're all dwarfed by this place. The books I spent those weeks reading were a single page in the book of his own knowledge. Ranger, I can feel what he's done in this place, and I cannot defeat him. Not in a direct fight."

Rew cringed.

"You've always known it would be this way. You've always known the only way would be to…"

He looked away.

"I thought I'd sacrifice myself in some grand display of virulent necromancy, a conflagration so powerful we'd both be destroyed. The books… I know the power I'll hold in my own death. I know I'll be something beyond this world, but it's not enough. I can see that now, but you've always known. Since Eastwatch?"

Rew's gaze fell to his feet, and he nodded. "I've known my father a long time. I suspected there was no power in this world that could surpass him."

"It's all right, Ranger," Cinda assured him. "What would we not sacrifice to defeat the king? But… what if it is not possible? What if we cannot do this?"

He looked at her. "I… I've considered that."

"We have to try, don't we? That is what you learned all those years in the wilderness, what you learned turning your back on

your family and the horror they've brought. It's not about them.
It's about us, and we have to try."

"You're right."

"What is your decision, then? Shall I take the walls and call the
wraiths, or do we slip away and run to Northguard?"

Looking around the cold, copper-sheathed room, Rew shook
his head. "I have a plan, but I'm not sure it will work."

"So we fight."

Rew crossed his arms over his chest and glanced around the
crypt then back at the young necromancer. "Our war is with my
father. We have to face him. Nothing else matters. We don't fight,
not exactly, but we might be able to buy the people some more
time."

"What is this final gamble of yours?"

Rew opened his mouth to tell her.

Cinda waved a hand and stooped to collect the belongings
she'd brought with her to the crypt. "No, don't bother telling me. I
don't want to spoil it before you tell Zaine. Let's go, Ranger. I
can't wait to see her face when you spew out whatever insane
caper you've concocted."

Turning toward the exit of the crypt, Rew put an arm on
Cinda's shoulder. "You jest, but I don't know the way. It might be
more likely to get us killed than to save us."

For the first time in weeks, Cinda laughed. "Ranger, we're
going to die. We won't all survive what's coming. I can feel it, like
looking into the future. Anne, Ang, Vurcell, they all sense it as
well. Look into their eyes, and you will know. Do you not feel it?"

"If I listened to what I felt in my gut, I'd still be in Eastwatch
having a cold ale right now."

Chapter Twenty-Four

The creche was a sprawling affair, like a cancer that continually encroached on its surroundings, consuming the hard, stone buildings and narrow streets that defined Mordenhold and drawing them into its ever-expanding circumference. The place, the story was, had started in an inn that Vaisius Morden the First commandeered as a place to raise and educate his children.

That he didn't raise his children in the massive keep he'd recently finished constructing was typically glossed over, but was an instructional bit of knowledge for those who considered it.

Over the generations, there were more children. There were more weapons masters, spellcasters, and serving staff. The wants of the creche rose on the back of the kingdom, which, once consolidated, proved to be an impressively lucrative organization. Vaisius Morden himself cared nothing for the baubles and totems of wealth that his domain brought in, but he cared deeply about power, and the products of the creche would be how Vaeldon's power marched on through the centuries.

But the finest confines imaginable still felt confining to those youths whose heads were stuffed full of their own importance. For a son of the king, who was being raised to wrest control of the kingdom through trickery, violence, and fratricide, rules were made to be broken. No length of lecture, no amount of punishment, was sufficient to keep the frothing spawn of the Mordens locked within the walls of the creche. While the creche's grasping tentacles snaked across the city, the reach of the future princes was greater.

It was sport, to them, to sneak out under the strictest guard, to explore the living city, to cause trouble, and eventually to sew their oats, planting a crop of future princes. They found the gambling halls, the dens of depravity, the stables of whores, and they drank everything that glinting gold coins could buy. They fought as well, testing themselves against mean thugs and even well-heeled merchants and nobles who were stupid enough to face them.

But for many of Vaisius Morden's children, the pleasures and foibles of the common and nobility only held their attention for so long because, after all, the pleasures of the common were common, and they were not. They were the blood of kings.

In the creche, they were students, and their teachers were the one group of people in the kingdom empowered to smack them into line. In their father's keep, they were shown polite deference, but their father's courtiers understood most of them would end up dead. It was never a good idea to anger a Morden, but when it came to the children, it could be just as dangerous to bind yourself to the wrong one.

Their teachers kept them at a distance to maintain authority. The people of the city were scared of them, and the staff of their father tried to avoid them to remain unentangled. They had difficulty making friends. It meant the denizens of the creche were drawn eventually to the one place they could be themselves. Arrogant, violent, alone.

They lurked in the tunnels that twisted beneath Mordenhold like the roots of some great, diseased tree. Those tunnels, the rumor was, had once been filled with massive veins of copper. Why Vaisius Morden built his city upon a wealth of magic-deadening metal wasn't clear, though the mountains for leagues

AC COBBLE

around were filled with the material. But the copper beneath the city was long gone, leaving gnarled caverns, narrow chutes, and snaking tunnels connecting it all. There were dangerous drops and tight squeezes that were difficult to return from and getting lost was easy.

It was the perfect place for young, adventurous youths to run wild, tormenting each other and learning to inhabit a world that was all their own.

Except the children weren't the only monsters in the tunnels. They called them cave bears, but the creatures had little resemblance to any bear which trod the soil beneath the sun above. These beasts were covered in thick, filthy fur. They had long, narrow bodies, which belied their incredible strength. Their legs ended in curving black claws, which had the ability to tear through rock.

It was often wondered if there was some ancient magic behind their power, but it was impossible to get close to one to study it. The things were ferocious hunters. They could not see well, but they could hear and smell, and if they sensed someone in their domain, they would come scrambling after them, keening a mournful wail.

Fighting and slaying the cave bears was a test of sorts, a coming of age for the denizens of the creche and the tunnels below. It was rare a boy left the creche into a princedom or the world without at least one cave bear skin stuffed in some forgotten closet, though it wasn't uncommon for the budding princes to overestimate their own abilities and to venture too deep into the caves and never return. Luckily, there were always younger brothers to fill any vacancies in the succession.

Less well known, even amongst the arcanists and weapons masters that raised the boys, was that quite often, when a lad went missing, it was because they had been lured too deep, or a clever sibling had somehow arranged a surprise encounter with a cave bear.

Eliminating a rival before it was time was against the few rules they were saddled with, but they had been raised to break rules, and you couldn't get in trouble if you weren't caught. A mauling by a cave bear was easier to pretend ignorance of than a knife in the back.

The network of tunnels also offered a way to move beneath the city undetected by tutors. There were a number of places the veins of copper had reached the surface. Some of the openings were blocked. Some were guarded. There were even a few places the network extended beyond the city walls, and there were openings which one could exit without coming within sight of the gates.

Secret tunnels that led from outside of the city into its heart were a security risk, but the rulers of Mordenhold throughout the years had taken precautions to ensure no enemies could approach from below.

Openings within the city had been sealed. Openings outside of the city had been hidden by both magical and mundane means. The main entrances were well-guarded and blocked by barriers that would be even more of a challenge than the city gates themselves. Huge volumes of rock were rigged to drop if necessary, completely sealing the exits. Enchantments had been laid in critical junctures, so no significant force could enter without alerting the king's spellcasters. Not to mention finding one's way through the twisting maze of tunnels while avoiding the cave bears was impossible without weeks of exploration.

In some terrain, sappers beneath the walls would have been a concern, but Mordenhold sat upon a foundation of solid granite, only pierced by the tunnels left from the copper. It would take more than the tools of man to undermine the granite and collapse one of Mordenhold's walls.

Evidently, the king felt secure enough he'd never bothered to fully close off the passageways. He'd left them open, a playground for his children. Maybe he'd understood, through his stolen memories, that those children needed an outlet. They needed a place to foment early plots against each other, to test themselves against something other than their instructors. The tunnels were a better place to do it than amongst the citizens of Mordenhold, or maybe it was just another way of sifting out the weakest of the brothers.

The difficulties of accessing the city through the tunnels was well enough known. They were a secret, but an open one. No army from Vaeldon would attempt such a feat, but the Dark Kind were not of Vaeldon. Could they be tempted into the tunnels and perhaps trapped there?

It was a long shot, but if Raif and his men couldn't hold the walls past sunset, and they still had hundreds of thousands of people to evacuate, and they couldn't use Cinda's talents for a number of reasons, and no help was coming from the kingdom's spellcasters and the black legion, there wasn't any other choice.

Rew told the others of the plan. He didn't tell them that if this didn't work, he intended to flee and leave Mordenhold on its own.

"Trick the Dark Kind into the tunnels and, I suppose, trap them there?" questioned Zaine. When Rew nodded confirmation, she allowed, "That sounds reasonable. What am I missing?"

"Bait," said Cinda, blinking owlishly in the light of day. They'd assembled half a block from the wall. It was the first time the necromancer had been out of the crypt in a cycle of a day and the first time Raif had been off the wall. Irremon and Hawn had joined as well, though they had to be carried to the location, and neither was contributing any valuable insight, so far. Continuing, Cinda surmised, "You believe that the Dark Kind are after you, and if they see you outside of the walls, they'll follow?"

Rew nodded again.

Raif shifted anxiously. "Showing yourself out there would be a risk, but the way they are climbing the walls, it won't be long before standing right here is as great a risk. The rangers have begun to join us, and that's helping, but an hour, two hours after dark, we're going to fail. I can feel it. I'm with Zaine. It sounds like it's worth a try unless I'm missing something?"

"There's no map to the tunnels," replied Rew. "They're dark, narrow, littered with places one could fall or put your weight on crumbling rock, and there are far more dead ends than open paths. It's easy to get lost down there. Some of my ancestors have marked the walls, which can help, but others have copied those marks to send people astray. You cannot trust what you see."

"But you recall the passages from your youth?" asked Anne. "You have confidence you could navigate them and find your way out?"

"No," replied Rew, "but I have to try."

He was going to leave Mordenhold. He wasn't going to fight. But he had to do something. He had to prove he was better than his father, or what was the point of it all?

"If you don't know the way out," warned Cinda, "then the risk is too great. We should put out efforts into slipping out of here and heading north."

"Why not ask one of the lads in the creche?" asked Irremon.

Rew blinked at the spellcaster.

The old man stared back placidly.

"The children in the creche?" questioned Rew. "Are they not... with my father? They are, aren't they? They were not on your inventory of spellcasters that you provided when we first arrived. I'm certain of that. I read the thing twice, and there wasn't a man or woman on there with fewer than seventy winters. You told me it was a complete inventory."

"Well of course they weren't on the list," retorted the old man. "They're just children."

"Children who have been bred for two hundred years to become the most talented men in the kingdom..."

"Yes, eventually."

"But they are still here in Mordenhold?" demanded Rew, leaning toward the aged spellcaster.

The old man nodded.

"Hold on," said Zaine. "You're going to ask Valchon's, Heindaw's, and Calb's children to help you navigate these dark, narrow tunnels where it's extremely easy to go astray, fall down a hole, or wander endlessly until you starve to death? And you think a few weeks after you murdered their fathers, that this is a great idea?"

Rew scratched his beard. "Well, great isn't the word I would use, but we're not exactly in position to turn down resources…"

"I guess it's not the worst plan you've ever shared with us. Probably."

"Good, because you're coming with me," said Rew. "There are places we'll need to climb, places a small, lithe body is best to scout, and I'll need help to get the Dark Kind's attention when we pop up."

Zaine snorted but held up her hands. "In for a copper, in for a gold, I suppose."

"I'll go as well," offered Raif.

Rew shook his head. "The men are used to seeing you on the wall, and in your armor, some areas of the tunnels would be difficult if not impossible to squeeze through. It was a close fit when I was a youth, now… I don't know if I can still fit, but I know you cannot."

The fighter grunted, but there was no argument.

"I'd like to stay as well," said Cinda. "I wish you luck, but in case you fail… I'd like to be here."

Rew sighed. He'd figured she would stay, but he didn't like her reasoning. He glanced at Anne. "You'll be needed here, too."

The empath looked uncomfortable but didn't protest.

Turning to Zaine, Rew said, "We'll gather Ang, Vurcell, Blythe, maybe a few of the others. As soon as they can meet us in the keep, we'll go in."

"A long walk in a dark maze. It won't be the worst thing you've had me do," said Zaine, trying to put a little cheer into her tone and failing. She hugged herself then suggested, "Is there a way to mark where we've gone in case we do get lost? There's a children's story about how they sprinkled breadcrumbs to find their way back from a forest. Maybe not bread, but…"

Rew shook his head. "No, any trail we leave will lead the cave bears right to us."

"The what?"

WALKING INTO THE CRECHE MADE REW'S SKIN CRAWL. PART OF IT was because the place was a piece of his past he would rather forget, a piece he would rather not have happened at all. Another piece was the macabre echo of Valchon's creche, where his brother had been raising a competing population of children. Those children were all dead now, the simulacra of his brother, but these children lived. What was Rew to do with them?

Dozens of them, the sons of his brothers—Valchon, Heindaw, Calb, and others who hadn't lived long enough to participate in the Investiture. Three brothers competed, but each generation usually had several dozen children. When cousins were factored in, there could be scores of them living in the creche. All boys. Rew hadn't put much thought into that when he'd lived there, but after seeing Valchon's brood, it gave him a squeamish feeling deep in his gut.

The majority of the children in the creche wouldn't live to see adulthood. They would be killed in training, in the tunnels, or by their siblings. The cousins would fare worse. Alsayer had been right when he'd estimated only one or two from Rew's generation had survived.

If they had any Morden blood at all, they could be powerful spellcasters. The king planted them in the creche with the intention of using them, but just as often, he forgot about them when they came of age. While the bastards and cousins were useful to any brother they allied with, they were dangerous to any they weren't close to. It was a precarious position.

When the Investiture ended, the cousins who'd chosen well were given positions in the keep or even baronies in rare cases. Those that had chosen poorly were like fattened lambs, there to whet the appetites of the wolves. Trying to appear useful but not too useful to any one heir to the throne could keep a cousin alive, but most did not survive for long once the Investiture ended.

Rew had considered that when walking to the expansive pile of buildings and courtyards. His brothers were dead. They'd had children. Spellcaster Irremon had confirmed, though Rew hadn't met any of them that he recalled. The ranger had no children. As far as he knew, he was the first instance a brother had won the Investiture without a litter of whelps already in the creche.

Frowning, he wondered what his nephews expected to happen. He'd won. Vaisius Morden had said as much, through the lips of Valchon's dead simulacra. Had the king told his grandchildren that? Did he select some to succeed Rew in another generation? Rew hadn't been a prince, but he was a son of the king, and he had killed his brothers. It was unprecedented.

It turned out his arrival in the creche was awkward but not in the way he'd anticipated. He'd thought he would face bitter accusations. He'd killed these boys' fathers, after all. Or perhaps he would see hope in their eyes, freedom from the shackles their family put on them and a release from the cold knowledge that eventually, they would have to face and kill their own brothers. Rew had prepared himself for those looks. He'd toyed with what to say, how to convince them to join his fight. He hadn't anticipated the naked hunger he witnessed.

The children, if they could be called that, were eager. He'd killed their fathers, but someone had to follow his path, and he had no heirs in the creche of his own. A child of royal blood had always become prince, inherited rule over Carff, Iyre, and Jabaan. His nephews, it seemed, had guessed that because he had no children, the next generation of princes would be called from their number.

When Rew strode through the open gate to the creche, he found someone had run ahead of them to warn the instructors, and the children were arrayed in a loose line, their masters standing nearby as if to proclaim the virtues of each applicant to the princely domains. Swallowing, the ranger let his gaze rove over the hopeful, greedy faces of his nephews.

They, in turn, tried to look either humble, or proud, or curious, but he caught dangerous looks toward Zaine. They might have heard about her by now, but they wouldn't understand. Young women wouldn't be unusual, hanging around their fathers, but they would sense she was different.

One lad in particular was fixated on her, and Rew understood. On Zaine's hips were the paired silver poignards that Valchon's spymaster had worn. They were enchanted weapons and could kill with a prick, though there'd been a cost alluded to Rew hadn't yet figured out. Some of these boys were the children of Valchon. They might recognize the blades his spymaster had carried.

Rew met the lad's gaze. He might have been the oldest of the group, one or two winters behind Zaine and Cinda, several years younger than the simulacra Rew had killed in Olsoth. The lad had the same look as them, but he wasn't a clone of Valchon. His nose was slightly upturned, and his eyes narrower than Valchon's. Rew wondered if he'd known the boy's mother.

Feeling Rew's gaze, the boy offered a shallow bow. "Welcome to Mordenhold."

Rew ignored the comment and raised his voice. "You've heard by now I've declared myself king. It's not the way things have been done before, nor the way they should be done, to be honest, but it's the way it is. We're pressed by tens of thousands of the Dark Kind, and my father has fled with his spellcasters and the black legion. Mordenhold—Vaeldon—needs a king, and that burden falls upon my shoulders. I am the king. Do you understand?"

The boys nodded, some quickly, some reluctantly, but one thing all Mordens understood was power. Rew had slain his brothers—their fathers. He'd claimed the throne, and no one was there to argue. The children would respect that, even if they didn't like it.

"Which of you knows the tunnels below this city the best?"

The boys looked at each other curiously, and one by one, several of them raised their hands.

"If you're up to it, I have a dangerous assignment for you," said Rew. He drew a deep breath and released it. "We're going to draw the Dark Kind into the tunnels. I need guides who can take us from here to outside the walls. We'll make ourselves known then retreat. I have reason to believe the Dark Kind will follow me."

"Is it true you've no high magic?" blurted a young man from the end of the line. He was half the size of the largest of the boys, and he looked excited. Too young and small to be a serious contender for the throne and too young and ignorant to understand what that meant for him.

An instructor stepped up and cuffed the lad on the back of the head. Rew frowned, and the instructor froze. Corporeal punishment was the way of things in the creche. Cuffs and kicks were constant. Much worse was delivered for serious transgressions. It was meant both to keep the children in line and to teach them how to handle pain, but there was a time when the children teetered on the edge of becoming adults, princes of the realm. They were dangerous then and able to fight back. Worse, striking a prince was a capital crime. The instructor must suddenly be wondering if one of his charges was about to be elevated.

"None of that," said Rew, his calm voice filling the open area.

"I know the ways beneath the city well, Your Majesty," said a youth. He wasn't the eldest of the group, but he was old enough. Fourteen winters, perhaps, though Rew had never paid attention to the ages of children. When Rew did not immediately respond, the boy added, "I can take you beyond the walls with confidence."

Rew glanced over the rest of the group. Some boys looked ready to speak, but none outright disputed the lad's claim.

"Good," said Rew. "Select two others who know the way almost as well as yourself, and in half an hour, you'll guide us.

Bring weapons and whatever armor you're comfortable with in the tunnels. Our task will be dangerous."

A flush and a small smile grew on the lad's face, and he bowed.

"Your Majesty," said the lad who'd spoken first, the one Rew guessed was the oldest child of Valchon. "Have you selected your heirs?"

Rew studied the boy before answering. "Not yet."

"You've been absent long from Mordenhold," continued the boy. "You may not know us well. I am not as familiar with the tunnels as Reymond, but I ask a chance to prove myself in another way. May I join the men on the wall? Allow me to defend this city and show you what I am capable of."

All around the boy, others spoke up in a rush, requesting or demanding the chance to prove themselves.

Rew stared at them, dumbfounded. He'd been a fool. The boys were children, but they'd spent their lives learning to kill. If he would risk Zaine and Cinda, just a few years older than these boys, why not make use of them as well? They had bloodlines as pure as any in the kingdom. They would be developing powers with high magic that rivaled their fathers and, in time, would exceed them. These boys had years of training left, but even so, they might be the most powerful surviving spellcasters in all of Vaeldon.

"Your name?" Rew asked the lad who'd spoken.

"Valjohn."

"You have your father's look," said Rew tightly. He glanced over the others then back to the instructors. He glared at them then asked Valjohn, "If you're eager to join the fight, why have you not done so already?"

The youth worked his mouth as if suddenly finding himself involved in a test he did not expect. Nervously, he offered, "The king, ah, your father I mean, instructed us to stay within the creche. We're young, Your Majesty, but we can fight! None of us would think of defying your father—or you—but if you allow us, we can show you what we're capable of."

Rew rubbed his face with his hands. Of course. Vaisius Morden wanted the city to fall. He wanted the surge of power the departing souls would grant him. He would hold back these children, making sure they didn't save the people. Had Irremon been following Vaisius Morden's will and hidden the presence of the children from Rew, or had the old man truly believed they were children and of no use in the fight?

Dropping his hands, Rew instructed, "Valjohn, gather all of your brothers who are at least thirteen winters and who will not be accompanying me into the tunnels. Join those on the wall, and report to a lad—a man—named Raif. He's big and has a big sword. You can't miss him."

Rew saw some of the faces purpling. They were eager to become princes, but Mordens did not report to anyone but their masters in the creche and their fathers.

"Raif, Baron of Falvar, has no high magic, but he's intimately familiar with the Dark Kind and their tactics. During the course of this battle, I expect you to listen to his instructions and to take his advice. You're to act on his commands as if they were from me. I recall from my time in the creche how my instructors taught me the importance of a prince following the king's command. They were right. While I'm underground, Raif will serve in my stead and will report on your actions. This is the first test I will judge you by. The second test is that the people of this city are paramount. They may be your subjects one day. Guard them."

The boys looked back at him, confusion and excitement passing over their faces like clouds in a winter sky.

Rew drew himself up and declared, "My third test is simple—kill as many Dark Kind as you can."

Predatory grins and wolfish smiles broke out, and the boys who were old enough looked eager, hungry.

Chapter Twenty-Five

❧❀❧

"Iff these children as so powerful, do we really need to be doing this?" complained Zaine. "That big one, Valjohn, could call down a maelstrom like his father and wipe the narjags out within an hour."

Rew shook his head. "Spellcasting doesn't work like that. Your only exposure has been Cinda, and she's… different. Girls, sorry, women, usually are. They mature faster."

"Everyone knows that."

Rew grinned. "Boys her age won't have her control, no matter how much they've practiced. Their powers are still growing, and understanding how to command that new strength takes time. Pfah, even Cinda has difficulty. Remember Jabaan? I don't want to be standing anywhere close if that lad Valjohn tried to rain down a maelstrom within paces of the city walls. Would you?"

"Fair point," conceded the thief, ducking low to slither beneath a protrusion of rock. "You don't think they're a match for the Dark Kind, then?"

"They'll give them a fight," said Rew, "but no, I don't think they'll be enough. Maybe if that fool Irremon had told us they were here earlier, they could have… It doesn't matter. It's too late now."

AC COBBLE

"I'm not sure we'll be enough," grumbled Zaine. "Tell me again why you think those creatures will follow us down into this death trap?"

"Because whoever summoned them wants us dead, and the only way that's going to happen is if they send the lot of them chasing after us. We've faced the Dark Kind before, and each time, we've survived. If they want the job finished, they'll send everything they have."

A hand trailing along the cold, dry granite above their heads, Zaine muttered, "Well, that's comforting."

Ahead of them, Rew saw the reflected eyes of Reymond. Apparently, he was Heindaw's second oldest. A schemer, guessed Rew. Had Heindaw won the Investiture, Reymond would be lobbying for whichever city he felt suited him best. He would be preparing to rule as prince and, in two or three decades, to face his brothers in mortal combat. But now, he was just a child.

Wasn't he?

The reflected eyes turned back, looking ahead down the dark tunnel toward where he was supposed to be taking them through the twisting paths to outside of the city's walls. Rew prayed the lad was actually doing so.

Beside Reymond, one of the other children from the creche crept along. Behind Rew and Zaine, Ang, Vurcell, and Blythe stepped soundlessly on the hard, granite floor of the tunnel. Behind them was another of Rew's nephews. The rangers and Zaine moved as quietly as the air. The children were not as silent, but they were not loud, and they did seem to know the direction they were taking.

Small hand lanterns lit their way, and each member of the party carried two additional torches on their backs, a coil of rope, some steel spikes which could be pounded into the walls, a heavy steel mallet to drive them, and their weapons.

Reymond and another of the children had longswords, similar to Rew's, and the one bringing up the rear had two hand axes. Unusual weapons for a future prince. The Mordens preferred grander arms, like a sword—or if an axe, a big one. The lad, an even younger son of Heindaw, Rew thought, seemed comfortable enough with his axes, but he had naturally assumed a position behind them, which made Rew uncomfortable. The ranger had tried to make conversation with the boy, but the youth demurred.

A shy prince?

Ahead of them, one of the children passed his hand lantern to another, and then he placed hands and feet on opposite sides of the wall. Using pressure to wedge himself there, he slowly crawled over a yawning gap in the floor.

Rew couldn't see how far the drop was below as the boys passed the lantern back over the gulf, but he recalled several such openings at various places in the tunnels. Some were shallow slopes. Some were immediate falls that would kill you at best or break a leg at worst. The latter was worse because with a broken leg, there was no hope of climbing out of the tunnels. The choice between slow starvation or being eaten by the cave bears wasn't a comfortable one.

Their spikes and ropes were meant to be a last resort if they did go tumbling down one of those chutes and managed to stay healthy. They could hammer the spikes in and climb out. Of course, the ring of steel on steel was a sure way to attract the cave bears. Reymond had strenuously impressed on them it was a last resort.

Rew handed his lantern to Zaine and, crawling like a spider, passed over the black hole below him. The thief shone the light down, and Rew glared at her over his shoulder. She could at least wait until he was past the hole and safe to show him how deep it ran.

They made it safely. Subdued, they kept walking. One hundred paces farther, they dropped to their bellies and shimmied ahead, just a hand's width of space above their heads to the low ceiling.

There were numerous routes through the tunnels. As a youth, Rew had avoided the tightest of the spaces, as he thought anyone sensible ought to do, but Reymond had promised a faster journey, and they had no time to spare. Even with the other children from the creche joining Raif on the walls, Rew didn't think the defenses would hold through the night.

He scraped under the last of the low-hanging section of tunnel and rose gratefully to his feet. Behind him, Ang and Vurcell were wriggling like twin worms. They carried on deeper into the tunnels.

THE WARM, FRESH AIR WAS LIKE A BALM FOR THEM ALL. REYMOND, sweat beading his brow, gave Rew a tentative smile in the pale light that trickled through the camouflage placed across the mouth of the tunnel.

It was a metal net, hung with fist-sized hunks of granite, but it could be parted easily. Behind it was a series of steel bars with a door that they'd already opened. None of it was high security, but outside the net, there was also an illusion cast by the king's best low magic users, and the entrance to the tunnels would be invisible to anyone who wasn't standing right atop it. Whether or not the illusion worked against the Dark Kind, Rew wasn't sure. He didn't think they were susceptible to low magic, but the disguise had held long enough.

They peered through the holes in the net. The entrance was half a league from the walls of Mordenhold, though the city was invisible from their angle. Below, hundreds of paces down a rocky slope, the gray bodies of narjags skittering over the lower fringes of a ridge, headed toward the city.

Whispering, Rew told the others, "Two hours left of daylight. We've got to make enough noise they see us and want to follow. It's me they need to see. Then, I don't think this needs to be said, but we're going to have to hurry. There are far more of those things out there than we can handle."

Ang and Vurcell nodded, and Zaine took Rew's place at the net.

Rew turned to the children from the creche. "What are your talents?"

"Enchanting," replied one of them, which was virtually useless in their circumstances. That was the one with the hatchets. Heindaw's younger son.

Another offered, "Invoking. My father was Valchon."

Rew wasn't sure why the youngling had added that, but he clapped the boy on the shoulder in response. It seemed the thing to do.

Reymond, Heindaw's elder, hesitantly admitted, "I have no high magic."

Rew raised an eyebrow. It was possible but uncommon. Throughout the history of the kingdom, children of the Mordens without high magic had renounced their claim to the throne. They didn't want to be standing between a talented younger sibling and the crown. As far as Rew knew, he was the only one who'd had the ability but had eschewed mastering his talent. Did Reymond have no gift, or had he followed in Rew's footsteps? The boy hadn't abdicated, which meant had Heindaw survived, Reymond would be in line to inherit one of the provinces.

"Brave of you to come with us, lad," said Ang when it became apparent Rew didn't have a response.

Shifting, crouched low in the tunnel, Reymond explained, "I'm not meant to be a prince, but that doesn't mean I'm nothing. I'd considered following in the path of the ranger. We're all called in unexpected ways."

"That we are," agreed Rew. He wondered if Reymond was telling the truth.

"Valaan," hissed Zaine.

"I'm not going to bother with a plan," said Rew, shuffling to peek out of cover beside Zaine. "We come out fast. I'm going to try to kill that valaan to get their attention. Then, we get back in the tunnels. Reymond, you and the others stay here with Blythe. No, don't argue. We need you alive and uninjured to guide us back to the keep. It's not the time to show off. We're dead without you."

Rew emerged first, followed by the twin rangers and then Zaine.

They were two hundred paces up a flat granite slope from the valaan and thousands of narjags. Rew swallowed. Fighting so many of the things was such a ludicrous idea that it cast the rest of the moment like it was in a dream. He'd never feared a narjag, not truly, but seeing the things flowing like a river below them sent a tremor down his spine.

"Don't think I'll need to tell you when it's time to run," he told the others then started a bouncing trot down the slope, bounding from rock to rock, and drawing his longsword.

He was halfway there when the valaan sensed him and turned its head to face him. It opened its mouth as if to call to the narjags, but it stood still, like it was confused or also walking a living dream. King's Sake, apparently even valaan could be surprised. He was twenty paces from it when it let out a wild, shrieking call. Immediately, the narjags nearby spun.

Rew was five paces away when the valaan moved. It'd been stunned by his reckless approach, but valaan were not meant for defense. The creature surged, and Rew was ready. He didn't so much stab it as angle his longsword to catch it. The sharp tip skewered the valaan, plunging through its dark skin and bursting out the back with a shower of orange blood. Rew slammed into the thing, its dying breaths spitting onto his cheek. He looked over its shoulder and saw a wave of narjags moving toward them.

He forced the valaan off his longsword and began to retreat. Already, at his flanks, Ang and Vurcell were engaged. Ang spun and leapt, his swordstaff cleaving the air and then the Dark Kind. He leapt back on light feet, the butt of the staff twirling, knocking the creatures away, and then the blade whipping around to chop into them or to jab just deep enough to cause a mortal wound. He fell back again.

"Run," growled Rew.

As he turned, he saw Vurcell. The man was like a tornado unleashed in a glassblower's shop. The paired falchions, which had belonged to Vyar Grund, were a blaze of gleaming steel. Long fans of narjag blood painted the hard stone.

Another valaan loomed out of the crowd, charging ahead of the bulk of the narjags, and the ranger flung one of the falchions at it. The blade wasn't weighted for throwing, and it was an awkward toss. The valaan, as sinuous as fog on a river, dodged out of the way then caught the falchion in a clawed hand.

Vurcell, moving up the slope, simply held out his hand, and the falchion tugged free of the valaan's grasp, severing several fingers as it came. It flew through the air and slapped into Vurcell's open palm.

The three rangers gave up their gracious withdrawal, turned, and ran. A score of paces behind them, Zaine was feverishly firing arrows. With so many of the Dark Kind below, she quite literally could not miss if she had any loft on the missiles, but when she saw the others coming, she began scrambling back up the hill as nimble as a goat.

The narjags were probably shouting, shrieking in rage, or something like that, but to Rew it all sounded like one continuous roar. It was as if the mountain itself was crawling up, climbing after them.

At the tunnel, Rew's nephews were still waiting. Reymond was holding the curtain open, and Zaine dropped and slid on her hip, disappearing into the hole and Blythe's waiting arms. The twins came after. Rew didn't bother to make his entry into the tunnel elegant. He plunged headfirst, crashing into the stone of the tunnel with his forearms, ignoring the pain, and crawling deeper.

Reymond slammed the gate shut, and the bolt fell into place. He came after Rew, calling, "Hurry! That won't hold them for more than a moment."

THE CLICK OF CLAWS, HEAVY BREATHING, AND THE OCCASIONAL
frustrated snarl echoed down the tunnel. A hundred paces, a
thousand paces? It was impossible to know how far away the
Dark Kind were. They couldn't see them, but that meant little, as
their hand lanterns only cast light twenty paces, and the Dark
Kind had rushed into the tunnels with no light at all.

In different circumstances, Rew might have gotten a laugh
thinking about the creatures blundering around in the pitch black.
They would take wrong turns, get lost, and fall down holes. It
would be a miserable experience, just as they'd planned, but at
the moment, all he could think of was how many he'd seen racing
up the slope after them. If nine out of ten get lost or killed—nine-
teen out of twenty even—there would still be enough to easily
overwhelm the small party. He was confident they'd drawn thousands of them away from the attack on the city, but was that
enough to save Mordenhold?

If they were overtaken, their swords and Ang's swordstaff
were nearly useless in some of the tighter confines. That they
would have to use them one-handed, holding their lantern in
the other hand, wouldn't make it any easier. While in some
places, the tunnels were wide enough three or four of them
could walk abreast, the most defensible positions were narrow,
and if they got stuck fighting there, it would be impossible to
switch out. Whoever was at the end of the line would have to
hold.

In time, Rew decided that if they were defending at all, they'd
already lost. Fighting a running battle against hundreds or thousands of narjags in the suffocating tunnels was unthinkable. Once
they made contact, there would be an effectively endless stream of
narjags. They had to stay ahead.

"If we get some distance, we ought to be able to lose them,"
suggested Reymond, calling back from where he'd taken the lead
at the front of the line. "There are some tricky turns up here, and

we'll lose the bulk of them as they go scampering down the wrong paths."

"Don't get overconfident," replied Rew, his voice coming in staccato bursts between sharp breaths.

They were all breathing and talking like that. He hoped it was from exertion and not the stifling terror he felt as the darkness swallowed them and the sounds of the narjags followed like hounds on their heels.

"These things smell like dogs," he continued. "The scents will be confusing enough in here from their own presence and all of your brothers who've been exploring, but at least some of them will guess right and follow us. And if they're anywhere close, they might see the glow of our light. We need more than a little distance."

The lad fell silent and scurried ahead.

The grim symphony behind them was suddenly interrupted with a chorus of squeals of anger and pain. A vicious, brutally violent fight had erupted somewhere hundreds of paces back.

"The narjags ripping into each other?" whispered Zaine, moving along at a crouch, her body silhouetted from her lantern, her legs illuminated by Rew's.

"Cave bear," replied the ranger. "We'd better hurry. If it catches our scent, it'll find us more appetizing than a narjag."

Zaine picked up her speed for a few paces but was slowed by those ahead of her.

They were rushing, but at each turn, Reymond was pausing and discussing the path forward with the son of Valchon. The second child on Heindaw hung back at a wide point in the tunnels. Rew looked at him in the dark.

The boy touched the axes on his belt. "These will be more effective in the tunnels than your sword. Shorter swings."

Grunting, the ranger moved on. He didn't think the lad was right, but the young man wanted to prove himself, and they didn't have time for a discussion about it. Though, the snarling battle behind them lasted a disturbingly long time. Finally, the deepest growls faded, and they were left listening to the clamor of the narjags again.

"I don't think I want to meet one of these cave bears," muttered Zaine.

No one responded.

Reymond pressed on, taking turns with growing confidence as they neared the exit into the keep. They reached a chute which Rew recalled from the way in. He knew the path from there. It was just several hundred paces farther to the exit.

Clustering at the bottom of the chute, Reymond angled his lantern up, and Rew sighed. He remembered it being much easier to climb down than it was going to be climbing up.

"Ladies first?" asked the child of Valchon.

"I'm not a lady," replied Zaine.

Blythe crossed her arms over her chest and raised an eyebrow at the boy.

Reymond unspooled a bit of rope, hooked his lantern to his belt, and began the climb up without asking anyone else. The others shone their lights after him, trying to help him find the hand- and toe-holds on the rough granite. The boy was an able climber, but the light was poor, and he moved steadily but slow.

Rew crouched near the tunnel they'd come from, listening. Whether it was because the ones in front had been delayed by the cave bear or because they weren't as close as they'd sounded, no narjags were pouring out after them, but he could hear the creatures. If they showed up now, it was going to be an ugly fight. Their party was pressed too close together, waiting on Reymond to reach the top and dangle the rope. They had no room to swing weapons. Their only hope would be to keep the narjags in the tunnel bottled up.

When Reymond reached the top, he called down in an exaggerated whisper, "I don't want to drive a spike in, but I should be able to hold the girl, and then she can help me support one of the rangers. Come on up, lass."

Muttering under her breath, Zaine reached for the rope and

scaled the chute, climbing twenty paces and then disappearing into the dark. Using the rope made it an easy climb. Valchon's whelp went next and then Ang and Vurcell.

Blythe shuffled over next to Rew and said, "You go next. I'll hold the tunnel."

Rew shook his head and said, "I go last."

"You're the king."

"Exactly. You have to do what I say."

"You're going to be an insufferable ruler, aren't you?"

Rew slapped the ranger on the shoulder, and Blythe moved to the rope.

Vurcell was clearing the top, and they whispered down for Blythe to start up. The ranger didn't argue. Dexterously, she ascended, leaving Rew and the younger child of Heindaw down below. They only had one lantern at the bottom of the well now, set in the middle of the room to give the climbers a little light from below.

A cacophony of screeches and bellows erupted again.

"Another cave bear," remarked the youth.

"They're getting close," responded Rew.

The boy paused a beat, and Rew opened his mouth to tell him to start climbing, when out of the darkness, a heavy shape barreled out of the tunnel.

Rew had been expecting narjags, but he'd been ready for anything. He got his longsword into the cave bear, but the beast was huge, and it was coming right at him and the child of Heindaw. He let go of his sword to shove the boy clear, then jumped, splaying his legs over the head and shoulders of the cave bear and grasping at the rock wall so he didn't fall down on top of the thing.

The bear roared as it passed below him, its cry reverberating in the close quarters of the tunnel. It scrambled around the base of the well they were climbing, claws extended down, scratching across the hard granite. The lantern was knocked over. It bounced against the wall, cracking and spilling oil across the stone floor of the well. The oil caught, and flared alight, illuminating the furious cave bear.

Showing surprising quickness, Heindaw's son had lunged at the rope and was already climbing. Ang was at the top of the chute, looking down like he was tempted to jump back and help Rew. Rew was hanging on the wall, on the opposite side from the rope, and his longsword was stuck awkwardly in the cave bear's shoulder.

"King's—Pfah." He needed some new curses.

The cave bear lunged after the climbing youth, who barely made it out of reach of the long, solid body of the bear.

Rew pulled out his hunting knife, leapt across the bottom of the floor of the tunnel, and landed on the back of the cave bear. He clutched its thick, matted fur and stabbed his hunting knife into its back. The bear's hide was as heavy as boiled leather armor, and beneath its skin were the hard planks of muscle it needed to claw its way through stone. It was like stabbing the side of a brick building.

Growling, Rew reared back and slammed his knife down again, putting all his effort behind it. The knife was crafted of the finest steel in the kingdom, and this time, it sank into the creature's shoulder. At the same moment, the cave bear bucked, spinning in a frenzied circle, trying to throw Rew off its back.

One hand gripped on its fur, one on his knife, Rew rode the thing like he was taming a wild stallion. The bear lurched about, roaring in pain, and then it staggered toward the wall and bent its shoulder, smashing against the granite.

Rew held on with one hand and kicked up with his legs, walking them up the wall as the cave bear rammed against it, trying to crush its unwanted passenger. It circled the room, rubbing against the stone, and Rew scrambled, his feet walking above the thing's body, his hands on its back.

Then, the bear flung itself the other way and started to roll.

Rew yanked the knife free and launched himself over the cave bear's head. He slid his knife along the blade of his longsword until it struck the hilt, and he tore the weapon free. He hit the ground hard and slapped a hand down, searching in the dark for the fallen longsword.

The cave bear stood, rising on its hind legs, roaring at him.

He found the sword and rolled out of the way just in time to avoid the bear crashing down on his prone body. The ranger rose to a knee and slashed up with his longsword, putting all his might into the blow. It was the kind of attack he would tell Raif to avoid, but his weapon bit into the elbow of the cave bear and sheared off the front leg of the creature.

It uttered a terrible cry and fell, scrambling in shock at its missing leg.

Over its back, Rew saw the gleaming pale eyes of a narjag lurking in the mouth of the tunnel.

He slid his longsword into the sheath, clamped down on the bone hilt of his hunting knife in his teeth, and started to climb hand over hand up the rope. He didn't spare a glance below, but he could hear the outraged roar of the bear and the gnashing cries of the narjags as they poured into the well of stone, confronting a wounded, and very angry, cave bear.

It was only twenty paces up the rope, and fueled by primal fear, Rew climbed it quickly. At the top, highlighted by the collection of lanterns, was Heindaw's youngest child. The lad was blocking the way into the tunnel at the top of the chute. Rew wanted to tell the boy to move, but he had his knife in his mouth.

The lad looked at him coldly, then swung one of his axes down onto the rope Rew was hanging from. The braided cord severed, and Rew fell.

IT WAS A TWENTY-PACE DROP, BUT HALFWAY TO THE BOTTOM, REW flung out his arms and legs, bashing them against the sides of the wall, skinning his knuckles, almost jerking his knee out of socket when he found a protrusion in the rock to wedge his boot against.

Fingers clasped at the opposite wall of the chute, and miraculously, he arrested his fall. His ligaments strained to the point of breaking, but he held.

He was hanging facing down, splayed out with hands and feet on opposite sides of the walls, ten paces above a horrific battle. The narjags had come into the bottom of the well and met the wounded cave bear there. All of them would have preferred to get at Rew, but they had each other. The horrible scene was lit from the burning oil of the smashed lantern.

Liquid pattered against Rew's face as the cave bear tore a narjag in two.

Gritting his teeth, which still held the hilt of his hunting knife, Rew tried to walk his hands up the wall, but when he lessened pressure, he almost fell down into the violent brawl below. He tried to move his foot and nearly slipped. Pressing with his fingers, he tried to inch them up the wall and moved a third of a pace before he had to pause, the strain on his hands too much.

Below, narjags leapt, trying to reach him but falling short. The cave bear was caught up in the swarm, thrashing chaotically to destroy the creatures that had invaded its domain, but already, Rew could see broken bits of swords sticking from the monster and ragged holes in its thick skin the narjags had somehow torn open.

He tried to move again but couldn't. He had no choice. He was going to have to drop down into the fray and hope he could spring back onto the wall before they caught him. It was a foolish hope, impossible now that the rope had been cut, but he couldn't fight all of the narjags and the cave bear together. The only chance would be speed. He could see more gleaming eyes in the tunnel. The narrow space was packed full of narjags pushing to get out, to get to him.

Then, Ang was there, hanging from a length of rope and grabbing Rew's arm. Quickly, Rew released with his other hand and wrapped it around Ang's waist. The ranger grunted at the weight, but any other way, Rew was going to drop.

Above, the rope tugged, and the pair of rangers was pulled higher until Rew was in position to grab the rope himself, and both of them walked their way up the wall.

Reymond, Zaine, and Valchon's child were holding the rope, all three of them lying down, bracing their legs against the wall or bumps on the floor. Vurcell was holding Heindaw's youngest by the scruff of his neck. He'd been disarmed, and in the lantern light, he looked livid.

Without a word, as soon as Rew and Ang cleared the chute, Vurcell shoved the boy into it. The child let out a startled squeak then disappeared into the tunnels.

Vurcell helped everyone to their feet and said, "We'd better hurry."

The sounds of fighting were fading, and in moments, the narjags would be crawling up the chute. The boy... Rew didn't look back. The lad had tried to kill him. He nearly had.

Chapter Twenty-Six

A hulking slab of stone was rolled into place to seal off the exit from the tunnels. A wedge was set beneath it on the city side, making the thing impossible to move. Ideally, they would have a way of sealing the other entrance to the tunnels as well, assuming enough narjags had ventured in after them, but Rew didn't figure sending someone through the gate to seal that side of it was going to work. There'd been a lot of narjags that had come after them, but had there been thousands? Tens of thousands? Was it enough to relieve pressure on the walls for long enough that the citizens of the city could evacuate?

Rew hurried out of the keep and jogged toward the walls, Zaine, the rangers, and Reymond at his heels. He was heartened by the sight of men on those walls instead of Dark Kind, but there still weren't many men, and on the way, they passed a serpentine line of people impatiently waiting to evacuate. It seemed the line had barely moved since they'd gone into the subterranean passages. Rew knew it was probably more people joining the line, which was a good thing, but it meant they still had a long time before the flight was complete.

Turning as they walked past the tail end of the refugees, Rew could hardly believe it. So many people, and if he had guessed right, Vaisius Morden had meant to sacrifice them all. His capital city, everyone. What was it Valchon had said? The people needed the king, and the king needed the people? They didn't need a king like that.

"What is it?" asked Zaine, walking briskly beside him.

"What is my father facing which is worth sacrificing everything for? What good is ruling a city of the dead?"

"I imagine it's more attractive if you're a necromancer." Rew snorted.

"It's the Dark Kind," said Ang. "He doesn't think he can destroy them."

Frowning, Rew asked, "Then, what hope do we have?"

"You've got to kill him," said Vurcell. "With the kingdom behind us, we have a chance."

Rew waved a hand, dismissing the comment, but he didn't respond. Did they have a chance?

They made it to the wall and climbed the stairwell, and he decided that today, they didn't. Dark Kind extended from the wall to the steep mountain passes they'd come from. Ten thousand of them, twenty? How many more could be lurking out of sight?

"Blessed Mother," choked Zaine. "Did any of them follow us? There are even more out here now than when we went below."

Raif, surrounded by a gaggle of erratically armored men and a few spellcasting children from the creche, came striding toward them. "I heard you'd returned." He looked at Zaine. "We were worried."

"Doesn't look like you needed to be," remarked the thief, gesturing at the sea of narjags. "It appears we didn't draw many after us."

Raif shook his head. "Several thousand must have gone down after you. Look, over against the slope, they're still going in. We saw when you popped out and attacked. The plan worked. It was like a tide of them were suddenly drawn toward you. For the last hour, they've been squeezing in there, like water circling a drain."

"But..."

"But there are a lot more of them than we realized," finished Raif. "More than it looks, even. Rew's nephews have been at work. They're boys, without a chin hair between them, but a few are capable invokers, and others have summoned a small army of tiny imps. The enchanters were able to activate some traps their elders had laid. Together, they gouged huge holes in the Dark Kind's forces. I can't begin to guess how many creatures were killed. I won't say it did no good. Since they arrived, the pressure has lessened. They bought us a chance to rest, and the lads are still at it. See down there, another pack of imps joining the fray. It's given us time, but I don't know what to do with it. The Dark Kind keep coming and the boys are getting tired. We can't win this fight."

"We have to," said Zaine.

Rew shook his head, staring at the narrow pass the road to Mordenhold cut through. It was still choked with Dark Kind where it wasn't blocked with shattered boulders. There were more of them back there. They were still coming. "No, Raif is right. We can't win this."

"We can buy time for—" began Vurcell.

"You saw the line of people we just passed," interrupted Rew. "What can we move through the portal stones, ten thousand in an hour? Twenty thousand? Even that will take us three days to get everyone evacuated. We've pulled the boys from the creche. Called in all of the rangers. Duke Vincent and Duke Findley are helping. I see a few other nobles down there by the trebuchet. They're here, helping. How many more nobles are out there that would be willing to come? How many spellcasters survived the Investiture? The Eastern Territory lost all of its nobility. Scores were killed in Jabaan, Carff. Over half the spellcasters of any talent in the entire kingdom are dead! The rest are with my father. If we had the black legion or more of the siege machines working, perhaps we could hold a few more days, but the legion is gone. These odds are beyond us."

"We can't quit," argued Zaine.

Rew stepped toward the battlement, resting his hands on a crenellation, staring out at the Dark Kind below. He did not respond.

The Dark Kind's faces were turned up toward the wall. With rolling eyes and glistening, foul teeth, they pressed against the stones, but without siege machinery, they couldn't breach the walls, and they couldn't craft ladders tall enough to reach the battlement. Occasionally, there was a flash as narjag shamans attempted a spell, but the enchantments on the wall held. It didn't matter. The Dark Kind didn't need to open holes in the walls. They were using their bodies, sacrificing themselves to form ramps. Hundreds of narjags had to die for each pathway up, but the valaan did not care. The narjags themselves didn't seem to care. They were in a frenzy.

Rew glanced down the walls and saw some of his nephews had been clever. They'd blasted away the ramps of dead narjags, stopping them from reaching the walls, but it was hopeless. More were coming. One of Valchon's maelstroms would have decimated the creatures, but could even the prince, after decades of refining the spell, cast it with such precision? If one of his children managed the effort, would it be enough? They didn't know how many more narjags clustered out of sight.

It was impossible to send scouts ranging across the bare stone to spy on the narrow valleys the road to Mordenhold ran through. They would be spotted, and ayres would run them down. As Rew studied the field, he decided it didn't matter. They couldn't risk some cataclysmic spell like the maelstrom so close to the city with the unprotected people lined up in the streets, and he could already see tens of thousands of narjags, with more coming.

They could hold out for a little longer. Every hour meant thousands more would live, but what then? Would the army of the Dark Kind move south, rampage through the disorganized duchies and baronies? He knew the nobles of Vaeldon well enough. None of them would rally to each other's defense.

He slammed a fist down on the stone wall. Could they find

enough good-hearted men to bolster the defense on the walls if they demanded support from the other sides of the portal stones? A few more mature spellcasters could make a big difference, but it would be impossible to get significant numbers of soldiers into position quickly, and if they tried, they would have to stop the evacuation so the soldiers could get out of the portal room.

Below him, the narjags screeched and wailed. They were climbing over each other, clawing at the wall, trying to climb it, though they didn't look to be very skilled at climbing. The awful creatures were staring at him, hundreds of them staring up at him, trying to get to him in vain.

Another ramp was forming at the base of the wall right below him as narjags crawled on the backs of their fellows, reaching for a little extra height, though they were still forty paces below.

"They want you," said Zaine. "Your theory was correct. They saw it was you and followed into the tunnels. They're trying to climb up to you now."

"Never thought that amongst the narjags is where I'd find fame."

"We should go," declared Cinda.

He glanced at her.

"They want you. If we leave, maybe they will too. This isn't our fight, Ranger. We're wasting our lives here, but worse, we may be wasting the lives of Mordenhold's people by staying."

Rew gave a short laugh. He didn't buy that line, and he didn't think she did either. It was their fight. Did she really mean to flee, or was she angling for him to release her necromancy?

He asked her, "What do you suggest? We walk out the gate?"

"Portal, obviously."

"Then how would these creatures know we left? Or do we shout down that we're evacuating as well and hope they leave the good people of Mordenhold alone?"

"Their master, your uncle or whatever he is, will send them after us if he knows where we are."

"We go to Northguard, confront him and my father?"

"We have to do it fast. Tonight. You want me to convince you, but you already know it's the only answer. What use is staying here?"

Rew grunted.

"She's right," said Raif, taking Rew's other side. "We cannot win this battle. It doesn't matter how brave we are, how hard we fight. We cannot win. Ranger, I can't hold this wall much longer."

Watching the narjags at the base of the barrier, Rew did not respond.

"Ranger, almost since the day we've met, you've chided me for not knowing when to retreat. You've cautioned me that if I extend too far, I'll end up dead. Believe it or not, I've been listening. This is our moment to fall back, to fight strategically, to take it somewhere we can win. I don't know what's in Northguard. Maybe we can't win that fight either, but if we're going to gamble, let's at least play a hand that gives us a chance."

Rew turned, eyeing Ang and Vurcell.

"Your uncle?" asked Ang.

"It's a long story."

Vurcell stepped close. "All of these people on the wall, all of the people in line to evacuate, are counting on you to do something. They know you killed your brothers, defied the king. They're expecting some cataclysmic magic to save them. A maelstrom. A legion of the dead. A forest of trees growing up and strangling all of these foul beasts. But we don't have any of that magic."

"We have to do something."

Down the wall from them, a man shouted in alarm, and Rew saw the black forms of valaan surging onto the battlement. Magic exploded. Lightning crackled. Men ran, and those who did not died. Then, after a sharp whistle, clouds billowed outward, sprinkled with shimmering sparks that tore into the valaan before they could react, blasting the creatures back from the wall.

"Lost a couple of spellcasters in that one," remarked Ang, leaning on his swordstaff and peering down below. "Spellcasters?

Pfah. They're just boys. Rew, in a quarter hour or less, those below
are going to be level with us. I'm not sure you standing on this
wall where they can see you is a good idea."

"That was Alsayer's spell," murmured Rew, still looking to
where the conflagration had exploded.

"Maybe he taught it to someone, or maybe they learned it like
he did. Too bad whoever cast that can't send it across this entire
field."

"That was Valjohn," supplied Reymond. "He can command a
star cloud, though I've never seen him cast one so extensive. He
tries to hide he can do it at all, but I've followed him, seen him.
You're right. Spellcaster Alsayer taught it to him. I don't know
why. Maybe he thought Valchon would prevail, and he was ingra-
tiating himself with his oldest son."

"Who knows why Alsayer did any of the things he did. Pfah, I
hate that bastard, but what I wouldn't give to question him, to
understand what he saw, what he was working toward."

"You could ask Valjohn," mentioned Raif.

"Not sure it's the time."

"Someone has to open the portal if we're going to Northguard.
Why not him?"

"Whatever we do, I advise we stop standing right here with
Rew in view," warned Ang, still looking down at the growing pile
of narjags.

Rew looked for Valjohn but did not see him. Why had Alsayer
taught the boy the star cloud spell? What else had Alsayer
told him?

Rew stepped back from the battlement, out of sight from the
narjags. His father had called him to Mordenhold. His father's
brother was sending an army to stop him. Alsayer had wanted
him in the capital as well. Why? There was only one place to find
the answer.

Rew gripped his longsword then told the others, "Gather
everyone. We're going to Northguard."

"SOMETHING HAS BEEN BOTHERING ME," SAID CINDA.

She was standing close beside Rew, whispering so that only he could hear. Before them, Valjohn was standing over a map, a finger to his lips, trying to figure out where he could open a portal to get them nearest to Northguard.

You could not portal into the keep itself. It was bound in copper, and the mountains around it were thick with the metal. There was a place outside where arrivals typically came, but if Vaisius Morden was waiting for them, he would have people there. They had to hurry, but Rew wasn't going to step into his father's arms and give themselves up that easily. It was worth at least trying stealth.

Rew glanced at the necromancer but didn't respond to her comment. There was a lot bothering him as well.

"Your father said to come to Mordenhold, right? He doesn't seem like the type to misspeak. That means he thought he'd be here. What changed? What made him leave?"

Rew shrugged. "The Dark Kind? His brother is closer to escape than expected? Us taking too long... I don't know."

"What'd they do with all of the copper that was in those tunnels? That much of it, they could have built an entire city out of the stuff."

Rew threw up his hands. "I don't know that either. It could have made all those breastplates that Valchon's soldiers wore. Maybe they did make a city out of it. Northguard is one solid hunk of the stuff, I'm told. It's why we can't portal directly there. Spellcasters loathe the place."

"Perhaps that is what has happened. Perhaps the door to the king's brother's prison has become weak."

"Sure. Maybe."

"It won't do us any good to defeat the king if his brother comes right out and takes control. If he can conjure tens of thousands of Dark Kind, you can't fight him. He'll be too strong. And my magic won't be sufficient either."

Rew didn't respond.

"When I act against your father, Ranger, I'll have one chance. When it's done, however it ends, I'll be done. We can't waste that effort."

He turned to her. She stared back at him, her eyes burning crisp emerald, her face blank. She didn't show fear, sorrow, anything he'd expect her to show.

He asked her, "Are you all right?"

"I'm going to die today, so no, I am not all right, but I've made my peace with it. I… I was comfortable in that knowledge. It's the way it has to be, and I've accepted that. Raif won't understand. When it happens… watch out for him, will you? He said he'll support me in what I have to do, but I don't think he will. He's going to try and interfere. You cannot let him stop me."

"It's useless," said Valjohn suddenly. "We should just go straight to the arrival point. If I try to bring us far enough away no one will see us, it will add hours to our journey. The woods around there… I am sorry. I'm not familiar with the terrain, and I'm still an apprentice at portaling. I can get us safely to the arrival point, but anywhere else is a risk."

"They'll be waiting for us there!" protested Reymond.

Valjohn raised his head and stared at his cousin before offering a defeated shrug.

"He's right," growled Rew. "We don't have time to spend half the day slinking through the woods. Within hours, Mordenhold may fall. We need to be within Northguard before that if we want any chance for my uncle to call off his Dark Kind. Everyone, ready yourselves for a fight. Valjohn, take us to the arrival point."

Anne joined Rew and Cinda and clutched his arm. He wanted to tell her to stay behind. She wasn't a warrior. She might be more of a hindrance than a help, and it wasn't wounds he was worried about. His father had the power to destroy any trace of them in a blink. He was going to kill them or inhabit their bodies and destroy their souls. He wasn't going to injure them.

But Rew felt comfort in Anne's presence. She was a soothing balm to his inflamed thoughts. She knew she couldn't fight, and likely even her empathy wouldn't help, but that was not why she insisted on accompanying them. They were family, she had said. Family went together.

Valjohn stood upright, raised his hands, and his brow creased in concentration. Then, in front of him, a purple and gold vortex began to form.

Chapter Twenty-Seven

The portal spun open, and without asking, Reymond leapt through first. Three steps later, a coruscating wave of brilliant blue energy scythed through him, slicing the lad into two ragged halves. Blood and gore exploded, and pieces of the boy went spinning out of view.

"They were watching for us, then," murmured Ang, his voice a dry rasp.

"So it seems," agreed Rew, his heart pounding.

Valjohn curled his fingers, preparing to close the portal.

Rew caught him on the wrist. "Hold it open."

Ang and Vurcell plunged through the opening. Anne gripped Rew's arm, and together, they went next. Raif, hovering protectively by Zaine's side, brought the reluctant thief through, followed by Cinda, who stepped across the threshold calmly.

They were in the middle of a road, surrounded by towering pine trees. There were empty flagpoles, where the king's pennant could be hung, and a squat, stone shack where guards would wait for arrivals. Around the structure, the boughs and trunks of the pines were unnaturally dark, as if saturated by woodsmoke. The ranks of trees formed stern shoulders alongside the road, and they could see nothing beneath the gloomy eaves the intertwined nettles formed.

Standing near the guard shack, were two spellcasters and a squadron of the black legion rushing to block the road toward Northguard. One of the spellcasters was clad in the black robes of an invoker and was drawing his hands back, building another blade of crackling blue. The second wore the green of a conjurer, and as Rew watched, he slapped his hands together. With a crack and a sulphureous billow of smoke, a man-sized imp appeared.

Without pause, the imp charged.

Ang took a hopping two step then launched his swordstaff at the invoker. The man squawked in surprise and caught the blade of the weapon in the center of his chest.

Vurcell ran to intercept the imp. The creature was bound in thick slabs of muscle. It had two enormous hands tipped with curved claws, and horns stood from its head in twisting spires. It had a narrow, equine jaw that was wrenched open as it bellowed a cry of attack.

The ranger was on it before it finished its call. Vurcell slid one of his enchanted falchions into its chest then spun and decapitated the imp with a sweeping blow from his second blade. The imp's head thumped to the hard, dirt road.

Rew, Raif, and Zaine were amongst the members of the black legion, though Rew had paused briefly to eviscerate the conjurer.

Raif smashed into their center, the soldiers' heavy chainmail doing little to slow the whirlwind of his greatsword. He crashed against them, striking aggressively, giving no thought to defense.

Rew took the fighter's right flank and, more elegantly, began engaging the chain-clad soldiers.

Zaine was on the left, but she held back, letting the legion-naires think they could circle behind Raif, and then she darted at them, her poignards held low. The thief didn't bother to get within their guards. She simply plunged the narrow blades into a wrist and then a thigh, and two of the soldiers toppled over dead.

Bursting through the line of armored men, Raif spun back and kept up his attack, but now the legionnaires were surrounded and panicked. Rew severed a man's leg at the ankle, plunged his longsword through the ribcage of another then drew his hunting knife, flipped it, and stabbed it into a third legionnaire's eye. In breaths, all ten of the legionnaires were dead.

"King's Sake!" screeched Valjohn. Rew glanced back and saw the young spellcaster had come through the portal as well and allowed it to close behind him. "You didn't even use high magic!"

Rew glanced at Cinda. "We're saving it for the real fight."

"I-I can't believe how fast that was. It was like a blur. All of you, it was incredible. It was like you were working together."

The party looked at each other, and grinning, Raif said, "Well, we—"

"Like a dancing troupe," continued the young spellcaster. "Like the ones that perform at the New Year, where all the girls twirl in time with each other. Amazing."

"Dancing girls…" muttered Raif, a dark scowl building as he looked at the younger boy.

Zaine put a hand on Raif's arm and winked. The fighter grumbled to himself but bent to clean his greatsword. Cinda ignored them all and began walking the road to Northguard. They scrambled to join her, Rew striding beside her but not speaking.

"They were waiting," she mentioned after they'd walked several hundred paces. "The king knows we're here."

Walking, half an eye on Ang who was still cleaning his swordstaff as they moved forward, Valjohn cleared his throat and said, "I knew that man, the invoker, Lucas. He was one of the king's— Vaisius Morden's, I mean—more talented spellcasters. He taught us sometimes. I didn't think he could be killed by a normal man."

"I'm tempted to tell you that rangers are not normal men," said Ang quietly, tossing aside the bloody rag he'd used to clean his weapon, "but the truth is, we are. Spellcasters are too. We all die just as easily. You nervous, lad? You could wait for us back at the arrival point."

Valjohn swallowed then shook himself. "I am ready. I've been training all of my life for this, but why would Lucas be waiting for us? If he wanted to kill us, he could have portaled to Mordenhold."

"He wasn't there to kill us," remarked Cinda. "He was there to get killed by us. One of the king's most talented invokers, you said? Vaisius Morden would have bound his soul then. The king will know that soul has departed."

"If he knows we're coming, how are we going to get inside?" worried Zaine, glancing around at the empty forest around them. "We could circle around the back, I suppose. Can the walls of Northguard be climbed? You said it's made of copper. Is that... good?"

"We don't have time for any of that," Rew told her. "We're going to walk in."

"Walk in?"

Rew nodded.

Zaine leaned in and declared, "Walking straight in is not a good plan, Ranger."

"I agree with her," said Cinda. She waved around them. "The air here is thick with death. It's almost physical. Your father could snuff us out before we even see him, and there's nothing I can do to stop him. If ever there was a time for stealth, this is it."

"The king needs us. In Havmark, he told me, 'Come to Mordenhold, spill the blood of family, cut out the rotten heart of the king.' He invited us. He won't stop us from walking into that fortress and confronting him."

"You've gone mad," muttered Zaine.

"It is madness, but it's time for this to end. The maelstrom Valchon cast over Carff, the army of Dark Kind outside of Mordenhold... It all has to stop. We have to stop it. I'm ready. Let's do this."

HALF A LEAGUE LATER, THEY EMERGED FROM THE FOREST AND SAW
Northguard perched on the opposite side of a steep valley. The
road ran like the arc of an arrow's flight, but the problem was the
valley was crowded with narjags and the heavily armored
soldiers of the black legion. The two sides were locked in an epic
conflict, bands of them swirling in a chaotic battle. At first glance,
it was like watching light dappled on a choppy sea. Pockets of
narjags would suddenly swarm, overwhelming the lines of the
black legion, but then a charge would break the clump of narjags,
trampling them beneath the hobnail boots of the soldiers.

There were gaps in the fight, and as Rew took in the scene, he
realized it sprawled outside of the valley, up the slopes, and for as
far as they could see. The battle completely encircled Northguard.
There were no clean lines where one side faced the other, no
central positions which the soldiers struggled to protect. It was a
wild melee, and it looked as if the entirety of the king's black
legion was involved, along with just as many narjags.

In the center of the raging battle, the keep thrust up like an
obelisk to his family's pride. In poor light, the structure looked
black, erratically slashed with bright turquoise. The keep was a
copper monolith, aged in the harsh northern clime for hundreds
of years. There was one gate and no windows. Rew knew the
inside was honeycombed with rooms for guards, kitchens, and a
bare great hall which rarely saw events or visitors.

He'd thought the place an unnecessary keep that sacrificed
comfort for security. He and his brothers had jested the time they
visited that it must be the worst assignment in the kingdom, a
place troublesome legionnaires were sent either to finish their
terms or to repent and change their ways. A stint in Northguard
would be enough to make one appreciate the small things in life
and learn a little discipline.

But now Rew saw it for what it was. A prison.

A prison for his uncle and a prison for his father as well.

They were locked in a feud that had lasted centuries. Vaisius

Morden had gotten the better of it in that time. He'd kept his brother sealed away, only able to affect the kingdom with sorties of Dark Kind he somehow conjured from within that massive, hunk of copper, but while the king had held the upper hand, he'd never been able to turn from his brother. He'd always had to keep one foot in Mordenhold, trusting his sons to rule the kingdom and the rangers to keep the monsters at bay. He'd been locked in Mordenhold nearly as effectively as he'd imprisoned his brother in Northguard.

The king hadn't been able to spare the time and energy to collect Rew. He had to focus all of his efforts on keeping his brother sealed away. They were like two dogs with their jaws clamped on each other. One was on top, but that didn't mean he couldn't have his throat ripped out by the one below, and now, their armies were locked together in an equally vicious struggle outside.

"All of those men are dead," remarked Cinda coolly. "Unfortunately, Vaisius Morden's hold on their souls is too tight for me to intervene and take control. That explains what I'd been feeling… Pfah, tens of thousands of them have died here over the last month. We must have finished off the last of them back at the arrival point."

"They're d-dead…" stammered Valjohn. "The entire black legion? But…"

"Can you portal us across this valley?" Rew asked the young spellcaster.

The boy's eyes closed, and his lips moved as he whispered under his breath. His hands quivered, but nothing happened. "It's like there is something in the way. I can raise a little power, a spark, but not enough for even a short hop through a portal. The power required to—"

"We know, lad. We're familiar with portals," interrupted Ang. He gestured at the keep with his swordstaff then rapped the butt on the ground beneath their feet. "Copper. Whole place is built from it, and no one's mined the hills around here. Bit of an effort,

AC COBBLE

don't you think, to haul all that metal way out here when it's as thick as a river below us."

Rew grunted but did not respond. His father had pulled the copper from beneath Mordenhold and used it to build here. Blessed Mother, what was the old man sealing away? Such effort... Wouldn't it have been easier to just kill his brother? Vaisius Morden wasn't a sentimental man, and he had the power to reach into the beyond and command departed souls, so why keep his brother alive? Why not just kill his grandest foe?"

"What now?" wondered Raif.

"The only way in is to walk," said Rew. He glanced at Zaine. "See? I told you."

She snorted and shook her head. Already, she'd drawn her poignards.

"Anne, anyone else, you can stay behind. You should stay behind."

The empath shook her head but did not speak.

Valjohn looked as if he was having second thoughts, but when neither Cinda nor Zaine backed down, he steeled himself. A young man was a young man even in the face of incredible danger. A young man was a fool.

"Ang, Vurcell, take my flanks. Raif, you've got the rear. Keep them off our backs. Cinda and Valjohn, in the center. Anne—"

"I'll be right behind you, Rew."

"Any advice?" asked Valjohn. "The only time I've faced Dark Kind was earlier today in Mordenhold."

"Try not to get killed," suggested Zaine.

Rew shrugged. "Aye, that pretty much covers it."

Then, he turned and began walking down the road. In front of him, spread as far as he could see, was chaos.

"It's a barrow," hissed Cinda as they descended toward the warring factions. "Northguard is one giant barrow."

"Does that help us?" wondered Zaine.

Cinda didn't answer.

Half a dozen of the black legion, their faces gaunt, bled of life, shuffled by, moving to meet a similar-sized pack of narjags. The soldiers ignored them, but the Dark Kind shifted, as if wanting to charge the party. Broken weapons and bodies crunched or squelched underfoot. The black legion fought soundlessly, and the Dark Kind were quiet as well.

Rew felt cold. Real or imagined, he was not sure. The sun shone down on them, but it brought no warmth. There was no smell either, just a dry, dusty odor that filled one's nostrils, threatening a sneeze. It made Rew think of old books or old graves. The copper keep had the tang of spilled blood, or was that the blood of the black legion, dead all around them? He'd had a dream like this before, he thought, or had that been in the enclosure, talking to Brian of the Brambles? He couldn't remember now, but it felt the same.

A narjag lurched toward him, its beady yellow eyes trembling, distracted. Its gaze washed over him, like it couldn't focus, but it stumbled closer and raised a sturdy-looking broadsword it must have taken off one of the fallen legionnaires.

Rew met the narjag's blow and tilted his longsword to the side, letting the Dark Kind's strike slip by him. He lashed out, cleaving into its skull. The narjag fell away without a cry. It fell soundlessly. The entire battle was eerily silent or muffled, but he knew the sounds of war. He knew them but could not hear them.

"Should I... do something?" asked Valjohn.

"It's a good idea to pick up a sword if you see one, but don't use high magic unless you're forced to," instructed Rew. "They're... dazed or something."

"This barrow is a portal to death," said Cinda. "This valley is a road. We're traveling to the beyond."

"What does that mean?"

"I don't know."

All around them, Dark Kind and legionnaires were locked in eddies of violence. The men were already dead, but they could be felled, and swarms of narjags crawled over some of them, tearing them to pieces, making sure there wasn't anything left that could rise.

When the narjags fell, they lay still. There were thousands of them already dead in the valley. Rew couldn't tell where they came from. There was no clear objective to the fight. No signs as to how long it'd been going, though the land was littered with detritus and the permanently fallen. Some of the bodies could have collapsed that morning. Others could have been there for weeks.

Neither side appeared to be storming the keep—or protecting it for that matter. In the distance, Rew could see looming steel gates that were left half-open. There were no standards waving atop the battlement, no men there, either. The giant copper keep could have been unoccupied from the way it looked, but he could feel it was where they needed to go. His father would be there, and his uncle. The end was behind those doors.

Three of the black legion, hounded by several times their number of narjags, careened toward the party. Ang slammed his swordstaff into the back of a legionnaire, trying to force it into the narjags, but the legionnaire spun.

The ranger leapt back, and the other two legionnaires turned and lurched toward Ang. The ranger defended a blow from one, dodged an attack from another, but the first one scored a slash across Ang's thigh. The ranger staggered out of reach.

Valjohn thrust his hand forward, and three thin tendrils of brilliant electrical energy snapped from him to the legionnaires. They jolted, and their flesh crackled and sizzled, but they kept coming after the wounded ranger.

Then, Raif was on them, and he smashed his greatsword against the soldiers, crumpling them with each blow. Rew and Vurcell moved to meet the narjags who had been attacking the legionnaires, and Anne took Ang's side.

The narjags were slow, deadened, and fell easily to Rew's and Vurcell's enchanted blades. Small groups of the lethargic beasts would be little threat to the party, but there were so many, and if the legionnaires turned on them as well...

Growling, Rew fell back into position. "Ang?"

"He can walk," answered Anne. "I can't... The connections are flimsy here. I know they're there, but it's like holding a fistful of water."

Rew started moving forward again without responding, taking the party off the road to avoid a scrum of Dark Kind and undead.

"Valjohn, the legionnaires are already dead. If you hit them, you've got to hit them hard enough they're destroyed. I mean completely obliterated. If you leave even a hand behind, that hand will still come at you."

"Or let me handle them," suggested Raif from the back. "My sword is enchanted and will sever the ties of their soul to their body."

The young spellcaster stammered, babbling wordlessly.

"You'll get used to it," assured Zaine, "or else you won't be with us long. Could be worse. You could be a necromancer. They always end up dying."

Rew stumbled. He felt Cinda's hand on his back. Her touch was cold but firm. Rew stood upright and walked farther into the deadened valley.

Chill fog began to swirl around their feet as they got closer to the looming keep. The mist moved reluctantly when they stepped through it and pulled at their ankles, making walking a chore. The temperature, either because of the fog or the weak sun overhead, continued to drop. The sounds of the battle... Rew shook his head. He knew steel and claw rang against each other. He knew what the sounds were, but he didn't hear them.

He didn't think about that. He kept moving.

The narjags were becoming even more desultory closer to the keep. They were quiet and stared with vacant eyes until something got close. Then, they moved to action and fought as hungrily as always, but slowed, like they were stiff on a freezing morning.

The black legion thinned near the doors, but they moved with more precision, working in squadrons effectively to corner narjags and surround them or forming into defensive squares when they faced a larger group.

Rew's jaw creaked, and he realized he was yawning. He shook himself and spared a glance back. The party was awake, more alert than the narjags, but their faces were incredulous, their eyes glassy. He thought they were awake.

Pushing forward, they encountered more of the narjags and several times bumped amidst the black legion. After being startled like waking from a nap, Zaine pounced on the corpses, punching her poignards through their armor, but whatever enchantments made her weapons so deadly to the living did nothing to those already dead.

Raif barely saved her when she'd struck without thinking, leaping over her as she fell back and brandishing his greatsword mightily. The lad went down, pressed too hard and too close by the soldiers. Valjohn's magic flickered impotently. The copper of the keep deadened his magic, but Rew's and Vurcell's blades cut through dead flesh as easily as living. They severed limbs and heads and crippled the legionnaires, though their arms and legs flopped still, jerking and scrabbling beneath the layer of fog. Rather than finishing the black-clad men, Rew hauled Raif to his feet and led them on.

His vision was getting dim. The sun no longer shone bright. The fog rose in thin curtains ahead of them, casting a haze over the battlefield. The dead below them crunched when they were stepped on, like burnt bread or frozen dew.

Always, they marched on, and the closer they got, the easier it was to avoid the combatants, though the simple act of walking became challenging. Rew's arms and legs ached. His breath was short, like he couldn't draw a lungful of air. His head throbbed as if he'd had too many drinks the night before. He was falling, the air motionless against his face, but he felt he was falling toward those open doors. Pressure and pain pressed against them.

"Anne, can you do something?" he asked, shaking his head to try to clear it, rubbing at his temples.

"I don't think so," she replied. "It's not a physical hurt. It's not mental either. It is not us that's damaged. The pain is coming from within the keep."

Rew didn't reply. He didn't know what she meant. He suspected she did not either.

His arms were fuzzy and appeared indistinct. When he looked around, his companions spoke, but he could not hear them. When he spoke, they did not act as if they'd heard, but they did not look panicked. He shouted. No one reacted, so he kept moving.

Shapes drifted through the fog, stepping in exaggerated motions like children pretending to be monsters. There was no source of light. He didn't know how he could see. He closed his eyes, but nothing changed. The fog was there, the indistinct shapes as well, a hazy penumbra defining their forms. He opened his eyes. Had they been closed?

Occasionally, a narjag or black legionnaire would come close, and they would fight. It was like stage fighting. Slower. Exaggerated. He used to have dreams like that, when he was young and spent every one of his daylight hours training. With movements, strange and stilted and familiar, he would fight faceless apparitions, parodying the work he put in during the day, until it was all a blur, dreaming and waking, always fighting.

Some of them took wounds as they progressed. Anne healed those, moving with the same puppet's grace they all did, though her healing was incomplete, like she would forget what she was doing and stop.

Valjohn disappeared during the course of one ugly brawl. They did not go looking for him.

Eventually, Cinda stepped beside Rew, putting a hand on him and taking the lead. The necromancer's face was blank as always, but her eyes blazed green, like lanterns on the deck of a merchant cog cutting through a stormy night, searching for the harbor.

He understood how slow he was when her steady steps took

her past him. He was a foal on ice. She was at home. She did not use her power, but he could feel it swelling around her. North-guard was sheathed in ancient copper, but from its open door, necromantic power bled like a gaping wound. A crypt? The king's own power seeping from his grasp?

Rew's thoughts were as fuzzy as his arms, and they slipped from him like a tab of butter on a hot pan. What were they doing there?

A man, dressed in black, wearing chainmail, thumped into him. The man's dead eyes stared straight ahead, but he clouted Rew with a metal-encased arm. Rew hit him back, not realizing he was holding his hunting knife until the blade gouged the man's face, cracking his orbital socket, tearing loose the black-clad man's eye. It hung from a cord of blood vessels, but there was no blood.

Rew hit the man again, carving another deep ravine across the armored man's face. The ranger blinked at the white bone exposed from the blow. The knife gleamed brightly. Rew turned it, looking at the steel. It wasn't right, he didn't think, that brilliant shine.

Steel, dark and filthy, punched into the armored man from the side, and he died bloodlessly. There was a big youth there, holding a massive sword. His eyes looked alert and concerned.

Rew stared at him dumbly. Should he thank this person? That armored man had been trying to kill him, he'd thought. He hoped so because he'd slashed the man across the face. He'd meant to do it and wished he hadn't, now.

Rew couldn't see his foe. Everything below his waist was obscured by a flowing white mist. What had happened to the armored man? The ranger did not believe he'd killed him, but he'd hurt him. If the man was hurt, he should find him.

He looked down at the hunting knife in his hand. The fog nearly obscured it, but he could see the light reflecting off the steel. Why wasn't the weapon bloody? He'd cut that man. He recalled that much but not why. It felt important. Violence had to have a reason. That was important to him once.

He raised his weapon, peering at it closer through the fog, but it wasn't fog. He trailed his hands through it, and they were dry. The blade was dry. No condensation beaded on the cold steel. The mist did not cling to it as he stirred it slowly in the air.

Was that strange?

A pair of black-clad men loomed closer, and the big lad with the greatsword charged them. Watching dispassionately, Rew saw the boy bash his way through the slower-moving soldiers. More of them came. The lad swung a giant sword, and the armored men fell like lifeless dolls. The fight, if that's what he was watching, vanished as another wall of the curious, dry fog rolled between them.

He couldn't hear the men any longer, but he knew the ring of their steel must be pealing loudly, like bells, calling the hours, those soothing reminders all was well through the night. Fog was beautiful then, drifting by the open door of a tavern, held at bay by a warm fire and the boisterous laughter brought on by too many ales. It was like a blanket, an embrace, that you were there, in that place in the world.

The ranger pushed forward with his hand, watching the dry mist swirl in the wake of his movement. He felt like he was stirring batter and moved his hand again in a broad circle then in a square.

Rew imagined himself stepping from square to square on a Kings and Queens board, moving across the board diagonal or vertical. Horizontal? That was stupid, he thought. What use, moving to the side? Straight ahead was too obvious. Diagonal was better. He looked down and couldn't see his feet, much less the squares on the board. He was holding a sword. That felt right. Who's side was he on, white or black? Which piece was he?

The slashing attackers? The stoic defenders? He giggled. The king?

A girl, wearing blood red robes, caught his arm and tugged him after her. He didn't know where she was taking him, but he didn't know where he was going, so it did not matter.

Chapter Twenty-Eight

❧❧❧

H
e coughed, and his body hurt. It tingled, a thousand, a million pricks from a needle, jabbing him from all sides. He rubbed his eyes with a fist then jerked his hand away. It was covered in gore. Rew spun and saw a giant door slightly open and, beyond, a wall of white. He was looking at a cloud from the inside. Eventually, he understood he was looking back out at the valley from the doorway to the keep.

He turned again, the realization bringing a wave of discomfort and fear. He was standing inside of the long, spartan entry hall of Northguard. The place was dark, dead, stone and steel. The ceiling was made of black tiles arching high above, lost in the gloom. In the walls, hanging in dull steel sconces, were spent torches. Ash lay below them in heaps. Soot stained the undecorated walls, but there was nothing else in the room. The only sign there'd ever been life was the spent flames.

Hearing a scuff, Rew turned, raising his weapons, but it was Cinda, emerging out of the white wall dragging Vurcell behind her. The ranger was staring stupidly at his feet. Blood coated one of his arms like a sleeve.

"Watch him," Cinda instructed Rew. Then, she turned on a heel and went back outside.

They'd been lost, like in a dream, out in the valley before Northguard. Cinda seemed unaffected. She was collecting the others. Without her... Rew knew he never would have awakened.

Raif stomped in, cursing, a hand wrapped around Anne's arm. The empath's mouth was open, stuck mid-yawn. Her eyes blinked owlishly, like she'd been dragged out of bed in the middle of the night, but not to a panic. She closed her mouth then rubbed at it with her hand. When she dropped her hand, she was frowning.

"I've got them," assured Rew.

Looking concerned, Raif nodded, then hurried back out into the murk.

Rew moved forward, checking Vurcell's bleeding arm, moving the ranger and Anne farther into the hallway, constantly looking over his shoulder, afraid at any moment they would be under attack. He was remembering, now, what was out there in the valley, the battle they'd walked through. He was remembering, as well, what was inside.

The ranger and the empath were ice cold, but already, Rew could see the blush of pink in their cheeks. They were breathing. Like him, they just needed time to recover.

Cinda brought Ang next and told Rew, "My brother is trying to find Zaine. Seems she wandered a bit farther than the rest of you. We lost Valjohn long ago, and I don't much fancy trying to locate him in that soup."

"We can't leave..." began Rew. He trailed off.

Wherever Valjohn was, he was on his own. Rew remembered the invoker disappearing early, or had it been? His memories were disjointed fragments. Time and duration were strange concepts.

He shook himself. Blessed Mother, he had to get his thoughts ordered. They were in the keep with the king and his brother. Wherever Valjohn had wandered, it might be safer than inside.

Cinda watched the wall of white dispassionately, seeming to see through it. Rew thought at first she would assist her brother finding Zaine, but she did not. She waited patiently.

"Did he…"

"He found her. They're coming," she said, glancing at Rew. "You know what it feels like to die now."

Rubbing his face, Rew shivered.

"Unpleasant?"

He looked at Cinda. "No, not really. It was… fuzzy. Like a dream."

She nodded. "That's not too bad."

"Cinda…"

"I'll feel it, soon enough."

He wanted to assure her all would be well, that they would figure a way to defeat the king, that they would prevail. But they wouldn't. He knew it, and she knew it.

Finally, Raif arrived with Zaine.

"She was taking a nap, I think, lying behind a pile of dead narjags. She was using one of their disemboweled stomachs as a pillow."

Rew looked at the gnarly mat of blood and filth caking the back of Zaine's hair and turned away. He asked Raif. "You weren't affected?"

"He has the same blood as I," murmured Cinda, "the same taint on our souls as the king and his brother. The barrowlands were filled with tombs. That's what we're in now. It feels like home."

Rew raised an eyebrow.

"It's not the same in size, but it has the same purpose. The barrowlands are studded with burial sites, but each of those mounds serves as a prison. They were built to hold the ghosts of a people before our own. The king's people. The wraiths that he and I both call upon."

"What was the purpose of all of that outside? Was that a… protection of sorts? I don't think we would have made it through without you two." Rew hugged himself then looked opposite of the entrance. There was a single door there, and it was ajar as well.

"I don't believe there was a purpose to the war in the valley," said Cinda. "Your ancestors have lost control of their minions. Their power spills out uncontrolled. Can you not feel it? They dream of death, it seems. You have enough latent ability you must feel something. It surges through this room like water pouring from a teapot. The valley is filled with it. Pfah, more than filled. The Dark Kind outside Mordenhold came from here. The potency of the energy here... it's going to wash over the entire kingdom if we don't stop it. Can you feel nothing?"

"I feel... ancient magic," said Rew, "the same as the pull of the Investiture, but you're right, it feels... unfocused, or maybe it's me who's unfocused."

"It's the same as it always is to me, the power of departing souls but not concentrated. It's all throughout this keep, all in the air here and outside. That's why the fog. The death you all just suffered... I wonder, are we sensing the same power or different? Was what you felt a true journey or a dream?"

"All dreams are true," murmured Zaine. "They're as true as waking, but that does not mean the two are the same. We believe what we see at that moment, but there's more to the world than that, facets of our existence we touch but do not witness." Suddenly, the thief slapped herself in the face, shuddered, and declared, "Blessed Mother, I need an ale. I think I'm going mad."

Cinda eyed the other girl, mouthing something about truth and dreams.

"We need to get going," said Anne. Rew turned and saw her holding Vurcell against the wall. Blood still leaked down his arm. "He doesn't have long."

"You can't heal him?"

She shook her head. "This place... whether it's truth, a dream, or we're all dead already, my power is suffocated. I couldn't heal a stubbed toe."

"Rew," said Vurcell, his voice quaking like a leaf in the wind. "When I fall, take the falchions. They should be yours."

"I have a sword."

"You have a prison. I've seen it. I see it now." The ranger slumped backward. "It's a prison. All of it. Everything. You cannot carry that forever."

"Anne, can you..."

The empath shook her head.

"Dying should hurt," mumbled Vurcell, rubbing surreptitiously at his bleeding arm. He glanced at his brother. "It'll take both of us to face the boy. I'll attack from the right, eh? It'll be easier with my arm."

"The right? The boy?" questioned Ang, coming beside his twin, supporting him. "What are you talking about?"

"You'll see."

Rew blinked at the pair of them. A prison? His sword was a prison? Rew had known that, but—

"The view is clear at the end," babbled Vurcell. His head rolled on his shoulders, and he looked to Cinda. "This is the end, isn't it? We're already gone. I can see."

The necromancer bowed her head then looked to the others. "We should go, but I believe he's right. He can see his own end. Listen to him. He may observe truths that we cannot yet view."

Anne clutched her hands at her chest, her lips trembling.

Ang looped his brother's arm over his shoulder and said, "Let's go."

Rew took the lead and was joined by Cinda. The necromancer's robes flowed as she strode across the cold entry hall.

He asked her, "You know what to do?"

"I don't know what to do, but I believe there is a path we can take. I can see the end as well. Death brings clarity, Ranger, a gift from the Blessed Mother. Anne would call it that. I don't know. I cannot see that far, but from what I can see, there is no mercy in death."

Halfway across the room, Rew hissed and asked her, "My father, Alsayer, they all wanted us here, but why? What are we meant to do?"

"What we are meant to do is the dream of our fathers, of our mothers. What we will do is up to us. To defeat your father, we must dream our own dream." Cinda spoke as if she was in that dream already, as if she was only half awake or as if she was already dead and her body had not yet realized it. "We were bred like livestock. We were raised by fathers, who had their own intentions, their own vision for what we would accomplish, but their dream is not our destiny. Do you understand?"

"No."

Still walking, Cinda looked over her shoulder at her brother. "Raif, it is our time to choose our own path, to lay the stones to build a bridge to our future. What stones shall we lay? What future shall we choose? Vurcell was right. At the end, the view is clear. We have no destiny, only our choices, whether we saddle ourselves with the dreams of our ancestors or whether we forge our own way. My choice, the choice we must both make for Vaeldon, is that it ends with us. Our line stops at us, Raif. Do you understand? This dream must end so that another may begin. We must end it."

"I don't know what you're saying."

"We will have no heirs. We are the end, but while my end is nigh, yours need not be. If we strive, all of us, it need not be. You should finish it—finish me when the time is right. That is your destiny if you choose it, but no matter what, remember what I ask, that the line ends with us. Our blood will spill, but may your seed never find purchase."

"What are you talking about?" demanded Raif, his eyes wide, his head shaking.

Rew figured that Raif knew exactly what she was talking about.

"I think I understand," mumbled Anne. "Cinda is feeling the grace of the Blessed Mother. The Mother offers wisdom in her embrace. Can you sense her spirit, its warmth?"

"I hope her embrace is as gentle as you believe," whispered the necromancer, "but it is not her spirit which I sense."

They reached the end of the entry hall and the heavy doors

that stood ajar, but before they could pass through them, six valaan emerged, led by a younger version of Valchon.

"A fraemoth? A simulacrum?" gasped Raif. "Or... is that the real thing? Are we really dead?"

"Not you. Not yet," rasped Vurcell, and he shrugged off his brother's assistance. "I was curious about these creatures. It is Valchon's child indeed. It feels just like he did—empty. None of them took their own path. They were bound by the dreams of their fathers. Their bridge always led back to the beginning. Only Rew journeyed alone. You all go on. I'll deal with this."

"Not alone," whispered Ang.

Vurcell glanced at his twin, his falchions gripped tightly, his own blood running down his arm then the blade and dripping onto the floor. "Bring these to Rew, will you? He will need them some day."

"Sleep in the Mother's Grace, Vurcell," intoned Anne.

The younger version of Valchon, a final simulacrum, spread its arms. In its hands, two blades of emerald green sparked to life. Ethereal, like Cinda's eyes, they cracked with cold electrical energy. The simulacrum settled its feet, blocking the doorway.

"It's using necromancy," warned Cinda. "No other magic may be cast within this place."

Grinning, the simulacrum told them, "Grandfather made me a deal. He shared his power with me, and all I have to do is kill you. The throne will be mine."

"A false deal," responded Cinda, "but it does not matter, for you will not succeed."

Vurcell raised his falchions and said, "Don't doubt your path, Rew. I can see now. It goes where it needs to, as uncomfortable as that may be."

The ranger struck, moving like he couldn't feel his wounds, moving like he did back in Eastwatch. Confident, fast, deadly.

The simulacrum was faster.

It shifted to the side, darting out of the charging ranger's path. One of the magical blades, trailing billowing mist like smoke over a barrow, carved a deep gash along the ranger's hip. Blood spurted, and the fog clung to Vurcell, swirling after him as he pivoted and chased after the simulacrum.

It was launching itself at Ang, who spun his swordstaff, knocking the strike aside. The younger Valchon ignored Vurcell like he was already dead, pressing its attack on Ang, until Vurcell slashed across its back, cutting a deep line into its flesh.

The simulacrum threw itself forward, narrowly avoiding a fatal wound but then catching the butt of Ang's quarterstaff on its chin. Bone cracked, but still, the thing rolled smoothly to its feet, its eyes flashing in anger.

"Your necromancy cannot kill what is already dead," cackled Vurcell, advancing on the simulacrum, blood soaking his hip and leg as well as his arm.

"Go," instructed Ang, turning from Rew and the others to walk with his brother, pursing the simulacrum. "We'll handle this thing and the valaan."

He shifted left, and Vurcell moved right. The simulacrum faltered. The valaan closed behind the two rangers. Rew led the party through the door into a long, empty hallway.

"Even with necromancy, he thought a single simulacrum and a few valaan was going to stop us?" scoffed Zaine. "How many of those things have we killed already? Dozens?"

"The king didn't think that would stop us," warned Cinda. "He's stripping away our allies. Stay close now. We can't lose anyone else. Not yet."

"We have to stay together," agreed Anne. "We're powerful together, while he is alone. Whatever happens, we stay together."

Chapter Twenty-Nine

The next room was a test of that. The room was dark. Light bled up from the floor, or maybe the illumination was a natural dark while the rest of the room was a black deeper than night. A cool wind blew over them, as if they were outside, but instead of stars or clouds in the inky sky, it was a void. There was simply nothing.

Hanging above the empty floor were five shapes, their forms like gossamer, casting the faintest of shadow. The presence of the figures was a scream of terror, a psychic shriek. Rew had felt it as an echo, when they'd seen the monsters before, but now it was more visceral. A punch. Here, in this place of death and dreams, the wraiths had more substance. Northguard was a barrow. They were comfortable there.

Rew readied his sword, wondering if it would bite in this time and this place or if he should sheathe it, and raise his fists. Marching to face his father, standing off against five wraiths, he kept his longsword in his grip. Even if it didn't hurt the apparitions, he couldn't bring himself to release the weapon. He didn't care what he'd been told and what had worked in the past, he wasn't going into this empty handed.

The wraiths' mournful cry continued, and they moved closer

but not quickly. Their faces were full, as they must have been in life. One was ancient with a beard that cascaded like a waterfall down its transparent chest. Three were in the thick of life with imperious stares and strong jaws. The fifth was of age with the three and had their look, but instead of proud, it appeared sad.

Family? Generations of spirits that had died together, been trapped upon the mortal plane? Rew frowned. He knew why they looked familiar. They looked like him. They looked like his father. And he knew they hadn't been trapped on the mortal plane through some terrible chance. They'd been imprisoned there by Vaisius Morden, like the king had kept his father, his brother, the souls locked within his crypts, everyone. From the barrowlands to the crypts of the Cursed Father to Northguard, how many souls were held by the king? What vile purpose could he have for accumulating such might, the fruits of so much life?

"I'll handle these," declared Raif.

The big fighter stepped beside Rew, his greatsword held confidently in his hands. The enchanted steel would cleave through these monsters, these ghosts of Rew's blood, but that was why the king had sent them. They were the shades that Baron Fedgley had called in Falvar, the ones Alsayer had taken and Vyar Grund had recovered.

"We stay together," instructed Rew.

"My sword can banish them," reminded Raif.

Rew shook his head. "We stay together."

"They'll—"

"My father wants me to continue. If he wants me, then he must face us all. These shades will not hurt us."

"You sure about that, Ranger?" worried Zaine. "I don't know if you remember…"

"They will not hurt us."

Cinda, stepping beside her brother, stared down the wraiths. "We are of them as much as we are of the king's line. The ranger is right. They won't hurt us."

"Family," said Raif.

"Have you met Rew's family?" argued the thief.

Rew walked forward, slow and steady. The wraiths hung motionless. Had they eyes? Had they shape? He could feel them watching him, but they did not attack. The bitter cold of their presence stung his skin, but when he moved through them, they drifted apart and allowed his companions to pass unmolested.

"Why aren't they doing anything?" worried Zaine.

"Because he needs me," answered Rew, trying to walk confidently, trying not to spin around and keep an eye on the wraiths as they moved away. "This is the path he wants me to walk, but it's my path as well. He'd face me alone, if he could, but he knows that is not his choice. We've decided to walk together, and thus, he will have to face us all."

They reached the end of the dark room, if it was a room they were still in, and entered another door. Through this one, they found a giant stone relief of a man. It was four times the height of a normal man, carved from a flat black stone that Rew did not recognize. In the dim light of the room, it was clear the relief was a detailed depiction of a man. He was long limbed and somber faced. A marvelous beard hung down his chest, and his hands rested on a massive mace. He was familiar, an echo of a dream.

A sound drew Rew's attention, and he tensed, crouching to spring into attack.

Standing from a chair, the sole furniture in the room, was King Vaisius Morden the Eighth. The king's soul was centuries old, and his current body was just entering its twilight years, but despite that, he looked healthy and vigorous. He had the best food and exercise in the kingdom. He had access to the most talented high magicians and most knowledgeable arcanists. He had a score of empaths at his beck and call. It showed.

His shoulders were broad, his stomach trim. He wore a black leather vest, which displayed corded muscles on his arms. His forearms were encased in gold vambraces that had been inscribed with swirling, chaotic patterns. Rew knew the armor to be enchanted, and for the first time, he wondered if perhaps those patterns were not as chaotic as they appeared.

The king was from a time before, a people before. They had their own language, practices, and customs. They had their own look as well. Rew could see it in the king's face, his father's face—the heavy brow and square chin, the sharp nose and firm lips. It was the look of an elder people, and the look Rew had grown accustomed to in the creche. His family, himself, bred through inter-familial bloodlines for centuries all had that look. It was most obvious in the eyes. Vaisius Morden had the eyes of a predator. They all did.

Rew blinked.

The statue looming behind his father could have been an uncle. Blessed Mother, maybe it was, eight generations removed. It was the same face that all of Vaeldon's nobility had, of a people whose time was over. The king had bred them for their magic, and to… change them, to recreate his own ancestors but in his new mold. A dead people rising again. It wasn't just magic the king craved but his people.

Cinda raised her hands, and flickering funeral fire began to dance on her fingers. She'd been waiting months for this moment, and there was no reason to wait any longer.

The king waved a hand dismissively, and her fire snuffed out.

The young necromancer grunted.

Ignoring her, Vaisius Morden's hungry eyes locked on Rew's face. His voice that of a gravestone being dragged over broken rock, he asked, "Come to take the crown, boy?"

"I already have," said Rew. "I sat your throne in Mordenhold. I commanded your people and took the responsibility you've eschewed."

The king's lips curled into a pleased grin. His beard, trim as the razor that cut it, moved as he shook with silent laughter. "Stubborn as you always were. All my children are, perhaps you more than any others. But, you foolish boy, my throne is not in Mordenhold. It is here."

Rew tried to hold his father's gaze, but he couldn't help but glance at the massive relief the king had been facing. How long had the king been sitting there, in the empty room, in the empty keep, staring at the forgotten stone? Forgotten, but... Rew recognized it. He'd seen that man before but not in Northguard.

Rew told his father, "I don't recall that statue being here the last time I visited this place."

Shaking his head, Vaisius Morden replied, "We're not in Northguard. We're not in Vaeldon or the world at all, as you know it. Coming here, walking the valley, you've passed into a different realm, though you have not entirely left the old one."

"You mean death? But no, we did not die. This is... false. A lie."

"Look behind you."

Hesitantly, Rew did. Another carved stone relief loomed where they must have walked. There was no longer a door or the hallway beyond. The second statue was like the first, different but familiar. Rew knew he'd seen this one before. In the temple in Iyre, the Cursed Father.

It was time for Zaine to make a pithy quip, but no one spoke. The door they'd just entered was gone. In its place was a massive statue of the god of death. Evidently, that oddity was enough to silence even the thief.

The king continued, "You may call this place death or a dream. Life, death, dreams, they are states of our own being. None are more true than the other. None reflect a world any more valid than the other. Our waking moments, our dreams, and yes, our deaths, they are all the same, but we see differently because it is us who changes. These states are facets on a gem, different faces that we look from but all of the same stone. Here... this place is the center of the gem, the point where your waking life, your dreams, and your death come together. It is not a lie, not false at all, my boy, but not truth as you expect it to be either. You've only ever seen a part of the whole."

Shaking his head, Rew adjusted his grip on his longsword. He wanted to attack, but he knew it wouldn't work. The king could snuff out his life as easily as he'd waved away Cinda's funeral fire. It had to be Cinda. She had the talent to defy this man, but the ease he'd shown smothering her magic was disconcerting. They didn't have the tools or the knowledge to beat him.

For them to defeat him, the king would have to show them how.

Vaisius Morden studied them all, his eyes lingering on Cinda. "I always had sons. I wonder if that's been a mistake? The girl has been touched by the Cursed Father, yet she persists. There is strength in the barrows, but it has crushed more than it's built. Crushed her as well but not entirely. Not yet. What is broken can be repaired, lass."

"There is no Cursed Father," snapped Rew, his eyes blazing.

The king spread his arms, his hands open. "There is a Cursed Father, and it is I."

"It is your invention, a figment of your fancy."

"Indeed, and why not? Death is another facet of our waking. The Cursed Father is another face of mine. Do you see his face behind you? My face?"

Rew, glancing rapidly between his father and the statue looming behind them, was startled to see the face was that of his father, but had it been? He couldn't remember.

"You're insane," growled Cinda.

"I view the world and all of its faces differently than you, lass. Perhaps that is insanity, or perhaps it is clarity. Your view is clear, is it not? In the end, do you see truth or madness? I see more than you and always have. Let me show you."

The king held up his hand, and Rew felt a wrenching jerk, as if his eyes had been yanked from his head, but instead, he was watching a dark, smoke-clouded image of Mordenhold. Flames roared through the granite buildings, and Dark Kind flooded the streets. Tens of thousands of narjags rampaged, valaan speckling the horde like raisins in porridge.

People fled from them, running and screaming in terror, but

not for long. There were so many of the Dark Kind. They were everywhere, and there was nowhere to run. The city was overwhelmed, overrun completely. Entirely lost.

"This is happening, but is it the waking truth or a dream? It doesn't matter, you see, because it will happen in both. Death is the final facet. The view is clear. Can't you see the Dark Kind, rampaging, destroying the kingdom I built? Mordenhold is fallen, dozens of smaller towns as well. I can't count the villages that have been consumed by the tide. Carff, Jabaan, Iyre, what will be next? Yes, I abandoned Mordenhold. As did you. Both of us could have fought off this attack. Both of us could have saved the city, but we came here because we knew."

"Knew what?"

"The fight is not with the Dark Kind but with their creator. Long ago, the Dark Kind were cast from the fevered dreams of my people. I've been fighting them ever since. I created a kingdom with the sole purpose of stopping it. I've gathered strength. I've sustained myself the only way I could, all to protect life, all life, because that is my face to this world, the face of the king, but there are other faces, other facets. Death. Dreams. I understand more now than I did two hundred years ago when I built this tomb. I cannot kill what is already dead, and I cannot sleep without dreaming. My plan did not work, but that does not mean loss. It means change. We change, but the truth is, always was, and always will be."

The vision of Mordenhold slowly faded, and they were yet again in the room with the king and the relief of his brothers.

"I came here to shatter these prisons. I need you, Rew. You are the key."

"Why me?"

"Because you passed the test. Because you have done it before."

Rew blinked at his father. "Erasmus?"

"You released him. Dozens of your ancestors have tried and failed. It's no shame to admit I failed as well. What we locked away, we could not release without destroying ourselves, but you can. You have the connection to life that I have lost. Alsayer told me, but I was not sure. Now I am. Only you can do this and withstand the onslaught."

"I won't help you," muttered Rew. He could feel the giant statues looming over them like they were living people. Giants. Brothers? Vaisius Morden himself? He'd called them brother, Brian of the Brambles—

Rew gasped. He knew where he'd seen the face on the statue before, the one of dreams. It wore his father's face now, but it'd worn another before. Vaisius Morden's brothers and Vaisius Morden were one in the same. The king was insane. He had been for centuries. He'd... he'd torn himself apart, locked away pieces of his soul, but those pieces were breaking out. Brian of the Brambles had dreamt of the waking world.

Vaisius Morden tilted his head, like he was studying a passage in a book he did not understand. He told them, "The kingdom will fall if you do not help me. Everyone will die."

"You could destroy the Dark Kind," responded Rew. "You've done it before. You could do it again. You could protect Mordenhold, your people."

"Yes, I could. If I did, more would come. I tire of the effort. No, we must release my brothers. I've been locked away for too long. It is time I'm whole."

"You have to face the Dark Kind. They are your dreams, your conjuring. It is your responsibility to stop them, to protect the kingdom you built."

"When you are king, you may face them," suggested Vaisius Morden. "I give you the crown. You will be king, Rew. All of Vaeldon's resources will be yours."

"Not if I'm your puppet. I know the price of your crown."

The king laughed again. "You are too stubborn to be completely subsumed by me. Your soul will remain in your body. You—I—will be the same. You'll have as much say in the future of this kingdom as I do, but with you, and only with you, will we have the strength to shatter the prison my brothers are entombed within. Then, death, dreams, and life will all be as one again. We'll rule all three planes, not just this one. I'll be whole, as will you, as will everything."

Rew took a step back. He didn't believe a word of what his father said. Of course he didn't. But should he attack the man? Should he shout at Cinda to… to do what? Maybe he could reseal the tomb, stop his ancestor from casting more Dark Kind from his dream into the world of the living, but he didn't know how. It was old magic, ancient magic he felt within the room. It was fueled by instinct and will, but he didn't know what to do. The way forward was obscured by his father's blazing madness.

"You brought Erasmus into your body, did you not?" pressed the king.

Rew took another step back and did not respond.

"You took knowledge from him. How to stop the maelstrom? Then you flung him aside, cast him into the beyond. What are you afraid of, boy? It is your magic, your connection with life, that we need now. My own ties to this world have been severed. I can no longer perform the old rituals, the ancient stirrings that I bound myself with all those years ago. All things have a cost, and my life has brought a steep one. It is you who will have the upper hand, now and forever. Let us complete the process. Let us make you king, and this will end."

"It will end, or it will change," hissed Zaine. "He's lying, Ranger. He doesn't need you to defeat the Dark Kind. He needs you to defeat everything else."

Vaisius Morden flung his hand out toward Zaine, and a spear of jet black leapt toward the thief. She yelped in surprise then screamed in pain.

Rew charged.

The king blurred and then separated. There were three of him. The one in the center swept a hand at Rew, and a scythe of utter darkness flew at the ranger. He jumped, hurdling the attack, but when he reached the king and swung, his sword met a shield of the same darkness. The king lashed out with another attack.

Vaisius Morden's fist was encapsulated in the void of the grave, and Rew scrambled away, certain he didn't want to get hit by whatever his father was swinging, but as he moved, he saw stark lines of muscle on the king's forearm. This king wasn't wearing the golden bracers.

"Fraemoths!" barked Anne. "He conjured himself. He is his own greatest fear."

Rew grunted and did not reply. The king feared himself. Fair enough. He was pretty damned terrifying to Rew, too. The king in front of him—the Cursed Father?—feinted, and Rew backed away. Would killing the king do them any good?

Raif went berserk.

Howling like a mindless beast, he charged the second bare-armed Vaisius Morden. It might be a conjuring of the king, but it moved with his grace, and it commanded his magic. In the king's hands, a giant mace materialized in a blink, and it swung at Raif.

The lad was mid-charge and didn't have time to react to the weapon appearing from nowhere. It smashed into his chest and sent him flying in a terrific cartwheel to crash in a clamor of steel.

Cinda threw her hands wide, and an icy cloud of death's breath flowed over the king and his fraemoths. They ignored it and began to approach Rew. He settled his feet. The king, with his bracers, would be the most dangerous, but the conjurings had almost killed him and they might have just killed Raif.

Death's breath evidently unable to harm them, Cinda tried again, this time throwing a blast of funeral fire. It struck the frae-moth on the right, the one who'd faced Rew, scalding the side of its face, but it turned to her, half its cheek melted and sloughing down. It smiled a ghastly grin and told her, "Lass, you cannot kill what is already dead. Your magic cannot hurt us."

And to speak truth to its claims, the fraemoth's face crawled back together, the skin knitting, covering the bone of its cheek, but blood still stained its neck and chest, and its skin was tight, twisting its lips in a mockery of mirth.

"Rew, I can slow them," said Cinda, "but I don't know how to stop them. He… I don't know how to stop him, do you understand?"

"I do," said the ranger, letting his sword dip down in front of him. "Father, I will give you my body, but you must spare my friends."

"The time for negotiation has passed."

"If we fight, this body will be damaged. You cannot take me unharmed. I promise you that."

"You have no idea of what I can do."

"And you've underestimated me at every turn. Shall we see how stubborn I truly am?"

The king paused his advance, his fraemoths stopping beside him. "Parents always underestimate their children, don't they?"

"The child is always stronger."

"Not always."

"Spare my friends or try me."

"They're half dead anyway," declared the king. "Very well. I will do them no further harm, but you must lay down your blade."

Rew waited a moment then dropped his sword. It gave a cold ring as it struck the stone floor. He could hear Anne's panicked breath behind him. She was trying to pray, he thought. Raif, or Zaine, was groaning, but he couldn't hear the other. Maybe they were already dead. Cinda stood calmly a dozen paces to his side, waiting.

"What do I do?" Rew asked his father.

"Kneel. Cut your hand with your knife then offer it to me."

"What then? How… how does it work?"

"Blood, our common blood, is a roadway. My soul will take that path and become one with you. Do not worry. The only pain will be the wound you cut into your hand."

"That's it?"

"It is ancient magic, son, instinct and will. Following the patterns of the world laid down far before even my time. You and your people want rules, but there are no rules. The only barriers are those you bind yourself with. Life, death, wake, dream, they're blinders you put on yourself to prevent you from truly seeing the possibilities. I've torn my blinders away. The view is clear now. It will be for you, too. Soon."

"When our blood mixes, the soul can pass through?"

The king held up a hand and, across it, drew a sharp line of utter black. Crimson blood welled in his palm, and he shoved it toward Rew.

Rew knelt, pulled his hunting knife, and sliced the blade across the meat of his palm just as the king had. He held his hand up and swallowed nervously as his father took another step closer.

"Be stubborn, Ranger," whispered Cinda.

"Be quiet," growled the king.

Vaisius Morden reached out and he grasped Rew's hand.

Immediately, Rew understood the king had lied.

THE GIANT STONE STATUE WAS NOT THE TOMB OF VAISIUS MORDEN'S brother or a prison where he'd hidden away a part of himself. It was the prison of each one of Rew's ancestors, the winners of the Investiture. This was their home, their jail, the throne room of the Mordens.

Zaine had been right. The King, the Cursed Father, and the Dreamer were all one man. They were all Vaisius Morden, but he had not imprisoned himself. He ruled the kingdom as king. He devoured the souls of the dead as the Cursed Father, and as the Dreamer, he conjured the Dark Kind. He had not hidden from the facets of his soul. He had embraced them.

But in doing so, he had spoken one truth. He'd lost his connection to life. His hold on the waking realm was slipping. That was why he'd fled to the fortress and Northguard, this realm beyond. His anchor to the waking world was tenuous, and he needed the ranger's skills to root himself back within the world, to return to Vaeldon. He needed those skills, but he did not need Rew, as he did not need his ancestors. If the king was successful, they would not share a body. Rew would share a stone prison with all of those who'd come before him.

He would be worse than dead.

As their blood mixed and the king's power flowed into Rew, he saw visions of the king's plan, like pages turning in a book. The king commanded the Dark Kind. He commanded the souls of the dead, and through Rew's communion, he would command the living as well. He was no longer keen to merely observe the world through his waking facet. He wanted to rule the world of the living, not as king, but as god.

The only truth he'd told? His connections were frayed. He'd lived too long. The ancient magic washed over him like a river over stone, wearing him to nothing. The king needed Rew's vibrancy, his connection to life. The king needed the blood of a ranger, the skill of communion, to nourish his dreams of conquest and immortality.

He did not care who survived within his realm. Life, death, and the dream would all be planes within his control, all facets of his command. It all flashed through Rew in an instant of under-standing as his father's soul came into contact with his own, and then he felt his father grasp his soul.

It felt as if cold bands of iron wrapped around him and then began to squeeze and pull. It was like being dragged through a hole that was half the size of his body. Immediately, he was in the thrall of his father. The king was experienced and powerful. There was no fighting him directly, and Rew could not grasp the wilder-ness, his home. He could not reach the wild in this place. So he held on. Not to himself. He held onto his friends, his chosen family.

Anne, warm comfort. Raif, hard determination. Zaine,

mischief and loyalty. Cinda, cold reason and sacrifice. They were his anchor, and he wrapped his mind around theirs just as his father closed on his own. Low magic. Ancient magic. All life was connected, and Rew held on as tightly as he could as his father began to strip his soul from his living flesh.

Then, Cinda put her hand on theirs. It was wet with her blood. The blood of Rew and the king mixed with that of the young necromancer.

"What—" began Vaisius Morden. Then, he cut off his words with an indignant snort. "Girl, you cannot."

Rew stood and punched his father in the stomach. The old man's eyes widened, but he didn't let go of Rew's hand, and Cinda did not let go of his. Rew punched the man in the side of the head, and the king's grip was broken.

Vaisius Morden cackled. "I don't need to be touching you, fool."

"Good to know," growled Cinda, and her eyes blazed. "I wouldn't know how to do any of this if you did not show me."

The king coughed and quivered.

"Only you know the pathways," said Rew. "Only you could guide us on how to walk them."

"Then watch," snarled the king.

The king clutched at Rew's soul while Cinda tugged on his. The ranger felt his grasp, his connection with the others, begin to slip, but they were there. They'd come with him, for him. They were his family, more so than any of those he'd grown up with in Mordenhold. The king sought the connection to Rew, the fruit of the Investiture, but Rew had already chosen. He was already bound.

The king had no one. His strength, his ties to life, death, and dream were frayed and breaking.

With a bestial shriek, Cinda cried out, and thin tendrils of glowing white peeled off the king and began to writhe, drawn toward her. She was connected as well, part of a thrumming circle, a family. In that, she had power.

The two fraemoths attacked.

Rew pitched himself forward, grabbing his longsword as he rolled, and he sprang up in between the creatures and Cinda. Ropes of the king's soul snaked around them, and Rew felt his own essence still under pressure, tugging from him, nearly pulling him from his feet, but he fought on instinct.

The creatures' fists were voids of utter darkness, and they swung them with fury. Rew dodged, but he had nowhere to go. He couldn't run, or he would expose Cinda. He attempted to deflect one of the strikes and gasped. The shock through his sword was like plunging into an icy mountain stream.

He ducked another blow, and he could feel the pull on his soul intensify. The voids were eroding the connection to the others, killing the bonds. If he no longer had those anchors, the king would rip him away in a blink. Cursing, Rew dropped to a knee and wheeled his longsword in a low sweep.

He caught one of the fraemoths at the ankles and severed both of its feet, but the second fraemoth leapt his attack and lashed out with a boot, catching Rew square in the face. The bone of his nose broke, and he was flung backward. As he skidded across the floor, hot blood poured from his nostrils, filling his mouth. He spit. There was nothing between the fraemoth and Cinda.

Raif bellowed and crashed into the side of the thing, knocking it away. Then, Zaine was at its back. She leapt on the creature, reaching around its head, thrusting back with her poignards, and plunging the blades into its eyes.

"I've got him!" cried Cinda, her eyes bright. Then, they faded. "I can see him."

Rew tried to stand, but he fell back, sitting. He looked down. His leg was a ruined mess. His knee was twisted, and halfway down his calf, the muscle was ripped away. Red blood and white bone. When had that... The first fraemoth had grabbed at him, the one he'd cut the legs from. It'd nearly ripped his own leg off. He tried to angle his longsword and use it to stand, but he couldn't.

"Raif," howled Cinda. "Now is the time. I've got him, but I cannot hold. You've got to banish us. Now!"

The fighter stood over the fraemoth he'd knocked aside, his greatsword in his hands, but he did not move toward Cinda. Instead, he thrust, driving his greatsword into the fraemoth's chest, killing it.

"Raif!" shouted Cinda.

The king had fallen onto his back. One of the fraemoths was dead. The other was trashing, dying impotently as blood pumped from its severed legs. Cinda was failing as well.

"He's stronger than I am," she quaked. "I can't—he's taking control. Raif! Your sword! Kill me, you fool!"

"Rew," hissed Anne. She pointed.

From the feet of the huge stone relief, the Dreamer, valaan were emerging. Five of them. Ten. Fifteen.

Rew tried to stand, but his leg collapsed under his weight. He searched for some thread of wild, some natural well of power he could draw upon, but where they were, there was nothing natural. They were in some figment of his father's dreams or his death, whatever difference that made. They were far from Rew's home, where he drew strength. They had each other, but as more valaan emerged, he knew it wasn't enough.

Twisting awkwardly, he called, "Anne, do you see Ang, Vurcell?"

"I don't see anything!" cried the empath. "There's no door, Rew. No one is coming. It's just us."

Raif moved to face the valaan, Zaine coming to take his side. The thief looked back, seeing Cinda's growing panic, but she stayed with Raif. The fighter ignored his sister and her pleading cries. He'd said he would support her. He'd said in the end he would be there, but he couldn't. Cinda was walking her path, but Raif could not follow.

Cinda staggered toward Rew then knelt in front of him. "He has to kill me. Tell him he has to kill me, or this is all for naught.

The enchantment on the sword can banish us both. Without... I cannot do this alone. The king is taking control!"

"Cinda... he can't." whispered Rew. "He can't."

"Ranger, I cannot hold. I have to die. We must all walk our own path. This is mine. Allow me to walk it. Tell him to kill me. He listens to you."

"If I force him, then it is not his path."

"Your father tried to choose for you. Would you do the same to me? It's the only way. Command him to slay me, or we're all going to die anyway."

Tears were rolling from Cinda's burning green eyes down her pale cheeks. She was trembling, and in her face, Rew saw fear eroding into triumph. Around her, like fog rising off a river, tendrils of Vaisius Morden's soul were writhing free. They were wrapping around her, taking control. She was right. She couldn't hold against the strength and knowledge of Vaisius Morden. She was going to lose this fight.

"Wait, what is she saying?" demanded Anne, crouching beside Rew. "What is happening?"

Rew and Cinda stared at each other. She tried to speak but couldn't. He could see the struggle marring her face. That calm face. That composed girl—no, a woman now—was being wracked by the battle taking place within. His father, a two-hundred-year-old soul, her a mere sixteen winters. How had they believed she could win?

He saw in her eyes that she was failing. The emerald green was streaked with virulent black. It was over. A croak, hardly a whisper, she pleaded, "He has to kill me."

"What is she saying?" cried Anne.

Rew tilted his longsword up, the razor-sharp point aimed toward the girl. "You each chose your own path. He walks his, but I can help you walk yours. Cinda, the sword is a prison, a tomb that not even Erasmus Morden could break from."

Holding his gaze, she slumped forward, the tip of the longsword piercing her breast then sliding through her, jutting out her back as she fell onto the enchanted steel. Her blood poured over his hands, hot and then cold. Her shoulder fell against his, and he felt desperate, strained gasps for air. Her blood was ice cold. The blood on the steel, sticking from her back, froze on his blade. Crimson crystals spread in blazing fractals and then began to disappear, absorbed into the blade.

"Rew!" screamed Anne, grabbing at Cinda's shoulder.

Raif and Zaine attacked the prone form of the king, striking his body, hacking and stabbing the man like a roasted hog. And like the hog, he was already dead. His soul was gone before they got to him. Before the feet of the statue of the Dreamer, the valaan were gone, as if they'd always been no more than a dream. Raif and Zaine spun, crying in victory and then in loss.

Rew fell back, dizzy, his body failing from loss of blood. Cinda slumped on top of him, her vacant eyes a hand-width from his own. Her body was still, and slowly, with each of his gasping breaths, the cold of the longsword began to fade.

Raif fell beside them, wrapping his sister in his arms. He was wailing, telling her it wasn't supposed to be like this, that he would have died for her, that he would have fought until the last breath left his body and then beyond. He would have—but in his own way. She had fought in her way.

Zaine and Anne were at Raif's back, trying to comfort him, but there was no comfort, not now.

Raif had fought his battle. Cinda had fought hers. It was the way it'd always had to be. The child was stronger than the parent. Cinda had been stronger than them all.

Rew laid back and closed his eyes. It was over.

Chapter Thirty

R aif scratched his beard.

Rew nodded approvingly. "Beard looks good."

"Saves time shaving each morning."

"Lose the hairs up top. You'll really be flying out the door."

Raif glanced at him suspiciously and unconsciously pushed his long, thick locks back from his face. "I may wait on that."

Rew shrugged and did not respond.

Raif dropped his arm, his armor rustling with the motion. He wore bright, gleaming chain beneath a solid steel breastplate embossed with a lacquered steed in ruby. Heavy pauldrons, thick gauntlets, and a kilt of overlapping steel completed the ensemble. The suit was new and untested. The lad sparkled like a gemstone. Rew didn't know where Raif had gotten the idea to use a horse as his sigil, but the color was to honor his sister.

Rew told him, "You could have someone else do this, you know."

Raif grunted. "I can't ask someone to do something I'm not willing to do myself. I learned that from you."

"You didn't learn much if you think I'd go tramping about the barrowlands for weeks, cracking open the tombs and peeking inside."

"You'd go off tramping through whatever wilderness you could find the moment you thought you could slip away without your guards noticing, Your Majesty. From what I heard, you nearly did. Anne caught you climbing out a window, didn't she, nothing but a traveler's pack on your back and a jug of ale in your hands?"

Rew crossed his arms over his chest. He would not respond to wild accusations, especially when they were true. He regretted the jug of ale. He figured that was how Anne learned he was escaping. Next time, he would get out then find ale in the city. An old dog could learn new tricks, no matter what they said.

Raif reached over his shoulder and touched the hilt of his giant, enchanted greatsword. "This blade is my family's legacy, but those wraiths out there are our legacy as well. The line ends with me, but there could be another, one day, with the strength to call upon those foul ghosts. No, I won't leave that for a future generation, whoever their sire is. I'm going to hunt down any remaining wraiths and banish them. It'll bring rest to these forgotten plains and give us a chance to move on from the past. The soil here is amongst the most fertile in Vaeldon, I'm told. Next spring, we could have settlers' wagons rolling across these grasslands."

"Expanding the duchy, eh?"

"Expanding your kingdom, my liege."

Rew grinned at the younger man. "How is Spinesend?"

"You could come visit."

"I don't want to step on your toes."

"Spinesend is well. The entire Eastern Province has been calm for a year, since we put down that last, ah, disagreement about who ought to control the highways south of the capital. We have peace and justice. My people are content with that for the moment. For what's next, maybe this new territory will bring prosperity."

"Some of the nobles' daughters hanging around your court

don't seem very content. They think you a bit strange, that you haven't been tripped into bed with any of them."

Raif glanced at Rew. "So you did visit."

"You're my bannerman. It's my duty to keep an eye on things."

"Secretly? On my love life?"

Rew shrugged.

"Well, let me spoil it for you. There isn't one. It was the last thing Cinda asked me, that the Fedgley line ends with us. I'll respect her wishes, and those daughters can think me strange all that they want. I owe my sister that, after... I owe her that."

Rew did not respond.

"Not going to try to talk me into marriage? It's known I'm close to you. You'd earn a great deal of good will by making a match for me. For a year, I've known eventually you would have to ask. The answer is no, Rew, for her, you understand?"

"I won't force you, but you know, your bloodline does not have to stop with you. Instead of the path ending, it can change course. Cinda would understand that. My advisors have managed some other arrangements. Noble blood paired with glittering gold. It seems to be going well, so far."

"Until the nobles realize you're mixing their blood with that of the merchants to wash away their magic."

"Ending the nobility in a marriage bed seemed more pleasant than doing it on the edge of a sword, but it turns out, nobles aren't as precious with their seed when there's a prominent merchant's daughter offering a dowry. After the Investiture, the Dark Kind... they need funds for rebuilding. Spellcasting had value in my father's kingdom, but not mine. That's only somewhat of a trick, and the cunning ones saw through it right away. Still, they've seen benefits, so they've kept quiet."

"They'll be back to their old ways sooner or later," warned Raif, "particularly if you abdicate, like you claim you will. That is still your plan, isn't it? I can't be the only one hearing questions about marriage and heirs."

Rew shifted uncomfortably, glancing back to make sure his dour-faced, black-clad guards were out of earshot. "Those plans are fluid. You're right. The nobles will be back to their old ways sooner or later. They're more stubborn about some things than I anticipated, and they'll grab any advantage they can take. I don't know that I'm a very good king, Raif, but who else is there?"

Raif snorted then answered, "I don't know. The nobility… aren't all like my father taught me they were. I suppose it's on us to change that, if anyone can."

Rew sighed but nodded in agreement.

"Truly," asked Raif, "you would bless a match with a commoner for me?"

"Zaine likes women, Raif."

The young duke scowled. "Last time I saw her, she gave some hints…"

"She likes women."

Frowning, the big youth questioned, "Is she with someone?"

Throwing up his hands, Rew backed away. "I'm not getting into the middle of this."

"She was last in Eastwatch, you know. I wrote her to come visit me. She hasn't sent a response yet. Perhaps I should go there?"

"I know she's in Eastwatch. I'm visiting there next. Touring the entire eastern half of the kingdom, actually. Anne insisted."

"To get you out of the keep, or punish you for trying to sneak off?"

"She didn't say."

"Tell Zaine I asked about her, will you? I'd like to see her, if she has the time. Do you think I should… No, this is important. I'll clear the barrows first, and then… will you ask her if she'll see me again?"

"Sure. I'll ask her."

Sighing, Raif put a hand on a longsword at his side. It was Rew's old blade, the weapon that had killed Raif's sister, the weapon that still held some piece of her, they both hoped.

"The pommel is cold sometimes, colder than it should be. Do you think that is her?"

"It could be."

"Could you feel Erasmus, his soul? Could you communicate with him before he... What was it like?"

Rew nodded. "I just felt him as a presence at first. For years, that was all. Just a sense. Eventually, yes, we shared some thoughts, some memories. It was uncomfortable because of who he was. There was a time we could speak, not quite like you and I are now, but it was true conversation. By then, I knew how dangerous he was. In time, as the connection grows..."

"That would be nice," said Raif, his voice dropping an octave. "It'd be nice to feel her again."

"I'm sorry, Raif."

"It was her choice," said the duke. "I hate it, but I don't know that she was wrong. Would any of this have been possible without her sacrifice? The king... I thought I'd killed him, you know. I thought I won a victory, stabbing my greatsword down into him, but he was already gone. She killed him the only way she knew how. Maybe that's the only way there was. She's the one who freed us. I'd like to thank her one day."

Rew reached out and gripped Raif's chainmail-clad arm.

"Pfah," said the duke. "I've got the wraiths to attend to. If I don't get going, we won't make the first barrow until after dark, and... Well, I'm committed, but I'm not that committed."

Rew nodded. "Be safe out there, lad."

"I'm not a child, you know."

"Old habits."

Raif gestured for a troop of his soldiers. A score of men wearing gleaming chain, thick leather jackets over it, and adorned in bright crimson piping started preparing to march.

"Anne will come in a month, when the weather warms," Rew told Raif.

The Duke of Spinesend nodded.

"Destroying the wraiths won't bring her back, Raif. Remember that. In time… you may feel her, but it will take time. Don't get yourself killed before that time has passed, eh."

Raif gripped the hilt of the longsword at his side. "I don't mean to get killed, but someone has to face the wraiths. It should be me. Perhaps that is how I can honor her."

Rew gave the lad a final nod. Raif and his men began marching out into the barrowlands, going to eradicate the last of the ghosts from Vaisius Morden's time. Rew, the former ranger, the king, waved to a young spellcaster who'd been loitering a dozen paces away.

The boy, his chin covered in an embarrassing peach fuzz, raised his hands, and in the middle of the air, a purple and gold vortex spun into a small portal.

Most of the spellcasters who could manage a big one were dead or had wisely fled from answering to the numerous atrocities they'd committed under the rule of Rew's family. If things went well, and the noble and common blood was thoroughly mixed in the next generation, there would be fewer spellcasters still who could manage a portal. Another generation past that, Rew hoped there wouldn't be any.

He stepped through the opening and smiled. It would be good for people to get out and walk a little.

ZAINE SAT BACK IN A STUFFED LEATHER CHAIR, ONE LEG COCKED jauntily over an arm of the chair, a half-full ale mug cradled in her lap. She was grinning mischievously, but Rew was fairly sure she hadn't stolen his coin purse. He rarely carried one these days. He had people for that.

He patted his belt and frowned. He was fairly certain he hadn't brought one. Pfah, had he? Had she stolen it? Her grin broadened, and he cursed to himself. He coughed and asked, "Your throat wet enough to give me a report now?"

Swirling the ale in her mug, Zaine drawled, "I figured Blythe was keeping you appraised of my whereabouts."

"She told me you two split up."

Zaine scowled. "We're taking a break."

"Umm hmm."

"What did she tell you? Did she send you here, hoping you'd talk me into something? Or out of something?"

"I'd never presume to give you relationship advice, Zaine."

"Yes you would. Go ahead. Let's hear it."

Rew laughed and drank deeply of his own ale. He wiped his lips with the back of his hand and told her, "Very well. Blythe is a good woman, a great woman, but she's ready to settle down, and you are not. Nothing wrong with that, but I don't see either of you changing in the near future. Perhaps a break is the right thing. Don't tell her I said that."

"That's it?"

Rew nodded.

Zaine sighed. "It's true enough. Not many prospects on the outskirts of the kingdom, though, you know? Not with a good woman, at least. Pfah, if I wanted a man, I could have any of them."

"I'm sure you could," he responded. He rubbed his scalp. Was that the time to mention Raif? No, he'd said he'd stay out of it, and he'd meant it. Instead, he asked, "How has the expedition gone? You find a wyvern yet?"

Shaking her head, Zaine told him, "No, and I rather hope we don't. Ah, don't tell Blythe I said that." She laughed then added, "Maybe we shouldn't tell her we spoke at all. It's been awkward, you know, working for her. Was fun at first. Sneaking away during meetings, touring the ranger's administrative offices, if you know what I mean. Even on the throne, once, when you were away. Sorry about that. She got too serious, though, when you named her commandant. Or maybe she just remembered what we did on the commandant's desk. Hard for her to tell me what to do when we're sitting there, and I'll be honest, hard for me to pay attention when I'm thinking about it."

Rew cleared his throat and responded, "Yes. Well, on that note, the commandant somewhat stiffly asked that your line of reporting skip her and go directly to me. I think she felt it was even more awkward than you do. Not that it's any better for me. My throne, really, Zaine?"

Zaine waved a hand dismissively then turned up her ale mug. When she lowered it, she at least had the decency to be flushing bright red. "Right. Forget I said anything about that. We paid complete attention when you were naming off all the new duchies and baronies, I swear. Anything that happened when all those folk left was strictly business."

Rew rolled his eyes. "I don't believe that for a moment. Tell me, what are you paying attention to? Are you even looking for the wyvern?"

"Oh, we're looking all right," assured Zaine, standing and ambling over to dip another mug of ale, "but they're not easy to find. You ever seen one?"

Rew shook his head.

"Well, if the legendary King's Ranger never spotted a wyvern out in the wilderness, how can I be expected to?"

"There's a real concern the natural beasts will come down from their hiding places now that the Dark Kind have been eliminated. A wyvern has no other predators. When I was a ranger here—"

Zaine pretended to cover a yawn with a balled fist. "We all know. When you were a ranger here, you left for each expedition walking uphill, and you returned uphill as well. I've heard the stories."

Rew snorted.

She assured him, "If there's a wyvern living within a week of Eastwatch, we'll find it. Sooner or later."

Glancing at the foam threatening to spill over the side of her ale mug, Rew rolled his eyes. He asked her, "How are the new recruits coming along?"

"Terrible. I don't think they're ever going to figure it out."

"You have to train them, you know."

"Or you could give me someone who's got a bit of experience. There was a woman I saw when I was last in Havmark. Pretty thing. Looked like just the type for—"

"I think I know who you're talking about, and she doesn't have the kind of experience you need."

"Need... want..."

"Zaine," said Rew, shaking his head at the woman's antics. "If you've been eyeing the recruits like that, you're lucky Blythe agreed to a break in your relationship rather than beating you from one end of the training yard to the other and breaking every bone in your body. Pfah, maybe I ought to ask her to do it and teach you a little discipline."

"Discipline? There's nothing else to do in Havmark except, ah, evaluate the new blood, you know. Come on, tell me that's not how Blythe ended up in your command? I won't believe you didn't give her a good look before you recruited her."

"Training, Zaine. Everyone is there to train. It's why we resettled the place. Give the rangers a proper home, a place they can develop into the organization Vaeldon needs."

"The place could use a few more taverns. That's all I'm saying."

Rew sat back, stretching his legs out. "I'm not disagreeing with that."

"Don't get your britches twisted, Your Majesty. We're leaving tomorrow at dawn on expedition again, looking for any signs of wyverns, or anything else out there. I got a tip, though if it turns out to be a good one, I'll eat my boot. Figured it'd be good for the lads, though, to venture deep in the wild. You know what? It might do our recruits some good seeing the man himself in action. Join us for a few days, for old time's sake?"

Shaking his head, Rew told her, "I've got to get back to Carff.

There'll be a stack of parchment on my desk that reaches the ceiling and a line of petitioners stretching along the beach."

"You mean Anne told you to be home in time for supper?"

"Something like that."

"We've got more ale if you want to stay the night. You can inspect the rangers in the morning. Isn't that something kings do, inspect the recruits? Stay a bit, your kingship. You can tell Anne I begged for your help."

"Inspecting the recruits is something the senior ranger is supposed to do…"

"I'll make a note of that. Another round while you share the rest of your wisdom with me?"

"Aye, I suppose someone's got to show you how it's done. Another round."

HE SLIPPED SILENTLY INTO HIS SITTING ROOM AND PAUSED. AT HIS desk, framed by open doors that led out to his patio overlooking the deep blue sea beyond, was Anne.

"You look tired," she said without looking up.

Frowning at the top of her head, he replied, "Well, I have been touring the eastern half of the kingdom. There was much to see, and—"

"Oh, really? And which part of the kingdom were you in last night?"

He coughed into his fist. "Eastwatch."

"With Zaine."

He nodded.

Though she still hadn't looked up at him, Anne snorted and declared, "Not tired, then, but hungover."

"She broke up with Blythe. She needed a shoulder to cry on, and I led the inspection of the rangers before she and her recruits went on expedition. Ruling a kingdom isn't all about paperwork, Anne. The people need to see me."

The empath finally glanced at him, her eyes narrow with suspicion. "Zaine, the same one I know, was crying on your shoulder over a breakup?"

"Sort of."

"You know, Zaine writes me letters," said Anne. "She told me she was ending it with Blythe. Said it was mutual. Sort of. In the same letter she inquired about a young healer that's getting attention here in town. She asked if the woman could be dispatched to Eastwatch and whether the woman was presently seeing anyone, and if she was, whether it was a man or a woman. That's the Zaine who was crying on your shoulder all night?"

"Well, I didn't say—Wait, Zaine writes letters?"

"She dictates them, I think."

"Who…" began Rew. Then, he trailed off, shaking his head. He didn't want to know.

The empath put a hand on a stack of papers she'd been reading. "Speaking of letters, you ought to peruse some of them yourself from time to time. Maybe running a kingdom isn't all about paperwork, but some of it is."

"That's why I have aides."

"I've decided to sell the inn."

"What?"

She sat back, crossing her hands over her stomach. "Every time you leave the city, I get a flood of courtiers showing up at my tables. They're never satisfied with the wine I serve, but don't want to pay coin for anything more expensive. They rarely eat my cooking, and worst of all, every one of them asks me where you are or what you think about some proposal that more often than not, I know nothing about. Pfah, if they wrote you a letter about it, you probably know even less than I do," she said, gesturing at the untouched pile on his desk. "But if I tell them that, they take it as an invitation to make the proposal directly to me."

"You should refer them to my administrators," suggested Rew. "They're the ones who can answer those queries."

"I do, but everyone knows you avoid your administrators with a tenacity that's quickly becoming legend."

"The kingdom runs better when professionals are managing it. I'm a ranger, Anne. I don't know anything about statecraft, negotiations, or any of the rest of it."

"What did they teach you in the creche? It wasn't all playing with swords and magic, was it?"

"That was a long time ago," he mumbled, "and my father didn't—"

"You want to be the same sort of king he was? What you don't know, you ought to learn. I bet you told something just like that to Zaine this morning when inspecting the recruits."

He shrugged and took at seat across from her on the opposite side of his desk. "If you close your inn, what will you do?"

"I thought of moving into the palace."

He blinked at her.

"I asked your seneschal to prepare me apartments."

"That will get people talking. The courtiers will be up in arms."

"Were you planning on marrying? If anything, this might shush them. You wouldn't believe some of the proposals I've heard…"

"Doesn't feel like I need to be married," complained Rew, staring at his old friend crossly.

Anne ignored his comment and continued, "I've been thinking. Your father—Vaisius Morden, whatever we ought to call him —failed because he had no one beside him. He truly had lost his connections to life. His children were in the creche. Their mothers were nothing more than warm vessels. His administrators were clutching scavengers, nipping at whatever power he let trickle from his fingers. I won't see you fall into the same trap. That's why I'm moving in. You need someone here who can support you. Keep you connected."

"Support me, or…" asked Rew, glancing pointedly at the paperwork she'd just asked him to read.

She ignored that comment as well. "The first order of business will be straightening up your rooms. You'll need a schedule, naturally, as half the problem is no one knows where you are or when they can reach you. A few hours of court each day ought to solve that. Your wardrobe will need a serious look as well, obviously."

"I have plenty of clothes."

"You have the clothes of a ranger. You're the king, Rew. It's time you dressed like it and act like it as well."

"I do my best."

"We'll see."

Rew sighed. He was doing a lot of that lately.

Anne pushed a piece of paper across the desk to him. "It seems Commandant Eckvar and the other retired rangers have completed their relocation to Havmark."

"That's good. The recruits are there to help them, if they admit a need for it. More so, they enjoy the climate along the coast better than the woods. Bright sunlight and a warm breeze." He shrugged. "Old people. They're like lizards."

"I'm sure you know there's still a portal stone down below which opens to the old ranger village. I sent some people to clean it up and check on the stores of supplies. The village is days from anywhere. Can't imagine there's another soul within twenty leagues of the place now that the rangers are gone. In a year or two, it will be a true wilderness."

Rew stared at her and did not respond.

"Address this paperwork. Attend to your administrators, and I won't tell anyone where you've gone when you need some time away. Go there. Stay in the village a few days or just wander around a bit in the woods. You're the king, and you have responsibilities because of that, but I know in your heart you're still a ranger."

Slowly, a smile crept onto his face.

"When you go, take those with you," said Anne, pointing above his mantle where two gleaming, silver falchions hung. "You never know when you might need them."

***

Hey, it's me, AC. Glad you made it this far, and thank you so much for taking this ride with me. Honestly, I never would have gotten past my first book without fans encouraging me to write more. So thank you, thank you.

Now take a deep breath, let things settle, and when you're ready, keep flipping pages because I've got a message for you about what comes next!

Thanks for reading!

My biggest thanks to the readers! If it wasn't for you, I wouldn't be doing this. Those of you who enjoyed the book, I can always use a good review—or even better—tell a friend.

My eternal gratitude to: Felix Ortiz for the breath-taking cover and social media illustrations. Shawn T King for his incredible graphic design. Kellerica for inking this world into reality. Nicole Zoltack coming back yet again as my long-suffering proofreader, joined by Anthony Holabird for the final polish. And of course, I'm honored to continue working with living legend Simon Vance on the audio. When you read my words, I hope it's in his voice.

Terrible 10… Always stay Terrible.

Thanks again, and hope to hear from you!
AC

TO LEARN WHAT IS NEXT OR CHECK OUT MY PREVIOUS BOOKS, FIND larger versions of the maps, series artwork, my newsletter, free short stories, and other goodies, go to accobble.com.

CPSIA information can be obtained
at www.ICGtesting.com
Printed in the USA
JSHW081040080523
41375JS00007B/3